The yellowbacks... classics of popular fiction

The yellowjackets or yellowbacks were a great series of bestselling adventure and crime thrillers that had its origins in the mid to late 19th century following on from the 'penny dreadfuls'. They virtually began the mass market revolution of the early 20th century with a clear standard format and imprint/series livery (what would today be called branding). Hodder & Stoughton published the yellowjackets in two main series with series run dates of: 1923-1939 and later 1949-1957.

As the tagline ('where thrillers really began') on the back cover implies, the imprint and series focused on thrillers that were the bestsellers of their time. This current reissue or retro revival if you will, brings back many of these masterpieces, now classics in their own way and extends it further by including key titles from that period that were either great crime or thriller or even general commercial fiction (including sub-genres of noir, horror, gothic, romance, westerns, etc.) influences of their time. There are some perennial favourites and many rarities either lost or not easily available being revived in the current series. Writers and characters ranged from adventure heroes like Bulldog Drummond, Allan Quatermain, Richard Hannay or the Saint through thriller grandmasters Edgar Wallace and E. Phillips Oppenheim, crime and mystery maestros like Patricia Wentworth, GK Chesterton, Agatha Christie and the Detection club, to western and swashbucklers like Zane Grey, Max Brand, Captain Blood and even romance or general fiction classics like Hermina Black, Denise Robins, Marie Corelli or Stella Morton. These were books that had storytelling at their heart and always entertained.

The yellowbacks had both hardback (with varying design elements) and paperback (which built the series look) versions with the latter still carrying the imprint 'yellowjacket'. The current reissues pay tribute to both and use an amalgam of elements from both editions while retaining the complete yellow (or 'mustard-plaster') livery with the author's name in blue beveled type with a 'simulated emboss' effect and a white outer 'outline', and the book title in black. These reissues retain the distinctive size of the original mass market paperback and follow the three main category variations— the thrillers (crime, westerns, mystery, adventure) had blue lettering for the author's name, while Romance and softer general fiction had red; and other categories like humour had green.

For more detail and a full list of titles visit https://www.hachetteindia.com/home/yellowbacks

THE COMPLETE THINKING MACHINE

VOLUME 1

THE COMPLETE THINKING MACHINE

Jacques Heath Futrelle (9 April 1875 – 15 April 1912) was an American journalist and mystery writer who achieved fame for his detective stories featuring 'The Thinking Machine' which were originally published in *The Saturday Evening Post* and the *Boston American*. Futrelle died at age 37 on 15 April 1912, on the RMS Titanic. He refused to board a lifeboat, insisting that his wife board instead. Interestingly Futrelle was used as the lead character in Max Allan Collins' disaster series novel *The Titanic Murders* (1999), which was about two murders aboard the Titanic.

THE
COMPLETE
THINKING MACHINE

Jacques Futrelle

VOLUME 1

hachette

The Complete Thinking Machine
First published by Chapman & Hall, Limited, London in 1907

This Hodder Yellowback edition © Hachette India 2023
(Registered Name: Hachette Book Publishing India Pvt. Ltd.)
An Hachette UK Company www.hachetteindia.com

1

All rights reserved. No part of the publication may be reproduced, stored in a retrieval system (including but not limited to computers, disks, external drives, electronic or digital devices, e-readers, websites), or transmitted in any form or by any means (including but not limited to cyclostyling, photocopying, docutech or other reprographic reproductions, mechanical, recording, electronic, digital versions) without the prior written permission of the publisher, nor be otherwise circulated in any form of binding or cover other than that in which it is published and without a similar condition being imposed on the subsequent purchaser.

The texts in these editions in most cases have been reprinted as is, with minimal editorial changes (including by and large no bowdlerizing for political correctness; though in some editions, a few words and phrases considered archaic, or those considered offensive now, along with archaic punctuation may have been modified in places to make the text more accessible to today's readers. The narratives, language, beliefs, social mores and/or cultural depictions, in these volumes are a reflection of their times and must be viewed as such. They may also contain certain cultural, racial and gender prejudices and stereotypes that may be outdated or clearly wrong then and wrong today; but their removal would be tantamount to claiming these prejudices never existed. The Publisher does not endorse or support those depictions or stereotypes; and these books have been made available for a discerning audience that will read it for entertainment value and a chronicle/record of popular fiction of past times.

Cover design by Priya Singh adapted from the original classic yellowjacket by Hodder & Stoughton.

Cover illustration by Ishan Trivedi.

Series note: Some of the books in the series (unless otherwise credited) may have cover or inside illustrations from the original yellowbacks or early editions, and while full restoration has been attempted, some images may be grainy or faded due to the condition of the original material. The end notes or bonus material or blurb details may have been sourced from the public domain or free use publications such as Wikipedia and attribution is hereby made also allowing similar free use reproduction from here. Sources requiring further specific attribution may write in and further detailing and/or corrections shall be made in subsequent printings/editions.

Reprint specifications may be subject to change including but not limited to finishes, paper, colour sections.

ISBN: 978-81-960269-2-9

Hachette Book Publishing India Pvt. Ltd.
4th & 5th Floors, Corporate Centre,
Plot No. 94, Sector 44, Gurugram - 122 003, India

Typeset in Electra LT STD 10/12.5 pt by Manipal Technologies Limited, Manipal

Printed and bound in India by Manipal Technologies Limited, Manipal

CONTENTS

1.	The Thinking Machine	1
2.	The First Problem	6
3.	The Problem of Cell 13	20
4.	My First Experience with the Great Logician	62
5.	Kidnapped Baby Blake, Millionaire	68
6.	Mystery of the Fatal Cipher	103
7.	Mystery of the Flaming Phantom	136
8.	The Tragedy of the Life Raft	172
9.	Problem of the Private Compartment	192
10.	Mystery of the Ralston Bank Burglary	206
11.	Mystery of the Scarlet Thread	239
12.	Problem of Convict No. 97	276
13.	Problem of the Broken Bracelet	294
14.	Problem of the Cross Mark	314
15.	The Jackdaw	328
16.	Problem of the Crystal Gazer	350
17.	Problem of the Deserted House	368

1

THE THINKING MACHINE

It was absolutely impossible. Twenty-five chess masters from the world at large, foregathered in Boston for the annual championships, unanimously declared it impossible, and unanimity on any given point is an unusual mental condition for chess masters. Not one would concede for an instant that it was within the range of human achievement. Some grew red in the face as they argued it, others smiled loftily and were silent; still others dismissed the matter in a word as wholly absurd.

A casual remark by the distinguished scientist and logician, Professor Augustus S. F. X. Van Dusen, provoked the discussion. He had, in the past, aroused bitter disputes by some chance remark; in fact had been once a sort of controversial centre of the sciences. It had been due to his modest announcement of a startling and unorthodox hypothesis that he had been invited to vacate the chair of Philosophy in a great university. Later that university had felt honoured when he accepted its degree of LL.D.

For a score of years, educational and scientific institutions of the world had amused themselves by crowding degrees upon him. He had initials that stood for things he couldn't pronounce; degrees from France, England, Russia, Germany, Italy, Sweden and Spain. These were expressed recognition of the fact that his was the foremost brain in the sciences. The imprint of his crabbed personality lay heavily on half a dozen of its branches. Finally there came a time when argument was respectfully silent in the face of one of his conclusions.

The remark which had arrayed the chess masters of the world into so formidable and unanimous a dissent was made by Professor Van Dusen in the presence of three other gentlemen of note. One of these, Dr Charles Elbert, happened to be a chess enthusiast.

"Chess is a shameless perversion of the functions of the brain," was Professor Van Dusen's declaration in his perpetually irritated voice. "It is a sheer waste of effort, greater because it is possibly the most difficult of all fixed abstract problems. Of course logic will solve it. Logic will solve any problem — not most of them but any problem. A thorough understanding of its rules would enable anyone to defeat your greatest chess players. It would be inevitable, just as inevitable as that two and two make four, not sometimes but all the time. I don't know chess because I never do useless things, but I could take a few hours of competent instruction and defeat a man who has devoted his life to it. His mind is cramped; bound down to the logic of chess. Mine is not; mine employs logic in its widest scope."

Dr Elbert shook his head vigorously. "It is impossible," he asserted.

"Nothing is impossible," snapped the scientist. "The human mind can do anything. It is all we have to lift us above the brute creation. For Heaven's sake leave us that."

The aggressive tone, the uncompromising egotism brought a flush to Dr Elbert's face. Professor Van Dusen affected many persons that way, particularly those fellow savants who, themselves men of distinction, had ideas of their own.

"Do you know the purposes of chess? Its countless combinations?" asked Dr Elbert.

"No," was the crabbed reply. "I know nothing whatever of the game beyond the general purpose which, I understand to be, to move certain pieces in certain directions to stop an opponent from moving his King. Is that correct?"

"Yes," said Dr Elbert slowly, "but I never heard it stated just that way before."

"Then, if that is correct, I maintain that the true logician can defeat the chess expert by the pure mechanical rules of logic. I'll take a few hours some time, acquaint myself with the moves of the pieces, and defeat you to convince you."

Professor Van Dusen glared savagely into the eyes of Dr Elbert.

"Not me," said Dr Elbert. "You say anyone – you for instance, might defeat the greatest chess player. Would you be willing to meet the greatest chess player after you 'acquaint' yourself with the game?"

"Certainly," said the scientist. "I have frequently found it necessary to make a fool of myself to convince people. I'll do it again."

This, then, was the acrimonious beginning of the discussion which aroused chess masters and brought open dissent from eminent men who had not dared for years to dispute any assertion by the distinguished Professor Van Dusen. It was arranged that at the conclusion of the championships Professor Van Dusen should meet the winner. This happened to be Tschaikowsky, the Russian, who had been champion for half a dozen years.

After this expected result of the tournament Hillsbury, a noted American master, spent a morning with Professor Van Dusen in the latter's modest apartments on Beacon Hill. He left there with a sadly puzzled face; that afternoon Professor Van Dusen met the Russian champion. The newspapers had said a great deal about the affair and hundreds were present to witness the game.

There was a little murmur of astonishment when Professor Van Dusen appeared. He was slight, almost child-like in body, and his thin shoulders seemed to droop beneath the weight of his enormous head. He wore a number eight hat. His brow rose straight and dome-like and a heavy shock of long, yellow hair gave him almost a grotesque appearance. The eyes were narrow slits of blue squinting eternally through thick spectacles; the face was small, clean shaven, drawn and white with the pallor of the student. His lips made a perfectly straight line. His hands were remarkable for their whiteness, their flexibility, and for the length of the slender fingers. One glance showed that physical development had never entered into the schedule of the scientist's fifty years of life.

The Russian smiled as he sat down at the chess table. He felt that he was humouring a crank. The other masters were grouped near by, curiously expectant. Professor Van Dusen began the game, opening with a Queen's gambit. At his fifth move, made without the slightest hesitation, the smile left the Russian's face. At the tenth, the masters grew intensely eager. The Russian champion was playing for honour now. Professor Van Dusen's fourteenth move was King's castle to Queen's four.

"Check," he announced.

After a long study of the board the Russian protected his King with a Knight. Professor Van Dusen noted the play then leaned back in his chair with finger tips pressed together. His eyes left the board and dreamily studied the ceiling. For at least ten minutes there was no sound, no movement, then:

"Mate in fifteen moves," he said quietly.

There was a quick gasp of astonishment. It took the practised eyes of the masters several minutes to verify the announcement. But the Russian champion saw and leaned back in his chair a little white and dazed. He was not astonished; he was helplessly floundering in a maze of incomprehensible things. Suddenly he arose and grasped the slender hand of his conqueror.

"You have never played chess before?" he asked.

"Never."

"Mon Dieu! You are not a man; you are a brain, a machine, a thinking machine."

"It's a child's game," said the scientist abruptly. There was no note of exultation in his voice; it was still the irritable, impersonal tone which was habitual.

This, then, was Professor Augustus S.F.X. Van Dusen, Ph.D., LL.D., F. R. S., M.D., etc., etc., etc. This is how he came to be known to the world at large as The Thinking Machine. The Russian's phrase had been applied to the scientist as a title by a newspaper reporter, Hutchinson Hatch. It had stuck.

2

THE FIRST PROBLEM

That strange, seemingly inexplicable chain of circumstances which had to do with the mysterious disappearance of a famous actress, Irene Wallack, from her dressing room in a Springfield theater in the course of a performance, while the echo of tumultuous appreciation still rang in her ears, was perhaps the first problem which was not purely scientific that The Thinking Machine was ever asked to solve. The scientist's aid was enlisted in this case by Hutchinson Hatch, reporter.

"But I am a scientist, a logician," The Thinking Machine had protested. "I know nothing whatever of crime."

"No one knows that a crime has been committed," the reporter hastened to say.

"There is something far beyond the ordinary in this affair. A woman has disappeared, evaporated into thin air in the hearing, almost in sight, of her friends. The police can make nothing of it. It is a problem for a greater mind than theirs."

Professor Van Dusen waved the newspaper man to a seat and himself sank back into a great cushioned chair in which his diminutive figure seemed even more child-like than it really was.

"Tell me the story," he said petulantly, "All of it."

THE FIRST PROBLEM

The enormous yellow head rested against the chair back, the blue eyes squinted steadily upward, the slender fingers were pressed tip to tip. The Thinking Machine was in a receptive mood. Hatch was triumphant; he had had only a vague hope that he could interest this man in an affair which was as bizarre as it was incomprehensible.

"Miss Wallack is thirty years old and beautiful," the reporter began. "As an actress she has won high recognition not only in this country but in England. You may have read something of her in the daily papers, and if—"

"I never read the papers," the other interrupted curtly. "Go on."

"She is unmarried, and as far as anyone knows, had no immediate intention of changing her condition," Hatch resumed, staring curiously at the thin face of the scientist. "I presume she had admirers—most beautiful women of the stage have – but she is one whose life has been perfectly clean, whose record is an open book. I tell you this because it might have a bearing on your conclusion as to a possible reason for her disappearance.

"Now the actual circumstances of that disappearance. Miss Wallack has been playing in Shakespearean repertoire. Last week she was in Springfield. On Saturday night, which concluded her engagement there, she appeared as Rosalind in 'As You Like It.' The house was crowded. She played the first two acts amid great enthusiasm, and this despite the fact that she was suffering intensely from headache to which she was subject at times. After the second act she returned to her dressing room and just before the curtain went up for the third the stage manager called her. She replied that she would be out immediately. There seems no possible shadow of doubt that it was her voice.

"Rosalind does not appear in the third act until the curtain has been up for six minutes. When Miss Wallack's cue came she did not answer it. The stage manager rushed to her door and again called her. There was no answer. Then, fearing that she might have fainted, he went in. She was not there. A hurried search was made without result, and the stage manager finally was compelled to announce to the audience that the sudden illness of the star would make it impossible to finish the performance.

"The curtain was lowered and the search resumed. Every nook and corner back of the footlights was gone over. The stage doorkeeper, William Meegan, had seen no one go out. He and a policeman had been standing at the stage door talking for at least twenty minutes. It is therefore conclusive that Miss Wallack did not leave by that exit. The only other way it was possible to leave the stage was over the footlights. Of course she didn't go that way. Yet no trace of her has been found. Where is she?"

"The windows?" asked The Thinking Machine.

"The stage is below the street level," explained Hatch. "The window of her dressing room, Room A, is small and barred with iron. It opens into an air shaft that goes straight up for ten feet, and that is covered with an iron grating fixed in the granite. The other windows on the stage are not only inaccessible but are also barred with iron. She could not have approached either of these windows without being seen by other members of the company or the stage hands."

"Under the stage?" suggested the scientist.

"Nothing," the reporter went on. "It is a large cemented basement which was vacant. It was searched, because there was of course a chance that Miss Wallack might have become temporarily unbalanced and wandered down there. There was even a search made of the flies – that is the galleries over the stage where the men who work the drop curtains are stationed."

There was silence for a long time. The Thinking Machine twiddled his fingers and continued to stare upward. He had not

THE FIRST PROBLEM

looked at the reporter. He broke the silence after a time. "How was Miss Wallack dressed at the time of her disappearance?"

"In doublet and hose, that is, tights," the newspaper man responded. "She wears that costume from the second act until practically the end of the play."

"Was all her street clothing in her room?"

"Yes, everything, spread across an unopened trunk of costumes. It was all as if she had left the room to answer her cue—all in order even to an open box of chocolate-cream candy on her table."

"No sign of a struggle, nor any noise heard?"

"No."

"Nor trace of blood?"

"Nothing."

"Her maid? Did she have one?"

"Oh, yes. I neglected to tell you that the maid, Gertrude Manning, had gone home immediately after the first act. She grew suddenly ill and was excused."

The Thinking Machine turned his squint eyes on the reporter for the first time.

"Ill?" he repeated. "What was the matter?"

"That I can't say," replied the reporter.

"Where is she now?"

"I don't know. Everyone forgot all about her in the excitement about Miss Wallack."

"What kind of candy was it?"

"I'm afraid I don't know that either."

"Where was it bought?"

The reporter shrugged his shoulders; that was something else he didn't know.

The Thinking Machine shot out the questions aggressively, staring meanwhile steadily at Hatch, who squirmed uncomfortably. "Where is the candy now?" demanded the scientist.

Again Hatch shrugged his shoulders.

"How much did Miss Wallack weigh?"

The reporter was willing to guess at this. He had seen her half a dozen times.

"Between a hundred and thirty and a hundred and forty," he ventured.

"Does there happen to be a hypnotist connected with the company?"

"I don't know," Hatch replied.

The Thinking Machine waved his slender hands impatiently; he was annoyed. "It is perfectly absurd, Mr Hatch," he expostulated, "to come to me with only a few facts and ask advice. If you had all the facts I might be able to do something; but this—"

The newspaper man was nettled. In his own profession he was accredited a man of discernment and acumen. He resented the tone, the manner, even the seemingly trivial questions, which the other asked. "I don't see," he began, "that the candy even if it had been poisoned as I imagine you think possible, or a hypnotist could have had anything to do with Miss Wallack's disappearance. Certainly neither poison nor hypnotism would have made her invisible."

"Of course you don't see!" blazed The Thinking Machine. "If you did, you wouldn't have come to me. When did this thing happen?"

"Saturday night, as I said," the reporter informed him a little more humbly. "It closed the engagement in Springfield. Miss Wallack was to have appeared here in Boston tonight."

"When did she disappear – by the clock, I mean?"

"The stage manager's time slip shows that the curtain for the third act went up at nine-forty-one—he spoke to her, say, one minute before, or at nine-forty. The action of the play before she appears in the third act takes six minutes; therefore—"

THE FIRST PROBLEM

"In precisely seven minutes a woman, weighing more than 130 pounds, certainly not dressed for the street, disappeared completely from her dressing room. It is now five-eighteen Monday afternoon. I think we may solve this crime within a few hours."

"Crime?" Hatch repeated eagerly. "Do you imagine there is a crime then?"

Professor Van Dusen didn't heed the question. Instead he rose and paced back and forth across the reception room half a dozen times, his hands behind his back and his eyes cast down. At last he stopped and faced the reporter, who had also risen.

"Miss Wallack's company, I presume, with the baggage, is now in Boston," he said. "See every male member of the company, talk to them and particularly study their eyes. Don't overlook anyone, however humble. Also find out what became of the box of chocolate candy, and if possible how many pieces are out of it. Then report here to me. Miss Wallack's safety may depend upon your speed and accuracy."

Hatch was frankly startled. "How—" he began.

"Don't stop to talk—hurry!" commanded The Thinking Machine. "I will have a cab waiting when you come back. We must get to Springfield."

The newspaper man rushed away to obey orders. He didn't understand them at all. Studying men's eyes was not in his line; but he obeyed nevertheless. An hour and a half later he returned, to be thrust unceremoniously into a waiting cab by The Thinking Machine. The cab rattled away toward South Station, where the two men caught a train, just about to move out for Springfield. Once settled in their seats, the scientist turned to Hatch, who was nearly suffocating with suppressed information.

"Well?" he asked.

"I found out several things," the reporter burst out. "First, Miss Wallack's leading man, Langdon Mason, who has been in love with her for three years, bought the candy at Schuyler's in Springfield early Saturday evening before he went to the theater. He told me so himself rather reluctantly; but I – I made him say it."

"Ah!" exclaimed The Thinking Machine. It was a most unequivocal ejaculation. "How many pieces of candy are out of the box?"

"Only three," explained Hatch. "Miss Wallack's things were packed into the open trunk in her dressing room, the candy with them. I induced the manager—"

"Yes, yes, yes!" interrupted The Thinking Machine impatiently. "What sort of eyes has Mason? What colour?"

"Blue, frank in expression, nothing unusual at all," said the reporter.

"And the others?"

"I didn't quite know what you meant by studying their eyes, so I got a set of photographs. I thought perhaps they might help."

"Excellent, Excellent!" commented The Thinking Machine. He shuffled the pictures through his fingers, stopping now and then to study one, and to read the name printed below. "Is that the leading man?" he asked at last, and handed one to Hatch.

"Yes."

Professor Van Dusen did not speak again. The train pulled into Springfield at nine-twenty. Hatch followed the scientist without a word into a cab.

"Schuyler's candy store," quickly commanded The Thinking Machine. "Hurry."

The cab rushed off through the night. Ten minutes later it stopped before a brilliantly lighted candy store. The Thinking Machine led the way inside and approached the girl behind the chocolate counter.

"Will you please tell me if you remember this man's face?" he asked as he produced Mason's photograph.

THE FIRST PROBLEM

"Oh, yes, I remember him," the girl replied. "He's an actor."

"Did he buy a small box of chocolates of you Saturday evening early?" was the next question.

"Yes. I recall it because he seemed to be in a hurry; in fact, I believe he said he was anxious to get to the theater to pack."

"And do you recall that this man ever bought chocolates here?" asked the scientist. He produced another photograph and handed it to the girl. She studied it a moment while Hatch craned his neck, vainly, to see.

"I don't recall that he ever did," the girl answered finally.

The Thinking Machine turned away abruptly and disappeared into a public telephone booth. He remained there for five minutes, then rushed out to the cab again, with Hatch following closely.

"City Hospital!" he commanded.

Again the cab dashed away. Hatch was dumb; there seemed to be nothing to say. The Thinking Machine was plainly pursuing some definite line of inquiry, yet the reporter didn't know what. The case was getting kaleidoscopic. This impression was strengthened when he found himself standing beside The Thinking Machine in City Hospital conversing with the house surgeon, Dr Carlton.

"Is there a Miss Gertrude Manning here?" was the scientist's first question.

"Yes," replied the surgeon. "She was brought here Saturday night, suffering from—"

"Strychnine poisoning, yes, I know," interrupted the other. "Picked up in the street, probably. I am a physician. If she is well enough I should like to ask her a couple of questions."

Dr Carlton agreed, and Professor Van Dusen, still followed faithfully by Hatch, was ushered into the ward where Miss Wallack's maid lay, pallid and weak. The Thinking Machine picked up her hand and his slender finger rested for a minute on her pulse. He nodded and seemed satisfied.

"Miss Manning, can you understand me?" he asked.

The girl nodded weakly.

"How many pieces of the candy did you eat?"

"Two," she replied. She stared into the face above her with dull eyes.

"Did Miss Wallack eat any of it up to the time you left the theatre?"

"No."

If the Thinking Machine had been in a hurry previously, he was racing now. Hatch trailed on dutifully behind, down the stairs, and into the cab, whence Professor Van Dusen shouted a word of thanks to Dr Carlton. This time their destination was the stage door of the theatre from which Miss Wallack had disappeared.

The reporter was muddled. He didn't know anything very clearly except that three pieces of candy were missing from the box. Of these the maid had eaten only two. She had been poisoned. Therefore, it seemed reasonable to suppose that if Miss Wallack had eaten the third piece she also would be poisoned. But poison would not make her invisible. At this point the reporter shook his head hopelessly.

William Meegan, the stage doorkeeper, was easily found.

"Can you inform me, please," began The Thinking Machine, "if Mr Mason left a box of candy with you last Saturday night for Miss Wallack?"

"Yes," Meegan replied good-naturedly. He was amused at the little man. "Miss Wallack hadn't arrived. Mason brought a box of candy for her nearly every night and usually left it here. I put the one Saturday night on the shelf here."

"Did Mr Mason come to the theatre before or after the others on Saturday night?"

"Before," replied Meegan. "He was unusually early, I suppose, to pack."

THE FIRST PROBLEM

"And the other members of the company coming in stop here, I imagine, to get their mail?" and the scientist squinted up at the mail box above the shelf.

"Sure, always."

The Thinking Machine drew a long breath. Up to this time there had been little perplexed wrinkles in his brow. Now they disappeared.

"Now, please," he went on, "was any package or box of any kind taken from the stage on Saturday night between nine and eleven o'clock?"

"No," said Meegan positively. "Nothing at all until the company's baggage was removed at midnight."

"Miss Wallack had two trunks in her dressing room?"

"Yes. Two whacking big ones too."

"How do you know?"

"Because I helped put 'em in and helped take 'em out," replied Meegan sharply. "What's it to you?"

Suddenly The Thinking Machine turned and ran out to the cab, with Hatch, his shadow, close behind.

"Drive, drive as fast as you know how to the nearest long-distance telephone!" the scientist instructed the cabby. "A woman's life is at stake."

Half an hour later Professor Van Dusen and Hutchinson Hatch were on a train rushing back to Boston. The Thinking Machine had been in the telephone booth for fifteen minutes. When he came out Hatch had asked several questions, to which the scientist vouchsafed no answer. They were perhaps thirty minutes out of Springfield before the scientist showed any disposition to talk. Then he began, without preliminary, much as he was resuming a former conversation.

"Of course if Miss Wallack didn't leave the stage of the theater she was there," he said. "We will admit that she did not become invisible. The problem therefore was to find her on the stage. The fact that no violence was used against her was conclusively proved by half a dozen instances. No one heard her scream; there was no struggle, no trace of blood. Ergo, we assume in the beginning that she must have consented to the first steps which led to her disappearance. Remember her attire was wholly unsuited to the street.

"Now let us shape a hypothesis which will fit all the circumstances. Miss Wallack had a severe headache. Hypnotic influence will cure headaches. Was there a hypnotist to whom Miss Wallack would have submitted herself? Assume there was. Then would that hypnotist take advantage of his control to place her in a cataleptic condition? Assume a motive and he would. Then, how would he dispose of her?

"From this point questions radiate in all directions. We will confine ourselves to the probable, granting for the moment that this hypothesis, the only one which fits all the circumstances, is correct. Obviously, a hypnotist would not have attempted to get her out of the dressing room. What remains? One of the two trunks in her room."

Hatch gasped. "You mean you think it possible that she was hypnotized and placed in that second trunk, the one that was strapped and locked?" he asked.

"It's the only thing that could have happened," said The Thinking Machine emphatically; "therefore that was just what did happen."

"Why, it's horrible!" exclaimed Hatch. "A live woman in a trunk for forty-eight hours? Even if she was alive then, she must be dead now."

The reporter shuddered a little and gazed curiously at the inscrutable face of his companion. He saw no pity, no horror, there; there was merely the reflection of the workings of a brain.

"It does not necessarily follow that she is dead," explained The Thinking Machine. "If she ate that third piece of candy before she was hypnotized she is probably dead. If it was placed in her mouth after she was in a cataleptic condition the chances are that she is not dead. The candy would not melt and her system could not absorb the poison."

"But she would be suffocated—her bones would be broken by the rough handling of the trunk-there are a hundred possibilities," the reporter suggested.

"A person in a cataleptic condition is singularly impervious to injury," replied the scientist. "There is of course a chance of suffocation, but a great deal of air may enter a trunk."

"And the candy?" Hatch asked.

"Yes, the candy. We know that two pieces of candy nearly killed the maid. Yet Mr Mason admitted having bought it. This admission indicated that this poisoned candy is not the candy he bought. Is Mr Mason a hypnotist? No. He hasn't the eyes. His picture tells me that. We know that Mr Mason did buy candy for Miss Wallack on several occasions. We know that sometimes he left it with the stage doorkeeper. We know that members of the company stopped there for mail. We instantly see that it is possible for one to take away that box and substitute poisoned candy. All the boxes are alike.

"Madness and the cunning of madness lie back of all this. It was a deliberate attempt to murder Miss Wallack, long pondered and due, perhaps, to unrequited or hopeless infatuation. It began with the poisoned candy, and that failing, went to a point immediately following the moment when the stage manager last spoke to the actress. The hypnotist was probably in her room then. You must remember that it would have been possible for him to ease the headache, and at the same time leave Miss Wallack free to play. She might have known this from previous experience."

"Is Miss Wallack still in the trunk?" asked Hatch after a silence.

"No," replied the Thinking Machine. "She is out now, dead or alive – I am inclined to believe alive."

"And the man?"

"I will turn him over to the police in half an hour after we reach Boston."

From South Station the scientist and Hatch were driven immediately to Police Headquarters. Detective Mallory, whom Hatch knew well, received them.

"We got your 'phone from Springfield—" he began.

"Was she dead?" interrupted the scientist.

"No," Mallory replied. "She was unconscious when we took her out of the trunk, but no bones are broken. She is badly bruised. The doctor says she's hypnotized."

"Was the piece of candy taken from her mouth?"

"Sure, a chocolate cream. It hadn't melted."

"I'll come back here in a few minutes and awake her," said The Thinking Machine. "Come with us now, and get the man."

Wonderingly the detective entered the cab and the three were driven to a big hotel a dozen blocks away. Before they entered the lobby The Thinking Machine handed a photograph to Mallory, who studied it under an electric light.

"That man is upstairs with several others," explained the scientist. "Pick him out and get behind him when we enter the room. He may attempt to shoot. Don't touch him until I say so."

In a large room on the fifth floor Manager Stanfeld of the Irene Wallack Company had assembled the men of her support. This was done at the 'phoned request of The Thinking Machine. There were no preliminaries when Professor Van Dusen entered. He squinted comprehensively about him, then went straight to Langdon Mason.

"Were you on the stage in the third act of your play before Miss Wallack was to appear – I mean the play last Saturday night?" he asked.

"I was," Mason replied, "for at least three minutes."

"Mr Stanfeld, is that correct?"

THE FIRST PROBLEM

"Yes," replied the manager.

There was a long tense silence broken only by the heavy footsteps of Mallory as he walked toward a distant corner of the room. A faint flush crept into Mason's face as he realized that the questions were almost an accusation. He started to speak, but the steady, impassive voice of The Thinking Machine stopped him.

"Mr Mallory, take your prisoner," it said.

Instantly there was a fierce, frantic struggle, and those present turned to see the detective with his great arms locked about Stanley Wightman, the melancholy Jaques of "As You Like It." The actor's face was distorted, madness blazed in the eyes, and he snarled like a beast at bay. By a sudden movement Mallory threw Wightman and manacled him, then looked up to find The Thinking Machine peering over his shoulder at the prostrate man.

"Yes, he's a hypnotist," the scientist remarked in self-satisfied conclusion. "It always tells in the pupils of the eyes."

This, then, was the beginning and end of the first problem. Miss Wallack was aroused, and told a story almost identical with that of The Thinking Machine. Stanley Wightman, whose brooding over a hopeless love for her made a maniac of him, raves and shrieks the lines of Jaques in the seclusion of a padded cell.

3

THE PROBLEM OF CELL 13

I

Practically all those letters remaining in the alphabet after Augustus S. F. X. Van Dusen was named were afterward acquired by that gentleman in the course of a brilliant scientific career, and, being honorably acquired, were tacked on to the other end. His name, therefore, taken with all that belonged to it, was a wonderfully imposing structure. He was a Ph.D., an LL.D., an F.R.S., an M.D., and an M.D.S. He was also some other things—just what he himself couldn't say—through recognition of his ability by various foreign educational and scientific institutions.

In appearance he was no less striking than in nomenclature. He was slender with the droop of the student in his thin shoulders and the pallor of a close, sedentary life on his clean-shaven face. His eyes wore a perpetual, forbidding squint—the squint of a man who studies little things—and when they could be seen at all through his thick spectacles, were mere slits of watery blue. But above his eyes was his most striking feature. This was a tall, broad brow, almost abnormal in height and width, crowned by a heavy shock of bushy, yellow hair. All these things conspired to give him a peculiar, almost grotesque, personality.

Professor Van Dusen was remotely German. For generations his ancestors had been noted in the sciences; he was the logical result, the master mind. First and above all he was a logician. At least thirty-five years of the half-century or so of his existence had been devoted exclusively to proving that two and two always equal four, except in unusual cases, where they equal three or five, as the case may be. He stood broadly on the general proposition that all things that start must go somewhere, and was able to bring the concentrated mental force of his forefathers to bear on a given problem. Incidentally it may be remarked that Professor Van Dusen wore a No. 8 hat.

The world at large had heard vaguely of Professor Van Dusen as the Thinking Machine. It was a newspaper catchphrase applied to him at the time of a remarkable exhibition at chess; he had demonstrated then that a stranger to the game might, by the force of inevitable logic, defeat a champion who had devoted a lifetime to its study. The Thinking Machine! Perhaps that more nearly described him than all his honorary initials, for he spent week after week, month after month, in the seclusion of his small laboratory from which had gone forth thoughts that staggered scientific associates and deeply stirred the world at large.

It was only occasionally that The Thinking Machine had visitors, and these were usually men who, themselves high in the sciences, dropped in to argue a point and perhaps convince themselves. Two of these men, Dr Charles Ransome and Alfred Fielding, called one evening to discuss some theory which is not of consequence here.

"Such a thing is impossible," declared Dr Ransome emphatically, in the course of the conversation.

"Nothing is impossible," declared The Thinking Machine with equal emphasis. He always spoke petulantly. "The mind is master of all things. When science fully recognizes that fact a great advance will have been made."

"How about the airship?" asked Dr Ransome.

"That's not impossible at all," asserted The Thinking Machine. "It will be invented some time. I'd do it myself, but I'm busy."

Dr Ransome laughed tolerantly.

"I've heard you say such things before," he said. "But they mean nothing. Mind may be master of matter, but it hasn't yet found a way to apply itself. There are some things that can't be thought out of existence, or rather which would not yield to any amount of thinking."

"What, for instance?" demanded The Thinking Machine.

Dr Ransome was thoughtful for a moment as he smoked.

"Well, say prison walls," he replied. "No man can think himself out of a cell. If he could, there would be no prisoners."

"A man can so apply his brain and ingenuity that he can leave a cell, which is the same thing," snapped The Thinking Machine.

Dr Ransome was slightly amused.

"Let's suppose a case," he said, after a moment. "Take a cell where prisoners under sentence of death are confined—men who are desperate and, maddened by fear, would take any chance to escape—suppose you were locked in such a cell. Could you escape?"

"Certainly," declared The Thinking Machine.

"Of course," said Mr Fielding, who entered the conversation for the first time, "you might wreck the cell with an explosive—but inside, a prisoner, you couldn't have that."

"There would be nothing of that kind," said The Thinking Machine. "You might treat me precisely as you treated prisoners under sentence of death, and I would leave the cell."

"Not unless you entered it with tools prepared to get out," said Dr Ransome.

The Thinking Machine was visibly annoyed and his blue eyes snapped.

"Lock me in any cell in any prison anywhere at any time, wearing only what is necessary, and I'll escape in a week," he declared, sharply.

Dr Ransome sat up straight in the chair, interested. Mr Fielding lighted a new cigar.

"You mean you could actually think yourself out?" asked Dr Ransome.

"I would get out," was the response.

"Are you serious?"

"Certainly I am serious."

Dr Ransome and Mr Fielding were silent for a long time.

"Would you be willing to try it?" asked Mr Fielding, finally.

"Certainly," said Professor Van Dusen, and there was a trace of irony in his voice. "I have done more asinine things than that to convince other men of less important truths."

The tone was offensive and there was an undercurrent strongly resembling anger on both sides. Of course it was an absurd thing, but Professor Van Dusen reiterated his willingness to undertake the escape and it was decided upon.

"To begin now," added Dr Ransome.

"I'd prefer that it begin tomorrow," said The Thinking Machine, "because—"

"No, now," said Mr Fielding, flatly. "You are arrested, figuratively, of course, without any warning locked in a cell with no chance to communicate with friends, and left there with identically the same care and attention that would be given to a man under sentence of death. Are you willing?"

"All right, now, then," said the Thinking Machine, and he arose.

"Say, the death-cell in Chisholm Prison."

"The death-cell in Chisholm Prison."

"And what will you wear?"

"As little as possible," said The Thinking Machine. "Shoes, stockings, trousers and a shirt."

"You will permit yourself to be searched, of course?"

I am to be treated precisely as all prisoners are treated," said The Thinking Machine. "No more attention and no less."

There were some preliminaries to be arranged in the matter of obtaining permission for the test, but all three were influential men and everything was done satisfactorily by telephone, albeit the prison commissioners, to whom the experiment was explained on purely scientific grounds, were sadly bewildered. Professor Van Dusen would be the most distinguished prisoner they had ever entertained.

When The Thinking Machine had donned those things which he was to wear during his incarceration he called the little old woman who was his housekeeper, cook and maid servant all in one.

"Martha," he said, "it is now twenty-seven minutes past nine o'clock. I am going away. One week from tonight, at half-past nine, these gentlemen and one, possibly two, others will take supper with me here. Remember Dr Ransome is very fond of artichokes."

The three men were driven to Chisholm Prison, where the Warden was awaiting them, having been informed of the matter by telephone. He understood merely that the eminent Professor Van Dusen was to be his prisoner, if he could keep him, for one week; that he had committed no crime, but that he was to be treated as all other prisoners were treated.

"Search him," instructed Dr Ransome.

The Thinking Machine was searched. Nothing was found on him; the pockets of the trousers were empty; the white, stiff-bosomed shirt had no pocket. The shoes and stockings were removed, examined, then replaced. As he watched all these preliminaries—the rigid search and noted the pitiful, childlike physical weakness of the man, the colorless face, and the thin, white hands—Dr Ransome almost regretted his part in the affair.

"Are you sure you want to do this?" he asked.

"Would you be convinced if I did not?" inquired The Thinking Machine in turn.

"No."

"All right. I'll do it."

What sympathy Dr Ransome had was dissipated by the tone. It nettled him, and he resolved to see the experiment to the end; it would be a stinging reproof to egotism.

"It will be impossible for him to communicate with anyone outside?" he asked.

"Absolutely impossible," replied the warden. "He will not be permitted writing materials of any sort."

"And your jailers, would they deliver a message from him?"

"Not one word, directly or indirectly," said the warden. "You may rest assured of that. They will report anything he might say or turn over to me anything he might give them."

"That seems entirely satisfactory," said Mr Fielding, who was frankly interested in the problem.

"Of course, in the event he fails," said Dr Ransome, "and asks for his liberty, you understand you are to set him free?"

"I understand," replied the warden.

The Thinking Machine stood listening, but had nothing to say until this was all ended, then:

"I should like to make three small requests. You may grant them or not, as you wish."

"No special favors, now," warned Mr Fielding.

"I am asking none," was the stiff response. "I would like to have some tooth powder—buy it yourself to see that it is tooth powder—and I should like to have one five-dollar and two ten-dollar bills."

Dr Ransome, Mr Fielding and the warden exchanged astonished glances. They were not surprised at the request for tooth powder, but were at the request for money.

"Is there any man with whom our friend would come in contact that he could bribe with twenty-five dollars?" asked Dr Ransome of the warden.

"Not for twenty-five hundred dollars," was the positive reply.

"Well, let him have them," said Mr Fielding. "I think they are harmless enough."

"And what is the third request?" asked Dr Ransome.

"I should like to have my shoes polished."

Again the astonished glances were exchanged. This last request was the height of absurdity, so they agreed to it. These things all being attended to, The Thinking Machine was led back into the prison from which he had undertaken to escape.

"Here is Cell 13," said the warden, stopping three doors down the steel corridor. "This is where we keep condemned murderers. No one can leave it without my permission; and no one in it can communicate with the outside. I'll stake my reputation on that. It's only three doors back of my office and I can readily hear any unusual noise."

"Will this cell do, gentlemen?" asked The Thinking Machine. There was a touch of irony in his voice.

"Admirably," was the reply.

The heavy steel door was thrown open, there was a great scurrying and scampering of tiny feet, and The Thinking Machine passed into the gloom of the cell. Then the door was closed and double locked by the warden.

"What is that noise in there?" asked Dr Ransome, through the bars.

"Rats—dozens of them," replied The Thinking Machine, tersely.

The three men, with final goodnights, were turning away when The Thinking Machine called:

"What time is it exactly, warden?"

"Eleven seventeen," replied the warden.

"Thanks. I will join you gentlemen in your office at half-past eight o'clock one week from tonight," said The Thinking Machine.

"And if you do not?"

"There is no 'if' about it."

II

Chisholm Prison was a great, spreading structure of granite, four stories in all, which stood in the center of acres of open space. It was surrounded by a wall of solid masonry eighteen feet high, and so smoothly finished inside and out as to offer no foothold to a climber, no matter how expert. Atop of this fence, as a further precaution, was a five-foot fence of steel rods, each terminating in a keen point. This fence in itself marked an absolute deadline between freedom and imprisonment, for, even if a man escaped from his cell, it would seem impossible for him to pass the wall.

The yard, which on all sides of the prison building was twenty-five feet wide, that being the distance from the building to the wall, was by day an exercise ground for those prisoners to whom was granted the boon of occasional semi-liberty. But that was not for those in Cell 13. At all times of the day there were armed guards in the yard, four of them, one patrolling each side of the prison building.

By night the yard was almost as brilliantly lighted as by day. On each of the four sides was a great arc light which rose above the prison wall and gave to the guards a clear sight. The lights, too, brightly illuminated the spiked top of the wall. The wires which fed the arc lights ran up the side of the prison building on insulators and from the top story led out to the poles supporting the arc lights.

All these things were seen and comprehended by The Thinking Machine, who was only enabled to see out his closely barred cell window by standing on his bed. This was on the morning following his incarceration. He gathered, too, that the river lay over there beyond the wall somewhere, because he heard faintly the pulsation of a motor boat and high up in the air saw a river bird. From that same direction came the shouts of boys at play and the occasional crack of a batted ball. He knew then that between the prison wall and the river was an open space, a playground.

Chisholm Prison was regarded as absolutely safe. No man had ever escaped from it. The Thinking Machine, from his perch on the bed, seeing what he saw, could readily understand why. The walls of the cell, though built he judged twenty years before, were perfectly solid, and the window bars of new iron had not a shadow of rust on them. The window itself, even with the bars out, would be a difficult mode of egress because it was small.

Yet, seeing these things, The Thinking Machine was not discouraged. Instead, he thoughtfully squinted at the great arc light—there was bright sunlight now—and traced with his eyes the wire which led from it to the building. That electric wire, he reasoned, must come down the side of the building not a great distance from his cell. That might be worth knowing.

Cell 13 was on the same floor with the offices of the prison— that is, not in the basement, nor yet upstairs. There were only four steps up to the office floor, therefore the level of the floor must be only three or four feet above the ground. He couldn't see the ground directly beneath his window, but he could see it further out toward the wall. It would be an easy drop from the window. Well and good.

Then The Thinking Machine fell to remembering how he had come to the cell. First, there was the outside guard's booth, a part of the wall. There were two heavily barred gates there, both of steel. At this gate was one man always on guard. He admitted persons to the prison after much clanking of keys and locks, and let them out when ordered to do so. The warden's office was in the prison building, and in order to reach that official from the prison yard one had to pass a gate of solid steel with only a peep-hole in it. Then coming from that inner office to Cell 13, where he was now, one must pass a heavy wooden door and two steel doors into the corridors of the prison; and always there was the double-locked door of Cell 13 to reckon with.

There were then, The Thinking Machine recalled, seven doors to be overcome before one could pass from Cell 13 into the outer world, a free man. But against this was the fact that he was rarely interrupted. A jailer appeared at his cell door at six in the morning with a breakfast of prison fare; he would come again at noon, and again at six in the afternoon. At nine o'clock at night would come the inspection tour. That would be all.

"It's admirably arranged, this prison system," was the mental tribute paid by The Thinking Machine. "I'll have to study it a little when I get out. I had no idea there was such great care exercised in the prisons."

There was nothing, positively nothing, in his cell, except his iron bed, so firmly put together that no man could tear it to pieces save with sledges or a file. He had neither of these. There was not even a chair, or a small table, or a bit of tin or crockery. Nothing! The jailer stood by when he ate, then took away the wooden spoon and bowl which he had used.

One by one these things sank into the brain of The Thinking Machine. When the last possibility had been considered he began an examination of his cell. From the roof, down the walls on all sides, he examined the stones and the cement between them. He stamped over the floor carefully time after time, but it was cement, perfectly solid. After the examination he sat on the edge of the iron bed and was lost in thought for a long time. For Professor Augustus S. F. X. Van Dusen, The Thinking Machine, had something to think about.

He was disturbed by a rat, which ran across his foot, then scampered away into a dark corner of the cell, frightened at its own daring. After awhile The Thinking Machine, squinting steadily into the darkness of the corner where the rat had gone, was able to make out in the gloom many little beady eyes staring at him. He counted six pair, and there were perhaps others; he didn't see very well.

Then The Thinking Machine, from his seat on the bed, noticed for the first time the bottom of his cell door. There was an opening there of two inches between the steel bar and the floor. Still looking steadily at this opening, The Thinking Machine backed suddenly into the corner where he had seen the beady eyes. There was a great scampering of tiny feet, several squeaks of frightened rodents, and then silence.

None of the rats had gone out the door, yet there were none in the cell. Therefore there must be another way out of the cell, however small. The Thinking Machine, on hands and knees, started a search for this spot, feeling in the darkness with his long, slender fingers.

At last his search was rewarded. He came upon a small opening in the floor, level with the cement. It was perfectly round and somewhat larger than a silver dollar. This was the way the rats had gone. He put his fingers deep into the opening; it seemed to be a disused drainage pipe and was dry and dusty.

Having satisfied himself on this point, he sat on the bed again for an hour, then made another inspection of his surroundings through the small cell window. One of the outside guards stood directly opposite, beside the wall, and happened to be looking at the window of Cell 13 when the head of The Thinking Machine appeared. But the scientist didn't notice the guard.

Noon came and the jailer appeared with the prison dinner of repulsively plain food. At home The Thinking Machine merely ate to live; here he took what was offered without comment.

THE PROBLEM OF CELL 13

Occasionally he spoke to the jailer who stood outside the door watching him.

"Any improvements made here in the last few years?" he asked.

"Nothing particularly," replied the jailer. "New wall was built four years ago."

"Anything done to the prison proper?"

"Painted the woodwork outside, and I believe about seven years ago a new system of plumbing was put in."

"Ah!" said the prisoner. "How far is the river over there?"

"About three hundred feet. The boys have a baseball ground between the wall and the river."

The Thinking Machine had nothing further to say just then, but when the jailer was ready to go he asked for some water.

"I get very thirsty here," he explained. "Would it be possible for you to leave a little water in a bowl for me?"

"I'll ask the warden," replied the jailer, and he went away. Half an hour later he returned with water in a small earthen bowl.

"The warden says you may keep this bowl," he informed the prisoner. "But you must show it to me when I ask for it. If it is broken, it will be the last."

"Thank you," said The Thinking Machine. "I shan't break it."

The jailer went on about his duties. For just the fraction of a second it seemed that The Thinking Machine wanted to ask a question, but he didn't.

Two hours later this same jailer, in passing the door of Cell No. 13, heard a noise inside and stopped. The Thinking Machine was down on his hands and knees in a corner of the cell, and from that same corner came several frightened squeaks. The jailer looked on interestedly.

"Ah, I've got you," he heard the prisoner say.

"Got what?" he asked, sharply.

"One of these rats," was the reply. "See?" And between the scientist's long fingers the jailer saw a small gray rat struggling. The prisoner brought it over to the light and looked at it closely. "It's a water rat," he said.

"Ain't you got anything better to do than to catch rats?" asked the jailer.

"It's disgraceful that they should be here at all," was the irritated reply. "Take this one away and kill it. There are dozens more where it came from."

The jailer took the wriggling, squirmy rodent and flung it down on the floor violently. It gave one squeak and lay still. Later he reported the incident to the warden, who only smiled.

Still later that afternoon the outside armed guard on Cell 13 side of the prison looked up again at the window and saw the prisoner looking out. He saw a hand raised to the barred window and then something white fluttered to the ground, directly under the window of Cell 13. It was a little roll of linen, evidently of white shirting material, and tied around it was a five-dollar bill. The guard looked up at the window again, but the face had disappeared.

With a grim smile he took the little linen roll and the five-dollar bill to the warden's office. There together they deciphered something which was written on it with a queer sort of ink, frequently blurred. On the outside was this:

"Finder of this please deliver to Dr Charles Ransome."

"Ah," said the warden, with a chuckle. "Plan of escape number one has gone wrong." Then, as an afterthought: "But why did he address it to Dr Ransome?"

"And where did he get the pen and ink to write with?" asked the guard.

The warden looked at the guard and the guard looked at the warden. There was no apparent solution of that mystery. The warden studied the writing carefully, then shook his head.

"Well, let's see what he was going to say to Dr Ransome," he said at length, still puzzled, and he unrolled the inner piece of linen.

"Well, if that—what—what do you think of that?" he asked, dazed.

The guard took the bit of linen and read this:

"Epa cseot d'net niiy awe htto n'si sih. "T."

III

The warden spent an hour wondering what sort of a cipher it was, and half an hour wondering why his prisoner should attempt to communicate with Dr Ransome, who was the cause of him being there. After this the warden devoted some thought to the question of where the prisoner got writing materials, and what sort of writing materials he had. With the idea of illuminating this point, he examined the linen again. It was a torn part of a white shirt and had ragged edges.

Now it was possible to account for the linen, but what the prisoner had used to write with was another matter. The warden knew it would have been impossible for him to have either pen or pencil, and, besides, neither pen nor pencil had been used in this writing. What, then? The warden decided to personally investigate. The Thinking Machine was his prisoner; he had orders to hold his prisoners; if this one sought to escape by sending cipher messages to persons outside, he would stop it, as he would have stopped it in the case of any other prisoner.

The warden went back to Cell 13 and found The Thinking Machine on his hands and knees on the floor, engaged in nothing more alarming than catching rats. The prisoner heard the warden's step and turned to him quickly.

"It's disgraceful," he snapped, "these rats. There are scores of them."

"Other men have been able to stand them," said the warden. "Here is another shirt for you — let me have the one you have on."

"Why?" demanded The Thinking Machine, quickly. His tone was hardly natural, his manner suggested actual perturbation.

"You have attempted to communicate with Dr Ransome," said the warden severely. "As my prisoner, it is my duty to put a stop to it."

The Thinking Machine was silent for a moment.

"All right," he said, finally. "Do your duty."

The warden smiled grimly. The prisoner arose from the floor and removed the white shirt, putting on instead a striped convict shirt the warden had brought. The warden took the white shirt eagerly, and then there compared the pieces of linen on which was written the cipher with certain torn places in the shirt. The Thinking Machine looked on curiously.

"The guard brought you those, then?" he asked.

"He certainly did," replied the warden triumphantly. "And that ends your first attempt to escape."

The Thinking Machine watched the warden as he, by comparison, established to his own satisfaction that only two pieces of linen had been torn from the white shirt.

"What did you write this with?" demanded the warden.

"I should think it a part of your duty to find out," said The Thinking Machine, irritably.

The warden started to say some harsh things, then restrained himself and made a minute search of the cell and of the prisoner instead. He found absolutely nothing; not even a match or toothpick which might have been used for a pen. The same mystery surrounded the fluid with which the cipher had been written. Although the warden left Cell 13 visibly annoyed, he took the torn shirt in triumph.

"Well, writing notes on a shirt won't get him out, that's certain," he told himself with some complacency. He put the linen scraps into his desk to await developments. "If that man escapes from that cell I'll—hang it—I'll resign."

On the third day of his incarceration The Thinking Machine openly attempted to bribe his way out. The jailer had brought his dinner and was leaning against the barred door, waiting, when The Thinking Machine began the conversation.

"The drainage pipes of the prison lead to the river, don't they?" he asked.

"Yes," said the jailer.

"I suppose they are very small?"

"Too small to crawl through, if that's what you're thinking about," was the grinning response.

There was silence until The Thinking Machine finished his meal. Then:

"You know I'm not a criminal, don't you?"

"Yes."

"And that I've a perfect right to be freed if I demand it?"

"Yes."

"Well, I came here believing that I could make my escape," said the prisoner, and his squint eyes studied the face of the jailer.

"Would you consider a financial reward for aiding me to escape?"

The jailer, who happened to be an honest man, looked at the slender, weak figure of the prisoner, at the large head with its mass of yellow hair, and was almost sorry.

"I guess prisons like these were not built for the likes of you to get out of," he said, at last.

"But would you consider a proposition to help me get out?" the prisoner insisted, almost beseechingly.

"No," said the jailer, shortly.

"Five hundred dollars," urged The Thinking Machine. "I am not a criminal."

"No," said the jailer.

"A thousand?"

"No," again said the jailer, and he started away hurriedly to escape further temptation. Then he turned back. "If you should give me ten thousand dollars I couldn't get you out. You'd have to pass through seven doors, and I only have the keys to two."

Then he told the warden all about it.

"Plan number two fails," said the warden, smiling grimly. "First a cipher, then bribery."

When the jailer was on his way to Cell 13 at six o'clock, again bearing food to The Thinking Machine, he paused, startled by the unmistakable scrape, scrape of steel against steel. It stopped at the sound of his steps, then craftily the jailer, who was beyond the prisoner's range of vision, resumed his tramping, the sound being apparently that of a man going away from Cell 13. As a matter of fact he was in the same spot.

After a moment there came again the steady scrape, scrape, and the jailer crept cautiously on tiptoes to the door and peered between the bars. The Thinking Machine was standing on the iron bed working at the bars of the little window. He was using a file, judging from the backward and forward swing of his arms.

Cautiously the jailer crept back to the office, summoned the warden in person, and they returned to Cell 13 on tiptoes. The steady scrape was still audible. The warden listened to satisfy himself and then suddenly appeared at the door.

"Well?" he demanded, and there was a smile on his face.

The Thinking Machine glanced back from his perch on the bed and leaped suddenly to the floor, making frantic efforts to hide something. The warden went in, with hand extended.

"Give it up," he said.

"No," said the prisoner, sharply.

"Come, give it up," urged the warden. "I don't want to have to search you again."

"No," repeated the prisoner.

"What was it, a file?" asked the warden.

The Thinking Machine was silent and stood squinting at the warden with something very nearly approaching disappointment on his face—nearly, but not quite. The warden was almost sympathetic.

"Plan number three fails, eh?" he asked, good-naturedly. "Too bad, isn't it?"

The prisoner didn't say.

"Search him," instructed the warden.

The jailer searched the prisoner carefully. At last, artfully concealed in the waist band of the trousers, he found a piece of steel about two inches long, with one side curved like a half moon.

"Ah," said the warden, as he received it from the jailer. "From your shoe heel," and he smiled pleasantly.

The jailer continued his search and on the other side of the trousers waist band found another piece of steel identical with the first. The edges showed where they had been worn against the bars of the window.

"You couldn't saw a way through those bars with these," said the warden.

"I could have," said The Thinking Machine firmly.

"In six months, perhaps," said the warden, good-naturedly.

The warden shook his head slowly as he gazed into the slightly flushed face of his prisoner.

"Ready to give it up?" he asked.

"I haven't started yet," was the prompt reply.

Then came another exhaustive search of the cell. Carefully the two men went over it, finally turning out the bed and searching that. Nothing. The warden in person climbed upon the bed and examined the bars of the window where the prisoner had been sawing. When he looked he was amused.

"Just made it a little bright by hard rubbing," he said to the prisoner, who stood looking on with a somewhat crestfallen air. The warden grasped the iron bars in his strong hands and tried to shake them. They were immovable, set firmly in the solid granite. He examined each in turn and found them all satisfactory. Finally he climbed down from the bed.

"Give it up, professor," he advised.

The Thinking Machine shook his head and the warden and jailer passed on again. As they disappeared down the corridor The Thinking Machine sat on the edge of the bed with his head in his hands.

"He's crazy to try to get out of that cell," commented the jailer.

"Of course he can't get out," said the warden. "But he's clever. I would like to know what he wrote that cipher with."

It was four o'clock next morning when an awful, heart-racking shriek of terror resounded through the great prison. It came from a cell somewhere about the center, and its tone told a tale of horror, agony, terrible fear. The warden heard and with three of his men rushed into the long corridor leading to Cell 13.

IV

As they ran there came again that awful cry. It died away in a sort of wail. The white faces of prisoners appeared at cell doors upstairs and down, staring out wonderingly, frightened.

"It's that fool in Cell 13," grumbled the warden.

He stopped and stared in as one of the jailers flashed a lantern. "That fool in Cell 13" lay comfortably on his cot, flat on his back with his mouth open, snoring. Even as they looked there came again the piercing cry, from somewhere above. The warden's face blanched a little as he started up the stairs. There on the top floor he found a man in Cell 43, directly above Cell 13, but two floors higher, cowering in a corner of his cell.

"What's the matter?" demanded the warden.

"Thank God you've come," exclaimed the prisoner, and he cast himself against the bars of his cell.

"What is it?" demanded the warden again.

He threw open the door and went in. The prisoner dropped on his knees and clasped the warden about the body. His face was white with terror, his eyes were widely distended, and he was shuddering. His hands, icy cold, clutched at the warden's.

"Take me out of this cell, please take me out," he pleaded.

"What's the matter with you, anyhow?" insisted the warden, impatiently.

"I heard something—something," said the prisoner, and his eyes roved nervously around the cell.

"What did you hear?"

"I—I can't tell you," stammered the prisoner. Then, in a sudden burst of terror: "Take me out of this cell—put me anywhere—but take me out of here."

The warden and the three jailers exchanged glances.

"Who is this fellow? What's he accused of?" asked the warden.

"Joseph Ballard," said one of the jailers. "He's accused of throwing acid in a woman's face. She died from it."

"But they can't prove it," gasped the prisoner. "They can't prove it. Please put me in some other cell."

He was still clinging to the warden, and that official threw his arms off roughly. Then for a time he stood looking at the cowering wretch, who seemed possessed of all the wild, unreasoning terror of a child.

"Look here, Ballard," said the warden, finally, "if you heard anything, I want to know what it was. Now tell me."

"I can't, I can't," was the reply. He was sobbing.

"Where did it come from?"

"I don't know. Everywhere—nowhere. I just heard it."

"What was it—a voice?"

"Please don't make me answer," pleaded the prisoner.

"You must answer," said the warden, sharply.

"It was a voice—but—but it wasn't human," was the sobbing reply.

"Voice, but not human?" repeated the warden, puzzled.

"It sounded muffled and—and far away—and ghostly," explained the man.

"Did it come from inside or outside the prison?"

"It didn't seem to come from anywhere—it was just here, here, everywhere. I heard it. I heard it."

For an hour the warden tried to get the story, but Ballard had become suddenly obstinate and would say nothing—only pleaded to be placed in another cell, or to have one of the jailers remain near him until daylight. These requests were gruffly refused.

"And see here," said the warden, in conclusion, "if there's any more of this screaming, I'll put you in the padded cell."

Then the warden went his way, a sadly puzzled man. Ballard sat at his cell door until daylight, his face, drawn and white with terror, pressed against the bars, and looked out into the prison with wide, staring eyes.

That day, the fourth since the incarceration of The Thinking Machine, was enlivened considerably by the volunteer prisoner, who spent most of his time at the little window of his cell. He began proceedings by throwing another piece of linen down to the guard, who picked it up dutifully and took it to the warden. On it was written:

"Only three days more."

The warden was in no way surprised at what he read; he understood that The Thinking Machine meant only three days more of his imprisonment, and he regarded the note as a boast.

But how was the thing written? Where had The Thinking Machine found this new piece of linen? Where? How? He carefully examined the linen. It was white, of fine texture, shirting material. He took the shirt which he had taken and carefully fitted the two original pieces of the linen to the torn places. This third piece was entirely superfluous; it didn't fit anywhere, and yet it was unmistakably the same goods.

"And where—where does he get anything to write with?" demanded the warden of the world at large.

Still later on the fourth day The Thinking Machine, through the window of his cell, spoke to the armed guard outside.

"What day of the month is it?" he asked.

"The fifteenth," was the answer.

The Thinking Machine made a mental astronomical calculation and satisfied himself that the moon would not rise until after nine o'clock that night. Then he asked another question: "Who attends to those arc lights?"

"Man from the company."

"You have no electricians in the building?"

"No."

"I should think you could save money if you had your own man."

"None of my business," replied the guard.

The guard noticed The Thinking Machine at the cell window frequently during that day, but always the face seemed listless and there was a certain wistfulness in the squint eyes behind the glasses. After a while he accepted the presence of the leonine head as a matter of course. He had seen other prisoners do the same thing; it was the longing for the outside world.

That afternoon, just before the day guard was relieved, the head appeared at the window again, and The Thinking Machine's hand held something out between the bars. It fluttered to the ground and the guard picked it up. It was a five-dollar bill.

"That's for you," called the prisoner.

As usual, the guard, took it to the warden. That gentleman looked at it suspiciously; he looked at everything that came from Cell 13 with suspicion.

"He said it was for me," explained the guard.

"It's a sort of a tip, I suppose," said the warden. "I see no particular reason why you shouldn't accept—"

Suddenly he stopped. He had remembered that The Thinking Machine had gone into Cell 13 with one five-dollar bill and two ten-dollar bills; twenty-five dollars in all. Now a five-dollar bill had been tied around the first pieces of linen that came from the cell. The warden still had it, and to convince himself he took it out and looked at it. It was five dollars; yet here was another five dollars, and The Thinking Machine had only had ten-dollar bills.

"Perhaps somebody changed one of the bills for him," he thought at last, with a sigh of relief.

But then and there he made up his mind. He would search Cell 13 as a cell was never before searched in this world. When a man could write at will, and change money, and do other wholly inexplicable things, there was something radically wrong with his prison. He planned to enter the cell at night— three o'clock would be an excellent time. The Thinking Machine must do all the weird things he did sometime. Night seemed the most reasonable.

Thus it happened that the warden stealthily descended upon Cell 13 that night at three-o'clock. He paused at the door and listened. There was no sound save the steady, regular breathing of the prisoner. The keys unfastened the double locks with scarcely a clank, and the warden entered, locking the door behind him. Suddenly he flashed his dark-lantern in the face of the recumbent figure.

If the warden had planned to startle The Thinking Machine he was mistaken, for that individual merely opened his eyes quietly, reached for his glasses and inquired, in a most matter-of-fact tone:

"Who is it?"

It would be useless to describe the search that the warden made. It was minute. Not one inch of the cell or the bed was overlooked. He found the round hole in the floor, and with a flash of inspiration thrust his thick fingers into it. After a moment of fumbling there he drew up something and looked at it in the light of his lantern.

"Ugh!" he exclaimed.

The thing he had taken out was a rat—a dead rat. His inspiration fled as a mist before the sun. But he continued the search. The Thinking Machine, without a word, arose and kicked the rat out of the cell into the corridor.

The warden climbed on the bed and tried the steel bars in the tiny window. They were perfectly rigid; every bar of the door was the same.

Then the warden searched the prisoner's clothing, beginning at the shoes. Nothing hidden in them! Then the trousers waist band. Still nothing! Then the pockets of the trousers. From one side he drew out some paper money and examined it.

"Five one-dollar bills," he gasped.

"That's right," said the prisoner.

"But the—you had two tens and a five—what the—how do you do it?"

"That's my business," said the Thinking Machine.

"Did any of my men change this money for you—on your word of honor?"

The Thinking Machine paused just a fraction of a second.

"No," he said.

"Well, do you make it?" asked the warden. He was prepared to believe anything.

"That's my business," again said the prisoner.

The warden glared at the eminent scientist fiercely. He felt—he knew—that this man was making a fool of him, yet he didn't know how. If he were a real prisoner he would get the truth—but, then, perhaps, those inexplicable things which had happened would not have been brought before him so sharply. Neither of the men spoke for a long time, then suddenly the warden turned fiercely and left the cell, slamming the door behind him. He didn't dare to speak, then.

He glanced at the clock. It was ten minutes to four. He had hardly settled himself in bed when again came that heart-breaking shriek through the prison. With a few muttered words, which, while not elegant, were highly expressive, he relighted his lantern and rushed through the prison again to the cell on the upper floor.

Again Ballard was crushing himself against the steel door, shrieking, shrieking at the top of his voice. He stopped only when the warden flashed his lamp in the cell.

"Take me out, take me out," he screamed. "I did it, I did it, I killed her. Take it away."

"Take what away?" asked the warden.

"I threw the acid in her face—I did it—I confess. Take me out of here."

Ballard's condition was pitiable; it was only an act of mercy to let him out into the corridor. There he crouched in a corner, like an animal at bay, and clasped his hands to his ears. It took half an hour to calm him sufficiently for him to speak. Then he told incoherently what had happened. On the night before at four o'clock he had heard a voice—a sepulchral voice, muffled and wailing in tone.

"What did it say?" asked the warden, curiously.

"Acid—acid—acid!" gasped the prisoner. "It accused me. Acid! I threw the acid, and the woman died. Oh!" It was a long, shuddering wail of terror.

"Acid?" echoed the warden, puzzled. The case was beyond him.

"Acid. That's all I heard—that one word, repeated several times. There were other things, too, but I didn't hear them."

"That was last night, eh?" asked the warden. "What happened to-night—what frightened you just now?"

"It was the same thing," gasped the prisoner. "Acid—acid—acid!" He covered his face with his hands and sat shivering. "It was acid I used on her, but I didn't mean to kill her. I just heard the words. It was something accusing me—accusing me." He mumbled, and was silent.

"Did you hear anything else?"

"Yes—but I couldn't understand—only a little bit—just a word or two."

"Well, what was it?"

"I heard 'acid' three times, then I heard a long, moaning sound, then—then—I heard 'No. 8 hat.' I heard that twice."

"No. 8 hat," repeated the warden. "What the devil—No. 8 hat? Accusing voices of conscience have never talked about No. 8 hats, so far as I ever heard."

"He's insane," said one of the jailers, with an air of finality.

"I believe you," said the warden. "He must be. He probably heard something and got frightened. He's trembling now. No. 8 hat! What the—"

V

When the fifth day of The Thinking Machine's imprisonment rolled around the warden was wearing a hunted look. He was anxious for the end of the thing. He could not help but feel that his distinguished prisoner had been amusing himself. And if this were so, The Thinking Machine had lost none of his sense of humor. For on this fifth day he flung down another linen note to the outside guard, bearing the words: "Only two days more." Also he flung down half a dollar.

Now the warden knew—he knew—that the man in Cell 13 didn't have any half dollars—he couldn't have any half dollars, no more than he could have pen and ink and linen, and yet he did have them. It was a condition, not a theory; that is one reason why the warden was wearing a hunted look.

That ghastly, uncanny thing, too, about "Acid" and "No. 8 hat" clung to him tenaciously. They didn't mean anything, of course, merely the ravings of an insane murderer who had been driven by fear to confess his crime, still there were so many things that "didn't mean anything" happening in the prison now since The Thinking Machine was there.

On the sixth day the warden received a postal stating that Dr Ransome and Mr Fielding would be at Chisholm Prison on the following evening, Thursday, and in the event Professor Van Dusen had not yet escaped—and they presumed he had not because they had not heard from him—they would meet him there.

"In the event he had not yet escaped!" The warden smiled grimly. Escaped!

The Thinking Machine enlivened this day for the warden with three notes. They were on the usual linen and bore generally on the appointment at half-past eight o'clock Thursday night, which appointment the scientist had made at the time of his imprisonment.

On the afternoon of the seventh day the warden passed Cell 13 and glanced in. The Thinking Machine was lying on the iron bed, apparently sleeping lightly. The cell appeared precisely as it always did to a casual glance. The warden would swear that no man was going to leave it between that hour—it was then four o'clock—and half-past eight o'clock that evening.

On his way back past the cell the warden heard the steady breathing again, and coming close to the door looked in. He wouldn't have done so if The Thinking Machine had been looking, but now—well, it was different.

A ray of light came through the high window and fell on the face of the sleeping man. It occurred to the warden for the first time that his prisoner appeared haggard and weary. Just then The Thinking Machine stirred slightly and the warden hurried on up the corridor guiltily. That evening after six o'clock he saw the jailer.

"Everything all right in Cell 13?" he asked.

"Yes, sir," replied the jailer. "He didn't eat much, though."

It was with a feeling of having done his duty that the warden received Dr Ransome and Mr Fielding shortly after seven o'clock. He intended to show them the linen notes and lay before them the full story of his woes, which was a long one. But before this came to pass, the guard from the river side of the prison yard entered the office.

"The arc light in my side of the yard won't light," he informed the warden.

"Confound it, that man's a hoodoo," thundered the official. "Everything has happened since he's been here."

The guard went back to his post in the darkness, and the warden 'phoned to the electric light company.

"This is Chisholm Prison," he said through the 'phone. "Send three or four men down here quick, to fix an arc light."

The reply was evidently satisfactory, for the warden hung up the receiver and passed out into the yard. While Dr Ransome and Mr Fielding sat waiting the guard at the outer gate came in with a special delivery letter. Dr Ransome happened to notice the address, and, when the guard went out, looked at the letter more closely.

"By George!" he exclaimed.

"What is it?" asked Mr Fielding.

Silently the doctor offered the letter. Mr Fielding examined it closely.

"Coincidence," he said. "It must be."

It was nearly eight o'clock when the warden returned to his office. The electricians had arrived in a wagon, and were now at work. The warden pressed the buzz-button communicating with the man at the outer gate in the wall.

"How many electricians came in?" he asked, over the short 'phone. "Four? Three workmen in jumpers and overalls and the manager? Frock coat and silk hat? All right. Be certain that only four go out. That's all."

He turned to Dr Ransome and Mr Fielding. "We have to be careful here—particularly," and there was broad sarcasm in his tone, "since we have scientists locked up."

The warden picked up the special delivery letter carelessly, and then began to open it.

"When I read this I want to tell you gentlemen something about how—Great Caesar!" he ended, suddenly, as he glanced at the letter. He sat with mouth open, motionless, from astonishment.

"What is it?" asked Mr Fielding.

"A special delivery from Cell 13," gasped the warden. "An invitation to supper."

"What?" and the two others arose, unanimously.

The warden sat dazed, staring at the letter for a moment, then called sharply to a guard outside in the corridor.

"Run down to Cell 13 and see if that man's in there."

The guard went as directed, while Dr Ransome and Mr Fielding examined the letter.

"It's Van Dusen's handwriting; there's no question of that," said Dr Ransome. "I've seen too much of it."

Just then the buzz on the telephone from the outer gate sounded, and the warden, in a semi-trance, picked up the receiver.

"Hello! Two reporters, eh? Let 'em come in." He turned suddenly to the doctor and Mr Fielding. "Why, the man can't be out. He must be in his cell."

THE PROBLEM OF CELL 13

Just at that moment the guard returned.

"He's still in his cell, sir," he reported. "I saw him. He's lying down."

"There, I told you so," said the warden, and he breathed freely again. "But how did he mail that letter?"

There was a rap on the steel door which led from the jail yard into the warden's office.

"It's the reporters," said the warden. "Let them in," he instructed the guard; then to the two other gentlemen: "Don't say anything about this before them, because I'd never hear the last of it."

The door opened, and the two men from the front gate entered.

"Goodevening, gentlemen," said one. That was Hutchinson Hatch; the warden knew him well.

"Well?" demanded the other, irritably. "I'm here."

That was The Thinking Machine.

He squinted belligerently at the warden, who sat with mouth agape. For the moment that official had nothing to say. Dr Ransome and Mr Fielding were amazed, but they didn't know what the warden knew. They were only amazed; he was paralyzed. Hutchinson Hatch, the reporter, took in the scene with greedy eyes.

"How—how—how did you do it?" gasped the warden, finally.

"Come back to the cell," said The Thinking Machine, in the irritated voice which his scientific associates knew so well.

The warden, still in a condition bordering on trance, led the way.

"Flash your light in there," directed The Thinking Machine.

The warden did so. There was nothing unusual in the appearance of the cell, and there—there on the bed lay the figure of The Thinking Machine. Certainly! There was the yellow hair! Again the warden looked at the man beside him and wondered at the strangeness of his own dreams.

With trembling hands he unlocked the cell door and The Thinking Machine passed inside.

"See here," he said.

He kicked at the steel bars in the bottom of the cell door and three of them were pushed out of place. A fourth broke off and rolled away in the corridor.

"And here, too," directed the erstwhile prisoner as he stood on the bed to reach the small window. He swept his hand across the opening and every bar came out.

"What's this in the bed?" demanded the warden, who was slowly recovering.

"A wig," was the reply. "Turn down the cover."

The warden did so. Beneath it lay a large coil of strong rope, thirty feet or more, a dagger, three files, ten feet of electric wire, a thin, powerful pair of steel pliers, a small tack hammer with its handle, and — and a Derringer pistol.

"'How did you do it?" demanded the warden.

"You gentlemen have an engagement to supper with me at halfpast nine o'clock," said The Thinking Machine. "Come on, or we shall be late."

"But how did you do it?" insisted the warden.

"Don't ever think you can hold any man who can use his brain," said The Thinking Machine. "Come on; we shall be late."

VI

It was an impatient supper party in the rooms of Professor Van Dusen and a somewhat silent one. The guests were Dr Ransome, Albert Fielding, the warden, and Hutchinson Hatch, reporter. The meal was served to the minute, in accordance with Professor Van Dusen's instructions of one week before; Dr Ransome found the artichokes delicious At last the supper was finished and The Thinking Machine turned full on Dr Ransome and squinted at him fiercely.

"Do you believe it now?" he demanded.

"I do," replied Dr Ransome.

"Do you admit that it was a fair test?"

"I do."

With the others, particularly the warden, he was waiting anxiously for the explanation.

"Suppose you tell us how—" began Mr Fielding.

"Yes, tell us how," said the warden.

The Thinking Machine readjusted his glasses, took a couple of preparatory squints at his audience, and began the story. He told it from the beginning logically; and no man ever talked to more interested listeners.

"My agreement was," he began, "to go into a cell, carrying nothing except what was necessary to wear, and to leave that cell within a week. I had never seen Chisholm Prison. When I went into the cell I asked for tooth powder, two ten and one five-dollar bills, and also to have my shoes blacked. Even if these requests had been refused it would not have mattered seriously. But you agreed to them."

"I knew there would be nothing in the cell which you thought I might use to advantage. So when the warden locked the door on me I was apparently helpless, unless I could turn three seemingly innocent things to use. They were things which would have been permitted to any prisoner under sentence of death, were they not, warden?"

"Tooth powder and polished shoes, yes, but not money," replied the warden.

"Anything is dangerous in the hands of a man who knows how to use it," went on The Thinking Machine. "I did nothing that first night but sleep and chase rats." He glared at the warden. "When the matter was broached I knew I could do nothing that night, so suggested next day. You gentlemen thought I wanted time to arrange an escape with outside assistance, but this was not true. I knew I could communicate with whom I pleased, when I pleased."

The warden stared at him a moment, then went on smoking solemnly.

"I was aroused next morning at six o'clock by the jailer with my breakfast," continued the scientist. "He told me dinner was at twelve and supper at six. Between these times, I gathered, I would be pretty much to myself. So immediately after breakfast I examined my outside surroundings from my cell window. One look told me it would be useless to try to scale the wall, even should I decide to leave my cell by the window, for my purpose was to leave not only the cell, but the prison. Of course, I could have gone over the wall, but it would have taken me longer to lay my plans that way. Therefore, for the moment, I dismissed all idea of that.

"From this first observation I knew the river was on that side of the prison, and that there was also a playground there. Subsequently these surmises were verified by a keeper. I knew then one important thing—that anyone might approach the prison wall from that side if necessary without attracting any particular attention. That was well to remember. I remembered it.

"But the outside thing which most attracted my attention was the feed wire to the arc light which ran within a few feet—probably three or four—of my cell window. I knew that would be valuable in the event I found it necessary to cut off that arc light."

"Oh, you shut it off tonight, then?" asked the warden.

"Having learned all I could from that window," resumed The Thinking Machine, without heeding the interruption, "I considered the idea of escaping through the prison proper. I recalled just how I had come into the cell, which I knew would be the only way. Seven doors lay between me and the outside. So, also for the time being I gave up the idea of escaping that way. And I couldn't go through the solid granite walls of the cell."

The Thinking Machine paused for a moment and Dr Ransome lighted a new cigar. For several minutes there was silence, then the scientific jail-breaker went on:

"While I was thinking about these things a rat ran across my foot. It suggested a new line of thought. There were at least half a dozen rats in the cell—I could see their beady eyes. Yet I had noticed none come under the cell door. I frightened them purposely and watched the cell door to see if they went out that way. They did not, but they were gone. Obviously they went another way. Another way meant another opening.

"I searched for this opening and found it. It was an old drain pipe, long unused and partly choked with dirt and dust. But this was the way the rats had come. They came from somewhere. Where? Drain pipes usually lead outside prison grounds. This one probably led to the river, or near it. The rats must therefore come from that direction. If they came a part of the way, I reasoned that they came all the way, because it was extremely unlikely that a solid iron or lead pipe would have any hole in it except at the exit.

"When the jailer came with my luncheon he told me two important things, although he didn't know it. One was that a new system of plumbing had been put in the prison seven years before; another that the river was only three hundred feet away. Then I knew positively that the pipe was a part of an old system; I knew, too, that it slanted generally toward the river. But did the pipe end in the water or on land?

"This was the next question to be decided. I decided it by catching several of the rats in the cell. My jailer was surprised to see me engaged in this work. I examined at least a dozen of them. They were perfectly dry; they had come through the pipe, and, most important of all, they were not house rats, but field rats. The other end of the pipe was on land, then, outside the prison walls. So far, so good.

"Then, I knew that if I worked freely from this point I must attract the warden's attention in another direction. You see, by telling the warden that I had come there to escape you made the test more severe, because I had to trick him by false scents."

The warden looked up with a sad expression in his eyes.

"The first thing was to make him think I was trying to communicate with you, Dr Ransome. So I wrote a note on a piece of linen I tore from my shirt, addressed it to Dr Ransome, tied a five-dollar bill around it and threw it out of the window. I knew the guard would take it to the warden, but I rather hoped the warden would send it as addressed. Have you that first linen note, warden?"

The warden produced the cipher.

"What the deuce does it mean, anyhow?" he asked.

"Read it backward, beginning with the 'T' signature and disregard the division into words," instructed The Thinking Machine.

The warden did so.

"T – h – i – s, this," he spelled, studied it a moment, then read it off, grinning:

"This is not the way I intend to escape."

"Well, now what do you think o' that?" he demanded, still grinning.

"I knew that would attract your attention, just as it did," said The Thinking Machine, "and if you really found out what it was, it would be a sort of gentle rebuke."

"What did you write it with?" asked Dr Ransome, after he had examined the linen and passed it to Mr Fielding.

"This," said the erstwhile prisoner, and he extended his foot. On it was the shoe he had worn in prison, though the polish was gone—scraped off clean. "The shoe blacking, moistened with water, was my ink; the metal tip of the shoe lace made a fairly good pen."

The warden looked up and suddenly burst into a laugh, half of relief, half of amusement.

"You're a wonder," he said, admiringly. "Go on."

"That precipitated a search of my cell by the warden, as I had intended," continued The Thinking Machine. "I was anxious to get the warden into the habit of searching my cell, so that finally, constantly finding nothing, he would get disgusted and quit. This at last happened, practically."

The warden blushed.

"He then took my white shirt away and gave me a prison shirt. He was satisfied that those two pieces of the shirt were all that was missing. But while he was searching my cell I had another piece of that same shirt, about nine inches square, rolled into a small ball in my mouth."

"Nine inches off that shirt?" demanded the warden. "Where did it come from?"

"The bosoms of all stiff white shirts are of triple thickness," was the explanation. "I tore out the inside thickness, leaving the bosom only two thicknesses. I knew you wouldn't see it. So much for that."

There was a little pause, and the warden looked from one to another of the men with a sheepish grin.

"Having disposed of the warden for the time being by giving him something else to think about, I took my first serious step toward freedom," said Professor Van Dusen. "I knew, within reason, that the pipe led somewhere to the playground outside; I knew a great many boys played there; I knew that rats came into my cell from out there. Could I communicate with some one outside with these things at hand?

"First was necessary, I saw, a long and fairly reliable thread, so—but here," he pulled up his trousers legs and showed that the tops of both stockings, of fine, strong lisle, were gone. "I unraveled those—after I got them started it wasn't difficult—and I had easily a quarter of a mile of thread that I could depend on.

"Then on half of my remaining linen I wrote, laboriously enough I assure you, a letter explaining my situation to this gentleman here," and he indicated Hutchinson Hatch. "I knew he would assist me for the value of the newspaper story. I tied firmly to this linen letter a ten-dollar bill—there is no surer way of attracting the eye of anyone—and wrote on the linen: 'Finder of this deliver to Hutchinson Hatch, Daily American, who will give another ten dollars for the information.'

"The next thing was to get this note outside on that playground where a boy might find it. There were two ways, but I chose the best. I took one of the rats—I became adept in catching them—tied the linen and money firmly to one leg, fastened my lisle thread to another, and turned him loose in the drain pipe. I reasoned that the natural fright of the rodent would make him run until he was outside the pipe and then out on earth he would probably stop to gnaw off the linen and money.

"From the moment the rat disappeared into that dusty pipe I became anxious. I was taking so many chances. The rat might gnaw the string, of which I held one end; other rats might gnaw it; the rat might run out of the pipe and leave the linen and money where they would never be found; a thousand other things might have happened. So began some nervous hours, but the fact that the rat ran on until only a few feet of the string remained in my cell made me think he was outside the pipe. I had carefully instructed Mr Hatch what to do in case the note reached him. The question was: Would it reach him?

"This done, I could only wait and make other plans in case this one failed. I openly attempted to bribe my jailer, and learned from him that he held the keys to only two of seven doors between me and freedom. Then I did something else to make the warden nervous. I took the steel supports out of the heels of my shoes and made a pretense of sawing the bars of my cell window. The warden raised a pretty row about that. He developed, too, the habit of shaking the bars of my cell window to see if they were solid. They were—then."

Again the warden grinned. He had ceased being astonished.

"With this one plan I had done all I could and could only wait to see what happened," the scientist went on. "I couldn't know whether my note had been delivered or even found, or whether the rat had gnawed it up. And I didn't dare to draw back through the pipe that one slender thread which connected me with the outside.

"When I went to bed that night I didn't sleep, for fear there would come the slight signal twitch at the thread which was to tell me that Mr Hatch had received the note. At half-past three o'clock, I judge, I felt this twitch, and no prisoner actually under sentence of death ever welcomed a thing more heartily."

The Thinking Machine stopped and turned to the reporter.

"You'd better explain just what you did," he said.

"The linen note was brought to me by a small boy who had been playing baseball," said Mr Hatch. "I immediately saw a big story in it, so I gave the boy another ten dollars, and got several spools of silk, some twine, and a roll of light, pliable wire. The professor's note suggested that I have the finder of the note show me just where it was picked up, and told me to make my search from there, beginning at two o'clock in the morning. If I found the other end of the thread I was to twitch it gently three times, then a fourth.

"I began the search with a small bulb electric light. It was an hour and twenty minutes before I found the end of the drain pipe, half hidden in weeds. The pipe was very large there, say twelve inches across. Then I found the end of the lisle thread, twitched it as directed and immediately I got an answering twitch.

"Then I fastened the silk to this and Professor Van Dusen began to pull it into his cell. I nearly had heart disease for fear the string would break. To the end of the silk I fastened the twine, and when that had been pulled in, I tied on the wire. Then that was drawn into the pipe and we had a substantial line, which rats couldn't gnaw, from the mouth of the drain into the cell."

The Thinking Machine raised his hand and Hatch stopped.

"All this was done in absolute silence," said the scientist. "But when the wire reached my hand I could have shouted. Then we tried another experiment, which Mr Hatch was prepared for. I tested the pipe as a speaking tube. Neither of us could hear very clearly, but I dared not speak loud for fear of attracting attention in the prison. At last I made him understand what I wanted immediately. He seemed to have great difficulty in understanding when I asked for nitric acid, and I repeated the word 'acid' several times.

"Then I heard a shriek from a cell above me. I knew instantly that some one had overheard, and when I heard you coming, Mr Warden, I feigned sleep. If you had entered my cell at that moment that whole plan of escape would have ended there. But you passed on. That was the nearest I ever came to being caught.

"Having established this improvised trolley it is easy to see how I got things in the cell and made them disappear at will. I merely dropped them back into the pipe. You, Mr Warden, could not have reached the connecting wire with your fingers; they are too large. My fingers, you see, are longer and more slender. In addition I guarded the top of that pipe with a rat—you remember how."

"I remember," said the warden, with a grimace.

"I thought that if any one were tempted to investigate that hole the rat would dampen his ardor. Mr Hatch could not send me anything useful through the pipe until next night, although he did send me change for ten dollars as a test, so I proceeded with other parts of my plan. Then I evolved the method of escape, which I finally employed.

"In order to carry this out successfully it was necessary for the guard in the yard to get accustomed to seeing me at the cell window. I arranged this by dropping linen notes to him, boastful in tone, to make the warden believe, if possible, one of his assistants was communicating with the outside for me. I would stand at my window for hours gazing out, so the guard could see, and occasionally I spoke to him. In that way I learned that the prison had no electricians of its own, but was dependent upon the lighting company if anything should go wrong.

"That cleared the way to freedom perfectly. Early in the evening of the last day of my imprisonment, when it was dark, I planned to cut the feed wire which was only a few feet from my window, reaching it with an acid-tipped wire I had. That would make that side of the prison perfectly dark while the electricians were searching for the break. That would also bring Mr Hatch into the prison yard.

"There was only one more thing to do before I actually began the work of setting myself free. This was to arrange final details with Mr Hatch through our speaking tube. I did this within half an hour after the warden left my cell on the fourth night of my imprisonment. Mr Hatch again had serious difficulty in understanding me, and I repeated the word 'acid' to him several times, and later the words: 'Number eight hat'—that's my size—and these were the things which made a prisoner upstairs confess to murder, so one of the jailers told me next day. This prisoner heard our voices, confused of course, through the pipe, which also went to his cell. The cell directly over me was not occupied, hence no one else heard.

"Of course the actual work of cutting the steel bars out of the window and door was comparatively easy with nitric acid, which I got through the pipe in thin bottles, but it took time. Hour after hour on the fifth and sixth and seven days the guard below was looking at me as I worked on the bars of the window with the acid on a piece of wire. I used the tooth powder to prevent the acid spreading. I looked away abstractedly as I worked and each minute the acid cut deeper into the metal. I noticed that the jailers always tried the door by shaking the upper part, never the lower bars, therefore I cut the lower bars, leaving them hanging in place by thin strips of metal. But that was a bit of dare-deviltry. I could not have gone that way so easily."

The Thinking Machine sat silent for several minutes. "I think that makes everything clear," he went on. "Whatever points I have not explained were merely to confuse the warden and jailers. These things in my bed I brought in to please Mr Hatch, who wanted to improve the story. Of course, the wig was necessary in my plan. The special delivery letter I wrote and directed in my cell with Mr Hatch's fountain pen, then sent it out to him and he mailed it. That's all, I think."

"But your actually leaving the prison grounds and then coming in through the outer gate to my office?" asked the warden.

"Perfectly simple," said the scientist. "I cut the electric light wire with acid, as I said, when the current was off. Therefore when the current was turned on, the arc light didn't light. I knew it would take some time to find out what was the matter and make repairs. When the guard went to report to you the yard was dark. I crept out the window — it was a tight fit, too — replaced the bars by standing on a narrow ledge and remained in a shadow until the force of electricians arrived. Mr Hatch was one of them.

"When I saw him I spoke and he handed me a cap, a jumper and overalls, which I put on within ten feet of you, Mr Warden, while you were in the yard. Later Mr Hatch called me, presumably as a workman, and together we went out the gate to get something out of the wagon. The gate guard let us pass out readily as two workmen who had just passed in. We changed our clothing and reappeared, asking to see you. We saw you. That's all."

There was silence for several minutes. Dr Ransome was first to speak. "Wonderful!" he exclaimed. "Perfectly amazing."

"How did Mr Hatch happen to come with the electricians?" asked Mr Fielding.

"His father is manager of the company," replied The Thinking Machine.

"But what if there had been no Mr Hatch outside to help?"

"Every prisoner has one friend outside who would help him escape if he could."

"Suppose—just suppose—there had been no old plumbing system there?" asked the warden, curiously.

"There were two other ways out," said The Thinking Machine, enigmatically.

Ten minutes later the telephone bell rang. It was a request for the warden. "Light all right, eh?" the warden asked, through the 'phone. "Good. Wire cut beside Cell 13? Yes, I know. One electrician too many? What's that? Two came out?"

The warden turned to the others with a puzzled expression.

"He only let in four electricians, he has let out two and says there are three left."

"I was the odd one," said The Thinking Machine.

"Oh," said the warden. "I see." Then through the 'phone: "Let the fifth man go. He's all right."

4

MY FIRST EXPERIENCE WITH THE GREAT LOGICIAN

It was once my good fortune to meet in person Professor Augustus S. F. X. Van Dusen, Ph.D., LL.D., F.R.S., M.D., etc. The meeting came about through a singular happening, which was as mystifying as it was dangerous to me—he saved my life in fact; and in process of hauling me back from eternity—the edge of that appalling mist which separates life and death—I had full opportunity of witnessing the workings of that marvelously keen, cold brain which has made him the most distinguished scientist and logician of his day. It was sometime afterward, however, that Professor Van Dusen was identified in my mind with The Thinking Machine.

I had dined at the Hotel Teutonic, taken a cigar from my pocket, lighted it, and started for a stroll across Boston Common. It was after eight o'clock on one of those clear, nippy evenings of winter. I was near the center of the Common on one of the many little by paths which lead toward Beacon Hill when I became conscious of an acute pain in my chest, a sudden fluttering of my heart, and a constriction in my throat. The lights in the distance began to waver and grow dim, and perspiration broke out all over me from an inward, gnawing agony which grew more intense each moment. I felt myself

MY FIRST EXPERIENCE

reeling, my cigar dropped from my fingers, and I clutched at a seat to steady myself. There was no one near me. I tried to call, then everything grew dark, and I sank down on the ground. My last recollection was of a figure approaching me; the last words I heard were a petulant, irritable "Dear me!" then I was lost to consciousness.

When I recovered consciousness I lay on a couch in a strange room. My eyes wandered weakly about and lingered with a certain childish interest on half a dozen spots which reflected glitteringly the light of an electric bulb set high up on one side. These bright spots, I came to realize after a moment, were metal parts of various instruments of a laboratory. For a time I lay helpless, listless, with trembling pulse and eardrums thumping, then I heard steps approaching, and some one bent over and peered into my face.

It was a man, but such a man as I had never seen before. A great shock of straw yellow hair tumbled about a broad, high forehead, a small, wrinkled, querulous face—the face of an aged child—a pair of watery blue eyes squinting aggressively through thick spectacles, and a thin lipped mouth as straight as the mark of a surgeon's knife, save for the drooping corners. My impression then was that it was some sort of hallucination, the distorted vagary of a disordered brain, but gradually my vision cleared and the grip of slender fingers on my pulse made me realize the actuality of the—the apparition.

"How do you feel?" The thin lips had opened just enough to let out the question, the tone was curt and belligerent, and the voice rasped unpleasantly. At the same time the squint eyes were focused on mine with a steady, piercing glare that made me uneasy. I tried to answer, but my tongue refused to move. The gaze continued for an instant, then the man—The Thinking Machine—turned away and prepared a particularly vile smelling concoction, which he poured into me. Then I was lost again.

After a time—it might have been minutes or hours—I felt again the hand on my pulse, and again The Thinking Machine favored me with a glare. An hour later I was sitting up on the couch, with unclouded brain, and a heartbeat which was nearly normal. It was then I learned why Professor Van Dusen, an eminent man of the sciences, had been dubbed The Thinking Machine; I understood first hand how material muddles were so unfailingly dissipated by unadulterated, infallible logic.

Remember that I had gone into that room an inanimate thing, inert, unconscious, mentally and physically dead to all practical intents—beyond the point where I might have babbled any elucidating fact. And remember, too, please, that I didn't know—had not the faintest idea—what had happened to me, beyond the fact that I had fallen unconscious. The Thinking Machine didn't ask questions, yet he supplied all the missing details, together with a host of personal, intimate things of which he could personally have had no knowledge. In other words, I was an abstruse problem, and he solved me. With head tilted back against the cushion of the chair—and such a head!—with eyes unwaveringly turned upward, and finger tips pressed idly together, he sat there, a strange, grotesque little figure in the midst of his laboratory apparatus. Not for a moment did he display the slightest interest in me, personally; it was all as if I had been written down on a slate, to be wiped off when I was solved.

"Did this ever happen to you before?" he asked abruptly.

"No," I replied. "What was it?"

"You were poisoned," he said. "The poison was a deadly one—corrosive sublimate, or bichlorid or mercury. The shock was very severe; but you will be all right in—"

"Poisoned!" I exclaimed, aghast. "Who poisoned me? Why?"

"You poisoned yourself," he replied testily. "It was your own carelessness. Nine out of ten persons handle poison as if it was candy, and you are like all the rest."

"But I couldn't have poisoned myself," I protested. "Why, I have had no occasion to handle poisons—not for—I don't know how long."

"I do know," he said. "It was nearly a year ago when you handled this; but corrosive sublimate is always dangerous."

The tone irritated me, the impassive arrogance of the little man inflamed my reeling brain, and I am not sure that I did not shake my finger in his face. "If I was poisoned," I declared with some heat, "it was not my fault. Somebody gave it to me; somebody tried to—"

"You poisoned yourself," said The Thinking Machine again impatiently. "You talk like a child."

"How do you know I poisoned myself? How do you know I ever handled a poison? And how do you know it was a year ago, if I did?"

The Thinking Machine regarded me coldly for an instant, and then those strange eyes of his wandered upward again. "I know those things," he said, "just as I know your name, address, and profession from cards I found in your pockets; just as I know you smoke, from half a dozen cigars on you; just as I know that you are wearing those clothes for the first time this winter; just as I know you lost your wife within a few months; that you kept house then; and that your house was infested with insects. I know just as I know everything else—by the rules of inevitable logic."

My head was whirling. I stared at him in blank astonishment. "But how do you know those things?" I insisted in bewilderment.

"The average person of today," replied the scientist, "knows nothing unless it is written down and thrust under his nose. I happen to be a physician. I saw you fall, and went to you, my first thought being of heart trouble. Your pulse showed it was not that, and it was obviously not apoplexy. Now, there was no visible reason why you should have collapsed like that. There had been no shot; there was no wound; therefore, poison. An examination confirmed this first hypothesis; your symptoms showed that the poison was bichlorid of mercury. I put you in a cab and brought you here. From the fact that you were not dead then I knew that your system had absorbed only a minute quantity of poison—a quantity so small that it demonstrated instantly that there had been no suicidal intent, and indicated, too, that no one else had administered it. If this was true, I knew—I didn't guess, I knew—that the poisoning was accidental. How accidental?

"My first surmise, naturally, was that the poison had been absorbed through the mouth. I searched your pockets. The only thing I found that you would put into your mouth were the cigars. Were they poisoned? A test showed they were, all of them. With intent to kill? No. Not enough poison was used. Was the poison a part of the gum used to bind the cigar? Possible, of course, but not probable. Then what?" He lowered his eyes and squinted at me suddenly, aggressively. I shook my head, and, as an afterthought, closed my gaping mouth.

"Perhaps you carried corrosive sublimate in your pocket. I didn't find any; but perhaps you once carried it. I tore out the coat pocket in which I found the cigars and subjected it to the test. At sometime there had been corrosive sublimate, in the form of powder or crystals, in the pocket, and in some manner, perhaps because of an imperfection in the package, a minute quantity was loose in your pocket.

"Here was an answer to every question, and more; here was how the cigars were poisoned, and, in combination with the tailor's tag inside your pocket, a short history of your life. Briefly it was like this: Once you had corrosive sublimate in your pocket. For what purpose? First thought—to rid your home of insects. Second thought—if you were boarding, married or unmarried, the task of getting rid of the insects would have been left to the servant; and this would possibly have been the case if you had been living at home. So I assumed for the instant that you were keeping house, and if keeping house, you were married—you bought the poison for use in your own house.

"Now, without an effort, naturally, I had you married, and keeping house. Then what? The tailor's tag, with your name, and the date your clothing was made—one year and three months ago. It is winter clothing. If you had worn it since the poison was loose in your pocket the thing that happened to you tonight would have happened to you before; but it never happened before, therefore I assume that you had the poison early last spring, when insects began to be troublesome, and immediately after that you laid away the suit until this winter. I know you are wearing the suit for the first time this winter, because, again, this thing has not happened before, and because, too, of the faint odor of moth balls. A band of crape on your hat, the picture of a young woman in your watch, and the fact that you are now living at your club, as your bill for last month shows, establish beyond doubt that you are a widower."

"It's perfectly miraculous!" I exclaimed.

"Logic, logic, logic," snapped the irritable little scientist. "You are a lawyer, you ought to know the correlation of facts; you ought to know that two and two make four, not sometimes but all the time."

5

KIDNAPPED BABY BLAKE, MILLIONAIRE

I

Douglas Blake, millionaire, sat flat on the floor and gazed with delighted eyes at the unutterable beauties of a highly colored picture book. He was only fourteen months old, and the picture book was quite the most beautiful thing he had ever beheld. Evelyn Barton, a lovely girl of twenty-two or three years, sat on the floor opposite and listened with a slightly amused smile as Baby Blake in his infinite wisdom discoursed learnedly on the astonishing things he found in the book.

The floor whereon Baby Blake sat was that of the library of the Blake home, in the outskirts of Lynn. This home, handsomely but modestly furnished, had been built by Baby Blake's father, Langdon Blake, who had died four months previously, leaving Baby Blake's beautiful mother, Elizabeth Blake, heart-broken and crushed by the blow, and removing her from the social world of which she had been leader.

Here, quietly, with but three servants and Miss Barton, the nurse, who could hardly be classed as a servant—rather a companion—Mrs Blake had lived on for the present.

The great house was gloomy, but it had been the scene of all her happiness, and she had clung to it. The building occupied relatively a central position in a plot of land facing the street for 200 feet or so, and stretching back about 300 feet. A stone wall inclosed it.

In Summer this plot was a great velvety lawn; now the first snow of the Winter had left an inch deep blanket over all, unbroken save the cement—paved walk which extended windingly from the gate in the street wall to the main entrance of the home. This path had been cleaned of snow and was now a black streak through the whiteness.

Near the front stoop this path branched off and led on around the building toward the back. This, too, had been cleared of snow, but beyond the back door entrance the white blanket covered everything back to the rear wall of the property. There against the rear wall, to the right as one stood behind the house, was a roomy barn and stable; in the extreme left hand corner of the property was a cluster of tall trees, with limbs outstretched fantastically.

The driveway from the front was covered with snow. It had been several weeks since Mrs Blake had had occasion to use either of her vehicles or horses, so she had closed the barn and stabled the horses outside. Now the barn was wholly deserted. From one of the great trees a swing, which had been placed there for the delight of Baby Blake, swung idly.

In the Summer Baby Blake had been wont to toddle the hundred or more feet from the house to the swing; but now that pleasure was forbidden. He was confined to the house by the extreme cold.

When the snow began to fall that day about two o'clock Baby Blake had shown enthusiasm. It was the first snow he remembered. He stood at a window of the warm library and, pointing out with a chubby finger, told Miss Barton:

"Me want doe."

Miss Barton interpreted this as a request to be taken out or permitted to go out in the snow.

"No, no," she said, firmly. "Cold. Baby must not go. Cold. Cold."

Baby Blake raised his voice in lusty protestation at this unkindness of his nurse, and finally Mrs Blake had to pacify him. Since then a hundred things had been used to divert Baby Blake's mind from the outside.

This snow had fallen for an hour, then stopped, and the clouds passed. Now, at fifteen minutes of six o'clock in the evening, the moon glittered coldly and clearly over the unbroken surface of the snow. Star points spangled the sky; the wind had gone, and extreme quiet lay over the place. Even the sound from the street, where an occasional vehicle passed, was muffled by the snow. Baby Blake heard a jingling sleigh bell somewhere in the distance and raised his head inquiringly.

"Pretty horse," said Miss Balton, quickly indicating a splash of color in the open book.

"Pitty horsie," said Baby Blake.

"Horse," said Miss Barton. "Four legs. One, two, three, four," she counted.

"Pitty horsie," said Baby Blake again.

He turned another page with a ruthless disregard of what might happen to it.

"Pitty kitty," he went on, wisely.

"Yes, pretty kitty," the nurse agreed.

"Pitty doggie, 'n' pitty ev'fing, ooo-o-oh," Baby Blake was gravely enthusiastic. "Ef'nit," he added, as his eye caught a full page picture.

"Elephant, yes," said Miss Barton. "Almost bedtime," she added.

"No, no," insisted Baby Blake, vigorously. "Pity ef 'nit."

Then Baby Blake arose from his seat on the floor and toddled over to where Miss Barton sat, plumping down heavily, directly in front of her. Here, with the picture book in his hands he lay back with his head resting against her knee. Mrs Blake appeared at the door.

KIDNAPPED BABY BLAKE, MILLIONAIRE 71

"Miss Barton, a moment please," she said. Her face was white and there was a strange note in her voice.

A little anxiously, the girl arose and went into the adjoining room with Mrs Blake, leaving Baby Blake with the picture book outspread on the floor. Mrs Blake handed her an open letter, written on a piece of wrapping paper in a scrawly, almost indecipherable hand.

"This came in the late afternoon mail," said the mother. "Read it."

"'We hav maid plans to kiddnap your baby,'" Miss Barton read slowly. "'Nothig cann bee dun to keep us from it so it wont do no good to tel the polece. If you will git me ten thousan dolers we will not, and will go away. Advertis YES or NOA ann sin your name in a Boston Amurikan. Then we will tell you wat to do. (sined) Three. (3)'"

Miss Barton was silent a moment as she realized what she had read and there was a quick-caught breath.

"A threat to kidnap," said the mother. "Evelyn, Evelyn, can you believe it?"

"Oh, Mrs Blake," and tears leaped to the girl's eyes quickly. "Oh, the monsters."

"I don't know what to do," said the mother, uncertainly.

"The police, I would suggest," replied the girl, quickly. "I should turn it over to the police immediately."

"Then the newspaper notoriety," said the mother, "and after all it may mean nothing. I think perhaps it would be better for us to leave here tomorrow, and go into Boston for the Winter. I could never live here with this horrible fear hanging over me—if I should lose my baby, too, it would kill me."

"As you say, but I would suggest the police, nevertheless," the girl insisted gently.

"Of course the money is nothing," she went on. "I would give every penny for the boy if I had to, but there's the fear and uncertainty of it. I think perhaps it would be better for you to pack up Douglas's little clothes tonight and tomorrow we will go to Boston to a hotel until we can make other arrangements for the Winter. You need not mention the matter to the others in the house."

"I think perhaps that would be best," said Miss Barton, "but I still think the police should be notified."

The two women left the room together and returned to the library after about ten minutes, where Baby Blake had been looking at the picture book. The baby was not there, and Miss Barton turned and glanced quickly at Mrs Blake. The mother apparently paid no attention, and the nurse passed into another room, thinking Douglas had gone there.

Within ten minutes the household was in an uproar—Baby Blake had disappeared. Miss Barton, the servants and the distracted mother raced through the roomy building, searching every nook and corner, calling for Douglas. No answer. At last Miss Barton and Mrs Blake met face to face in the library over the picture book the baby had been admiring.

"I'm afraid it's happened," said the nurse.

"Kidnapped!" exclaimed the mother. "Oh," and with waxen white face she sank back on a couch in a dead faint.

Regardless of the mother, Evelyn ran to the telephone and notified the police. They responded promptly, three detectives and two uniformed officers. The threatening letter was placed in their hands, and one of them laid its contents before his chief by 'phone, a general alarm was sent out.

While the uniformed men searched the house again from attic to cellar the two other plain clothes men searched outside. Together they went over the ground, but the surface of the snow was unbroken save for their own footprints and the paved path. From the front wall, which faced the street, the detectives walked slowly back, one on each side of the house, searching in the snow for some trace of a footprint.

There was nothing to reward this vigilance, and they met behind the house. Each shook his head. Then one stopped suddenly and pointed to the snow which lay at their feet and spreading away over the immense back yard. The other detective looked intently then stopped and stared.

What he saw was the footprint of a child—a baby. The tracks led straight away through the snow toward the back wall, and without a word the two men followed them, one by one; the regular toddling steps of a baby who is only fairly certain of his feet. Ten, twenty, thirty feet they went on in a straight line and already the detectives saw a possible solution. It was that Baby Blake had wandered away of his own free will.

Then, as they were following the tracks, they stopped suddenly astounded. Each dropped on his knees in the snow and sought vainly for something, sought over a space of many feet, then turned back to the tracks again.

"Well, if that—" one began.

The footprints, going steadily forward across the yard, had stopped. There was the last, made as if Baby Blake had intended to go forward, but there were no more tracks—no more traces of tracks—nothing. Baby Blake had walked to this point, and then—

"Why he must have gone straight up in the air," gasped one of the detectives. He sank down on a small wooden box three or four feet from where the tracks ended, and wiped the perspiration from his face.

II

"All problems may be reduced to an arithmetical basis by a simple mental process," declared Professor Augustus S. F. X. Van Dusen, emphatically. "Once a problem is so reduced, no matter what it is, it may be solved. If you play chess, Mr Hatch, you will readily grasp what I mean. Our great chess masters are really our greatest logicians and mathematicians, yet their efforts are directed in a way which can be of no use save to demonstrate, theatrically, I may say, the unlimited possibilities of the human mind."

Hutchinson Hatch, reporter, leaned back in his chair and watched the great scientist and logician as he pottered around the long workbench beside the big window of his tiny laboratory. It was here that Professor Van Dusen had achieved some of those marvels which had attracted the attention of the world at large and had won for him a long list of honorary initials.

Hatch doubted if the Professor himself could recall these — that is beyond the more common ones of Ph.D., LL.D., M.D., and M.A. There were strange combinations of letters bestowed by French, Italian, German and English educational and scientific institutions, which were delighted to honor so eminent a scientist as Professor Van Dusen, so-called The Thinking Machine.

The slender body of the scientist, bowed from close study and minute microscopic observation, gave the impression of physical weakness — an impression which was wholly correct — and made the enormous head which topped the figure seem abnormal. Added to this was the long yellow hair of the scientist, which sometimes as he worked fell over his face and almost obscured the keen blue eyes perpetually squinting through unusually thick glasses.

"By the reduction of a problem to an arithmetical basis," The Thinking Machine went on, "I mean the finding of the cause of an effect. For instance, a man is dead. We know only that. Reason tells us that he died naturally or was killed.

"If killed, it may have been an accident, design or suicide. There are no alternatives. The average mind grasps those possibilities instantly as facts because the average mind has to do with death and understands. We may call this primary reasoning instinct.

"In the higher reasoning which can only come from long study and experiment, imagination is necessary to supply temporarily gaps caused by absence of facts. Imagination is the backbone of the scientific mind. Marconi had to imagine wireless telegraphy before he accomplished it. It is the same with the telephone, the telegraph, the steam engine and those scores of commonplace marvels which are a part of our everyday life.

"The higher scientific mind is, perforce, the mind of a logician. It must possess imagination to a remarkable extent. For instance, science proved that all matter is composed of atoms—the molecular theory. Having proven this, scientific imagination saw that it was possible that atoms were themselves composed of more minute atoms, and sought to prove this. It did so.

"Therefore we know atoms make atoms, and that more minute atoms make those atoms, and so on down to the point of absolute indivisibility. This is logic.

"Applied in the other direction this imagination—really logic—leads to amazing possibilities. It would grade upward something like this: Man is made of atoms; man and his works as other atoms make cities; cities and nature as atoms make countries; countries and oceans as atoms make worlds.

"Then comes the supreme imaginative leap which would make worlds merely atoms, pin point parts of a vast solar system; the vast solar system itself merely an atom in some greater scheme of creation which the imagination refuses to grasp, which staggers the mind. It is all logic, logic, logic."

The irritated voice stopped as the scientist lifted a graded measuring glass to the light and squinted for an instant at its contents, which, under the amazed eyes of Hutchinson Hatch, swiftly changed from a brilliant scarlet to a pure white.

"You have heard me say frequently, Mr Hatch," The Thinking Machine resumed, "that two and two make four, not sometimes, but all the time—atoms make atoms, therefore atoms make creations." He paused. "That change of color in this chemical is merely a change of atoms; it has in no way affected the consistency or weight of the liquid. Yet the red atoms have disappeared, eliminated by the white."

"The logic being that the white atoms are the stronger?" asked Hatch, almost timidly.

"Precisely," said The Thinking Machine, "and also constant and victorious enemies of the red atoms. In other words that was a war between red and white atoms you just witnessed. Who shall say that a war on this earth is not as puny to the observer of this earth as an atom in the greater creation, as was that little war to us?"

Hatch blinked a little at the question. It opened up something bigger than his mind had ever struggled with before, and he was a newspaper reporter, too. Professor Van Dusen turned away and stirred up more chemicals in another glass, then poured the contents of one glass into another.

Hatch heard the telephone bell ring in the next room, and after a moment Martha, the aged woman who was the household staff of the scientist's modest home, appeared at the door.

"Some one to speak to Mr Hatch at the 'phone," she said.

Hatch went to the 'phone. At the other end was his city editor bursting with impatience.

"A big kidnapping story," the city editor said. "A wonder. I've been looking for you everywhere. Happened tonight about 6 o'clock—It's now 8:30. Jump up to Lynn quick and get it."

Then the city editor went on to detail the known points of the mystery, as the police of Lynn had learned them; the child left alone for only two or three minutes, the letter threatening kidnapping, the demand for $10,000 and the footsteps in the snow which led to—nothing.

Thoroughly alive with the instinct of the reporter Hatch returned to the laboratory where The Thinking Machine was at work.

"Another mystery," he said, persuasively.

"What is it?" asked The Thinking Machine, without turning.

Hatch repeated what information he had and The Thinking Machine listened without comment, down to the discovery of the tracks in the snow, and the abrupt ending of these.

"Babies don't have wings, Mr Hatch," said The Thinking Machine, severely.

"I know," said Hatch. "Would—would you like to go out with me and look it over?"

"It's silly to say the tracks end there," declared The Thinking Machine aggressively. "They must go somewhere. If they don't, they are not the boy's tracks."

"If you'd like to go," said Hatch, coaxingly, "we could get there by half-past nine. It's half-past eight now."

"I'll go," said the other suddenly.

An hour later, they were at the front gate of the Blake home in Lynn. The Thinking Machine saw the kidnappers' letter. He looked at it closely and dismissed it apparently with a wave of his hand. He talked for a long time to the mother, to the nurse, Evelyn Barton, to the servants, then went out into the back yard where the tiny tracks were found.

Here, seeing perfectly by the brilliant light of the moon, The Thinking Machine remained for in hour. He saw the last of the tiny footprints which led nowhere, and he sat on the box where the detective had sat. Then he arose suddenly and examined the box. It was, he found, of wood, approximately two feet square, raised only four or five inches above the ground. It was built to cover and protect the main water connection with the house. The Thinking Machine satisfied himself on this point by looking inside.

From this box he sought in every direction for footprints-tracks which were not obviously those of the detectives or his own or Hatch's. No one else had been permitted to go over the ground, the detectives objecting to this until they had completed their investigations.

No other tracks or footprints appeared; there was nothing to indicate that there had been tracks which had been skillfully covered up by whoever made them.

Again The Thinking Machine sat down on the box and studied his surroundings. Hatch watched him curiously. First he looked away toward the stone wall, nearly a hundred feet in front of him. There was positively no indentation in the snow of any kind so far as Hatch could see. Then the scientist looked back toward the house—one of the detectives had told him it was just forty-eight feet from the box—but there were no tracks there save those the detectives and Hatch and himself had made.

Then The Thinking Machine looked toward the back of the lot. Here in the bright moonlight he could see the barn and the clump of trees, several inside the enclosure made by the stone wall and others outside, extending away indefinitely, snow laden and grotesque in the moonlight. From the view in this direction The Thinking Machine turned to the other stone wall, a hundred feet or so. Here, too, he vainly sought footprints in the snow.

Finally he arose and walked in this direction with an expression of as near bewilderment on his face as Hatch had ever seen. A small dark spot in the snow had attracted his attention. It was eight or ten feet from the box. He stopped and looked at it; it was a stone of flat surface, perhaps a foot square and devoid of snow.

"Why hasn't this any snow on it?" he asked Hatch.

Hatch started and shook his head. The Thinking Machine, bowed almost to the ground, continued to stare at the stone for a moment, then straightened up and continued walking toward the wall. A few feet further on a rope, evidently a clothes line, barred his way. Without stopping, he ducked his head beneath it and walked on toward the wall, still staring at the ground.

From the wall he retraced his steps to the clothes line, then walked along under that, still staring at the snow, to its end, sixty or seventy feet toward the back of the enclosure. Two or three supports placed at regular intervals beneath the line were closely examined.

"Find anything?" asked Hatch, finally.

The Thinking Machine shook his head impatiently.

"It's amazing," he exclaimed petulantly, like a disappointed child.

"It is," Hatch agreed, cheerfully.

The Thinking Machine turned and walked back toward the house as he had come, Hatch following.

"I think we'd better go back to Boston," he said tartly.

Hatch silently acquiesced. Neither spoke until they were in the train, and The Thinking Machine turned suddenly to the wondering reporter.

"Did it seem possible to you that those are not the footprints of Baby Blake at all, only the prints of his shoes?" he demanded suddenly.

"How did they get there?" asked Hatch, in turn.

The Thinking Machine shook his head.

On the afternoon of the next day, when the newspapers were full of the mystery, Mrs Blake received this letter, signed "Three" as before:

"We hav the baby and will bring him bak for twenny fiv thousan dolers. Will you give it. Advertis as befour dereckted, YES or NOA."

III

When Hutchinson Hatch went to inform The Thinking Machine of the appearance of this second letter late in the afternoon, he found the scientist sitting in his little laboratory, finger tips pressed together, squinting steadily at the ceiling. There was a little puzzled line on the high brow, a line Hatch never saw there before, and frank perplexity was in the blue eyes.

The Thinking Machine listened without changing his position as Hatch told him of the letter and its contents.

"What do you make of it all, professor?" asked the reporter.

"I don't know," was the reply — one which was a little startling to Hatch. "It's most perplexing."

"The only known facts seem to be that Baby Blake was kidnapped, and is now in the possession of the kidnappers," said Hatch.

"Those tracks — the footprints in the snow, I mean — furnish the real problem in this case," said the other after a moment. "Presumably they were made by the baby — yet they might not have been. They might have been put there merely to mislead anyone who began a search. If the baby made them — how and why do they stop as they do? If they were made merely with the baby's shoes, to mislead investigation, the same question remains — how?

"Let's see a moment. We will dismiss the seeming fact that the baby walked on off into the air and disappeared, granting that those tracks were made by the baby. We will also dismiss the possibility that the baby was with anyone when it made the tracks, if it did make them. There were certainly no other footprints but those. There were no footprints leading from or to that point where the baby tracks stopped.

"What are the possibilities? What remains? A balloon? If we accept the balloon as a possibility we must at the same time relinquish the theory of a preconceived plan of abduction. Why? Because no successful plan could have been arranged so that that baby, of its own will, would have been in that particular spot at that particular moment. Therefore a balloon might have been floated over the place a thousand times without success, and balloons are large – they attract attention, therefore are to be avoided.

"There is a possibility – a bare one – that a balloon with a trailing anchor or hook did pass over the place, and that this hook caught up the baby by its clothing, lifting it clear of the ground. But in that event it was not kidnapping – it was accident. But here against the theory of accident we have the kidnappers' letters.

"If not a balloon, then an eagle? Hardly possible. It would take a bird of exceptional strength to have lifted a fourteen-month child, and besides there are a thousand things against such a possibility. Certainly the winged man is not known to science, yet there is every evidence of his handiwork here. Briefly, the problem is – granting that the baby itself made the tracks – how was a baby lifted out of the relative centre of a large yard?

"Consider for a moment that the baby did not make the tracks – that they were placed there by some one else. Then we are confronted by the same question – how? A person might have fastened shoes to a long pole and rigged up some arrangement of the sort, and made the tracks for a distance say of twenty feet out into the snow, but remember the tracks run out forty-eight feet to the box you say.

"If it would have been possible for a person to stand on that box without leaving a track to it or from it, he might have finished the tracks with the shoes on a pole, but nobody went to that box."

The Thinking Machine was silent for several minutes. Hatch had nothing to say. The Thinking Machine seemed to have covered the possibilities thoroughly.

"Of course, it might have been possible for a person in a balloon to have put the tracks there, but it would have been a senseless proceeding," the scientist went on. "Certainly there could have been no motive for it strong enough to make a person invite discovery by sailing about the house in a balloon even at night. We face a stone wall, Mr Hatch – a stone wall. It is possible for the mind to follow it only to a certain point as it now stands."

He arose and disappeared into an adjoining room, returning in a few minutes with his hat and overcoat.

"Of course," he said to Hatch, "if the baby is alive and in the possession of the kidnappers, it is possible to recover it, and we'll do that, but the real problem remains."

"If it is alive?" Hatch repeated.

"Yes, if," said the other shortly. "There are in my mind grave doubts on that point."

"But the kidnappers' letters?" said Hatch

"Let's go find out who wrote them," said the other, enigmatically.

Together the two men went to Lynn, and there for half an hour The Thinking Machine talked to Mrs Blake. He came out finally with a package in his hand.

Miss Barton, with eyes red, apparently from weeping, and evident sorrow imprinted on her pretty face, entered the room almost at the same moment.

"Miss Barton," the scientist asked, "could you tell me how much the baby Douglas weighed – relatively, I mean?"

The girl gazed at him a moment as if startled. "About thirty pounds, I should say," she answered.

"Thanks," said The Thinking Machine, and turned to Hatch. "I have twenty-five thousand dollars in this package," he said.

Miss Barton turned and glanced quickly toward him, then passed out of the room.

"What are you going to do with it?" asked Hatch.

"It's for the kidnappers," was the reply. "The police advised Mrs Blake not to try to make terms – I advised her the other way and she gave me this."

"What's the next step?" Hatch asked.

"To put the advertisement 'Yes' signed by Mrs Blake in the newspaper," said The Thinking Machine. "That's in accordance with the stipulations of the letters."

An hour later the two men were in Boston. The advertisement was inserted in the Boston American as directed. The next day Mrs Blake received a third letter.

"Rapp the munny in a ole nuspaipr ann thow it onn the trash – heape at the addge of the vakant lott one blok down the street frum wear you liv," it directed. "Putt it on topp. We wil gett it ann yore baby wil be in yore armms two ours latter. Three (3)."

This letter was immediately placed in the hands of The Thinking Machine. Mrs Blake's face flushed with hope, and believing that the child would be restored to her, she waited in a fever of impatience.

"Now, Mr Hatch," instructed The Thinking Machine. "Do with this package as directed. A man will come for it some time. I shall leave the task of finding out who he is, where he goes and all about him to you. He is probably a man of low mentality, though not so low as the misspelled words of his letter would have you believe. He should be easily trapped. Don't interfere with him – merely report to me when you find out these things."

Alone The Thinking Machine returned to Boston. Thirty-six hours later, in the early morning, a telegram came for him. It was as follows:

"Have man located in Lynn and trace of baby. Come quick, if possible, to — Hotel. Hatch."

IV

The Thinking Machine answered the telegraphic summons immediately, but instead of elation on his face there was another expression – possibly surprise. On the train he read and re-read the telegram.

"Have trace of baby," he mused. "Why, it's perfectly astonishing."

White-faced from exhaustion, and with eyes drooping from lack of sleep, Hutchinson Hatch met The Thinking Machine in the hotel lobby and they immediately went to a room, which the reporter had engaged on the third floor.

The Thinking Machine listened without comment as Hatch told the story of what he had done. He had placed the bundle, then hired a room overlooking the vacant lot and had remained there at the window for hours. At last night came, but there were clouds which effectively hid the moon. Then Hatch had gone out and secreted himself near the trash pile.

Here from six o'clock in the evening until four in the morning he had remained, numbed with cold and not daring to move. At last his long vigil was rewarded. A man suddenly appeared near the trash heap, glanced around furtively, and then picked up the newspaper package, felt of it to assure himself that it contained something, and then started away quickly.

The work of following him Hatch had not found difficult. He had gone straight to a tenement in the eastern end of Lynn and disappeared inside. Later in the morning, after the occupants of the house were about, Hatch made inquiries which established the identity of the man without question.

His name was Charles Gates and he lived with his wife on the fourth floor of the tenement. His reputation was not wholly savory, and he drank a great deal. He was a man of some education, but not of such ignorance as the letters he had written would indicate.

"After learning all these facts," Hatch went on, "my idea was to see the man and talk to him or to his wife. I went there this morning about nine o'clock, as a book agent." The reporter smiled a little. "His wife, Mrs Gates, didn't want any books, but I nearly sold her a sewing machine.

"Anyway, I got into the apartments and remained there for fifteen or twenty minutes. There was only one room which I didn't enter, of the four there. In that room, the woman explained, her husband was asleep. He had been out late the night before, she said. Of course I knew that.

"I asked if she had any babies and received a negative. From other people in the house I learned that this was true so far as they knew. There was not and has not been a baby in the apartments so far as anyone could tell me. And in spite of that fact I found this."

Hatch drew something from his pocket and spread it on his open hand. It was a baby stocking of fine texture. The Thinking Machine took it and looked at it closely.

"Baby Blake's?" he asked.

"Yes," replied the reporter. "Both Mrs Blake and the nurse, Miss Barton, identify it."

"Dear me! Dear me!" exclaimed the scientist, thoughtfully. Again the puzzled expression came into his face.

"Of course, the baby hasn't been returned?" went on the scientist.

"Of course not!" said Hatch.

"Did Mrs Gates behave like a woman who had suddenly received a share of twenty-five thousand dollars?" asked The Thinking Machine.

"No," Hatch replied. "She looked as if she had attended a mixed ale party. Her lip was cut and bruised and one eye was black."

"That's what her husband did when he found out what was in the newspaper," commented The Thinking Machine, grimly.

"It wasn't money, at all, then?" asked Hatch.

"Certainly not."

Neither said anything for several minutes. The Thinking Machine sat idly twisting the tiny stocking between his long, slender fingers with the little puzzled line in his brow.

"How do you account for that stocking in Gates's possession?" asked the reporter at last.

"Let's go talk to Mrs Blake," was the reply. "You didn't tell her anything about this man Gates getting the package?"

"No," said the reporter.

"It would only worry her," explained the scientist. "Better let her hope, because—"

Hatch looked at The Thinking Machine quickly, startled. "Because, what?" he asked.

"There seems to be a very strong probability that Baby Blake is dead," the other responded.

Pondering that, yet conceiving no motive which would cause the baby's death, Hatch was silent as he and the scientist together went to the house of Mrs Blake. Miss Barton, the nurse, answered the door.

"Miss Barton," said The Thinking Machine, testily as they entered, "just when did you give this stocking," – and he produced it—"to Charles Gates?"

The girl flushed quickly, and she stammered a little.

"I – I don't know what you mean," she said. "Who is Charles Gates?"

"May we see Mrs Blake?" asked the scientist. He squinted steadily into the girl's eyes.

"Yes – of course – that is, I suppose so," she stammered.

She disappeared, and in a few minutes Mrs Blake appeared. There was an eager, expectant look in her face. It was hope. It faded when she saw the solemn face of The Thinking Machine.

"What recommendations did Miss Barton have when you engaged her?" he began pointedly.

KIDNAPPED BABY BLAKE, MILLIONAIRE

"The best I could ask," was the reply. "She was formerly a governess in the family of the Governor – General of Canada. She is well educated, and came to me from that position."

"Is she well acquainted in Lynn?" asked the scientist.

"That I couldn't say," replied Mrs Blake. "If you are thinking that she might have some connection with this affair—"

"Ever go out much?" interrupted her questioner.

"Rarely, and then usually with me. She is more of a companion than servant."

"How long have you had her?"

"Since a week or so after my baby" – and the mother's lips trembled a little – "was born. She has been devoted to me since the death of my husband. I would trust her with my life."

"This is your baby's stocking?"

"Beyond any doubt," she replied as she again examined it.

"I suppose he had several pairs like this?"

"I really don't know. I should think so."

"Will you please have Miss Barton, or someone else, find those stockings and see if all the pairs like this are complete," instructed The Thinking Machine.

Wonderingly, Mrs Blake gave the order to Miss Barton, who as wonderingly received it and went out of the room with a quick, resentful look at the bowed figure of the scientist.

"Did you ever happen to notice, Mrs Blake, whether or not your baby could open a door? For instance, the front door?"

"I believe he could," she replied. "He could reach them because the handles are low, as you see," and she indicated the knob on the front door, which was visible through the reception hall room where they stood.

The Thinking Machine turned suddenly and strode to the window of the library, looking out on the back yard. He was debating something in his own mind. It was whether or not he should tell this mother his fear of her son's death, or should hide it from her until such time as it would appear itself. For some reason known only to himself he considered the child's death not only a possibility, but a probability.

Whatever might have resulted from this mental debate was not to be known then, for suddenly, as he stood staring out the rear window overlooking the spot where the baby's tracks had been seen in the snow – now melted – he started a little and peered eagerly out. It was the first sight he had had of the yard since the night he had examined it by moonlight.

"Dear me, dear me," he exclaimed suddenly.

Turning abruptly he left the room, and a moment later Hatch saw him in the back yard. Mrs Blake at the window watched curiously. Outside The Thinking Machine walked straight out to the spot where the baby's tracks had been, and from there Hatch saw him stop and stare at the slightly raised box which covered the water connections.

From this box the scientist took five steps toward a flat-topped stone – the one he had noticed previously – and Hatch saw that it was about ten feet. Then from this he saw The Thinking Machine take four steps to where the sagging clothes-line hung. It was probably eight feet. Then the bowed figure of The Thinking Machine walked on out toward the rear wall of the enclosure, under the clothes-line.

When he stopped at the end of the line he was within fifteen feet of the dangling swing which had been Baby Blake's. This swing was attached to a limb twenty feet above – a stout limb which jutted straight out from the tree trunk for fifteen feet. The Thinking Machine studied this for a moment, then passed on beyond the tree, still looking up, until he disappeared.

Fifteen minutes later he returned to the library where Mrs Blake awaited him. There was a question in Hatch's eyes.

"I've got it," snapped The Thinking Machine, much as if there had been a denial. "I've got it."

V

On the following day, by direction of The Thinking Machine, Mrs Blake ordered the following advertisement inserted in all Boston and Lynn newspapers, to occupy one-quarter of a page.

TO THE PERSONS WHO NOW HOLD DOUGLAS BLAKE:

"Your names, residence and place of concealment of Douglas Blake, fourteen months old, and the manner in which he came into your possession are now known.

"Mrs Blake, the mother, does not desire to prosecute for reasons you know, and will give you twenty-four hours in which to return the baby safely to its home in Lynn.

"Any attempt to escape of either person concerned will be followed instantly by arrest. Meanwhile you are closely watched, and will be for twenty-four hours, at which time arrest and prosecution will follow.

"No questions will he asked when the child is returned and your names will be fully protected. There will also be a reward of $1,000 for the person who returns the baby."

Hutchinson Hatch read this when The Thinking Machine had completed it and had stared at the scientist in wonderment.

"Is it true?" he asked.

"I am afraid the child is dead," repeated The Thinking Machine evasively. "I am very much afraid of it."

"What gives you that impression?" Hatch asked.

"I know now how the child was taken from that back yard, if we grant that the child itself made the tracks," was the rejoinder. "And knowing how it was taken away makes me more fearful than I have been that it is not alive; in fact, that it may never be seen again."

"How did the child leave the yard?"

"If the child does not appear within twenty-four hours," was the reply, "I shall tell you. It is a hideous story."

Hatch had to be content with that statement of the case for the moment. None knew better than he how useless it would be to question The Thinking Machine.

"Did you happen to know, Mr Hatch," The Thinking Machine asked, "that in the event of the death of Douglas Blake, his fortune of nearly three million dollars left in trust by his father would be divided among four relatives of Mrs Blake?"

"What?" asked Hatch, a little startled.

"Suppose for instance, Baby Blake was never found, as seems possible," went on the other. "After a certain number of years, I believe, in a case of that kind there is an assumption of death and property passes to heirs. You see then, there was a motive, and a strong one, underlying this entire affair."

"But, surely there wouldn't be murder?"

"Not murder," responded The Thinking Machine tartly. "I haven't even suggested murder. I said I believe the child is dead. If it is not dead who would benefit by his disappearance? The four whom I named. Well, suppose Baby Blake fell into the hands of those people. It would be comparatively an easy matter for them to lose it in some way—not necessarily kill it—have it adopted in some orphan asylum, place it anywhere to hide its identity. That's the main thing."

Hatch began to see light faintly, he thought.

"Then this advertisement is to the people who may be holding the child now?" he asked.

"It is so addressed," was the other's reply.

"But, but—" Hatch began.

"Once upon a time a noted wit, who was of necessity a student of human nature," The Thinking Machine began, "declared there was one thing carefully hidden in every man's life which would ruin him should it be known, or land him in prison. He volunteered to prove this, taking any man whose name was suggested. An eminent minister of the gospel was named as the victim. The wit sent a telegram to the minister, who was attending a banquet: 'All is discovered. Flee while there is opportunity,' signed 'Friend.' The minister read it, arose and left the room, and from that day to this he has never been seen again."

Hatch laughed, and The Thinking Machine glanced at him with an annoyed expression on his face.

"I had no intention of arousing your laughter," he said sharply. "I merely intended to illustrate the possible effect of a guilty conscience."

When the flaming advertisement in the newspapers was called to the attention of the police, they were first surprised, then amused. Then they grew serious. After a while an officer went to Mrs Blake and asked what it meant. She informed him that she had acted at the suggestion of Professor Van Dusen. Then the police were amused again; they are wont to feign an amusement which they never feel in the presence of a superior mind.

That afternoon, Hatch, who by direction of The Thinking Machine, was on watch again near the Blake home, received a strange request from the scientist by telephone. It was: "Go to the Blake home immediately, see the picture book which Baby Blake was looking at just before his disappearance, and report to me by 'phone just what's in it."

"The picture book?" Hatch repeated.

"Certainly, the picture book," said the scientist, irritably. "Also find out for me from the nurse and Mrs Blake if the baby cried easily, that is from a slight hurt or anything of that kind."

With these things in his mind Hatch went to the Blake house, had a look at the picture book, asked the questions as to Baby Blake's propensity to weep on slight provocation, and returned to the 'phone. Feeling singularly foolish, he enumerated to The Thinking Machine the things he had seen in the picture book.

"There's a horse, and a cat with three kittens," he explained. "Also a pale purple rhinoceros, and a dog, an elephant, a deer, an alligator, a monkey, three chicks, and a whole lot of birds."

"Any eagle?" queried the other.

"Yes, an eagle among them, with a rabbit in its claws."

"And the monkey. What is it doing?"

"Hanging by its tail to a blue tree with a coconut in its hands," replied the reporter. The humor of the situation was beginning to appeal to him.

"And about the baby crying?" the scientist asked.

"He does not cry easily, both the mother and nurse say," replied Hatch. "They both describe him as a brave little chap, who cries sometimes when he can't have his own way, but never from fright or a minor hurt."

"Good," he heard The Thinking Machine say. "Watch in front of the Blake house tonight until half past eight. If the child returns it will probably be earlier than that. Speak to the person who brings him, as he leaves the house, and he will tell you his story I think, if you can make him understand that he is in no danger. Immediately after that come to my home in Boston."

Hatch was treading on air; when The Thinking Machine gave positive directions of that sort it usually meant that the final curtain was to be drawn aside. He so construed this.

Thus it came to pass that Hutchinson Hatch planted himself, carefully hidden so he might command a view of the front of the Blake home, and waited there for many hours.

Mrs Blake, the mother of the millionaire baby, had just finished her dinner and had retired to a small parlor off the library, where she reclined on a couch. It was ten minutes of seven o'clock in the evening. After a moment Miss Barton entered the room.

The girl heard a sob from the couch and impulsively ran to Mrs Blake, who was weeping softly—she was always weeping now. A few comforting words, a little consolation such as one woman is able to give to another, and the girl arose from her knees and started into the library, where a dim light burned.

As she was entering that room again, she paused, screamed and without a word sank down on the floor, fainting. Mrs Blake rose from the couch and rushed toward the door. She screamed too, but that scream was of a different tone from that of the girl—it was a fierce scream of mother-love satisfied.

For there on the floor of the library sat Baby Blake, millionaire, gazing with enraptured eyes at his brilliantly colored picture book.

"Pitty hossie," he said to his mother. "See! See!"

VI

It was an affecting scene Hutchinson Hatch witnessed in the Blake home about half-past seven o'clock. It was that of a mother clasping a baby to her breast while tears of joy and hysteria streamed from her eyes. Baby Blake struggled manfully to free himself, but the mother clung to him.

"My boy, my boy," she sobbed again and again.

Miss Barton sat on the floor beside the mother and wept too. Hatch saw it, and received some thanks, heartfelt, but broken with a little sobbing laughter. Then he had to dry his eyes, too, and Hutchinson Hatch was not a sentimental man.

"There will be no prosecution, Mrs Blake, I suppose?" he asked.

"No, no, no," was the half laughing, half tearful reply. "I am content."

"I would like to ask a favor, if you don't mind?" he suggested.

"Anything—anything for you and Professor Van Dusen," was the reply.

"Will you lend me the baby's picture book until tomorrow?" he asked.

"Certainly," and in her happiness the mother forgot to note the strangeness of the request.

Hatch's purpose in borrowing the book was not clear even to himself; in his mind had grown the idea that in some way The Thinking Machine connected this book with the disappearance of the child, and he was burning with curiosity to get the book and return to Boston, where The Thinking Machine might throw some light on the mystery. For it was still a mystery—a perplexing, baffling mystery that he could in no way grasp, even now that the baby was safe at home again.

In Boston the reporter went straight to the home of The Thinking Machine. The scientist was pottering about the little laboratory and only turned to look at Hatch when he entered.

"Baby back home?" he asked, shortly.

"Yes," said the reporter.

"Good," said the other, and he rubbed his slender hands together briskly. "Sit down, Mr Hatch. It was a little better after all than I hoped for. Now your story first. What happened when the baby was brought back home?"

"I waited as you directed from afternoon until a few minutes to seven," Hatch explained. "I could plainly see anyone who approached the front gate of the Blake place, although I could not be seen well, remaining in the shadow of the building opposite.

"I saw two or three people go up to the gate and enter the yard, but they were tradespeople. I spoke to them as they came out and ascertained this for myself. At last I saw a man approaching carrying something closely wrapped in his arms. He stopped at the gate, stared up the path a moment, glanced around several times and entered the yard. He was carrying Baby Blake. I knew it instinctively.

"He went to the front door of the house and there I lost him in the shadow for a moment. Subsequent developments showed that he opened this front door, which was not locked, put the baby down and closed the door softly. Then he came rapidly down the path toward the gate. An instant later I heard two screams from the house. I knew then that the baby was there, dead or alive—probably alive.

"The man who had brought it also heard the screams and accelerated his pace somewhat, so that I had to run. He heard me coming and he ran, too. It was a two-block chase before I caught him, and when I did he turned on me. I thought it was to fight.

"'There was a promise of no arrest or prosecution,' he said.

"I assured him hurriedly, and then walked on down the street beside him. He told me a queer story—it might be true or it might not, but I believe it. This was that the baby had been in his and his wife's care from about half-past six o'clock of the evening it disappeared until a few minutes before when he had returned it to its home.

"The man's name is Sheldon—Michael Sheldon—and he is an ex-convict. He served four years for burglary, and at one time had a pretty nasty record. He told me of it in explanation of his reasons for not turning the baby over to the police. Now he has reformed and is leading a new life. He is a clerk in a store here in Lynn, and despite his previous record is, I ascertained, a trusted and reliable man.

"Now here comes the queer part of the story. It seems that Sheldon and his wife live on the third floor of a tenement in northern Lynn. Their dining room has one window, which leads to a fire escape. He and his wife were at supper about half-past six—in other words, a little more than half an hour from the time the baby disappeared from the Blake home.

"After awhile they heard a noise – they didn't know what— on the fire escape. They paid no attention. Finally they heard another noise from the fire escape—that of a baby crying. Then Sheldon went to the window and opened it. There on the fire escape was Baby Blake. How he got there no human being knows."

"I know now," said The Thinking Machine. "Go on."

"Puzzled and bewildered they took the child off the iron structure, where only the barest chance had prevented it from falling and being killed on the pavement below. The baby was apparently uninjured save for a few bruises, but his clothing was soiled and rumpled, and he was terribly cold. The wife, mother-like, set out to warm the little fellow and make him comfortable with hot milk and a steaming bath. The husband, Sheldon, says he went out to find how it was possible for the baby to have reached the fire escape. He knew no baby lived in the building.

"He looked long and carefully. There was no possible way by which a man could have climbed the fire escape to the third floor, and therefore certainly no way by which a fourteen-month-old baby could climb there. There is a fence there which is pretty tall, say six feet, but even standing on this a man would have had to leap straight up in the air for five feet, and nobody I know could do it with a baby in his arms, particularly when the snow was there and everything was so slippery a person could hardly hold on.

"It seems that then Sheldon made inquiries of some of his neighbors, occupants of the house, but no one could throw any light on the subject. He did not tell them then of the baby, indeed, never told them. First, from the fine quality of the clothing, there had been an idea in his mind that the baby was one of a well-to-do family, and he remained quiet that night hoping that next day he might be able to learn something and possibly get a reward for the return of the child. He had given up the problem of how it got where he found it."

Hatch paused a moment and lighted a cigar.

"Well, next day," he went on, "Sheldon and his wife both saw the newspaper account of the mysterious disappearance of Baby Blake. The photographs of the missing child convinced them that Baby Blake was the child they had—the child they had really saved from death. Then came the question of returning the child to its home or turning it over to the police.

"Instantly the fact that a threat had been made to kidnap the child and a demand for ten thousand dollars made was borne in on Sheldon he became frightened. Remember he had a bad record. He was afraid of the police. He did not believe that he—however innocent he might be—could go to the police, turn over the baby and make them believe the strange story. I readily see how some wooden-headed department officials would have made his life a burden. I know the police. It is ninety-nine dollars to a cent they would have made him a prisoner and perhaps railroaded him for the kidnapping."

"Yes, I see," interrupted The Thinking Machine.

"So then he and his wife tried to devise a method of getting the baby back home. They thought of all sorts of things, but none satisfied them entirely. And they were still debating this point and considering it when your advertisement promised immunity. As a matter of fact it scared Sheldon. He imagined that you knew, and knew if he were even remotely connected with the matter it would get him in trouble. Then he resolved to take the baby back home on the promise of immunity."

There was a little pause. The Thinking Machine sat staring steadily at the ceiling.

"Is that all?" he asked at last.

"I think so," replied Hatch. "And now how—how in the name of all that's good or evil did that baby disappear from the middle of its own back yard and then suddenly appear on a fire escape three blocks away, to be taken in by strangers?"

"It's quite the most remarkable thing I have ever come across," The Thinking Machine said. "A balloon anchor, which picked up the child by its clothing, through accident, and then dropped it safely on the fire escape might answer the question in a way. But it does not fully answer it. The baby was carried there.

"Frankly I will say that I could see no possible explanation of the affair until the day you and I were talking to Mrs Blake and I stood looking out of the library window. Then it all flashed on me instantly. I went out and satisfied myself. When I returned to the library I was satisfied in all reason that Baby Blake was dead; I had had such an idea before. I was firmly convinced the child was dead when I put those advertisements in the newspapers. But there was still a chance that he was not.

"Several seemingly unanswerable questions faced me when I found the end of the baby's footprints in the snow. I instantly saw that if the baby had made those tracks it had been lifted suddenly from the ground, but by what? From where? How had it been taken away? The balloon I could not consider seriously, although as I say it offered a possible solution. An eagle? I could not consider that seriously. Eagles are rare; eagles powerful enough to lift a baby weighing thirty pounds are extremely rare, practically unknown save in the far West; certainly I never heard of one doing such a thing as this. Therefore I passed the eagle by as an improbability.

"I satisfied myself that there were no other footsteps save the baby's in the yard. Then – what? It occurred to me that someone standing on the little box might have reached over and lifted the child out of its tracks. But it was too far away, I thought, and if someone did stand there and lift the child that someone could not have leaped from that box over the stone wall, which was approximately a hundred feet away in all directions.

"I saw the stone ten feet away. Could a man stand on the box and leap to the stone? Generally, no. And from the stone, where could he have gone? Obviously nowhere. I considered this matter not minutes, but hours and days, and no light came to me. I was convinced, though, that the box was the starting point if the baby had made the tracks. I was now fairly certain that the baby did make the tracks. He wanted to get out in the snow, was left alone, opened the front door and wandered out.

"Then it all occurred to me in a new light. What living animal could have stood on the box and lifted the child clear four feet away, then leaped from there to the stone, and from the stone where? The clothes line is eight feet or so from the stone. It is a pretty sturdy rope and capable of bearing a considerable weight, supported as it is."

He stopped and turned his eyes toward Hatch, who listened eagerly.

"Do you see it now?" he asked.

The reporter shook his head, bewildered.

"The thing that lifted Baby Blake from the snow stood on the box, leaped from there to the stone, from there to the clothes line, along which it climbed to the end. From the wooden support at the end it is a clear distance of fifteen feet to the nearest thing – the swing. This thing made that leap, climbed the swing rope, disappeared into the trees, moving through the branches freely from one tree to another, and dropped to the ground nearly a block away."

"A monkey?" suggested Hatch.

"An orang-outang," nodded The Thinking Machine.

"An orang-outang?" gasped Hatch, and he shuddered a little. "I see now why you were positive the child was dead."

"An orang-outang is the only living thing within the knowledge of man which could have done all these things — therefore an orang-outang did them," said the other emphatically. "Remember a full-sized orang-outang is nearly as tall as a man, has a reach relatively a third longer than a very tall man would have, and a strength which is enormous. It could have made the leaps and probably would have made them rather than step in the snow. They despise snow, being from the tropics themselves, and will not step in it unless they are compelled to. The leap of fifteen feet to the swing rope from the clothes line would have been comparatively easy, even with a child in its arms.

"Where could it have come from? I don't know. Possibly escaped from a ship, because sailors have strange pets; might have gotten away from a menagerie somewhere, or a circus. I only knew that an orang-outang was the actual abductor. The difficulties of a man climbing the fire escape where the baby was found were nothing to an orang-outang. There it would have merely been a leap up of five feet."

The Thinking Machine stopped as if he had finished. Hatch respected this silence for a moment, but he had questions yet to be answered.

"Who wrote the kidnapping letters demanding money?" was the first.

"You found him — Charles Gates," was the reply.

"And the letter written after the abduction demanding twenty-five thousand dollars?"

"Was written by him, of course — but this was a bluff. This poor deluded fool imagined that someone would actually go out and toss $25,000 on a trash-heap where he could find it, and then he could escape. That was his purpose. He knew nothing of the whereabouts of the baby. He beat his wife when he found, instead of money, I had put some good advice in the newspaper bundle for him."

"But the stocking in his room, and your question to Miss Barton?"

"This man did write a letter threatening kidnapping before the baby disappeared. It was perfectly possible that after the kidnapping he stole the little stocking and two or three other things from the laundry, for Miss Barton noticed they were missing, or got someone to do so for him. And, the baby being gone, he was intending to send these to the mother, one at a time, I imagine, to make her believe he had the child. That is transparent. I asked Miss Barton the question about giving them to Gates to see if she did—her manner would have told me. I instantly saw she did not—had never even heard of him, as a matter of fact. I also dropped that remark about there being $25,000 in the package to see what effect it would have on her."

"And the facts you had about the baby's fortune going to relatives of Mrs Blake in the event of the baby's death?"

"I got from her, by a casual question as to the succession of the estate. There was still a possibility that the baby was in their hands despite the manner of its disappearance. As it transpired they had nothing whatever to do with it. The advertisement I put in the paper was a palpable trick—but it had the desired effect. It touched a guilty conscience. The guilty conscience feared it was trapped and acted accordingly."

"It seems perfectly incomprehensible that the baby should have come out of it alive," mused Hatch. "I had always imagined orang-outangs to be extremely ferocious."

"Read up on them a bit, Mr Hatch," said The Thinking Machine. "You will find they are of strangely contradictory and mischievous natures. Where this child was permitted to escape safely others might have been torn limb from limb."

There was silence for a time. Hatch considered the matter all explained, until suddenly the picture book occurred to him.

"You 'phoned to me to see the picture book and tell you what's in it," he said. "Why?"

"Suppose there was a picture of a monkey in it," rejoined the other. "I merely wanted to know if the baby would know a monkey, in other words an orang-outang, if it saw one. Why? Because if the baby knew one it would not necessarily be afraid of one in the flesh, and would not of necessity cry out when the orang-outang picked it up. As a matter of fact no one heard it scream when taken away."

"Oh, I see," said Hatch. "There was a picture of a monkey in the book. I told you." He took out the book and looked at it. "Here," and he extended it to the scientist who glanced at it casually, and nodded.

"If you want to prove this just as I have told it," said The Thinking Machine, "go to the Blake home tomorrow, put your finger on that picture and show it to Baby Blake. He will prove it."

It came to pass that Hatch did this very thing.

"Pitty monkey," said Baby Blake. "Doe, doe."

"He means he wants to go," Miss Barton exclaimed to Hatch.

Hatch was satisfied.

Two days later the Boston American carried a dispatch from a village near Lynn stating that a semi-tame orang-outang had been killed by a policeman. It had belonged to a sailor, from whose vessel it had escaped more than two weeks before.

6

MYSTERY OF THE FATAL CIPHER

I

For the third time Professor Augustus S. F. X. Van Dusen-so-called The Thinking Machine – read the letter. It was spread out in front of him on the table, and his blue eyes were narrowed to mere slits as he studied it through his heavy eyeglasses. The young woman who had placed the letter in his hands, Miss Elizabeth Devan, sat waiting patiently on the sofa in the little reception room of The Thinking Machine's house. Her blue eyes were opened wide and she stared as if fascinated at this man who had become so potent a factor in the solution of intangible mysteries.

Here is the letter:

To those Concerned:

Tired of it all I seek the end, and am content. Ambition now is dead; the grave yawns greedily at my feet, and with the labor of my own hands lost I greet death of my own will, by my own act.

To my son I leave all, and you who maligned me, you who discouraged me, you may read this and know I punish you thus. It's for him, my son, to forgive.

I dared in life and dare dead your everlasting anger, not alone that you didn't speak but that you cherished secret, and my ears are locked forever against you. My vault is my resting place.

On the brightest and dearest page of life I wrote (7) my love for him. Family ties, binding as the Bible itself, bade me give all to my son.

Goodbye. I die.

Pomeroy Stockton

"Under just what circumstances did this letter come into your possession, Miss Devan?" The Thinking Machine asked. "Tell me the full story; omit nothing."

The scientist sank back into his chair with his enormous yellow head pillowed comfortably against the cushion and his long, steady fingers pressed tip to tip. He didn't even look at his pretty visitor. She had come to ask for information; he was willing to give it, because it offered another of those abstract problems which he always found interesting. In his own field — the sciences — his fame was worldwide. This concentration of a brain which had achieved so much on more material things was perhaps a sort of relaxation.

Miss Devan had a soft, soothing voice, and as she talked it was broken at times by what seemed to be a sob. Her face was flushed a little, and she emphasized her points by a quick clasping and unclasping of her daintily gloved hands.

"My father, or rather my adopted father, Pomeroy Stockton, was an inventor," she began. "We lived in a great, old-fashioned house in Dorchester. We have lived there since I was a child. When I was only five or six years old, I was left an orphan and was adopted by Mr Stockton, then a man of forty years. I am now twenty-three. I was raised and cared for by Mr Stockton, who always treated me as a daughter. His death, therefore, was a great blow to me.

"Mr Stockton was a widower with only one child of his own, a son, John Stockton, who is now about thirty-one years old.

He is a man of irreproachable character, and has always, since I first knew him, been religiously inclined. He is the junior partner in a great commercial company, Dutton & Stockton, leather men. I suppose he has an immense fortune, for he gives largely to charity, and is, too, the active head of a large Sunday school.

"Pomeroy Stockton, my adopted father, almost idolized this son, although there was in his manner toward him something akin to fear. Close work had made my father querulous and irritable. Yet I don't believe a better hearted man ever lived. He worked most of the time in a little shop, which he had installed in a large back room on the ground floor of the house. He always worked with the door locked. There were furnaces, moulds, and many things that I didn't know the use of."

"I know who he was," said The Thinking Machine. "He was working to re-discover the secret of hardened copper – a secret which was lost in Egypt. I knew Mr Stockton very well by reputation. Go on."

"Whatever it was he worked on," Miss Devan resumed, "he guarded it very carefully. He would permit no one at all to enter the room. I have never seen more than a glimpse of what was in it. His son particularly I have seen barred out of the shop a dozen times and every time there was a quarrel to follow.

"Those were the conditions at the time Mr Stockton first became ill, six or seven months ago. At that time he double-locked the doors of his shop, retired to his rooms on the second floor, and remained there in practical seclusion for two weeks or more. These rooms adjoined mine, and twice during that time I heard the son and the father talking loudly, as if quarreling. At the end of the two weeks, Mr Stockton returned to work in the shop and shortly afterward the son, who had also lived in the house, took apartments in Beacon Street and removed his belongings from the house.

"From that time up to last Monday – this is Thursday – I never saw the son in the house. On Monday the father was at work as usual in the shop. He had previously told me that the work he was engaged in was practically ended and he expected a great fortune to result from it. About 5 o'clock in the afternoon on Monday the son came to the house. No one knows when he went out. It is a fact, however, that Father did not have dinner at the usual time, 6:30. I presumed he was at work, and did not take time for his dinner. I have known him to do this many times."

For a moment the girl was silent and seemed to be struggling with some deep grief which she could not control.

"And next morning?" asked The Thinking Machine gently.

"Next morning," the girl went on, "Father was found dead in the workshop. There were no marks on his body, nothing to indicate at first the manner of death. It was as if he had sat in his chair beside one of the furnaces and had taken poison and died at once. A small bottle of what I presume to be prussic acid was smashed on the floor, almost beside his chair. We discovered him dead after we had rapped on the door several times and got no answer. Then Montgomery, our butler, smashed in the door, at my request. There we found Father.

"I immediately telephoned to the son, John Stockton, and he came to the house. The letter you now have was found in my father's pocket. It was just as you see it. Mr Stockton seemed greatly agitated and started to destroy the letter. I induced him to give it to me, because instantly it occurred to me that there was something wrong about all of it. My father had talked too often to me about the future, what he intended to do and his plans for me. There may not be anything wrong. The letter may be just what it purports to be. I hope it is – oh – I hope it is. Yet everything considered –"

"Was there an autopsy?" asked The Thinking Machine.

"No. John Stockton's actions seemed to be directed against any investigation. He told me he thought he could do certain things which would prevent the matter coming to the attention of the police. My father was buried on a death certificate issued by a Dr Benton, who has been a friend of John Stockton since their college days. In that way the appearance of suicide or anything else was covered up completely.

"Both before and after the funeral John Stockton made me promise to keep this letter hidden or else destroy it. In order to put an end to this I told him I had destroyed the letter. This attitude on his part, the more I thought of it, seemed to confirm my original idea that it had not been suicide. Night after night I thought of this, and finally decided to come to you rather than to the police. I feel that there is some dark mystery behind it all. If you can help me now—"

"Yes, yes," broke in The Thinking Machine. "Where was the key to the workshop? In Pomeroy's pocket? In his room? In the door?"

"Really, I don't know," said Miss Devan. "It hadn't occurred to me."

"Did Mr Stockton leave a will?"

"Yes, it is with his lawyer, a Mr Sloane."

"Has it been read? Do you know what is in it?"

"It is to be read in a day or so. Judging from the second paragraph of the letter, I presume he left everything to his son."

For the fourth time The Thinking Machine read the letter. At its end he again looked up at Miss Devan.

"Just what is your interpretation of this letter from one end to the other?" he asked.

"Speaking from my knowledge of Mr Stockton and the circumstances surrounding him," the girl explained, "I should say the letter means just what it says. I should imagine from the first paragraph that something he invented had been taken away from him, stolen perhaps. The second paragraph and the third,

I should say, were intended as a rebuke to certain relatives – a brother and two distant cousins – who had always regarded him as a crank and took frequent occasion to tell him so. I don't know a great deal of the history of that other branch of the family. The last two paragraphs explain themselves except—"

"Except the figure seven," interrupted the scientist. "Do you have any idea whatever as to the meaning of that?"

The girl took the letter and studied it closely for a moment.

"Not the slightest," she said. "It does not seem to be connected with anything else in the letter."

"Do you think it possible, Miss Devan, that this letter was written under coercion?"

"I do," said the girl quickly, and her face flamed. "That's just what I do think. From the first I have imagined some ghastly, horrible mystery back of it all."

"Or, perhaps Pomeroy Stockton never saw this letter at all," mused The Thinking Machine. "It may be a forgery?"

"Forgery!" gasped the girl. "Then John Stockton—"

"Whatever it is, forged or genuine," The Thinking Machine went on quietly, "it is a most extraordinary document. It might have been written by a poet. It states things in such a roundabout way. It is not directly to the point, as a practical man would have written."

There was silence for several minutes and the girl sat leaning forward on the table, staring into the inscrutable eyes of the scientist.

"Perhaps, perhaps," she said, "there is a cipher of some sort in it?"

"That is precisely correct," said The Thinking Machine emphatically. "There is a cipher in it, and a very ingenious one."

II

It was twenty-four hours later that The Thinking Machine sent for Hutchinson Hatch, reporter, and talked over the matter with him. He had always found Hatch a discreet, resourceful individual, who was willing to aid in any way in his power. Hatch read the letter, which The Thinking Machine had said contained a cipher, and then the circumstances as related by Miss Devan were retold to the reporter.

"Do you think it is a cipher?" asked Hatch in conclusion.

"It is a cipher," replied The Thinking Machine. "If what Miss Devan has said is correct, John Stockton cannot have said anything about the affair. I want you to go and talk to him, find out all about him and what division of the property is made by the will. Does this will give everything to the son?

"Also find out what personal enmity there is between John Stockton and Miss Devan, and what was the cause of it. Was there a man in it? If so, who? When you have done all this, go to the house in Dorchester and bring me the family Bible, if there is one there. It's probably a big book. If it is not there, let me know immediately by 'phone. Miss Devan will, I suppose, give it to you, if she has it."

With these instructions Hatch went away. Half an hour later he was in the private office of John Stockton at the latter's place of business. Mr Stockton was a man of long visage, rather angular and clerical in appearance. There was a smug satisfaction about the man that Hatch didn't quite approve of, and yet it was a trait which found expression only in a soft voice and small acts of needless courtesy.

A deprecatory look passed over Stockton's face when Hatch asked the first question, which bore on his relationship with Pomeroy Stockton.

"I had hoped that this matter would not come to the attention of the press," said Stockton in an oily, gentle tone.

"It is something which can only bring disgrace upon my poor father's memory, and his has been a name associated with distinct achievements in the progress of the world. However, if necessary, I will state my knowledge of the affair, and invite the investigation which, frankly, I will say, I tried to stop."

"How much was your father's estate?" asked Hatch.

"Something more than a million," was the reply. "He made most of it through a device for coupling cars. This is now in use on practically all the railroads."

"And the division of this property by will?" asked Hatch.

"I haven't seen the will, but I understand that he left practically everything to me, settling an annuity and the home in Dorchester on Miss Devan, whom he had always regarded as a daughter."

"That would give you then, say, two-thirds or three-quarters of the estate."

"Something like that, possibly $800,000."

"Where is this will now?"

"I understand in the hands of my father's attorney, Mr Sloane."

"When is it to be read?"

"It was to have been read today, but there has been some delay about it. The attorney postponed it for a few days."

"What, Mr Stockton, was the purpose in making it appear that your father died naturally, when obviously he committed suicide and there is even a suggestion of something else?" demanded Hatch.

John Stockton sat up straight in his chair with a startled expression in his eyes. He had been rubbing his hands together complacently; now he stopped and stared at the reporter.

"Something else?" he asked. "Pray what else?"

Hatch shrugged his shoulders, but in his eyes there lay almost an accusation. "Did any motive ever appear for your father's suicide?"

"I know of none," Stockton replied. "Yet, admitting that this is suicide, without a motive, it seems that the only fault I have committed is that I had a friend report it otherwise and avoided a police inquiry."

"It's just that. Why did you do it?"

"Naturally to save the family name from disgrace. But this something else you spoke of? Do you mean that anyone else thinks that anything other than suicide or natural death is possible?"

As he asked the question there came some subtle change over his face. He leaned forward toward the reporter. All trace of the sanctimonious smirk about the thin-lipped mouth had gone now.

"Miss Devan has produced the letter found on your father at death and has said—" began the reporter.

"Elizabeth! Miss Devan!" exclaimed John Stockton. He arose suddenly, paced several times across the room, then stopped in front of the reporter. "She gave me her word of honor that she would not make the existence of that letter known."

"But she has made it public," said Hatch. "And further she intimates that your father's death was not even what it appeared to be, suicide."

"She's crazy, man, crazy," said Stockton in deep agitation. "Who could have killed my father? What motive could there have been?"

There was a grim twitching of Hatch's lips.

"Was Miss Devan legally adopted by your father?" he asked, irrelevantly.

"Yes."

"In that event, disregarding other relatives, doesn't it seem strange even to you that he gives three-quarters of the estate to you – you have a fortune already – and only a small part to Miss Devan, who has nothing?"

"That's my father's business."

There was a pause. Stockton was still pacing back and forth.

Finally he sank down in his chair at the desk, and sat for a moment looking at the reporter.

"Is that all?" he asked.

"I should like to know, if you don't mind telling me, what direct cause there is for ill feeling between Miss Devan and you?"

"There is no ill feeling. We merely never got along well together. My father and I have had several arguments about her for reasons which it is not necessary to go into."

"Did you have such an argument on the night before your father was found dead?"

"I believe there was something said about her."

"What time did you leave the shop that night?"

"About 10 o'clock."

"And you had been in the room with your father since afternoon, had you not?"

"Yes."

"No dinner?"

"No."

"How did you come to neglect that?"

"My father was explaining a recent invention he had perfected, which I was to put on the market."

"I suppose the possibility of suicide or his death in any way had not occurred to you?"

"No, not at all. We were making elaborate plans for the future."

Possibly it was some prejudice against the man's appearance which made Hatch so dissatisfied with the result of the interview. He felt that he had gained nothing, yet Stockton had been absolutely frank, as it seemed. There was one last question.

"Have you any recollection of a large family Bible in your father's house?" he asked.

"I have seen it several times," Stockton said.

"Is it still there?"

"So far as I know, yes."

That was the end of the interview, and Hatch went straight to the house in Dorchester to see Miss Devan. There, in accordance with instructions from The Thinking Machine, he asked for the family Bible.

"There was one here the other day," said Miss Devan, "but it has disappeared."

"Since your father's death?" asked Hatch.

"Yes, the next day."

"Have you any idea who took it?"

"Not unless—unless—"

"John Stockton! Why did he take it?" blurted Hatch.

There was a little resigned movement of the girl's hands, a movement which said, "I don't know."

"He told me, too," said Hatch indignantly, "that he thought the Bible was still here."

The girl drew close to the reporter and laid one white hand on his sleeve. She looked up into his eyes and tears stood in her own. Her lips trembled.

"John Stockton has that book," she said. "He took it away from here the day after my father died, and he did it for a purpose. What, I don't know."

"Are you absolutely positive he has it?" asked Hatch

"I saw it in his room, where he had hidden it," replied the girl.

III

Hatch laid the results of the interviews before the scientist at the Beacon Hill home. The Thinking Machine listened without comment up to that point where Miss Devan had said she knew the family Bible to be in the son's possession.

"If Miss Devan and Stockton do not get along well together, why should she visit Stockton's place at all?" demanded The Thinking Machine.

"I don't know," Hatch replied, "except that she thinks he must have had some connection with her father's death, and is investigating on her own account. What has this Bible to do with it anyway?"

"It may have a great deal to do with it," said The Thinking Machine enigmatically. "Now, the thing to do is to find out if the girl told the truth and if the Bible is in Stockton's apartment. Now, Mr Hatch, I leave that to you. I would like to see that Bible. If you can bring it to me, well and good. If you can't bring it, look at and study the seventh page for any pencil marks in the text, anything whatever. It might be even advisable, if you have the opportunity, to tear out that page and bring it to me. No harm will be done, and it can be returned in proper time."

Perplexed wrinkles were gathering on Hatch's forehead as he listened. What had page 7 of a Bible to do with what seemed to be a murder mystery? Who had said anything about a Bible, anyway? The letter left by Stockton mentioned a Bible, but that didn't seem to mean anything. Then Hatch remembered that same letter carried a figure seven in parentheses which had apparently nothing to do and no connection with any other part of the letter. Hatch's introspective study of the affair was interrupted by The Thinking Machine.

"I shall await your report here, Mr Hatch. If it is what I expect, we shall go out late tonight on a little voyage of discovery. Meanwhile see that Bible and tell me what you find."

Hatch found the apartments of John Stockton on Beacon Street without any difficulty. In a manner best known to himself he entered and searched the place. When he came out there was a look of chagrin on his face as he hurried to the house of The Thinking Machine nearby.

"Well?" asked the scientist.

"I saw the Bible," said Hatch.

"And page 7?"

"Was torn out, missing, gone," replied the reporter.

"Ah," exclaimed the scientist. "I thought so. Tonight we will make the little trip I spoke of. By the way, did you happen to notice if John Stockton had or used a fountain pen?"

"I didn't see one," said Hatch.

"Well, please see for me if any of his employees have ever noticed one. Then meet me here tonight at 10 o'clock."

Thus Hatch was dismissed. A little later he called casually on Stockton again. There, by inquiries, he established to his own satisfaction that Stockton did not own a fountain pen. Then with Stockton himself he took up the matter of the Bible again.

"I understand you to say, Mr Stockton," he began in his smoothest tone, "that you knew of the existence of a family Bible, but you did not know if it was still at the Dorchester place."

"That's correct," said Stockton.

"How is it then," Hatch resumed, "that that identical Bible is now at your apartments, carefully hidden in a box under a sofa?"

Mr Stockton seemed to be amazed. He arose suddenly and leaned over toward the reporter with hands clenched. There was a glitter of what might have been anger in his eyes.

"What do you know about this? What are you talking about?" he demanded.

"I mean that you had said you did not know where this book was, and meanwhile have it hidden. Why?"

"Have you seen the Bible in my rooms?" asked Stockton.

"I have," said the reporter coolly.

Now a new determination came into the face of the merchant. The oiliness of his manner was gone, the sanctimonious smirk had been obliterated, the thin lips closed into a straight, rigid line.

"I shall have nothing further to say," he declared almost fiercely.

"Will you tell me why you tore out the seventh page of the Bible?" asked Hatch.

Stockton stared at him dully, as if dazed for a moment. All the color left his face. There came a startling pallor instead. When next he spoke, his voice was tense and strained.

"Is — is — the seventh page missing?"

"Yes," Hatch replied. "Where is it?"

"I'll have nothing further to say under any circumstances. That's all."

With not the slightest idea of what it might mean or what bearing it had on the matter, Hatch had brought out statements which were wholly at variance with facts. Why was Stockton so affected by the statement that page seven was gone? Why had the Bible been taken from the Dorchester home? Why had it been so carefully hidden? How did Miss Devan know it was there?

These were only a few of the questions that were racing through the reporter's mind. He did not seem to be able to grasp anything tangible. If there were a cipher hidden in the letter, what was it? What bearing did it have on the case?

Seeking a possible answer to some of these questions, Hatch took a cab and was soon back at the Dorchester house. He was somewhat surprised to see The Thinking Machine standing on the stoop waiting to be admitted. The scientist took his presence as a matter of course.

"What did you find out about Stockton's fountain pen?" he asked.

"I satisfied myself that he had not owned a fountain pen, at least recently enough for the pen to have been used in writing that letter. I presume that's what inquiries in that direction mean."

The two men were admitted to the house and after a few minutes Miss Devan entered. She understood when The Thinking Machine explained that they merely wished to see the shop in which Mr Stockton had been found dead.

"And also if you have a sample of Mr Stockton's handwriting," asked the scientist.

"It's rather peculiar," Miss Devan explained, "but I doubt if there is an authentic sample in existence large enough, that is, to be compared with that letter. He had a certain amount of correspondence, but this I did for him on the typewriter. Occasionally he would prepare an article for a scientific paper, but these were also dictated to me. He has been in the habit of doing so for years."

"This letter seems to be all there is?"

"Of course his signature appears to checks and in other places. I can produce some of those for you. I don't think, however, that there is the slightest doubt that he wrote this letter. It is his handwriting."

"I suppose he never used a fountain pen?" asked The Thinking Machine.

"Not that I know of," the girl replied. "I have one," and she took it out of a little gold fascinator she wore at her bosom.

The scientist pressed the point of the pen against his thumb nail, and a tiny drop of blue ink appeared. The letter was written in black. The Thinking Machine seemed satisfied.

"And now the shop," he suggested.

Miss Devan led the way through the long wide hall to the back of the building. There she opened a door, which showed signs of having been battered in, and admitted them. Then, at the request of The Thinking Machine, she rehearsed the story in full, showed him where Stockton had been found, where the prussic acid had been broken, and how the servant, Montgomery, had broken in the door at her request.

"Did you ever find the key to the door?"

"No. I can't imagine what became of it."

"Is this room precisely as it was when the body was found? That is, has anything been removed from it?"

"Nothing," replied the girl.

"Have the servants taken anything out? Did they have access to this room?"

"They have not been permitted to enter it at all. The body was removed and the fragments of the acid bottle were taken away, but nothing else."

"Have you ever known of pen and ink being in this room?"

"I hadn't thought of it."

"You haven't taken them out since the body was found, have you?"

"I-I-er-have not," the girl stammered.

Miss Devan left the room, and for an hour Hatch and The Thinking Machine conducted the search.

"Find a pen and ink," The Thinking Machine instructed.

They were not found.

At midnight, which was six hours later, The Thinking Machine and Hutchinson Hatch were groping through the cellar of the Dorchester house by the light of a small electric lamp which shot a straight beam aggressively through the murky, damp air. Finally the ray fell on a tiny door set in the solid wall of the cellar.

There was a slight exclamation from The Thinking Machine, and this was followed immediately by the sharp, unmistakable click of a revolver somewhere behind them in the dark.

"Down, quick," gasped Hatch, and with a sudden blow he dashed aside the electric light, extinguishing it. Simultaneously with this there came a revolver shot, and a bullet was buried in the wall behind Hatch's head.

IV

The reverberation of the pistol shot was still ringing in Hatch's ears when he felt the hand of The Thinking Machine on his arm, and then through the utter blackness of the cellar came the irritable voice of the scientist:

"To your right, to your right," it said sharply.

Then, contrary to this advice Hatch felt the scientist drawing him to the left. In another moment there came a second shot, and by the flash Hatch could see that it was aimed at a point a dozen feet to the right of the point where they had been when the first shot was fired. The person with the revolver had heard the scientist and had been duped.

Firmly the scientist drew Hatch on until they were almost to the cellar steps. There, outlined against a dim light which came down the stairs, they could see a tall figure peering through the darkness toward a spot opposite where they stood. Hatch saw only one thing to do and did it. He leaped forward and landed on the back of the figure, bearing the man to the ground. An instant later his hand closed on the revolver and he wrested it away.

"All right," he sang out. "I've got it."

The electric light which he had dashed from the hand of The Thinking Machine gleamed again through the cellar and fell upon the face of John Stockton, helpless and gasping in the hands of the reporter.

"Well?" asked Stockton calmly. "Are you burglars or what?"

"Let's go upstairs to the light," suggested The Thinking Machine.

It was under these peculiar circumstances that the scientist came face to face for the first time with John Stockton. Hatch introduced the two men in a most matter-of-fact tone and restored to Stockton the revolver. This was suggested by a nod of the scientist's head. Stockton laid the revolver on a table.

"Why did you try to kill us?" asked The Thinking Machine.

"I presumed you were burglars," was the reply. "I heard the noise down stairs and came down to investigate."

"I thought you lived on Beacon Street," said the scientist.

"I do, but I came here tonight on a little business, which is all my own, and happened to hear you. What were you doing in the cellar?"

"How long have you been here?"

"Five or ten minutes."

"Have you a key to this house?"

"I have had one for many years. What is all this, anyway? How did you get in this house? What right had you here?"

"Is Miss Devan in the house tonight?" asked The Thinking Machine, entirely disregarding the other's questions.

"I don't know. I suppose so."

"You haven't seen her, of course?"

"Certainly not."

"And you came here secretly without her knowledge?"

Stockton shrugged his shoulders and was silent. The Thinking Machine raised himself on the chair on which he had been sitting and squinted steadily into Stockton's eyes. When he spoke it was to Hatch, but his gaze did not waver.

"Arouse the servants, find where Miss Devan's room is, and see if anything has happened to her," he directed.

"I think that will be unwise," broke in Stockton quickly.

"Why?"

"If I may put it on personal grounds," said Stockton, "I would ask as a favor that you do not make known my visit here, or your own for that matter, to Miss Devan."

There was a certain uneasiness in the man's attitude, a certain eagerness to keep things away from Miss Devan that spurred Hatch to instant action. He went out of the room hurriedly and ten minutes later Miss Devan, who had dressed quickly, came into the room with him. The servants stood outside in the hall,

all curiosity. The closed door barred them from knowledge of what was happening.

There was a little dramatic pause as Miss Devan entered and Stockton arose from his seat. The Thinking Machine glanced from one to the other. He noted the pallor of the girl's face and the frank embarrassment of Stockton

"What is it?" asked Miss Devan, and her voice trembled a little. "Why are you all here? What has happened?"

"Mr Stockton came here tonight," The Thinking Machine began quietly, "to remove the contents from the locked vault in the cellar. He came without your knowledge and found us ahead of him. Mr Hatch and myself are here in the course of our inquiry into the matter which you placed in my hands. We also came without your knowledge. I considered this best. Mr Stockton was very anxious that his visit should be kept from you. Have you anything to say now?"

The girl turned on Stockton with magnificent scorn. Accusation was in her very attitude. Her small hand was pointed directly at Stockton and into his face there came a strange emotion, which he struggled to repress.

"Murderer! Thief!" the girl almost hissed.

"Do you know why he came?" asked The Thinking Machine.

"He came to rob the vault, as you said," said the girl, fiercely. "It was because my father would not give him the secret of his last invention that this man killed him. How he compelled him to write that letter I don't know."

"Elizabeth, for God's sake what are you saying?" asked Stockton with ashen face.

"His greed is so great that he wanted all of my father's estate," the girl went on impetuously. "He was not content that I should get even a small part of it."

"Elizabeth, Elizabeth!" said Stockton, as he leaned forward with his head in his hands.

"What do you know about this secret vault?" asked the scientist.

"I – I – have always thought there was a secret vault in the cellar," the girl explained. "I may say I know there was one because those things my father took the greatest care of were always disposed of by him somewhere in the house. I can imagine no other place than the cellar."

There was a long pause. The girl stood rigid, staring down at the bowed figure of Stockton with not a gleam of pity in her face. Hatch caught the expression and it occurred to him for the first time that Miss Devan was vindictive. He was more convinced than ever that there had been some long-standing feud between these two. The Thinking Machine broke the long silence.

"Do you happen to know, Miss Devan, that page seven of the Bible which you found hidden in Mr Stockton's place is missing?"

"I didn't notice," said the girl.

Stockton had arisen with the words and now stood with white face and listening intently. "Did you ever happen to see a page seven in that Bible?" the scientist asked.

"I don't recall."

"What were you doing in my rooms?" demanded Stockton of the girl.

"Why did you tear out page seven?" asked The Thinking Machine.

Stockton thought the question was addressed to him and turned to answer. Then he saw it was unmistakably a question to Miss Devan and turned again to her.

"I didn't tear it out," exclaimed Miss Devan. "I never saw it. I don't know what you mean."

The Thinking Machine made an impatient gesture with his hands; his next question was to Stockton.

"Have you a sample of your father's handwriting?"

"Several," said Stockton. "Here are three or four letters from him."

Miss Devan gasped a little as if startled and Stockton produced the letters and handed them to The Thinking Machine. The latter glanced over two of them.

"I thought, Miss Devan, you said your father always dictated his letters to you?"

"I did say so," said the girl. "I didn't know of the existence of these."

"May I have these?" asked The Thinking Machine.

"Yes. They are of no consequence."

"Now let's see what is in the secret vault," the scientist went on.

He arose and led the way again into the cellar, lighting his path with the electric bulb. Stockton followed immediately behind, then came Miss Devan, her white dressing gown trailing mystically in the dim light, and last came Hatch. The Thinking Machine went straight to that spot where he and Hatch had been when Stockton had fired at them. Again the rays of the light revealed the tiny door set into the wall of the cellar. The door opened readily at his touch; the small vault was empty.

Intent on his examination of this, The Thinking Machine was oblivious for a moment to what was happening. Suddenly there came again a pistol shot, followed instantly by a woman's scream.

"My God, he's killed himself. He's killed himself."

It was Miss Devan's voice.

V

When The Thinking Machine flashed his light back into the gloom of the cellar, he saw Miss Devan and Hatch leaning over the prostrate figure of John Stockton. The latter's face was perfectly white save just at the edge of the hair, where there was a trickle of red. In his right hand he clasped a revolver.

"Dear me! Dear me!" exclaimed the scientist. "What is it?"

"Stockton shot himself," said Hatch, and there was excitement in his tone.

On his knees the scientist made a hurried examination of the wounded man, then suddenly – it may have been inadvertently—he flashed the light in the face of Miss Devan.

"Where were you?" he demanded quickly.

"Just behind him," said the girl. "Will he die? Is it fatal?"

"Hopeless," said the scientist. "Let's get him upstairs."

The unconscious man was lifted and with Hatch leading was again taken to the room which they had left only a few minutes before. Hatch stood by helplessly while The Thinking Machine, in his capacity of physician, made a more minute examination of the wound. The bullet mark just above the right temple was almost bloodless; around it there were the unmistakeable marks of burned powder.

"Help me just a moment, Miss Devan," requested The Thinking Machine, as he bound an improvised handkerchief bandage about the head. Miss Devan tied the final knots of the bandage and The Thinking Machine studied her hands closely as she did so. When the work was completed he turned to her in a most matter of fact way.

"Why did you shoot him?" he asked.

"I – I—" stammered the girl, "I didn't shoot him, he shot himself."

"How come those powder marks on your right hand?"

Miss Devan glanced down at her right hand, and the color which had been in her face faded as if by magic. There was fear, now, in her manner.

"I – I don't know," she stammered. "Surely you don't think that I—"

"Mr Hatch, 'phone at once for an ambulance and then see if it is possible to get Detective Mallory here immediately. I shall give Miss Devan into custody on the charge of shooting this man."

The girl stared at him dully for a moment and then dropped back into a chair with dead white face and fear-distended eyes. Hatch went out, seeking a telephone, and for a time Miss Devan sat silent, as if dazed. Finally, with an effort, she aroused herself and facing The Thinking Machine defiantly, burst out:

"I didn't shoot him. I didn't, I didn't. He did it himself."

The long, slender fingers of The Thinking Machine closed on the revolver and gently removed it from the hand of the wounded man.

"Ah, I was mistaken," he said suddenly, "he was not as badly wounded as I thought. See! He is reviving."

"Reviving," exclaimed Miss Devan. "Won't he die, then?"

"Why?" asked The Thinking Machine sharply.

"It seems so pitiful, almost a confession of guilt," she hurriedly exclaimed. "Won't he die?"

Gradually the color was coming back into Stockton's face. The Thinking Machine bending over him, with one hand on the heart, saw the eyelids quiver and then slowly the eyes opened. Almost immediately the strength of the heartbeat grew perceptibly stronger. Stockton stared at him a moment, then wearily his eyelids drooped again.

"Why did Miss Devan shoot you?" The Thinking Machine demanded.

There was a pause and the eyes opened for the second time. Miss Devan stood within range of the glance, her hands outstretched entreatingly toward Stockton.

"Why did she shoot you?" repeated The Thinking Machine.

"She-did-not," said Stockton slowly. "I-did-it-myself."

For an instant there was a little wrinkle of perplexity on the brow of The Thinking Machine and then it passed.

"Purposely?" he asked.

"I did it myself."

Again the eyes closed and Stockton seemed to be passing into unconsciousness. The Thinking Machine glanced up to find an infinite expression of relief on Miss Devan's face. His own manner changed; became almost abject, in fact, as he turned to her again.

"I beg your pardon," he said. "I made a mistake."

"Will he die?"

"No, that was another mistake. He will recover."

Within a few moments a City Hospital ambulance rattled up to the door and John Stockton was removed. It was with a feeling of pity that Hatch assisted Miss Devan, now almost in a fainting condition, to her room. The Thinking Machine had previously given her a slight stimulant. Detective Mallory had not answered the call by 'phone.

The Thinking Machine and Hatch returned to Boston. At the Park Street subway they separated, after The Thinking Machine had given certain instructions. Hatch spent most of the following day carrying out these instructions. First he went to see Dr Benton, the physician who issued the death certificate on which Pomeroy Stockton was buried. Dr Benton was considerably alarmed when the reporter broached the subject of his visit. After a time he talked freely of the case.

"I have known John Stockton since we were in college together," he said, "and I believe him to be one of the few really good men I know. I can't believe otherwise. Singularly enough, he is also one of the few good men who has made his own fortune. There is nothing hypocritical about him.

"Immediately after his father was found dead, he 'phoned to me and I went out to the house in Dorchester. He explained then that it was apparent Pomeroy Stockton had committed suicide. He dreaded the disgrace that public knowledge would bring on an honored name, and asked me what could be done.

I suggested the only thing I knew – that was the issuance of a death certificate specifying natural causes – heart disease, I said. This act was due entirely to my friendship for him.

"I examined the body and found a trace of prussic acid on Pomeroy's tongue. Beside the chair on which he sat a bottle of prussic acid had been broken. I made no autopsy, of course. Ethically I may have sinned, but I feel that no real harm has been done. Of course, now that you know the real facts my entire career is at stake."

"There is no question in your mind but that it was suicide?" asked Hatch.

"Not the slightest. Then, too, there was the letter, which was found in Pomeroy Stockton's pocket. I saw that and if there had been any doubt then it was removed. This letter, I think, was then in Miss Devan's possession. I presume it is still."

"Do you know anything about Miss Devan?"

"Nothing, except that she is an adopted daughter, who for some reason retained her own family name. Three or four years ago she had a little love affair, to which John Stockton objected. I believe he was the cause of it being broken off. As a matter of fact, I think at one time he was himself in love with her and she refused to accept him as a suitor. Since that time there has been some slight friction, but I know nothing of this except in a general way from what he has said to me."

Then Hatch proceeded to carry out the other part of The Thinking Machine's instructions. This was to see the attorney in whose possession Pomeroy Stockton's will was supposed to be and to ask him why there had been a delay in the reading of the will.

Hatch found the attorney, Frederick Sloane, without difficulty. Without reservation Hatch laid all the circumstances as he knew them before Mr Sloane. Then came the question of why the will had not been read. Mr Sloane, too, was frank.

"It's because the will is not now in my possession," he said. "It has either been mislaid, lost, or possibly stolen. I did not care for the family to know this just now, and delayed the reading of the will while I made a search for it. Thus far I have found not a trace. I haven't even the remotest idea where it is."

"What does the will provide?" asked Hatch.

"It leaves the bulk of the estate to John Stockton, settles an annuity of $5,000 a year on Miss Devan, gives her the Dorchester house, and specifically cuts off other relatives whom Pomeroy Stockton once accused of stealing an invention he made. The letter, found after Mr Stockton's death—"

"You knew of that letter, too?" Hatch interrupted.

"Oh, yes, this letter confirms the will, except, in general terms, it also cuts off Miss Devan."

"Would it not be to the interest of the other immediate relatives of Stockton, those who were specifically cut off, to get possession of that will and destroy it?"

"Of course it might be, but there has been no communication between the two branches of the family for several years. That branch lives in the far West and I have taken particular pains to ascertain that they could not have had anything to do with the disappearance of the will."

With these new facts in his possession, Hatch started to report to The Thinking Machine. He had to wait half an hour or so. At last the scientist came in.

"I've been attending an autopsy," he said.

"An autopsy? Whose?"

"On the body of Pomeroy Stockton."

"Why, I had thought he had been buried."

"No, only placed in a receiving vault. I had to call the attention of the Medical Examiner to the case in order to get permission to make an autopsy. We did it together."

"What did you find?" asked Hatch.

"What did you find?" asked The Thinking Machine, in turn.

Briefly Hatch told him of the interview with Dr Benton and Mr Sloane. The scientist listened without comment and at the end sat back in his big chair squinting at the ceiling.

"That seems to finish it," he said. "These are the questions which were presented: First, In what manner did Pomeroy Stockton die? Second, If not suicide, as appeared, what motive was there for anything else? Third, If there was a motive, to whom does it lead? Fourth, What was in the cipher letter? Now, Mr Hatch, I think I may make all of it clear. There was a cipher in the letter — what may be described as a cipher in five, the figure five being the key to it.

VI

"First, Mr Hatch," The Thinking Machine resumed, as he drew out and spread on a table the letter which had been originally placed in his hands by Miss Devan, "the question of whether there was a cipher in this letter was to be definitely decided.

"There are a thousand different kinds of ciphers. One of them, which we will call the arbitrary cipher, is excellently illustrated in Poe's story, 'The Gold Bug'. In that cipher, a figure or symbol is made to represent each letter of the alphabet.

"Then, there are book ciphers, which are, perhaps, the safest of all ciphers, because without a clue to the book from which words may be chosen and designated by numbers, no one can solve it.

"It would be useless for me to go into this matter at any length, so let us consider this particular letter as a cipher possibility. A careful study of the letter develops three possible starting points. The first of these is the general tone of the letter. It is not a direct, straight-away statement such as a man about to commit suicide would write unless he had a purpose — that is, a purpose beyond the mere apparent meaning of the letter itself. Therefore we will suppose there was another purpose hidden behind a cipher.

"The second starting point is that offered by the absence of one word. You will see that the word 'in' should appear between the word 'cherished' and 'secret'. This, of course, may have been an oversight in writing, the sort of thing anyone might do. But further down we find the third starting point.

"This is the figure seven in parentheses. It apparently has no connection whatever with what precedes or follows. It could not have been an accident. Therefore what did it mean? Was it a crude outward indication of a hurriedly constructed cipher?

"I took the figure seven at first to be a sort of key to the entire letter, always presuming there was a cipher. I counted seven words down from that figure and found the word 'binding'. Seven words from that down made the next word 'give'. Together the two words seemed to mean something.

"I stopped there and started back. The seventh word up is 'and'. The seventh word from 'and', still counting backward, seemed meaningless. I pursued that theory of seven all the way through the letter and found only a jumble of words. It was the same way counting seven letters. These letters meant nothing unless each letter was arbitrarily taken to represent another letter. This immediately led to intricacies. I believe always in exhausting simple possibilities first, so I started over again.

"Now what word nearest to the seven meant anything when taken together with it? Not 'family', not 'Bible', not 'son', as the vital words appear from the seven down. Going up from the seven, I did find a word which applied to it and meant something. That was the word 'page'. I had immediately 'page seven'. 'Page' was the fifth word up from the seven.

"What was the next fifth word, still going up? This was 'on'. Then I had 'on page seven' – connected words appearing in order, each being the fifth from the other. The fifth word down from seven I found was 'family'; the next fifth word was 'Bible'; thus, 'on page seven family Bible'.

MYSTERY OF THE FATAL CIPHER

"It is unnecessary to go further into the study I made of the cipher. I worked upward from the seven, taking each fifth word until I had all the cipher words. I have underscored them here. Read the words underscored and you have the cipher."

Hatch took the letter marked as follows:

To those Concerned:

Tired of it all I seek the end, and am content. Ambition is dead; the grave yawns greedily at my feet, and with the labor of my own hands lost I greet death of my own will, by my own act.

To my son I leave all, and you who maligned me, you who discouraged me, you may read this and know I punish you thus. It's for him, my son, to forgive.

I dared in life and dare dead your everlasting anger, not alone that you didn't speak, but that you cherished secret, and my ears are locked forever against you. My vault is my resting place.

On the brightest and dearest page of life I wrote (7) my love for him. Family ties, binding as the Bible itself, bade me give all to my son.

Goodbye. I die.

Pomeroy Stockton

Slowly Hatch read this:

"I am dead at the hands of my son. You who read punish him. I dare not speak. Secret locked vault on page 7 family Bible."

"Well, by George!" exclaimed the reporter. It was a tribute to The Thinking Machine, as well as an expression of amazement at what he read.

"You see," explained The Thinking Machine, "if the word 'in' had appeared between 'cherished' and 'secret', as it would naturally have done, it would have lost the order of the cipher, therefore it was purposely left out."

"It's enough to send Stockton to the electric chair," said Hatch.

"It would be if it were not a forgery," said the scientist testily.

"A forgery," gasped Hatch. "Didn't Pomeroy Stockton write it?"

"No."

"Surely not John Stockton?"

"No."

"Well, who then?"

"Miss Devan."

"Miss Devan!" Hatch repeated in amazement. "Then, Miss Devan killed Pomeroy Stockton?"

"No, he died a natural death."

Hatch's head was whirling. A thousand questions demanded an immediate answer. He stared mouth agape at The Thinking Machine. All his ideas of the case were tumbling about him. Nothing remained.

"Briefly, here is what happened," said The Thinking Machine. "Pomeroy Stockton died a natural death of heart disease. Miss Devan found him dead, wrote this letter, put it in his pocket, put a drop of prussic acid on his tongue, smashed the bottle of acid, left the room, locked the door, and next day had it broken down.

"It was she who shot John Stockton. It was she who tore out page seven of that family Bible, and then hid the book in Stockton's room. It was she who in some way got hold of the will. She either has it or destroyed it. It was she who took advantage of her aged benefactor's sudden death to further as weird and inhuman a plot against another as a woman can devise. There is nothing on God's earth as bad as a bad woman, and nothing as good as a good one. I think that has been said before."

"But as to this case," Hatch interrupted. "How? what? why?"

"I read the cipher within a few hours after I got the letter," replied The Thinking Machine. "Naturally I wanted to find out then who and what this son was.

"I had Miss Devan's story, of course – a story of disagreement between father and son, quarrelling and all that. It was also a story which showed a certain underlying animosity despite Miss Devan's cleverness. She had so mingled fact with fiction that it was not altogether easy to weed out the truth, therefore I believed what I chose.

"Miss Devan's idea, as expressed to me, was that the letter was written under coercion. Men who are being murdered don't write cipher letters as intricate as that; and men who are committing suicide have no obvious reasons for writing such letters. The line 'I dare not speak' was silly. Pomeroy Stockton was not a prisoner. If he had feared a conspiracy to kill him why shouldn't he speak?

"All these things were in my mind when I asked you to see Stockton. I was particularly anxious to hear what he had to say as to the family Bible. And yet I may say I knew that page seven had been torn out of the book and was then in Miss Devan's possession.

"I may say, too, that I knew that the secret vault was empty. Whatever these two things contained, supposing she wrote the cipher, had been removed or she would not have called attention to them in this cipher. I had an idea that she might have written it from the mere fact that it was she who first called my attention to the possibility of a cipher.

"Assuming then that the cipher was a forgery, that she wrote it, that it directly accused John Stockton, that she brought it to me, I had fairly conclusive proof that if Pomery Stockton had been murdered she had had a hand in it. John Stockton's motive in trying to suppress the fact of a suicide, as he thought it, was perfectly clear. It was, as he said, to avoid disgrace. Such things are done frequently.

"From the moment you told him of the possibility of murder, he suspected Miss Devan. Why? Because, above all, she had the opportunity, because she wanted the bulk of the estate, because there was some animosity against John Stockton.

"This now proves to have been a broken-off love affair. John Stockton broke it off. He himself had loved Miss Devan. She had refused him. Later, when he broke off the love affair, she hated him.

"Her plan for revenge was almost diabolical. It was intended to give her full revenge and the estate at the same time. She hoped, she knew, that I would read that cipher. She planned that it would send John Stockton to the electric chair."

"Horrible!" commented Hatch with a little shudder.

"It was a fear that this plan might go wrong that induced her to try to kill Stockton by shooting him. The cellar was dark, but she forgot that ninety-nine revolvers out of a hundred leave slight powder stains on the hand of the person who fires them. Stockton said that she did not shoot him, because of that inexplicable loyalty which some men show to a woman they love or have loved.

"Stockton made his secret visit to the house that night to get what was in that vault without her knowledge. He knew of its existence. His father had probably told him. The thing that appeared on page seven of the family Bible was in all probability the copper hardening process he was perfecting. I should think it had been written there in invisible ink. John Stockton knew this was there. His father told him. If his father told it, Miss Devan probably overheard it. She knew it, too.

"Now the actual circumstances of the death. The girl must have had and used a key to the work room. After John Stockton left the house that Monday night she entered that room. She found his father dead of heart disease. The autopsy proved this.

"Then the whole scheme was clear to her. She forged that cipher letter – as Pomeroy Stockton's secretary she probably knew the handwriting better than anyone else in the world – placed it in his pocket, and the rest of it you know."

"But the Bible in John Stockton's room?" asked Hatch.

"Was placed there by Miss Devan," replied The Thinking Machine. "It was a part of the general scheme to hopelessly implicate Stockton. She is a clever woman. She showed that when she produced the fountain pen, having carefully filled it with blue instead of black ink."

"What was in the locked vault?"

"That I can only conjecture. It is not impossible that the inventor had only part of the formula he so closely guarded written on the Bible leaf and the other part of it in that vault, together with other valuable documents.

"I may add that the letters which John Stockton had were not forged. They were written without Miss Devan's knowledge. There was a vast difference in the handwriting of the cipher letter which she wrote and those others which the father wrote.

"Of course it is obvious that the missing will is now, or was, in Miss Devan's possession. How she got it, I don't know. With that out of the way and this cipher unravelled apparently proving the son's guilt, at least half, possibly all, of the estate would have gone to her."

Hatch lighted a cigarette thoughtfully and was silent for a moment.

"What will be the end of it all?" he asked. "Of course, I understand that John Stockton will recover."

"The result will be that the world will lose a great scientific achievement – the secret of hardening copper, which Pomeroy Stockton had rediscovered. I think it safe to say that Miss Devan has burned every scrap of this."

"But what will become of her?"

"She knows nothing of this. I believe she will disappear before Stockton recovers. He wouldn't prosecute anyway. Remember he loved her once."

John Stockton was convalescent two weeks later, when a nurse in the City Hospital placed an envelope in his hands. He opened it and a little cloud of ashes filtered through his fingers onto the bed clothing. He sank back on his pillow, weeping.

7

MYSTERY OF THE FLAMING PHANTOM

I

Hutchinson Hatch, reporter, stood beside the City Editor's desk, smoking and waiting patiently for that energetic gentleman to dispose of several matters in hand. City Editors always have several matters in hand, for the profession of keeping count of the pulse-beat of the world is a busy one. Finally this City Editor emerged from a mass of other things and picked up a sheet of paper on which he had scribbled some strange hieroglyphics, these representing his interpretation of the art of writing.

"Afraid of ghosts?" he asked.

"Don't know," Hatch replied, smiling a little. "I never happened to meet one."

"Well, this looks like a good story," the City Editor explained. "It's a haunted house. Nobody can live in it; all sorts of strange happenings, demoniacal laughter, groans and things. House is owned by Ernest Weston, a broker. Better jump down and take a look at it. If it is promising, you might spend a night in it for a Sunday story. Not afraid, are you?"

"I never heard of a ghost hurting anyone," Hatch replied, still smiling a little. "If this one hurts me it will make the story better."

Thus attention was attracted to the latest creepy mystery of a small town by the sea, which in the past had not been wholly lacking in creepy mysteries.

Within two hours Hatch was there. He readily found the old Weston house, as it was known, a two-story, solidly built frame structure, which had stood for sixty or seventy years high upon a cliff overlooking the sea, in the center of a land plot of ten or twelve acres. From a distance it was imposing, but close inspection showed that, outwardly, at least, it was a ramshackle affair.

Without having questioned anyone in the village, Hatch climbed the steep cliff road to the old house, expecting to find some one who might grant him permission to inspect it. But no one appeared; a settled melancholy and gloom seemed to overspread it; all the shutters were closed forbiddingly.

There was no answer to his vigorous knock on the front door, and he shook the shutters on a window without result. Then he passed around the house to the back. Here he found a door and dutifully hammered on it. Still no answer. He tried it, and passed in. He stood in the kitchen, damp, chilly and darkened by the closed shutters.

One glance about this room and he went on through a back hall to the dining-room, now deserted, but at one time a comfortable and handsomely furnished place. Its hardwood floor was covered with dust; the chill of disuse was all-pervading. There was no furniture, only the litter which accumulates of its own accord.

From this point, just inside the dining-room door, Hatch began a sort of study of the inside architecture of the place. To his left was a door, the butler's pantry. There was a passage through, down three steps into the kitchen he had just left.

Straight before him, set in the wall, between two windows, was a large mirror, seven, possibly eight, feet tall and proportionately wide. A mirror of the same size was set in the wall at the end of the room to his left. From the dining-room he passed through a wide archway into the next room. This archway made the two rooms almost as one. This second, he presumed, had been a sort of living-room, but here, too, was nothing save accumulated litter, an old-fashioned fireplace and two long mirrors. As he entered, the fireplace was to his immediate left, one of the large mirrors was straight ahead of him and the other was to his right.

Next to the mirror in the end was a passageway of a little more than usual size which had once been closed with a sliding door. Hatch went through this into the reception-hall of the old house. Here, to his right, was the main hall, connected with the reception-hall by an archway, and through this archway he could see a wide, old-fashioned stairway leading up. To his left was a door, of ordinary size, closed. He tried it and it opened. He peered into a big room beyond. This room had been the library. It smelled of books and damp wood. There was nothing here — not even mirrors.

Beyond the main hall lay only two rooms, one a drawing-room of the generous proportions our old folks loved, with its gilt all tarnished and its fancy decorations covered with dust. Behind this, toward the back of the house, was a small parlour. There was nothing here to attract his attention, and he went upstairs. As he went he could see through the archway into the reception-hall as far as the library door, which he had left closed.

Upstairs were four or five roomy suites. Here, too, in small rooms designed for dressing, he saw the owner's passion for mirrors again. As he passed through room after room he fixed the general arrangement of it all in his mind, and later on paper, to study it, so that, if necessary, he could leave any part of the house in the dark. He didn't know but what this might be necessary, hence his care – the same care he had evidenced downstairs.

After another casual examination of the lower floor, Hatch went out the back way to the barn. This stood a couple of hundred feet back of the house and was of more recent construction. Above, reached by outside stairs, were apartments intended for the servants. Hatch looked over these rooms, but they, too, had the appearance of not having been occupied for several years. The lower part of the barn, he found, was arranged to house half a dozen horses and three or four traps.

"Nothing here to frighten anybody," was his mental comment as he left the old place and started back toward the village. It was three o'clock in the afternoon. His purpose was to learn then all he could of the "ghost," and return that night for developments.

He sought out the usual village bureau of information, the town constable, a grizzled old chap of sixty years, who realized his importance as the whole police department, and who had the gossip and information, more or less distorted, of several generations at his tongue's end.

The old man talked for two hours – he was glad to talk – seemed to have been longing for just such a glorious opportunity as the reporter offered. Hatch sifted out what he wanted, those things which might be valuable in his story.

It seemed, according to the constable, that the Weston house had not been occupied for five years, since the death of the father of Ernest Weston, present owner. Two weeks before the reporter's appearance there Ernest Weston had come down with a contractor and looked over the old place.

"We understand here," said the constable, judicially, "that Mr Weston is going to be married soon, and we kind of thought he was having the house made ready for his Summer home again."

"Whom do you understand he is to marry?" asked Hatch, for this was news.

"Miss Katherine Everard, daughter of Curtis Everard, a banker up in Boston," was the reply. "I know he used to go around with her before the old man died, and they say since she came out in Newport he has spent a lot of time with her."

"Oh, I see," said Hatch. "They were to marry and come here?"

"That's right," said the constable. "But I don't know when, since this ghost story has come up."

"Oh, yes, the ghost," remarked Hatch. "Well, hasn't the work of repairing begun?"

"No, not inside," was the reply. "There's been some work done on the grounds—in the daytime – but not much of that, and I kind of think it will be a long time before it's all done."

"What is the spook story, anyway?"

"Well," and the old constable rubbed his chin thoughtfully. "It seems sort of funny. A few days after Mr Weston was down here a gang of laborers, mostly Italians, came down to work and decided to sleep in the house—sort of camp out – until they could repair a leak in the barn and move in there. They got here late in the afternoon and didn't do much that day but move into the house, all upstairs, and sort of settle down for the night. About one o'clock they heard some sort of noise downstairs, and finally all sorts of a racket and groans and yells, and they just naturally came down to see what it was.

"Then they saw the ghost. It was in the reception-hall, some of 'em said, others said it was in the library, but anyhow it was there, and the whole gang left just as fast as they knew how. They slept on the ground that night. Next day they took out their things and went back to Boston. Since then nobody here has heard from 'em."

"What sort of a ghost was it?"

"Oh, it was a man ghost, about nine feet high, and he was blazing from head to foot as if he was burning up," said the constable. "He had a long knife in his hand and waved it at 'em. They didn't stop to argue. They ran, and as they ran they heard the ghost a-laughing at them."

"I should think he would have been amused," was Hatch's somewhat sarcastic comment. "Has anybody who lives in the village seen the ghost?"

"No; we're willing to take their word for it, I suppose," was the grinning reply, "because there never was a ghost there before. I go up and look over the place every afternoon, but everything seems to be all right, and I haven't gone there at night. It's quite a way off my beat," he hastened to explain.

"A man ghost with a long knife," mused Hatch "Blazing, seems to be burning up, eh? That sounds exciting. Now, a ghost who knows his business never appears except where there has been a murder. Was there ever a murder in that house?"

"When I was a little chap I heard there was a murder or something there, but I suppose if I don't remember it nobody else here does," was the old man's reply. "It happened one Winter when the Westons weren't there. There was something, too, about jewelry and diamonds, but I don't remember just what it was."

"Indeed?" asked the reporter.

"Yes, something about somebody trying to steal a lot of jewelry – a hundred thousand dollars' worth. I know nobody ever paid much attention to it. I just heard about it when I was a boy, and that was at least fifty years ago."

"I see," said the reporter.

That night at nine o'clock, under cover of perfect blackness, Hatch climbed the cliff toward the Weston house. At one o'clock he came racing down the hill, with frequent glances over his shoulder. His face was pallid with a fear which he had never known before and his lips were ashen. Once in his room in the village hotel Hutchinson Hatch, the nerveless young man, lighted a lamp with trembling hands and sat with wide, staring eyes until the dawn broke through the east.

He had seen the flaming phantom.

II

It was ten o'clock that morning when Hutchinson Hatch called on Professor Augustus S. F. X. Van Dusen – The Thinking Machine. The reporter's face was still white, showing that he had slept little, if at all. The Thinking Machine squinted at him a moment through his thick glasses, then dropped into a chair.

"Well?" he queried.

"I'm almost ashamed to come to you, Professor," Hatch confessed, after a minute, and there was a little embarrassed hesitation in his speech. "It's another mystery."

"Sit down and tell me about it."

Hatch took a seat opposite the scientist.

"I've been frightened," he said at last, with a sheepish grin; "horribly, awfully frightened. I came to you to know what frightened me."

"Dear me! Dear me!" exclaimed The Thinking Machine. "What is it?"

Then Hatch told him from the beginning the story of the haunted house as he knew it; how he had examined the house by daylight, just what he had found, the story of the old murder and the jewels, the fact that Ernest Weston was to be married. The scientist listened attentively.

"It was nine o'clock that night when I went to the house the second time," said Hatch. "I went prepared for something, but not for what I saw."

"Well, go on," said the other, irritably.

"I went in while it was perfectly dark. I took a position on the stairs because I had been told the – the THING – had been seen from the stairs, and I thought that where it had been seen once it would be seen again. I had presumed it was some trick of a shadow, or moonlight, or something of the kind. So I sat waiting calmly. I am not a nervous man – that is, I never have been until now.

"I took no light of any kind with me. It seemed an interminable time that I waited, staring into the reception-room in the general direction of the library. At last, as I gazed into the darkness, I heard a noise. It startled me a bit, but it didn't frighten me, for I put it down to a rat running across the floor.

"But after awhile I heard the most awful cry a human being ever listened to. It was neither a moan nor a shriek – merely a – a cry. Then, as I steadied my nerves a little, a figure – a blazing, burning white figure – grew out of nothingness before my very eyes, in the reception-room. It actually grew and assembled as I looked at it."

He paused, and The Thinking Machine changed his position slightly.

"The figure was that of a man, apparently, I should say, eight feet high. Don't think I'm a fool – I'm not exaggerating. It was all in white and seemed to radiate a light, a ghostly, unearthly light, which, as I looked, grew brighter. I saw no face to the THING, but it had a head. Then I saw an arm raised and in the hand was a dagger, blazing as was the figure.

"By this time I was a coward, a cringing, frightened coward – frightened not at what I saw, but at the weirdness of it. And then, still as I looked, the – the THING – raised the other hand, and there, in the air before my eyes, wrote with his own finger – on the very face of the air, mind you – one word: 'Beware!'"

"Was it a man's or woman's writing?" asked The Thinking Machine.

The matter-of-fact tone recalled Hatch, who was again being carried away by fear, and he laughed vacantly.

"I don't know," he said. "I don't know."

"Go on."

"I have never considered myself a coward, and certainly I am not a child to be frightened at a thing which my reason tells me is not possible, and, despite my fright, I compelled myself to action. If the THING were a man I was not afraid of it, dagger and all; if it were not, it could do me no injury.

"I leaped down the three steps to the bottom of the stairs, and while the THING stood there with upraised dagger, with one hand pointing at me, I rushed for it. I think I must have shouted, because I have a dim idea that I heard my own voice. But whether or not I did I—"

Again he paused. It was a distinct effort to pull himself together. He felt like a child; the cold, squint eyes of The Thinking Machine were turned on him disapprovingly.

"Then – the THING disappeared just as it seemed I had my hands on it. I was expecting a dagger thrust. Before my eyes, while I was staring at it, I suddenly saw only half of it. Again I heard the cry, and the other half disappeared – my hands grasped empty air.

"Where the THING had been there was nothing. The impetus of my rush was such that I went right on past the spot where the THING had been, and found myself groping in the dark in a room which I didn't place for an instant. Now I know it was the library.

"By this time I was mad with terror. I smashed one of the windows and went through it. Then from there, until I reached my room, I didn't stop running. I couldn't. I wouldn't have gone back to the reception-room for all the millions in the world."

The Thinking Machine twiddled his fingers idly; Hatch sat gazing at him with anxious, eager inquiry in his eyes.

"So when you ran and the – the THING moved away or disappeared you found yourself in the library?" The Thinking Machine asked at last.

"Yes."

"Therefore you must have run from the reception-room through the door into the library?"

"Yes."

"You left that door closed that day?"
"Yes."
Again there was a pause.
"Smell anything?" asked The Thinking Machine.
"No."
"You figure that the THING, as you call it, must have been just about in the door?"
"Yes."
"Too bad you didn't notice the handwriting – that is, whether it seemed to be a man's or a woman's."
"I think, under the circumstances, I would be excused for omitting that," was the reply.
"You said you heard something that you thought must be a rat," went on The Thinking Machine. "What was this?"
"I don't know."
"Any squeak about it?"
"No, not that I noticed."
"Five years since the house was occupied," mused the scientist. "How far away is the water?"
"The place overlooks the water, but it's a steep climb of three hundred yards from the water to the house."
That seemed to satisfy The Thinking Machine as to what actually happened.
"When you went over the house in daylight, did you notice if any of the mirrors were dusty?" he asked.
"I should presume that all were," was the reply. "There's no reason why they should have been otherwise."
"But you didn't notice particularly that some were not dusty?" the scientist insisted.
"No. I merely noticed that they were there."
The Thinking Machine sat for a long time squinting at the ceiling, then asked, abruptly:
"Have you seen Mr Weston, the owner?"
"No."

"See him and find out what he has to say about the place, the murder, the jewels, and all that. It would be rather a queer state of affairs if, say, a fortune in jewels should be concealed somewhere about the place, wouldn't it?"

"It would," said Hatch. "It would."

"Who is Miss Katherine Everard?"

"Daughter of a banker here, Curtis Everard. Was a reigning belle at Newport for two seasons. She is now in Europe, I think, buying a trousseau, possibly."

"Find out all about her, and what Weston has to say, then come back here," said The Thinking Machine, as if in conclusion. "Oh, by the way," he added, "look up something of the family history of the Westons. How many heirs were there? Who are they? How much did each one get? All those things. That's all."

Hatch went out, far more composed and quiet than when he entered, and began the work of finding out those things The Thinking Machine had asked for, confident now that there would be a solution of the mystery.

That night the flaming phantom played new pranks. The town constable, backed by half a dozen villagers, descended upon the place at midnight, to be met in the yard by the apparition in person. Again the dagger was seen; again the ghostly laughter and the awful cry were heard.

"Surrender or I'll shoot," shouted the constable, nervously.

A laugh was the answer, and the constable felt something warm spatter in his face. Others in the party felt it, too, and wiped their faces and hands. By the light of the feeble lanterns they carried they examined their handkerchiefs and hands. Then the party fled in awful disorder.

The warmth they had felt was the warmth of blood—red blood, freshly drawn.

MYSTERY OF THE FLAMING PHANTOM

III

Hatch found Ernest Weston at luncheon with another gentleman at one o'clock that day. This other gentleman was introduced to Hatch as George Weston, a cousin. Hatch instantly remembered George Weston for certain eccentric exploits at Newport a season or so before; and also as one of the heirs of the original Weston estate.

Hatch thought he remembered, too, that at the time Miss Everard had been so prominent socially at Newport, George Weston had been her most ardent suitor. It was rumored that there would have been an engagement between them, but her father objected. Hatch looked at him curiously; his face was clearly a dissipated one, yet there was about him the unmistakable polish and gentility of the well-bred man of society.

Hatch knew Ernest Weston as Weston knew Hatch; they had met frequently in the ten years Hatch had been a newspaper reporter, and Weston had been courteous to him always. The reporter was in doubt as to whether to bring up the subject on which he had sought out Ernest Weston, but the broker brought it up himself, smilingly.

"Well, what is it this time?" he asked, genially. "The ghost down on the South Shore, or my forth-coming marriage?"

"Both," replied Hatch.

Weston talked freely of his engagement to Miss Everard, which he said was to have been announced in another week, at which time she was due to return to America from Europe. The marriage was to be three or four months later, the exact date had not been set.

"And I suppose the country place was being put in order as a Summer residence?" the reporter asked.

"Yes. I had intended to make some repairs and changes there, and furnish it, but now I understand that a ghost has taken a hand in the matter and has delayed it. Have you heard much about this ghost story?" he asked, and there was a slight smile on his face.

"I have seen the ghost," Hatch answered.

"You have?" demanded the broker.

George Weston echoed the words and leaned forward, with a new interest in his eyes, to listen. Hatch told them what had happened in the haunted house—all of it. They listened with the keenest interest, one as eager as the other.

"By George!" exclaimed the broker, when Hatch had finished. "How do you account for it?"

"I don't," said Hatch, flatly. "I can offer no possible solution. I am not a child to be tricked by the ordinary illusion, nor am I of the temperament which imagines things, but I can offer no explanation of this."

"It must be a trick of some sort," said George Weston.

"I was positive of that," said Hatch, "but if it is a trick, it is the cleverest I ever saw."

The conversation drifted on to the old story of missing jewels and a tragedy in the house fifty years before. Now Hatch was asking questions by direction of The Thinking Machine; he himself hardly saw their purport, but he asked them.

"Well, the full story of that affair, the tragedy there, would open up an old chapter in our family which is nothing to be ashamed of, of course," said the broker, frankly; "still it is something we have not paid much attention to for many years. Perhaps George here knows it better than I do. His mother, then a bride, heard the recital of the story from my grandmother."

Ernest Weston and Hatch looked inquiringly at George Weston, who lighted a fresh cigarette and leaned over the table toward them. He was an excellent talker. "I've heard my mother tell of it, but it was a long time ago," he began. "It seems, though, as I remember it, that my great-grandfather, who built the house, was a wealthy man, as fortunes went in those days, worth probably a million dollars.

"A part of this fortune, say about one hundred thousand dollars, was in jewels, which had come with the family from England. Many of those pieces would be of far greater value now than they were then, because of their antiquity. It was only on state occasions, I might say, when these were worn, say, once a year.

"Between times the problem of keeping them safely was a difficult one, it appeared. This was before the time of safety deposit vaults. My grandfather conceived the idea of hiding the jewels in the old place down on the South Shore, instead of keeping them in the house he had in Boston. He took them there accordingly.

"At this time one was compelled to travel down the South Shore, below Cohasset anyway, by stagecoach. My grandfather's family was then in the city, as it was Winter, so he made the trip alone. He planned to reach there at night, so as not to attract attention to himself, to hide the jewels about the house, and leave that same night for Boston again by a relay of horses he had arranged for. Just what happened after he left the stagecoach, below Cohasset, no one ever knew except by surmise."

The speaker paused a moment and relighted his cigarette.

"Next morning my great-grandfather was found unconscious and badly injured on the veranda of the house. His skull had been fractured. In the house a man was found dead. No one knew who he was; no one within a radius of many miles of the place had ever seen him.

"This led to all sorts of surmises, the most reasonable of which, and the one which the family has always accepted, being that my grandfather had gone to the house in the dark, had there met some one who was stopping there that night as a shelter from the intense cold, that this man learned of the jewels, that he had tried robbery and there was a fight.

"In this fight the stranger was killed inside the house, and my great-grandfather, injured, had tried to leave the house for aid. He collapsed on the veranda where he was found and died without having regained consciousness. That's all we know or can surmise reasonably about the matter."

"Were the jewels ever found?" asked the reporter.

"No. They were not on the dead man, nor were they in the possession of my grandfather."

"It is reasonable to suppose, then, that there was a third man and that he got away with the jewels?" asked Ernest Weston.

"It seemed so, and for a long time this theory was accepted. I suppose it is now, but some doubt was cast on it by the fact that only two trails of footsteps led to the house and none out. There was a heavy snow on the ground. If none led out it was obviously impossible that anyone came out."

Again there was silence. Ernest Weston sipped his coffee slowly.

"It would seem from that," said Ernest Weston, at last, "that the jewels were hidden before the tragedy, and have never been found."

George Weston smiled.

"Off and on for twenty years the place was searched, according to my mother's story," he said. "Every inch of the cellar was dug up; every possible nook and corner was searched. Finally the entire matter passed out of the minds of those who knew of it, and I doubt if it has ever been referred to again until now."

"A search even now would be almost worth while, wouldn't it?" asked the broker.

George Weston laughed aloud.

"It might be," he said, "but I have some doubt. A thing that was searched for twenty years would not be easily found."

So it seemed to strike the others after awhile and the matter was dropped.

"But this ghost thing," said the broker, at last. "I'm interested in that. Suppose we make up a ghost party and go down tonight. My contractor declares he can't get men to work there."

"I would be glad to go," said George Weston, "but I'm running over to the Vandergrift ball in Providence tonight."

"How about you, Hatch?" asked the broker.

"I'll go, yes," said Hatch, "as one of several," he added with a smile.

"Well, then, suppose we say the constable and you and I?" asked the broker; "tonight?"

"All right."

After making arrangements to meet the broker later that afternoon he rushed away—away to The Thinking Machine. The scientist listened, then resumed some chemical test he was making.

"Can't you go down with us tonight?" Hatch asked.

"No," said the other. "I'm going to read a paper before a scientific society and prove that a chemist in Chicago is a fool. That will take me all evening."

"Tomorrow night?" Hatch insisted.

"No – the next night."

This would be on Friday night—just in time for the feature which had been planned for Sunday. Hatch was compelled to rest content with this, but he foresaw that he would have it all, with a solution. It never occurred to him that this problem, or, indeed, that any problem, was beyond the mental capacity of Professor Van Dusen.

Hatch and Ernest Weston took a night train that evening, and on their arrival in the village stirred up the town constable.

"Will you go with us?" was the question.

"Both of you going?" was the counter-question.

"Yes."

"I'll go," said the constable promptly. "Ghost!" and he laughed scornfully. "I'll have him in the lockup by morning."

"No shooting, now," warned Weston. "There must be somebody back of this somewhere; we understand that, but there is no crime that we know of. The worst is possibly trespassing."

"I'll get him all right," responded the constable, who still remembered the experience where blood—warm blood—had been thrown in his face. "And I'm not so sure there isn't a crime."

That night about ten the three men went into the dark, forbidding house and took a station on the stairs where Hatch had sat when he saw the THING – whatever it was. There they waited. The constable moved nervously from time to time, but neither of the others paid any attention to him.

At last the – the THING appeared. There had been a preliminary sound as of something running across the floor, then suddenly a flaming figure of white seemed to grow into being in the reception-room. It was exactly as Hatch had described it to The Thinking Machine.

Dazed, stupefied, the three men looked, looked as the figure raised a hand, pointing toward them, and wrote a word in the air—positively in the air. The finger merely waved, and there, floating before them, were letters, flaming letters, in the utter darkness. This time the word was: "Death."

Faintly, Hatch, fighting with a fear which again seized him, remembered that The Thinking Machine had asked him if the handwriting was that of a man or woman; now he tried to see. It was as if drawn on a blackboard, and there was a queer twist to the loop at the bottom. He sniffed to see if there was an odor of any sort. There was not.

Suddenly he felt some quick, vigorous action from the constable behind him. There was a roar and a flash in his ear; he knew the constable had fired at the THING. Then came the cry and laugh—almost a laugh of derision—he had heard them before. For one instant the figure lingered and then, before their eyes, faded again into utter blackness. Where it had been was nothing—nothing.

The constable's shot had had no effect.

IV

Three deeply mystified men passed down the hill to the village from the old house. Ernest Weston, the owner, had not spoken since before the – the THING appeared there in the reception-room, or was it in the library? He was not certain – he couldn't have told. Suddenly he turned to the constable.

"I told you not to shoot."

"That's all right," said the constable. "I was there in my official capacity, and I shoot when I want to."

"But the shot did no harm," Hatch put in.

"I would swear it went right through it, too," said the constable, boastfully. "I can shoot."

Weston was arguing with himself. He was a cold-blooded man of business; his mind was not one to play him tricks. Yet now he felt benumbed; he could conceive no explanation of what he had seen. Again in his room in the little hotel, where they spent the remainder of the night, he stared blankly at the reporter.

"Can you imagine any way it could be done?"

Hatch shook his head.

"It isn't a spook, of course," the broker went on, with a nervous smile; "but—but I'm sorry I went. I don't think probably I shall have the work done there as I thought."

They slept only fitfully and took an early train back to Boston. As they were almost to separate at the South Station, the broker had a last word.

"I'm going to solve that thing," he declared, determinedly. "I know one man at least who isn't afraid of it—or of anything else. I'm going to send him down to keep a lookout and take care of the place. His name is O'Heagan, and he's a fighting Irishman. If he and that—that – THING ever get mixed up together—"

Like a schoolboy with a hopeless problem, Hatch went straight to The Thinking Machine with the latest developments. The scientist paused just long enough in his work to hear it.

"Did you notice the handwriting?" he demanded.

"Yes," was the reply; "so far as I could notice the style of a handwriting that floated in air."

"Man's or woman's?"

Hatch was puzzled.

"I couldn't judge," he said. "It seemed to be a bold style, whatever it was. I remember the capital D clearly."

"Was it anything like the handwriting of the broker—what's – his – name? – Ernest Weston?"

"I never saw his handwriting."

"Look at some of it, then, particularly the capital D's," instructed The Thinking Machine. Then, after a pause: "You say the figure is white and seems to be flaming?"

"Yes."

"Does it give out any light? That is, does it light up a room, for instance?"

"I don't quite know what you mean."

"When you go into a room with a lamp," explained The Thinking Machine, "it lights the room. Does this thing do it? Can you see the floor or walls or anything by the light of the figure itself?"

"No," replied Hatch, positively.

"I'll go down with you tomorrow night," said the scientist, as if that were all.

"Thanks," replied Hatch, and he went away.

Next day about noon he called at Ernest Weston's office. The broker was in.

"Did you send down your man O'Heagan?" he asked.

"Yes," said the broker, and he was almost smiling.

"What happened?"

"He's outside. I'll let him tell you."

The broker went to the door and spoke to some one and O'Heagan entered. He was a big, blue-eyed Irishman, frankly freckled and red-headed – one of those men who look trouble in the face and are glad of it if the trouble can be reduced to a fighting basis. An everlasting smile was about his lips, only now it was a bit faded.

"Tell Mr Hatch what happened last night," requested the broker.

O'Heagan told it. He, too, had sought to get hold of the flaming figure. As he ran for it, it disappeared, was obliterated, wiped out, gone, and he found himself groping in the darkness of the room beyond, the library. Like Hatch, he took the nearest way out, which happened to be through a window already smashed.

"Outside," he went on, "I began to think about it, and I saw there was nothing to be afraid of, but you couldn't have convinced me of that when I was inside. I took a lantern in one hand and a revolver in the other and went all over that house. There was nothing; if there had been we would have had it out right there. But there was nothing. So I started out to the barn, where I had put a cot in a room.

"I went upstairs to this room – it was then about two o'clock – and went to sleep. It seemed to be an hour or so later when I awoke suddenly – I knew something was happening. And the Lord forgive me if I'm a liar, but there was a cat – a ghost cat in my room, racing around like mad. I just naturally got up to see what was the matter and rushed for the door. The cat beat me to it, and cut a flaming streak through the night.

"The cat looked just like the thing inside the house—that is, it was a sort of shadowy, waving white light like it might be afire. I went back to bed in disgust, to sleep it off. You see, sir," he apologized to Weston, "that there hadn't been anything yet I could put my hands on."

"Was that all?" asked Hatch, smilingly.

"Just the beginning. Next morning when I awoke I was bound to my cot, hard and fast. My hands were tied and my feet were tied, and all I could do was lie there and yell. After awhile, it seemed years, I heard some one outside and shouted louder than ever. Then the constable come up and let me loose. I told him all about it – and then I came to Boston. And with your permission, Mr Weston, I resign right now. I'm not afraid of anything I can fight, but when I can't get hold of it – well—"

Later Hatch joined The Thinking Machine. They caught a train for the little village by the sea. On the way The Thinking Machine asked a few questions, but most of the time he was silent, squinting out the window. Hatch respected his silence, and only answered questions.

"Did you see Ernest Weston's handwriting?" was the first of these.

"Yes."

"The capital D's?"

"They are not unlike the one the – the THING wrote, but they are not wholly like it," was the reply.

"Do you know anyone in Providence who can get some information for you?" was the next query.

"Yes."

"Get him by long-distance 'phone when we get to this place and let me talk to him a moment."

Half an hour later The Thinking Machine was talking over the long-distance 'phone to the Providence correspondent of Hatch's paper. What he said or what he learned there was not revealed to the wondering reporter, but he came out after several minutes, only to re-enter the booth and remain for another half an hour.

"Now," he said.

Together they went to the haunted house. At the entrance to the grounds something else occurred to The Thinking Machine.

"Run over to the 'phone and call Weston," he directed. "Ask him if he has a motor-boat or if his cousin has one. We might need one. Also find out what kind of a boat it is – electric or gasoline."

Hatch returned to the village and left the scientist alone, sitting on the veranda gazing out over the sea. When Hatch returned he was still in the same position.

"Well?" he asked.

"Ernest Weston has no motor-boat," the reporter informed him. "George Weston has an electric, but we can't get it because it is away. Maybe I can get one somewhere else if you particularly want it."

"Never mind," said The Thinking Machine. He spoke as if he had entirely lost interest in the matter.

Together they started around the house to the kitchen door.

"What's the next move?" asked Hatch.

"I'm going to find the jewels," was the startling reply.

"Find them?" Hatch repeated.

"Certainly."

They entered the house through the kitchen and the scientist squinted this way and that, through the reception-room, the library, and finally the back hallway. Here a closed door in the flooring led to a cellar.

In the cellar they found heaps of litter. It was damp and chilly and dark. The Thinking Machine stood in the center, or as near the center as he could stand, because the base of the chimney occupied this precise spot, and apparently did some mental calculation.

From that point he started around the walls, solidly built of stone, stooping and running his fingers along the stones as he walked. He made the entire circuit as Hatch looked on. Then he made it again, but this time with his hands raised above his head, feeling the walls carefully as he went. He repeated this at the chimney, going carefully around the masonry, high and low.

"Dear me, dear me!" he exclaimed, petulantly. "You are taller than I am, Mr Hatch. Please feel carefully around the top of this chimney base and see if the rocks are all solidly set."

Hatch then began a tour. At last one of the great stones which made this base trembled under his hand.

"It's loose," he said.

"Take it out."

It came out after a deal of tugging.

"Put your hand in there and pull out what you find," was the next order. Hatch obeyed. He found a wooden box, about eight inches square, and handed it to The Thinking Machine.

"Ah!" exclaimed that gentleman.

A quick wrench caused the decaying wood to crumble. Tumbling out of the box were the jewels which had been lost for fifty years.

V

Excitement, long restrained, burst from Hatch in a laugh— almost hysterical. He stooped and gathered up the fallen jewelry and handed it to The Thinking Machine, who stared at him in mild surprise.

"What's the matter?" inquired the scientist.

"Nothing," Hatch assured him, but again he laughed.

The heavy stone which had been pulled out of place was lifted up and forced back into position, and together they returned to the village, with the long-lost jewelry loose in their pockets.

"How did you do it?' asked Hatch.

"Two and two always make four," was the enigmatic reply. "It was merely a sum in addition." There was a pause as they walked on, then: "Don't say anything about finding this, or even hint at it in any way, until you have my permission to do so."

Hatch had no intention of doing so. In his mind's eye he saw a story, a great, vivid, startling story spread all over his newspaper about flaming phantoms and treasure trove — $100,000 in jewels. It staggered him. Of course he would say nothing about it – even hint at it, yet. But when he did say something about it—!

In the village The Thinking Machine found the constable. "I understand some blood was thrown on you at the Weston place the other night?"

"Yes. Blood – warm blood."

"You wiped it off with your handkerchief?"

"Yes."

"Have you the handkerchief?"

"I suppose I might get it," was the doubtful reply. "It might have gone into the wash."

"Astute person," remarked The Thinking Machine. "There might have been a crime and you throw away the one thing which would indicate it—the blood stains."

The constable suddenly took notice.

"By ginger!" he said. "Wait here and I'll go see if I can find it."

He disappeared and returned shortly with the handkerchief. There were half a dozen blood stains on it, now dark brown.

The Thinking Machine dropped into the village drug store and had a short conversation with the owner, after which he disappeared into the compounding room at the back and remained for an hour or more—until darkness set in. Then he came out and joined Hatch, who, with the constable, had been waiting.

The reporter did not ask any questions, and The Thinking Machine volunteered no information.

"Is it too late for anyone to get down from Boston tonight?" he asked the constable.

"No. He could take the eight o'clock train and be here about half-past nine."

"Mr Hatch, will you wire to Mr Weston—Ernest Weston — and ask him to come tonight, sure. Impress on him the fact that it is a matter of the greatest importance."

Instead of telegraphing, Hatch went to the telephone and spoke to Weston at his club. The trip would interfere with some other plans, the broker explained, but he would come. The Thinking Machine had meanwhile been conversing with the constable and had given some sort of instructions which evidently amazed that official exceedingly, for he kept repeating "By ginger!" with considerable fervor.

"And not one word or hint of it to anyone," said The Thinking Machine. "Least of all to the members of your family."

"By ginger!" was the response, and the constable went to supper.

The Thinking Machine and Hatch had their supper thoughtfully that evening in the little village "hotel." Only once did Hatch break this silence.

"You told me to see Weston's handwriting," he said. "Of course you knew he was with the constable and myself when we saw the THING, therefore it would have been impossible—"

"Nothing is impossible," broke in The Thinking Machine. "Don't say that, please."

"I mean that, as he was with us—"

"We'll end the ghost story tonight," interrupted the scientist.

Ernest Weston arrived on the nine-thirty train and had a long, earnest conversation with The Thinking Machine, while

Hatch was permitted to cool his toes in solitude. At last they joined the reporter.

"Take a revolver by all means," instructed The Thinking Machine.

"Do you think that necessary?" asked Weston.

"It is – absolutely," was the emphatic response.

Weston left them after awhile. Hatch wondered where he had gone, but no information was forthcoming. In a general sort of way he knew that The Thinking Machine was to go to the haunted house, but he didn't know when; he didn't even know if he was to accompany him.

At last they started, The Thinking Machine swinging a hammer he had borrowed from his landlord. The night was perfectly black, even the road at their feet was invisible. They stumbled frequently as they walked on up the cliff toward the house, dimly standing out against the sky. They entered by way of the kitchen, passed through to the stairs in the main hall, and there Hatch indicated in the darkness the spot from which he had twice seen the flaming phantom.

"You go in the drawing-room behind here," The Thinking Machine instructed. "Don't make any noise whatever."

For hours they waited, neither seeing the other. Hatch heard his heart thumping heavily; if only he could see the other man; with an effort he recovered from a rapidly growing nervousness and waited, waited. The Thinking Machine sat perfectly rigid on the stair, the hammer in his right hand, squinting steadily through the darkness.

At last he heard a noise, a slight nothing; it might almost have been his imagination. It was as if something had glided across the floor, and he was more alert than ever. Then came the dread misty light in the reception-hall, or was it in the library? He could not say. But he looked, looked, with every sense alert.

Gradually the light grew and spread, a misty whiteness which was unmistakably light, but which did not illuminate anything around it. The Thinking Machine saw it without the tremor of a nerve; saw the mistiness grow more marked in certain places, saw these lines gradually grow into the figure of a person, a person who was the center of a white light.

Then the mistiness fell away and The Thinking Machine saw the outline in bold relief. It was that of a tall figure, clothed in a robe, with head covered by a sort of hood, also luminous. As The Thinking Machine looked he saw an arm raised, and in the hand he saw a dagger. The attitude of the figure was distinctly a threat. And yet The Thinking Machine had not begun to grow nervous; he was only interested.

As he looked, the other hand of the apparition was raised and seemed to point directly at him. It moved through the air in bold sweeps, and The Thinking Machine saw the word "Death," written in air luminously, swimming before his eyes. Then he blinked incredulously. There came a wild, demoniacal shriek of laughter from somewhere. Slowly, slowly the scientist crept down the steps in his stocking feet, silent as the apparition itself, with the hammer still in his hand. He crept on, on toward the figure. Hatch, not knowing the movements of The Thinking Machine, stood waiting for something, he didn't know what. Then the thing, he had been waiting for happened. There was a sudden loud clatter as of broken glass, the phantom and writing faded, crumbled up, disappeared, and somewhere in the old house there was the hurried sound of steps. At last the reporter heard his name called quietly. It was The Thinking Machine.

"Mr Hatch, come here."

The reporter started, blundering through the darkness toward the point whence the voice had come. Some irresistible thing swept down upon him; a crashing blow descended on his head, vivid lights flashed before his eyes; he fell. After awhile, from a great distance, it seemed, he heard faintly a pistol shot.

VI

When Hatch, fully recovered consciousness it was with the flickering light of a match in his eyes – a match in the hand of The Thinking Machine, who squinted anxiously at him as he grasped his left wrist. Hatch, instantly himself again, sat up suddenly.

"What's the matter?" he demanded.

"How's your head?" came the answering question.

"Oh," and Hatch suddenly recalled those incidents which had immediately preceded the crash on his head. "Oh, it's all right, my head, I mean. What happened?"

"Get up and come along," requested The Thinking Machine, tartly. "There's a man shot down here."

Hatch arose and followed the slight figure of the scientist through the front door, and toward the water. A light glimmered down near the water and was dimly reflected; above, the clouds had cleared somewhat and the moon was struggling through.

"What hit me, anyhow?" Hatch demanded, as they went. He rubbed his head ruefully.

"The ghost," said the scientist. "I think probably he has a bullet in him now – the ghost."

Then the figure of the town constable separated itself from the night and approached.

"Who's that?"

"Professor Van Dusen and Mr Hatch."

"Mr Weston got him all right," said the constable, and there was satisfaction in his tone. "He tried to come out the back way, but I had that fastened, as you told me, and he came through the front way. Mr Weston tried to stop him, and he raised the knife to stick him; then Mr Weston shot. It broke his arm, I think. Mr Weston is down there with him now."

The Thinking Machine turned to the reporter.

"Wait here for me, with the constable," he directed. "If the man is hurt he needs attention. I happen to be a doctor; I can aid him. Don't come unless I call."

For a long while the constable and the reporter waited. The constable talked, talked with all the bottled-up vigor of days. Hatch listened impatiently; he was eager to go down there where The Thinking Machine and Weston and the phantom were.

After half an hour the light disappeared, then he heard the swift, quick churning of waters, a sound as of a powerful motor-boat maneuvering, and a long body shot out on the waters.

"All right down there?" Hatch called.

"All right," came the response.

There was again silence, then Ernest Weston and The Thinking Machine came up.

"Where is the other man?" asked Hatch.

"The ghost—where is he?" echoed the constable.

"He escaped in the motor-boat," replied Mr Weston, easily.

"Escaped?" exclaimed Hatch and the constable together.

"Yes, escaped," repeated The Thinking Machine, irritably. "Mr Hatch, let's go to the hotel."

Struggling with a sense of keen disappointment, Hatch followed the other two men silently. The constable walked beside him, also silent. At last they reached the hotel and bade the constable, a sadly puzzled, bewildered and crestfallen man, goodnight.

"By ginger!" he remarked, as he walked away into the dark.

Upstairs the three men sat, Hatch impatiently waiting to hear the story. Weston lighted a cigarette and lounged back; The Thinking Machine sat with finger tips pressed together, studying the ceiling.

"Mr Weston, you understand, of course, that I came into this thing to aid Mr Hatch?" he asked.

"Certainly," was the response. "I will only ask a favor of him when you conclude."

The Thinking Machine changed his position slightly, readjusted his thick glasses for a long, comfortable squint, and told the story, from the beginning, as he always told a story. Here it is:

"Mr Hatch came to me in a state of abject, cringing fear and told me of the mystery. It would be needless to go over his examination of the house, and all that. It is enough to say that he noted and told me of four large mirrors in the dining-room and living-room of the house; that he heard and brought to me the stories in detail of a tragedy in the old house and missing jewels, valued at a hundred thousand dollars, or more.

"He told me of his trip to the house that night, and of actually seeing the phantom. I have found in the past that Mr Hatch is a cool, level-headed young man, not given to imagining things which are not there, and controls himself well. Therefore I knew that anything of charlatanism must be clever, exceedingly clever, to bring about such a condition of mind in him.

"Mr Hatch saw, as others had seen, the figure of a phantom in the reception-room near the door of the library, or in the library near the door of the reception-room, he couldn't tell exactly. He knew it was near the door. Preceding the appearance of the figure he heard a slight noise which he attributed to a rat running across the floor. Yet the house had not been occupied for five years. Rodents rarely remain in a house – I may say never – for that long if it is uninhabited. Therefore what was this noise? A noise made by the apparition itself? How?

"Now, there is only one white light of the kind Mr Hatch described known to science. It seems almost superfluous to name it. It is phosphorus, compounded with Fuller's earth and glycerine and one or two other chemicals, so it will not instantly flame as it does in the pure state when exposed to air. Phosphorus has a very pronounced odor if one is within, say, twenty feet of it. Did Mr Hatch smell anything? No.

"Now, here we have several facts, these being that the apparition in appearing made a slight noise; that phosphorus was the luminous quality; that Mr Hatch did not smell phosphorus even when he ran through the spot where the phantom had appeared. Two and two make four; Mr Hatch saw phosphorus, passed through the spot where he had seen it, but did not smell it, therefore it was not there. It was a reflection he saw – a reflection of phosphorus. So far, so good.

"Mr Hatch saw a finger lifted and write a luminous word in the air. Again he did not actually see this; he saw a reflection of it. This first impression of mine was substantiated by the fact that when he rushed for the phantom a part of it disappeared, first half of it, he said – then the other half. So his extended hands grasped only air.

"Obviously those reflections had been made on something, probably a mirror as the most perfect ordinary reflecting surface. Yet he actually passed through the spot where he had seen the apparition and had not struck a mirror. He found himself in another room, the library, having gone through a door which, that afternoon, he had himself closed. He did not open it then.

"Instantly a sliding mirror suggested itself to me to fit all these conditions. He saw the apparition in the door, then saw only half of it, then all of it disappeared. He passed through the spot where it had been. All of this would have happened easily if a large mirror, working as a sliding door, and hidden in the wall, were there. Is it clear?"

"Perfectly," said Mr Weston.

"Yes," said Hatch, eagerly. "Go on."

"This sliding mirror, too, might have made the noise which Mr Hatch imagined was a rat. Mr Hatch had previously told me of four large mirrors in the living – and dining-rooms. With these, from the position in which he said they were, I readily saw how the reflection could have been made.

"In a general sort of way, in my own mind, I had accounted for the phantom. Why was it there? This seemed a more difficult problem. It was possible that it had been put there for amusement, but I did not wholly accept this. Why? Partly because no one had ever heard of it until the Italian workmen went there. Why did it appear just at the moment they went to begin the work Mr Weston had ordered? Was it the purpose to keep the workmen away?

"These questions arose in my mind in order. Then, as Mr Hatch had told me of a tragedy in the house and hidden jewels, I asked him to learn more of these. I called his attention to the fact that it would be a queer circumstance if these jewels were still somewhere in the old house. Suppose some one who knew of their existence were searching for them, believed he could find them, and wanted something which would effectually drive away any inquiring persons, tramps or villagers, who might appear there at night. A ghost? Perhaps.

"Suppose some one wanted to give the old house such a reputation that Mr Weston would not care to undertake the work of repair and refurnishing. A ghost? Again perhaps. In a shallow mind this ghost might have been interpreted even as an effort to prevent the marriage of Miss Everard and Mr Weston. Therefore Mr Hatch was instructed to get all the facts possible about you, Mr Weston, and members of your family. I reasoned that members of your own family would be more likely to know of the lost jewels than anyone else after a lapse of fifty years.

"Well, what Mr Hatch learned from you and your cousin, George Weston, instantly, in my mind, established a motive for the ghost. It was, as I had supposed possible, an effort to drive workmen away, perhaps only for a time, while a search was made for the jewels. The old tragedy in the house was a good pretext to hang a ghost on. A clever mind conceived it and a clever mind put it into operation.

"Now, what one person knew most about the jewels? Your cousin George, Mr Weston. Had he recently acquired any new information as to these jewels? I didn't know. I thought it possible. Why? On his own statement that his mother, then a bride, got the story of the entire affair direct from his grandmother, who remembered more of it than anybody else—who might even have heard his grandfather say where he intended hiding the jewels."

The Thinking Machine paused for a little while, shifted his position, then went on:

"George Weston refused to go with you, Mr Weston, and Mr Hatch, to the ghost party, as you called it, because he said he was going to a ball in Providence that night. He did not go to Providence; I learned that from your correspondent there, Mr Hatch; so George Weston might, possibly, have gone to the ghost party after all.

"After I looked over the situation down there it occurred to me that the most feasible way for a person, who wished to avoid being seen in the village, as the perpetrator of the ghost did, was to go to and from the place at night in a motor-boat. He could easily run in the dark and land at the foot of the cliff, and no soul in the village would be any the wiser. Did George Weston have a motor-boat? Yes, an electric, which runs almost silently.

"From this point the entire matter was comparatively simple. I knew—the pure logic of it told me—how the ghost was made to appear and disappear; one look at the house inside convinced me beyond all doubt. I knew the motive for the ghost – a search for the jewels. I knew, or thought I knew, the name of the man who was seeking the jewels; the man who had fullest knowledge and fullest opportunity, the man whose brain was clever enough to devise the scheme. Then, the next step to prove what I knew. The first thing to do was to find the jewels."

"Find the jewels?" Weston repeated, with a slight smile.

"Here they are," said The Thinking Machine, quietly.

And there, before the astonished eyes of the broker, he drew out the gems which had been lost for fifty years. Mr Weston was

MYSTERY OF THE FLAMING PHANTOM 169

not amazed; he was petrified with astonishment and sat staring at the glittering heap in silence. Finally he recovered his voice.

"How did you do it?" he demanded. "Where?"

"I used my brain, that's all," was the reply. "I went into the old house seeking them where the owner, under all conditions, would have been most likely to hide them, and there I found them."

"But – but—" stammered the broker.

"The man who hid these jewels hid them only temporarily, or at least that was his purpose," said The Thinking Machine, irritably. "Naturally he would not hide them in the woodwork of the house, because that might burn; he did not bury them in the cellar, because that has been carefully searched. Now, in that house there is nothing except woodwork and chimneys above the cellar. Yet he hid them in the house, proven by the fact that the man he killed was killed in the house, and that the outside ground, covered with snow, showed two sets of tracks into the house and none out. Therefore he did hide them in the cellar. Where? In the stonework. There was no other place.

"Naturally he would not hide them on a level with the eye, because the spot where he took out and replaced a stone would be apparent if a close search were made. He would, therefore, place them either above or below the eye level. He placed them above. A large loose stone in the chimney was taken out and there was the box with these things."

Mr Weston stared at The Thinking Machine with a new wonder and admiration in his eyes.

"With the jewels found and disposed of, there remained only to prove the ghost theory by an actual test. I sent for you, Mr Weston, because I thought possibly, as no actual crime had been committed, it would be better to leave the guilty man to you. When you came I went into the haunted house with a hammer – an ordinary hammer – and waited on the steps.

"At last the ghost laughed and appeared. I crept down the steps where I was sitting in my stocking feet. I knew what it was. Just when I reached the luminous phantom I disposed of it for all time by smashing it with a hammer. It shattered a large sliding mirror which ran in the door inside the frame, as I had thought. The crash startled the man who operated the ghost from the top of a box, giving it the appearance of extreme height, and he started out through the kitchen, as he had entered. The constable had barred that door after the man entered; therefore the ghost turned and came toward the front door of the house. There he ran into and struck down Mr Hatch, and ran out through the front door, which I afterwards found was not securely fastened. You know the rest of it; how you found the motor-boat and waited there for him; how he came there, and—"

"Tried to stab me," Weston supplied. "I had to shoot to save myself."

"Well, the wound is trivial," said The Thinking Machine. "His arm will heal up in a little while. I think then, perhaps, a little trip of four or five years in Europe, at your expense, in return for the jewels, might restore him to health."

"I was thinking of that myself," said the broker, quietly. "Of course, I couldn't prosecute."

"The ghost, then, was—?" Hatch began.

"George Weston, my cousin," said the broker. "There are some things in this story which I hope you may see fit to leave unsaid, if you can do so with justice to yourself."

Hatch considered it.

"I think there are," he said, finally, and he turned to The Thinking Machine. "Just where was the man who operated the phantom?"

"In the dining-room, beside the butler's pantry," was the reply. "With that pantry door closed he put on the robe already covered with phosphorus, and merely stepped out. The figure was reflected in the tall mirror directly in front, as you enter the dining-room from the back, from there reflected to the mirror on the opposite wall in the living-room, and thence reflected to the sliding mirror in the door which led from the reception-hall to the library. This is the one I smashed."

"And how was the writing done?"

"Oh, that? Of course that was done by reversed writing on a piece of clear glass held before the apparition as he posed. This made it read straight to anyone who might see the last reflection in the reception-hall."

"And the blood thrown on the constable and the others when the ghost was in the yard?" Hatch went on.

"Was from a dog. A test I made in the drug store showed that. It was a desperate effort to drive the villagers away and keep them away. The ghost cat and the tying of the watchman to his bed were easily done."

All sat silent for a time. At length Mr Weston arose, thanked the scientist for the recovery of the jewels, bade them all goodnight and was about to go out. Mechanically Hatch was following. At the door he turned back for the last question.

"How was it that the shot the constable fired didn't break the mirror?"

"Because he was nervous and the bullet struck the door beside the mirror," was the reply. "I dug it out with a knife. Goodnight."

8

THE TRAGEDY OF THE LIFE RAFT

'Twas a shabby picture altogether—old Peter Ordway in his office; the man shriveled, bent, cadaverous, aquiline of feature, with skin like parchment, and cunning, avaricious eyes; the room gaunt and curtainless, with smoke-grimed windows, dusty, cheerless walls, and threadbare carpet, worn through here and there to the rough flooring beneath. Peter Ordway sat in a swivel chair in front of an ancient roll-top desk. Opposite, at a typewriter upon a table of early vintage, was his secretary—one Walpole, almost a replica in middle age of his employer, seedy and servile, with lips curled sneeringly as a dog's.

Familiarly in the financial district, Peter Ordway was "The Usurer," a title which was at once a compliment to his merciless business sagacity and an expression of contempt for his methods. He was the money lender of the Street, holding in cash millions which no one dared to estimate. In the last big panic the richest man in America, the great John Morton in person, had spent hours in the shabby office, begging for the loan of the few millions in currency necessary to check the market. Peter Ordway didn't fail to take full advantage of his pressing need. Mr Morton got the millions on collateral worth five times the sum borrowed, but Peter Ordway fixed the rate of interest, a staggering load.

THE TRAGEDY OF THE LIFE RAFT

Now we have the old man at the beginning of a day's work. After glancing through two or three letters which lay open on his desk, he picked up at last a white card, across the face of which was scribbled in pencil three words only:

One million dollars!

Ordinarily it was a phrase to bring a smile to his withered lips, a morsel to roll under his wicked old tongue; but now he stared at it without comprehension. Finally he turned to his secretary, Walpole.

"What is this?" he demanded querulously, in his thin, rasping voice.

"I don't know, sir," was the reply. "I found it in the morning's mail, sir, addressed to you."

Peter Ordway tore the card across, and dropped it into the battered wastebasket beside him, after which he settled down to the ever-congenial occupation of making money.

On the following morning the card appeared again, with only three words, as before:

One million dollars!

Abruptly the aged millionaire wheeled around to face Walpole, who sat regarding him oddly.

"It came the same way, sir," the seedy little secretary explained hastily, "in a blank envelope. I saved the envelope, sir, if you would like to see it."

"Tear it up!" Peter Ordway directed sharply.

Reduced to fragments, the envelope found its way into the wastebasket. For many minutes Peter Ordway sat with dull, lusterless eyes, gazing through the window into the void of a leaden sky. Slowly, as he looked, the sky became a lashing, mist-covered sea, a titanic chaos of water; and upon its troubled bosom rode a life raft to which three persons were clinging. Now the frail craft was lifted up, up to the dizzy height of a giant wave; now it shot down sickeningly into the hissing trough beyond; again, for minutes it seemed altogether lost in the far-plunging spume. Peter Ordway shuddered and closed his eyes.

On the third morning the card, grown suddenly ominous, appeared again:

One million dollars!

Peter Ordway came to his feet with an exclamation that was almost a snarl, turning, twisting the white slip nervously in his talonlike fingers. Astonished, Walpole half arose, his yellow teeth bared defensively, and his eyes fixed upon the millionaire.

"Telephone Blake's Agency," the old man commanded, "and tell them to send a detective here at once."

Came in answer to the summons a suave, smooth-faced, indolent-appearing young man, Fragson by name, who sat down after having regarded with grave suspicion the rickety chair to which he was invited. He waited inquiringly.

"Find the person – man or woman – who sent me that!"

Peter Ordway flung the card and the envelope in which it had come upon a leaf of his desk. Fragson picked them up and scrutinized them leisurely. Obviously the handwriting was that of a man, an uneducated man, he would have said. The postmark on the envelope was Back Bay; the time of mailing seven p.m. on the night before. Both envelope and card were of a texture which might be purchased in a thousand shops.

"'One million dollars!'" Fragson read. "What does it mean?"

"I don't know," the millionaire answered.

"What do you think it means?"

"Nor do I know that, unless—unless it's some crank, or—or blackmailer. I've received three of them—one each morning for three days."

Fragson placed the card inside the envelope with irritating deliberation, and thrust it into his pocket, after which he lifted his eyes quite casually to those of the secretary, Walpole. Walpole, who had been staring at the two men tensely, averted his shifty gaze, and busied himself at his desk.

THE TRAGEDY OF THE LIFE RAFT

"Any idea who sent them?" Fragson was addressing Peter Ordway, but his eyes lingered lazily upon Walpole.

"No." The word came emphatically, after an almost imperceptible instant of hesitation.

"Why" – and the detective turned to the millionaire curiously – "why do you think it might be blackmail? Has any one any knowledge of any act of yours that—"

Some swift change crossed the parchment like face of the old man. For an instant he was silent; then his avaricious eyes leaped into flame; his fingers closed convulsively on the arms of his chair.

"Blackmail may be attempted without reason," he stormed suddenly. "Those cards must have some meaning. Find the person who sent them."

Fragson arose thoughtfully, and drew on his gloves.

"And then?" he queried.

"That's all!" curtly. "Find him, and let me know who he is."

"Do I understand that you don't want me to go into his motives? You merely want to locate the man?"

"That understanding is correct – yes."

...a lashing, mist-covered sea; a titanic chaos of water, and upon its troubled bosom rode a life raft to which three persons were clinging...

Walpole's crafty eyes followed his millionaire employer's every movement as he entered his office on the morning of the fourth day. There was nervous restlessness in Peter Ordway's manner; the parchment face seemed more withered; the pale lips were tightly shut. For an instant he hesitated, as if vaguely fearing to begin on the morning's mail. But no fourth card had come! Walpole heard and understood the long breath of relief which followed upon realization of this fact.

Just before ten o'clock a telegram was brought in. Peter Ordway opened it:

One million dollars!

Three hours later at his favorite table in the modest restaurant where he always went for luncheon, Peter Ordway picked up his napkin, and a white card fluttered to the floor:

One million dollars!

Shortly after two o'clock a messenger boy entered his office, whistling, and laid an envelope on the desk before him:

One million dollars!

Instinctively he had known what was within.

At eight o'clock that night, in the shabby apartments where he lived with his one servant, he answered an insistent ringing of the telephone bell.

"What do you want?" he demanded abruptly.

"One million dollars!" The words came slowly, distinctly.

"Who are you?"

"One million dollars!" faintly, as an echo.

Again Fragson was summoned, and was ushered into the cheerless room where the old millionaire sat cringing with fear, his face reflecting some deadly terror which seemed to be consuming him. Incoherently he related the events of the day. Fragson listened without comment, and went out.

On the following morning – Sunday – he returned to report. He found his client propped upon a sofa, haggard and worn, with eyes feverishly aglitter.

"Nothing doing," the detective began crisply. "It looked as if we had a clew which would at least give us a description of the man, but–" He shook his head.

"But that telegram – some one filed it?" Peter Ordway questioned huskily. "The message the boy brought–"

"The telegram was inclosed in an envelope with the money necessary to send it, and shoved through the mail slot of a telegraph office in Cambridge," the detective informed him explicitly. "That was Friday night. It was telegraphed to you on Saturday morning. The card brought by the boy was handed

THE TRAGEDY OF THE LIFE RAFT

in at a messenger agency by some street urchin, paid for, and delivered to you. The telephone call was from an automatic station in Brookline. A thousand persons use it every day."

For the first time in many years, Peter Ordway failed to appear at his office Monday morning. Instead he sent a note to his secretary:

Bring all important mail to my apartment tonight at eight o'clock. On your way uptown buy a good revolver with cartridges to fit.

Twice that day a physician – Doctor Anderson – was hurriedly summoned to Peter Ordway's side. First there had been merely a fainting spell; later in the afternoon came complete collapse. Doctor Anderson diagnosed the case tersely.

"Nerves," he said. "Overwork, and no recreation."

"But, doctor, I have no time for recreation!" the old millionaire whined. "My business—"

"Time!" Doctor Anderson growled indignantly. "You're seventy years old, and you're worth fifty million dollars. The thing you must have if you want to spend any of that money is an ocean trip – a good, long ocean trip – around the world, if you like."

"No, no, no!" It was almost a shriek. Peter Ordway's evil countenance, already pallid, became ashen; abject terror was upon him... a lashing, mist-covered sea; a titanic chaos of water, and upon its troubled bosom rode a life raft to which three persons were clinging...

"No, no, no!" he mumbled, his talon fingers clutching the physician's hand convulsively. "I'm afraid, afraid!"

The slender thread which held sordid soul to withered body was severed that night by a well-aimed bullet. Promptly at eight o'clock Walpole had arrived, and gone straight to the room where Peter Ordway sat propped up on a sofa. Nearly an hour later the old millionaire's one servant, Mrs Robinson, answered the doorbell, admitting Mr Franklin Pingree, a well-known financier. He had barely stepped into the hallway when there came a reverberating crash as of a revolver shot from the room where Peter Ordway and his secretary were.

Together Mr Pingree and Mrs Robinson ran to the door. Still propped upon the couch, Peter Ordway sat—dead. A bullet had penetrated his heart. His head was thrown back, his mouth was open, and his right hand dangled at his side. Leaning over the body was his secretary, Walpole. In one hand he held a revolver, still smoking. He didn't turn as they entered, but stood staring down upon the man blankly. Mr Pingree disarmed him from behind.

Hereto I append a partial transcript of a statement made by Frederick Walpole immediately following his arrest on the charge of murdering his millionaire employer. This statement he repeated in substance at the trial:

I am forty-eight years old. I had been in Mr Ordway's employ for twenty-two years. My salary was eight dollars a week… I went to his apartments on the night of the murder in answer to a note. (Note produced.) I bought the revolver and gave it to him. He loaded it and thrust it under the covering beside him on the sofa… He dictated four letters and was starting on another. I heard the door open behind me. I thought it was Mrs Robinson, as I had not heard the front-door bell ring.

Mr Ordway stopped dictating, and I looked at him. He was staring toward the door. He seemed to be frightened. I looked around. A man had come in. He seemed very old. He had a flowing white beard and long white hair. His face was ruddy, like a seaman's.

"Who are you?" Mr Ordway asked.

"You know me all right," said the man. "We were together long enough on that craft." (Or "raft," prisoner was not positive.)

"I never saw you before," said Mr Ordway. "I don't know what you mean."

"I have come for the reward," said the man.

"What reward?" Mr Ordway asked.

"One million dollars!" said the man.

Nothing else was said. Mr Ordway drew his revolver and fired. The other man must have fired at the same instant, for Mr Ordway fell back dead. The man disappeared. I ran to Mr Ordway and picked up the revolver. He had dropped it. Mr Pingree and Mrs Robinson came in...

Reading of Peter Ordway's will disclosed the fact that he had bequeathed unconditionally the sum of one million dollars to his secretary, Walpole, for "loyal services." Despite Walpole's denial of any knowledge of this bequest, he was immediately placed under arrest. At the trial, the facts appeared as I have related them. The district attorney summed up briefly. The motive was obvious – Walpole's desire to get possession of one million dollars in cash. Mr Pingree and Mrs Robinson, entering the room directly after the shot had been fired, had met no one coming out, as they would have had there been another man – there was no other egress. Also, they had heard only one shot – and that shot had found Peter Ordway's heart. Also, the bullet which killed Peter Ordway had been positively identified by experts as of the same make and same caliber as those others in the revolver Walpole had bought. The jury was out twenty minutes. The verdict was guilty. Walpole was sentenced to death.

It was not until then that "The Thinking Machine" – otherwise Professor Augustus S.F.X. Van Dusen, Ph.D., F.R.S., M.D., LL.D., et cetera, et cetera, logician, analyst, master mind in the sciences – turned his crabbed genius upon the problem.

Five days before the date set for Walpole's execution, Hutchinson Hatch, newspaper reporter, introduced himself into The Thinking Machine's laboratory, bringing with him a small roll of newspapers. Incongruously enough, they were old friends, these two — on one hand, the man of science, absorbed in that profession of which he was already the master, small, almost grotesque in appearance, and living the life of a recluse; on the other, a young man of the world, worldly, enthusiastic, capable, indefatigable.

So it came about The Thinking Machine curled himself in a great chair, and sat for nearly two hours partially submerged in newspaper accounts of the murder and of the trial. The last paper finished, he dropped his enormous head back against his chair, turned his petulant, squinting eyes upward, and sat for minute after minute staring into nothingness.

"Why," he queried, at last, "do you think he is innocent?"

"I don't know that I do think it," Hatch replied. "It is simply that attention has been attracted to Walpole's story again because of a letter the governor received. Here is a copy of it."

The Thinking Machine read it:

You are about to allow the execution of an innocent man. Walpole's story on the witness stand was true. He didn't kill Peter Ordway. I killed him for a good and sufficient reason.

"Of course," the reporter explained, "the letter wasn't signed. However, three handwriting experts say it was written by the same hand that wrote the 'One million dollar' slips. Incidentally the prosecution made no attempt to connect Walpole's handwriting with those slips. They couldn't have done it, and it would have weakened their case."

"And what," inquired the diminutive scientist, "does the governor purpose doing?"

"Nothing," was the reply. "To him it is merely one of a thousand crank letters."

"He knows the opinions of the experts?"

"He does. I told him."

"The governor," remarked The Thinking Machine gratuitously, "is a fool." Then: "It is sometimes interesting to assume the truth of the improbable. Suppose we assume Walpole's story to be true, assuming at the same time that this letter is true – what have we?"

Tiny, cobwebby lines of thought furrowed the domelike brow as Hatch watched; the slender fingers were brought precisely tip to tip; the pale-blue eyes narrowed still more.

"If," Hatch pointed out, "Walpole's attorney had been able to find a bullet mark anywhere in that room, or a single isolated drop of blood, it would have proven that Peter Ordway did fire as Walpole says he did, and—"

"If Walpole's story is true," The Thinking Machine went on serenely, heedless of the interruption, "we must believe that a man – say, Mr X—entered a private apartment without ringing. Very well. Either the door was unlocked, he entered by a window, or he had a false key. We must believe that two shots were fired simultaneously, sounding as one. We must believe that Mr X was either wounded or the bullet mark has been overlooked; we must believe Mr X went out by the one door at the same instant Mr Pingree and Mrs Robinson entered. We must believe they either did not see him, or they lied."

"That's what convicted Walpole," Hatch declared. "Of course, it's impossible—"

"Nothing is impossible, Mr Hatch," stormed The Thinking Machine suddenly. "Don't say that. It annoys me exceedingly."

Hatch shrugged his shoulders, and was silent. Again minute after minute passed, and the scientist sat motionless, staring now at a plan of Peter Ordway's apartment he had found in a newspaper, the while his keen brain dissected the known facts.

"After all," he announced, at last, "there's only one vital question: Why Peter Ordway's deadly fear of water?"

The reporter shook his head blankly. He was never surprised any more at The Thinking Machine's manner of approaching a problem. Never by any chance did he take hold of it as any one else would have.

"Some personal eccentricity, perhaps," Hatch suggested hopefully. "Some people are afraid of cats, others of—"

"Go to Peter Ordway's place," The Thinking Machine interrupted tartly, "and find if it has been necessary to replace a broken windowpane anywhere in the building since Mr Ordway's death."

"You mean, perhaps, that Mr X, as you call him, may have escaped—" the newspaper man began.

"Also find out if there was a curtain hanging over or near the door where Mr X must have gone out."

"Right!"

"We'll assume that the room where Ordway died has been gone over inch by inch in the search for a stray shot," the scientist continued. "Let's go farther. If Ordway fired, it was probably toward the door where Mr X entered. If Mr X left the door open behind him, the shot may have gone into the private hall beyond, and may be buried in the door immediately opposite." He indicated on the plan as he talked. "This second door opens into a rear hall. If both doors chanced to be open—"

Hatch came to his feet with blazing eyes. He understood. It was a possibility no one had considered. Ordway's shot, if he had fired one, might have lodged a hundred feet away.

"Then if we find a bullet mark—" he questioned tensely.

"Walpole will not go to the electric chair."

"And if we don't?"

"We will look farther," said The Thinking Machine. "We will look for a wounded man of perhaps sixty years, who is now, or has been, a sailor; who is either clean – shaven or else has a close-cropped beard, probably dyed – a man who may have a false key to the Ordway apartment – the man who wrote this note to the governor."

"You believe, then," Hatch demanded, "that Walpole is innocent?"

"I believe nothing of the sort," snapped the scientist. "He's probably guilty. If we find no bullet mark, I'm merely saying what sort of man we must look for."

"But—but how do you know so much about him—what he looks like?" asked the reporter, in bewilderment.

"How do I know?" repeated the crabbed little scientist. "How do I know that two and two make four, not sometimes, but all the time? By adding the units together. Logic, that's all – logic, logic!"

While Hatch was scrutinizing the shabby walls of the old building where Peter Ordway had lived his miserly life, The Thinking Machine called on Doctor Anderson, who had been Peter Ordway's physician for a score of years. Doctor Anderson couldn't explain the old millionaire's aversion to water, but perhaps if the scientist went farther back in his inquiries there was an old man, John Page, still living who had been Ordway's classmate in school. Doctor Anderson knew of him because he had once treated him at Peter Ordway's request. So The Thinking Machine came to discuss this curious trait of character with John Page. What the scientist learned didn't appear, but whatever it was it sent him to the public library, where he spent several hours pulling over the files of old newspapers.

All his enthusiasm gone, Hatch returned to report.

"Nothing," he said. "No trace of a bullet."

"Any windowpanes changed or broken?"

"Not one."

"There were curtains, of course, over the door through which Mr X entered Ordway's room." It was not a question.

"There were. They're there yet."

"In that case," and The Thinking Machine raised his squinting eyes to the ceiling, "our sailorman was wounded."

"There is a sailorman, then?" Hatch questioned eagerly.

"I'm sure I don't know," was the astonishing reply. "If there is, he answers generally the description I gave. His name is Ben Holderby. His age is not sixty; it's fifty-eight."

The newspaper man took a long breath of amazement. Surely here was the logical faculty lifted to the nth power! The Thinking Machine was describing, naming, and giving the age of a man whose existence he didn't even venture to assert – a man who never had been in existence so far as the reporter knew! Hatch fanned himself weakly with his hat.

"Odd situation, isn't it?" asked The Thinking Machine. "It only proves that logic is inexorable – that it can only fail when the units fail; and no unit has failed yet. Meantime, I shall leave you to find Holderby. Begin with the sailors' lodging houses, and don't scare him off. I can add nothing to the description except that he is probably using another name."

Followed a feverish two days for Hatch – a hurried, nightmarish effort to find a man who might or might not exist, in order to prevent a legal murder. With half a dozen other clever men from his office, he finally achieved the impossible.

"I've found him!" he announced triumphantly over the telephone to The Thinking Machine. "He's stopping at Werner's, in the North End, under the name of Benjamin Goode. He is clean-shaven, his hair and brows are dyed black, and he is wounded in the left arm."

"Thanks," said The Thinking Machine simply. "Bring Detective Mallory, of the bureau of criminal investigation, and come here to-morrow at noon prepared to spend the day. You might go by and inform the governor, if you like, that Walpole will not be electrocuted Friday."

Detective Mallory came at Hatch's request – came with a mouthful of questions into the laboratory, where The Thinking Machine was at work.

"What's it all about?" he demanded.

"Precisely at five o'clock this afternoon a man will try to murder me," the scientist informed him placidly, without lifting his eyes. "I'd like to have you here to prevent it."

THE TRAGEDY OF THE LIFE RAFT

Mallory was much given to outbursts of amazement; he humored himself now:

"Who is the man? What's he going to try to kill you for? Why not arrest him now?"

"His name is Benjamin Holderby," The Thinking Machine answered the questions in order. "He'll try to kill me because I shall accuse him of murder. If he should be arrested now, he wouldn't talk. If I told you whom he murdered, you wouldn't believe it."

Detective Mallory stared without comprehension.

"If he isn't to try to kill you until five o'clock," he asked, "why send for me at noon?"

"Because he may know you, and if he watched and saw you enter he wouldn't come. At half past four you and Mr Hatch will step into the adjoining room. When Holderby enters, he will face me. Come behind him, but don't lift a finger until he threatens me. If you have to shoot—kill! He'll be dangerous until he's dead."

It was just two minutes of five o'clock when the bell rang, and Martha ushered Benjamin Holderby into the laboratory. He was past middle age, powerful, with deep-bronzed face and the keen eyes of the sea. His hair and brows were dyed—badly dyed; his left arm hung limply. He found The Thinking Machine alone.

"I got your letter, sir," he said respectfully. "If it's a yacht, I'm willing to ship as master; but I'm too old to do much—"

"Sit down, please," the little scientist invited courteously, dropping into a chair as he spoke. "There are one or two questions I should like to ask. First" – the petulant blue eyes were raised toward the ceiling; the slender fingers cametogether precisely, tip to tip – "first: Why did you kill Peter Ordway?"

Fell an instant's amazed silence. Benjamin Holderby's muscles flexed, the ruddy face was contorted suddenly with hideous anger, the sinewy right hand closed until great knots appeared in the tendons. Possibly The Thinking Machine had never been nearer death than in that moment when the sailorman towered above him – 'twas giant and weakling. The tiger was about to spring. Then, suddenly as it had come, anger passed from Holderby's face; came instead curiosity, bewilderment, perplexity.

The silence was broken by the sinister click of a revolver. Holderby turned his head slowly, to face Detective Mallory, stared at him oddly, then drew his own revolver, and passed it over, butt foremost.

No word had been spoken. Not once had The Thinking Machine lowered his eyes.

"I killed Peter Ordway," Holderby explained distinctly, "for good and sufficient reasons."

"So you wrote the governor," the scientist observed. "Your motive was born thirty-two years ago?"

"Yes." The sailor seemed merely astonished.

"On a raft at sea?"

"Yes."

"There was murder done on that raft?"

"Yes."

"Instigated by Peter Ordway, who offered you—"

"One million dollars – yes."

"So Peter Ordway is the second man you have killed?"

"Yes."

With mouth agape, Hutchinson Hatch listened greedily; he had – they had – saved Walpole! Mallory's mind was a chaos. What sort of tommyrot was this? This man confessing to a murder for which Walpole was to be electrocuted! His line of thought was broken by the petulant voice of The Thinking Machine.

"Sit down, Mr Holderby," he was saying, "and tell us precisely what happened on that raft."

THE TRAGEDY OF THE LIFE RAFT

'Twas a dramatic story Benjamin Holderby told – a tragedy tale of the sea – a tale of starvation and thirst, torture and madness, and ceaseless battling for life – of crime and greed and the power of money even in that awful moment when death seemed the portion of all. The tale began with the foundering of the steamship Neptune, Liverpool to Boston, ninety-one passengers and crew, some thirty-two years ago. In mid-ocean she was smashed to bits by a gale, and went down. Of those aboard only nine persons reached shore alive.

Holderby told the story simply:

"God knows how many of us went through that storm; it raged for days. There were ten of us on our raft when the ship settled, and by dusk of the second day there were only six—one woman, and one child, and four men. The waves would simply smash over us, and when we came to daylight again there was some one missing. There was little enough food and water aboard, anyway, so the people dropping off that way was really what saved – what saved two of us at the end. Peter Ordway was one, and I was the other.

"The first five days were bad enough-short rations, little or no water, no sleep, and all that; but what came after was hell! At the end of that fifth day there were only five of us—Ordway and me, the woman and child, and another man. I don't know whether I went to sleep or was just unconscious; anyway, when I came to there were only the three of us left. I asked Ordway where the woman and child was. He said they were washed off while I was asleep.

"'And a good thing,' he says.

"'Why?' I says.

"'Too many mouths to feed,' he says. 'And still too many.' He meant the other man. 'I've been looking at the rations and the water,' he says.

'There's enough to keep three people alive three days, but if there were only two people – me and you, for instance?' he says.

"'You mean throw him off?' I says.

"'You're a sailor,' says he. 'If you go, we all go. But we may not be picked up for days. We may starve or die of thirst first. If there were only two of us, we'd have a better chance. I'm worth millions of dollars,' he says. 'If you'll get rid of this other fellow, and we ever come out alive, I'll give you one million dollars!' I didn't say anything. 'If there were only two of us,' says he, 'we would increase our chances of being saved one-third. One million dollars!' says he. 'One million dollars!'

"I expect I was mad with hunger and thirst and sleeplessness and exhaustion. Perhaps he was, too. I know that, regardless of the money he offered, his argument appealed to me. Peter Ordway was a coward; he didn't have the nerve; so an hour later I threw the man overboard, with Peter Ordway looking on.

"Days passed somehow – God knows – and when I came to I had been picked up by a sailing vessel. I was in an asylum for months. When I came out, I asked Ordway for money. He threatened to have me arrested for murder. I pestered him a lot, I guess, for a little later I found myself shanghaied, on the high seas. I didn't come back for thirty years or so. I had almost forgotten the thing until I happened to see Peter Ordway's name in a paper. Then I wrote the slips and mailed them to him. He knew what they meant, and set a detective after me. Then I began hating him all over again, worse than ever. Finally I thought I'd go to his house and make a holdup of it – one million dollars! I don't think I intended to kill him; I thought he'd give me money. I didn't know there was any one with him. I talked to him, and he shot me. I killed him."

Fell a long silence. The Thinking Machine broke it:

"You entered the apartment with a skeleton key?"

"Yes."

"And after the shot was fired, you started out, but dodged behind the curtain at the door when you heard Mr Pingree and Mrs Robinson coming in?"

"Yes."

Suddenly Hatch understood why The Thinking Machine had asked him to ascertain if there were curtains at that door. It was quite possible that in the excitement Mr Pingree and Mrs Robinson would not have noticed that the man who killed Peter Ordway actually passed them in the doorway.

"I think," said The Thinking Machine, "that that is all. You understand, Mr Mallory, that this confession is to be presented to the governor immediately, in order to save Walpole's life?" He turned to Holderby. "You don't want an innocent man to die for this crime?"

"Certainly not," was the reply. "That's why I wrote to the governor. Walpole's story was true. I was in court, and heard it." He glanced at Mallory curiously. "Now, if necessary, I'm willing to go to the chair."

"It won't be necessary," The Thinking Machine pointed out. "You didn't go to Peter Ordway's place to kill him – you went there for money you thought he owed you – he fired at you – you shot him. It's hardly self-defense, but it was not premeditated murder."

Detective Mallory whistled. It was the only satisfactory vent for the tangled mental condition which had befallen him. Shortly he went off with Holderby to the governor's office; and an hour later Walpole, deeply astonished, walked out of the death cell – a free man.

Meanwhile Hutchinson Hatch had some questions to ask of The Thinking Machine.

"Logic, logic, Mr Hatch!" the scientist answered, in that perpetual tone of irritation. "As an experiment, we assumed the truth of Walpole's story. Very well. Peter Ordway was afraid of water. Connect that with the one word 'raft' or 'craft' in Walpole's statement of what the intruder had said. Connect that with his description of that man – 'ruddy, like a seaman.' Add them up, as you would a sum in arithmetic. You begin to get a glimmer of cause and effect, don't you? Peter Ordway was afraid of the water because of some tragedy there in which he had played a part. That was a tentative surmise. Walpole's description of the intruder said white hair and flowing white beard. It is a common failing of men who disguise themselves to go to the other extreme. I went to the other extreme in conjecturing Holderby's appearance—clean—shaven or else close-cropped beard and hair-dyed. Since no bullet mark was found in the building – remember, we are assuming Walpole's statement to be true – the man Ordway shot at carried the bullet away with him. Ergo, a seaman with a pistol wound. Seamen, as a rule, stop at the sailors' lodging houses. That's all."

"But – but you knew Holderby's name – his age!" the reporter stammered.

"I learned them in my effort to account for Ordway's fear of water," was the reply. "An old friend, John Page, whom I found through Doctor Anderson, informed me that he had seen some account in a newspaper thirty-two years before, at the time of the wreck of the Neptune, of Peter Ordway's rescue from a raft at sea. He and one other man were picked up. The old newspaper files in the libraries gave me Holderby's name as the other survivor, together with his age. You found Holderby. I wrote to him that I was about to put a yacht in commission, and he had been recommended to me – that is, Benjamin Goode had been recommended. He came in answer to the advertisement. You saw everything else that happened."

"And the so – called 'one million dollar' slips?"

"Had no bearing on the case until Holderby wrote to the governor," said The Thinking Machine. "In that note he confessed the killing; ergo I began to see that the 'One million dollar' slips probably indicated some enormous reward Ordway had offered Holderby. Walpole's statement, too, covers this point. What happened on the raft at sea? I didn't know. I followed an instinct, and guessed." The distinguished scientist arose. "And now," he said, "begone about your business. I must go to work."

Hatch started out, but turned at the door. "Why," he asked, "were you so anxious to know if any windowpane in the Ordway house had been replaced or was broken?"

"Because," the scientist didn't lift his head, "because a bullet might have smashed one, if it was not to be found in the woodwork. If it smashed one, our unknown Mr X was not wounded."

Upon his own statement, Benjamin Holderby was sentenced to ten years in prison; at the end of three months he was transferred to an asylum after an examination by alienists.

9

PROBLEM OF THE PRIVATE COMPARTMENT

Leaning forward in his seat, the driver lashed his horses into a gallop. The carriage had barely halted at the railroad station, when a woman leaped out. She was closely veiled; but her slender figure revealed the fact that she was little more than a girl. She paused just long enough to hand the driver a bill, then hurried to a train.

When the conductor passed through the cars he found the slender young woman sitting in one of the day coaches. She paid her fare in cash through to Albany, and made inquiry about accommodations in the sleeping car. He volunteered to arrange the matter for her; and so it came to pass that half an hour after she had boarded the train she was ushered into the more exclusive rear car.

"We have only one upper berth," the conductor there apologized.

"Oh, well, it doesn't really matter," she remarked listlessly, and was shown to a seat.

Then for the first time she raised her veil. Her pretty face was still flushed from the excitement of catching the train; but a haunting, furtive fear mingled with a shade of sorrow in the shadowy, dark eyes, and the red lips expressed a sullen defiance. For a long time she sat moodily thoughtful, staring out of the window; then the growing dusk obliterated the flying landscape, and the porter came through to light the lamps.

After awhile the door of the drawing room compartment at one end of the car opened, and a young woman glanced out. It might have been idle curiosity which caused her to scrutinize the lounging passengers; but her eyes paused, with a flash of recognition, on the crisp, brown hair of the slender young woman just half a dozen seats ahead, and she went forward.

"Why, Julia!" she exclaimed. "I hadn't the faintest idea you were on the train!"

First there came an embarrassed surprise into the face of the slender young woman; but it was instantly followed by an expression of relief.

"Oh, Mary! How you startled me!"

There was a little interchange of greetings, which ended by Miss Mary Langham leading Miss Julia Farrar back into the snug little drawing room. They had been classmates at Vassar, these two, and there were a thousand things to talk about; yet in the manner of each was a certain restraint, a vague, indefinable reserve. As a breaking point of a sudden silence which fell between them, Miss Farrar mentioned the upper berth that she had been given.

"Well, don't worry about that a moment, my dear," urged Miss Langham cheerfully. "I have this whole big compartment, and there are two lower berths. You shall take one, and I'll take the other." There was silence for a moment. "But, my dear girl, where are you going?"

"I'm going to Albany – now," was the reply.

"Right on the eve of your—"

"I'm not going to marry Mr Devore!" interrupted Miss Farrar with quick passion.

Miss Langham lifted her arched brows in astonishment. "Why, Julia, you amaze me!" she exclaimed.

"I'm running away from him now," she went on.

Miss Langham stared at her blankly for an instant. Defiance flamed in Miss Farrar's face; there were tense little lines about the mouth, and the lips were pressed sternly together. But at last some glimmer of comprehension seemed to reach Miss Langham, and with it came an expression which might almost have been of relief. With a quick movement she seized Miss Farrar's hand.

"I think I understand, dear," she said sympathetically at last. "Under all circumstances, I don't know that I can blame you either. Mr Devore must know that you don't love him."

"Well, if he doesn't, it isn't because I haven't told him so, goodness knows!" replied Miss Farrar.

Miss Langham laughed lightly, and her eyes reflected some strange, new born light, a glimmer of satisfaction.

"Poor fellow!" she mused. "And he is so devoted!"

"I don't want his devotion!" blazed Miss Farrar. "The mere sight of him is intolerable to me. It's all just like – like I was being sold to him. It's perfectly hideous, and I won't – I won't – I won't!"

Defiance melted into tears of anger and mortification, and Miss Farrar lay against Miss Langham's shoulder while her slender figure was shaken by a storm of sobs. Miss Langham stroked the crisp, brown hair back from the white temples, and continued to stare dreamily out of the window.

"Even my father and mother and brother conspired with him against me," Miss Farrar sobbed after a time. "They insisted on the marriage from the first, merely because Mr Devore happens to be wealthy. I don't know why I ever agreed, unless it was just desperation. I detest the man, and yet the members of my own family, knowing that, could only think of the brilliant match, the money, and social position which marriage would bring."

"Tomorrow it was to have been," mused Miss Langham vacantly.

"Yes, tomorrow. For weeks and weeks it has been a nightmare to me, and last night, somehow, I seemed to go all to pieces.

The sight of the wedding gown made me perfectly furious. All today I thought of it, and thought of it, until my head seemed bursting. Then late this afternoon I could stand it no longer; so I – I ran away. I suppose it's horrid of me, and I know my father and mother will never forgive me for the scandal it will cause; but I don't care. They've made me almost hate them. I'm going to my aunt's in Albany and remain there for a few days. Of course, my father will be furious, and will try to force me to return; but she's a dear loyal soul and won't let them take me away. Then I shall decide about the future."

"I can't imagine a worse fate than marriage with a man whom you don't love," said Miss Langham after a pause. "I don't blame you at all. But remember, my dear, in giving up your family you will have to look out for yourself — perhaps earn your own living?"

"I don't care," continued Miss Farrar passionately. "I have fifty or sixty dollars now, and before that is gone surely I can get a place as teacher, or governess, or something. I will do something."

"And I have no doubt that everything will come right," Miss Langham assured her. She raised the tear stained face between her hands and printed a kiss on each damp cheek. "And now, my dear, you need repose. Lie down and rest for awhile."

With the obedience of a child Miss Farrar lay across the berth, and after awhile, with Miss Langham's hand clasped between her own, closed her red, swollen eyes in sleep.

It was perhaps half an hour later that Miss Langham pressed her call button beside the door. A porter appeared.

"What is the next stop?" she inquired.

"East Newlands," was the reply.

"Can I send a telegram from there?"

"Yes, ma'am."

Miss Langham gently detached her fingers from the clinging clasp of the sleeping girl, and scribbled a telegram on a blank which the porter offered. It was addressed to J. Charles Wingate, in a small city, just beyond Albany, and said:

Have changed my mind. This is irrevocable. M.

When the train pulled into Albany the following morning Miss Julia Farrar was found dead in her berth, fully dressed, except for her hat. A thirty-two caliber bullet had entered her body just below the left shoulder. Miss Langham herself gave the alarm. When physicians came they agreed that Miss Farrar had been dead for at least two hours.

Professor Augustus S. F. X. Van Dusen – The Thinking Machine – absorbed, digested, and assimilated all the known facts in the problem of the private compartment. Instantly that singular, penetrating brain beneath the mop of tangled, straw yellow hair was alive with questions.

"Who is Miss Langham?" was the first query.

"She is the daughter of Daniel Eustace Langham, president of a national bank in his home city," replied Hutchinson Hatch, reporter.

"She and Miss Farrar were classmates in Vassar, and met by accident on the train."

"Do you know they met by accident?"

"It seems to have been by accident," the reporter amended. "As a matter of fact, Miss Langham was on the train first—in fact, had engaged the drawing room compartment a couple of days ahead."

"Does she know – Miss Langham, I mean – know Devore?"

"Very well indeed," responded the reporter. "A couple of years ago he was rather assiduous in his attentions to her. That was before Devore met Miss Farrar."

The Thinking Machine turned suddenly in his chair and squinted into the eyes of the newspaper man. Faint corrugations in the dome – like brow were swept away.

"Oh!" he exclaimed. "An old love affair! How did it come to be broken off?"

"I imagine it was Devore who broke it off," replied Hatch. "When he met Miss Farrar it resulted in a quick transfer of attentions. As a matter of fact, he doesn't seem to be a very pleasant sort of person, anyway—spoiled son and sole heir of a man worth millions. You know what that means."

"And where was Miss Langham going at the time of the tragedy?" inquired the scientist.

"To visit some friends just beyond Albany."

For a long time The Thinking Machine was silent, while Hatch turned over those vague impressions which the scientist's manner and words had created.

"That seems to simplify the matter somewhat," mused The Thinking Machine at last.

"You don't mean," blurted Hatch quickly – "you don't mean that Miss Langham could have had anything to do with Miss Farrar's death?"

"Why not?" demanded The Thinking Machine coldly.

"But her social position, her wealth, everything, would seem to remove her beyond the range of suspicion," Hatch protested.

The Thinking Machine regarded him with frank disapproval. "Two and two always make four, Mr Hatch," he said shortly. "We have here a motive for the crime – jealousy—and practically exclusive opportunity. Social position and wealth do not deter criminals; they only make them more cunning. In this case two and two make four so obviously that I am surprised Miss Langham wasn't arrested immediately. Where is she now, by the way?"

"With her father and mother at the Hotel Bellevoir in town here," Hatch responded. "Immediately after the tragedy was reported she returned here, and her father and mother joined her. She is now suffering from shock, and inaccessible – at least to reporters."

"Any physician?"

"Dr Barrow and Dr Curtis are attending her."

"I may call on her in person," remarked The Thinking Machine. "And now about this man Devore? Have you seen him?"

"He was the first man the police wanted to see," explained the reporter. "They have already made him account for his every move on the night of the murder. Of course, a motive in his case would be obvious—anger, revenge, jealousy, anything."

"And where was he between, say, midnight and breakfast that night?"

"He says he was asleep at home."

"He says!" snapped The Thinking Machine abruptly. "Don't you know?"

"Not of my knowledge."

"Well, find out!" was the curt instruction. "That isn't one of the things that we can be at all uncertain about."

Hatch opened his eyes again. Here were two lines of investigation laid out by the scientist, either one of which might, if pursued to a logical conclusion, convict a person of wealth and position of a terrible crime.

"And Miss Farrar's family?" continued The Thinking Machine mercilessly. "Where were her father and brother that night?"

"Surely you can't believe that—"

"I never believe anything, Mr Hatch, until I know it. I merely wanted to know where they were; for on that side too it is possible to conceive a motive for Miss Farrar's death."

"There has been no inquiry in that direction at all," explained the bewildered reporter. "I'll begin one."

Then for a time The Thinking Machine sat with fingertips pressed idly together, squinting blankly at the ceiling.

"While a motive is never absolutely essential to the solution of any criminal problem," he observed after awhile, "it will frequently indicate a line of investigation. Now, in the usual case when a motive appears the solution is inevitable. But this case differs from the usual case in that we have too many motives—three excellent ones that we know – a jealous woman, a suitor discarded on the eve of his wedding, and perhaps a vengeful father or brother. And beyond those there are other possibilities."

Hatch went about his business with turbulent, troubled thoughts – a vague sense of treading on dangerous ground – while The Thinking Machine turned to the telephone. Five minutes later he picked up his hat and went to the Hotel Bellevoir.

"Did Dr Curtis telephone you?" he inquired of the clerk.

"Yes. Is this Mr Van Dusen?"

The Thinking Machine bobbed his head, and was ushered into Miss Langham's apartments.

Pallid as the sheets, resistlessly inert, the girl lay staring upward as if fascinated by the brilliant scintillating point which floated backward and forward rhythmically before her eyes as The Thinking Machine slowly waved his arm. It was like some weird exorcism, some uncanny incantation, but it compelled attention.

"Watch it closely, please!"

The scientist's tone was low, almost a whisper, yet it carried a command. The swing of his arm shortened gradually, almost imperceptibly, and slowly the bright spot passed upward in little erratic circles until it was directly before her eyes. And there it stopped for a moment. After awhile it moved on again, still farther upward, in a straight line, until the girl was aware of a queerly strained feeling in her eyes. It paused again, then very, very slowly began to move round and round.

After awhile the fascination in the girl's eyes gave way to a vacant staring, and the pupils distended, as a mist crept over them. Slowly, slowly, the swing of the bright spot decreased, until at last it hung motionless, suspended in air, between the slim fingers of the scientist. Thus for a time, and the vacant staring became glassy-dead. Then the bright spot was withdrawn, materializing as the lower part of the bowl of a silver spoon which The Thinking Machine laid on the table beside him. One hand passed over the girl's white face once. The long fingers lingered caressingly on the lids, and pressed them together.

The Thinking Machine passed round from the head of the couch where the girl lay and took a seat, with his hand on her wrist. The pulse fluttered a little, but he nodded his head as if satisfied.

"You are on a train – in a private compartment," he said, still in a voice that was almost a whisper.

"Yes," breathed the girl. It was nearly inaudible.

"A young woman is sleeping there."

"Yes," came the sigh again.

"You hate her."

"No."

It was a flat, unequivocal denial, and the dreamy, sighing tone hardened suddenly. Again The Thinking Machine pressed his fingers down on her eyelids, and sat silent for a time.

"You dislike her," he suggested.

"No," the girl denied once more dreamily. "She and I were—" and the phrase drifted off into intangible incoherency.

"You have a revolver in your traveling bag."

"Yes."

The petulant, crabbed face of The Thinking Machine lighted suddenly, exultantly. But when he spoke again it was in the same whispering monotone. "You always carry a revolver when traveling."

"No."

"Your revolver is thirty-two caliber."

"I don't know."

"The sleeping woman loves the man you love."

"Yes."

"She is at your mercy; therefore you will kill her."

"No, no, no!"

There was a sudden horror in the voice, a strange, convulsive working of the face, and the eyelids fluttered. Thrice The Thinking Machine passed his hands over her face, and she became calm again.

"You are back in your own apartments at the Hotel Bellevoir," he continued after a minute.

"Yes," she answered readily.

"Your revolver is in the traveling bag."

"No."

The Thinking Machine glanced quickly round the room, and again his eyes settled on the pallid face.

"It is in the dressing table."

"Yes."

With set, inscrutable face, the scientist arose and went to the table. In the drawer lay a handsomely mounted weapon. He picked it up, examined it closely as he whirled the barrel in his fingers, and then replaced it, after which he returned to the girl.

"You have fainted," he said. "You will return to consciousness in a moment."

He leaned forward and blew gently into the closed eyes, and the girl sighed. Thrice he did this, then a trace of color appeared in the face, and she raised her eyelids. For an instant she stared into the drawn face of the scientist.

"Why, I must have fainted," she said.

Hutchinson Hatch burst into the laboratory, where The Thinking Machine was at work, with an air of excitement which caused the eminent scientist to turn and squint at him in disapproval.

"That man Devore lied about where—" he began.

"Just a moment, Mr Hatch," interrupted The Thinking Machine curtly. "Did you see the sleeping car in which Miss Farrar was killed?"

"Yes," replied the reporter, and, somewhat abashed, sat down.

"I suppose the windows were all screened, as is usually the case?"

"Why, I suppose so," was the reply.

"Was there any hole of any sort in the screen of the window in the private compartment?"

"Oh, I see what you mean. Shot from the outside. No, there was no hole."

The brow of the scientist had been smooth and unruffled as the summer sea; but now the minute corrugations which Hatch knew so well appeared again, and he sat silent for a time.

"When you came in you started to say—" he remarked at last.

"That Devore lied as to where he was the night Miss Farrar was killed," Hatch hastened to explain. "He said he was at home in bed. I have the word of two servants that he was not, and have learned that he was at Troy that night."

"Well?" inquired the scientist impassively.

"Troy is just a short distance from Albany," the reporter rushed on. "The train had to pass so near there, don't you see, that Devore might have boarded it, and—"

He paused. The Thinking Machine arose suddenly, and paced back and forth across the room twice.

"Why was he in Troy?" he asked.

"It was some sort of dinner – a stag affair, I imagine – the night before the day of the wedding," said Hatch.

"And I dare say young Farrar, Miss Farrar's brother, was with him?"

"Yes, he was. You didn't give me time."

The Thinking Machine passed into the adjoining room, and Hatch heard the telephone bell. Fifteen minutes later he came out.

"Devore and Farrar spent the night – that is from midnight until eight o'clock in the morning of the murder – in adjoining rooms at a hotel in Troy," explained the scientist. "They were asleep there. So that makes the affair perfectly clear."

"Perfectly clear?" exclaimed Hatch. "Perfectly clear? I don't see how you make that out, when—"

The Thinking Machine started out, with Hatch following. They went straight to the Hotel Bellevoir, and sent their cards to Langham. He was staring blankly at a telegram when they entered. He recognized The Thinking Machine by name as a physician who had called on his daughter.

"Your daughter is engaged to be married, isn't she, Mr Langham?" inquired the scientist.

"Yes, she was," he replied wonderingly. "Why?"

"And she was, I believe, on her way to visit some friends in a small city just beyond Albany when this – this unhappy event occurred?"

"Yes," Langham assented again.

"Perhaps the family of the man to whom she was betrothed?"

Again Langham assented.

"And what is the man of this man, please?"

"J. Charles Wingate," was the reply. "I've just got a telegram from him. Here it is."

The Thinking Machine glanced at the yellow slip of paper. The message was dated at New York city, and said tersely:

Wedding impossible. I cannot explain. Wingate.

"It's an outrage," declared Langham.

"It's a confession," remarked The Thinking Machine.

"When we remove Miss Langham as a possibility," The Thinking Machine told Hatch and Detective Mallory, "we inevitably bring the murder of Miss Farrar down to a man. And I may say that I personally demonstrated Miss Langham's innocence by a little experiment in mechanical hypnotism. She confessed that she had a revolver on the train. But her revolver was a twenty-two caliber, and the bullet that killed

Miss Farrar was a thirty-two. So there was no further need to consider her.

"I also removed Devore by establishing an alibi for him even after he had lied to the police as to his whereabouts on the night of the crime. Why he lied doesn't appear, and is of no consequence now. I proved his whereabouts conclusively by telephone, and at the same time proved the whereabouts of Miss Farrar's brother, thus eliminating both at the same time. Then what?

"Everyone had presumed – and I also did at first – that the person who killed Miss Farrar was in the private compartment with her. And yet, if that was true, why didn't the shot awake Miss Langham? When I knew that she was innocent the logic of the thing indicated that the shot came from the outside.

"It was a warm night, and we shall suppose the window was open. Was the screen in it? It did not have a hole in it; so I presumed it was not. Then the possibilities became infinite. The first thing to do was dispose of Devore and Miss Farrar's brother. I did that. Both you gentlemen recall, I dare say, the peculiar circumstances surrounding the murder of the young woman in a box at the opera? Yes. Instantly that came to me – perhaps the wrong woman had been killed. If so, we must look for a motive for the murder of Miss Langham.

"Well, we know that there had once been a love affair between Miss Langham and Devore. Was it possible that, despite her engagement to another man, Miss Langham still loved Devore? – that she learned Miss Farrar's story, and then and there decided to jilt the man to whom she was engaged, because of this love for Devore, who was now, by the act of Miss Farrar, cast aside? If so, would she have telegraphed to him this change of mind? If we suppose that she was expecting to meet him in a few hours – in other words, visit his family – we can imagine her telegraphing from the train, while her intention was to go no further than Albany, where she would turn back.

"That hypothesis made the entire matter perfectly clear. She did telegraph her decision to J. Charles Wingate, and a motive for her murder was instantly created – revenge. Now, he probably knew what train she was on, that she had taken the private compartment in a certain sleeping car on that train, and it is not only possible but probable that he took a train to meet it.

"Some time between the moment he received the telegram and met the train on which she was a passenger he resolved upon murder. The method? What better than firing through the window while the train was standing at some small station? The shot might not attract attention, particularly as the sleeping car was the last on the train, and it was, say, four o'clock in the morning. He did fire through the window; therefore the shot, being outside, did not disturb Miss Langham, already accustomed to the roar and clatter of the train. Wingate merely looked in, saw a woman asleep, and fired. He did not know that he had killed the wrong woman, perhaps, until the matter got into the newspapers."

There was a long silence. Detective Mallory and Hatch exchanged glances; then the detective turned to The Thinking Machine.

"And where is Wingate?" he inquired.

"Mr Langham received a telegram from him dated at New York," was the reply. "I imagine it was sent on the eve of his flight, perhaps abroad. I should advise, anyway, that a watch be kept on the steamers as they arrive on the other side."

And eight days later J. Charles Wingate was arrested as he walked down the gangplank of a steamer at Liverpool. He had gone over in the steerage.

10

MYSTERY OF THE RALSTON BANK BURGLARY

I

With expert fingers Phillip Dunston, receiving teller, verified the last package of one-hundred-dollar bills he had made up – ten thousand dollars in all – and tossed it over on the pile beside him, while he checked off a memorandum. It was correct; there were eighteen packages of bills, containing $107,231. Then he took the bundles, one by one, and on each placed his initials, "P. D." This was a system of checking in the Ralston National Bank.

It was care in such trivial details, perhaps, that had a great deal to do with the fact that the Ralston National had advanced from a small beginning to the first rank of those banks which were financial powers. President Quinton Fraser had inaugurated the system under which the Ralston National had so prospered, and now, despite his seventy-four years, he was still its active head. For fifty years he had been in its employ; for thirty-five years of that time he had been its president.

Publicly the aged banker was credited with the possession of a vast fortune, this public estimate being based on large sums he had given to charity. But as a matter of fact the private

MYSTERY OF THE RALSTON BANK

fortune of the old man, who had no one to share it save his wife, was not large; it was merely a comfortable living sum for an aged couple of simple tastes.

Dunston gathered up the packages of money and took them into the cashier's private office, where he dumped them on the great flat-top desk at which that official, Randolph West, sat figuring. The cashier thrust the sheet of paper on which he had been working into his pocket and took the memorandum which Dunston offered.

"All right?" he asked.

"It tallies perfectly," Dunston replied.

"Thanks. You may go now."

It was an hour after closing time. Dunston was just pulling on his coat when he saw West come out of his private office with the money to put it away in the big steel safe which stood between depositors and thieves. The cashier paused a moment to allow the janitor, Harris, to sweep the space in front of the safe. It was the late afternoon scrubbing and sweeping.

"Hurry up," the cashier complained, impatiently.

Harris hurried, and West placed the money in the safe. There were eighteen packages.

"All right, sir?" Dunston inquired.

"Yes."

West was disposing of the last bundle when Miss Clarke – Louise Clarke – private secretary to President Fraser, came out of his office with a long envelope in her hand. Dunston glanced at her and she smiled at him.

"Please, Mr West," she said to the cashier, "Mr Fraser told me before he went to put these papers in the safe. I had almost forgotten."

She glanced into the open safe and her pretty blue eyes opened wide. Mr West took the envelope, stowed it away with the money without a word, the girl looking on interestedly, and then swung the heavy door closed. She turned away with a quick, reassuring smile at Dunston, and disappeared inside the private office.

West had shot the bolts of the safe into place and had taken hold of the combination dial to throw it on, when the street door opened and President Fraser entered hurriedly.

"Just a moment, West," he called. "Did Miss Clarke give you an envelope to go in there?"

"Yes. I just put it in."

"One moment," and the aged president came through a gate which Dunston held open and went to the safe. The cashier pulled the steel door open, unlocked the money compartment where the envelope had been placed, and the president took it out.

West turned and spoke to Dunston, leaving the president looking over the contents of the envelope. When the cashier turned back to the safe the president was just taking his hand away from his inside coat pocket.

"It's all right, West," he instructed. "Lock it up."

Again the heavy door closed, the bolts were shot and the combination dial turned. President Fraser stood looking on curiously; it just happened that he had never witnessed this operation before.

"How much have you got in there tonight?" he asked.

"One hundred and twenty-nine thousand," replied the cashier. "And all the securities, of course."

"Hum," mused the president. "That would be a good haul for some one—if they could get it, eh, West?" and he chuckled dryly.

"Excellent," returned West, smilingly. "But they can't."

Miss Clarke, dressed for the street, her handsome face almost concealed by a veil which was intended to protect her pink cheeks from boisterous winds, was standing in the door of the president's office.

MYSTERY OF THE RALSTON BANK

"Oh, Miss Clarke, before you go, would you write just a short note for me?" asked the president.

"Certainly," she responded, and she returned to the private office. Mr Fraser followed her.

West and Dunston stood outside the bank railing, Dunston waiting for Miss Clarke. Every evening he walked over to the subway with her. His opinion of her was an open secret. West was waiting for the janitor to finish sweeping.

"Hurry up, Harris," he said again.

"Yes, sir," came the reply, and the janitor applied the broom more vigorously. "Just a little bit more. I've finished inside."

Dunston glanced through the railing. The floor was spick and span and the hardwood glistened cleanly. Various bits of paper came down the corridor before Harris's broom. The janitor swept it all up into a dustpan just as Miss Clarke came out of the president's room. With Dunston she walked up the street. As they were going they saw Cashier West come out the front door, with his handkerchief in his hand, and then walk away rapidly.

"Mr Fraser is doing some figuring," Miss Clarke explained to Dunston. "He said he might be there for another hour."

"You are beautiful," replied Dunston, irrelevantly.

These, then, were the happenings in detail in the Ralston National Bank from 4:15 o'clock on the afternoon of November 11. That night the bank was robbed. The great steel safe which was considered impregnable was blown and $129,000 was missing.

The night watchman of the bank, William Haney, was found senseless, bound and gagged, inside the bank. His revolver lay beside him with all the cartridges out. He had been beaten into insensibility; at the hospital it was stated that there was only a bare chance of his recovery.

The locks, hinges and bolts of the steel safe had been smashed by some powerful explosive, possibly nitro-glycerine. The tiny dial of the time-lock showed that the explosion came at 2:39; the remainder of the lock was blown to pieces.

Thus was fixed definitely the moment at which the robbery occurred. It was shown that the policeman on the beat had been four blocks away. It was perfectly possible that no one heard the explosion, because the bank was situated in a part of the city wholly given over to business and deserted at night.

The burglars had entered the building through a window of the cashier's private office, in the full glare of an electric light. The window sash here had been found unfastened and the protecting steel bars, outside from top to bottom, seemed to have been dragged from their sockets in the solid granite. The granite crumbled away, as if it had been chalk.

Only one possible clew was found. This was a white linen handkerchief, picked up in front of the blown safe. It must have been dropped there at the time of the burglary, because Dunston distinctly recalled it was not there before he left the bank. He would have noticed it while the janitor was sweeping.

This handkerchief was the property of Cashier West. The cashier did not deny it, but could offer no explanation of how it came there. Miss Clarke and Dunston both said that they had seen him leave the bank with a handkerchief in his hand.

II

President Fraser reached the bank at ten o'clock and was informed of the robbery. He retired to his office, and there he sat, apparently stunned into inactivity by the blow, his head bowed on his arms. Miss Clarke, at her typewriter, frequently glanced at the aged figure with an expression of pity on her face. Her eyes seemed weary, too. Outside, through the closed door, they could hear the detectives.

MYSTERY OF THE RALSTON BANK

From time to time employees of the bank and detectives entered the office to ask questions. The banker answered as if dazed; then the board of directors met and voted to personally make good the loss sustained. There was no uneasiness among depositors, because they knew the resources of the bank were practically unlimited.

Cashier West was not arrested. The directors wouldn't listen to such a thing; he had been cashier for eighteen years, and they trusted him implicitly. Yet he could offer no possible explanation of how his handkerchief had come there. He asserted stoutly that he had not been in the bank from the moment Miss Clarke and Dunston saw him leave it.

After investigation the police placed the burglary to the credit of certain expert cracksmen, identity unknown. A general alarm, which meant a rounding up of all suspicious persons, was sent out, and this drag-net was expected to bring important facts to light. Detective Mallory said so, and the bank officials placed great reliance on his word.

Thus the situation at the luncheon hour. Then Miss Clarke, who, wholly unnoticed, had been waiting all morning at her typewriter, arose and went over to Fraser.

"If you don't need me now," she said, "I'll run out to luncheon."

"Certainly, certainly," he responded, with a slight start. He had apparently forgotten her existence.

She stood silently looking at him for a moment.

"I'm awfully sorry," she said, at last, and her lips trembled slightly.

"Thanks," said the banker, and he smiled faintly. "It's a shock, the worst I ever had."

Miss Clarke passed out with quiet tread, pausing for a moment in the outer office to stare curiously at the shattered steel safe. The banker arose with sudden determination and called to West, who entered immediately.

"I know a man who can throw some light on this thing," said Fraser, positively. "I think I'll ask him to come over and take a look. It might aid the police, anyway. You may know him? Professor Van Dusen."

"Never heard of him," said West, tersely, "but I'll welcome anybody who can solve it. My position is uncomfortable."

President Fraser called Professor Van Dusen – The Thinking Machine – and talked for a moment through the 'phone. Then he turned back to West.

"He'll come," he said, with an air of relief. "I was able to do him a favor once by putting an invention on the market."

Within an hour The Thinking Machine, accompanied by Hutchinson Hatch, reporter, appeared. President Fraser knew the scientist well, but on West the strange figure made a startling, almost uncanny, impression. Every known fact was placed before The Thinking Machine. He listened without comment, then arose and wandered aimlessly about the offices. The employees were amused by his manner; Hatch was a silent looker-on.

"Where was the handkerchief found?" demanded The Thinking Machine, at last.

"Here," replied West, and he indicated the exact spot.

"Any draught through the office — ever?"

"None. We have a patent ventilating system which prevents that."

The Thinking Machine squinted for several minutes at the window which had been unfastened – the window in the cashier's private room – with the steel bars guarding it, now torn out of their sockets, and at the chalklike softness of the granite about the sockets. After awhile he turned to the president and cashier.

"Where is the handkerchief?"

"In my desk," Fraser replied. "The police thought it of no consequence, save, perhaps – perhaps —," and he looked at West.

MYSTERY OF THE RALSTON BANK

"Except that it might implicate me," said West, hotly.

"Tut, tut, tut," said Fraser, reprovingly. "No one thinks for a—"

"Well, well, the handkerchief?" interrupted The Thinking Machine, in annoyance.

"Come into my office," suggested the president.

The Thinking Machine started in, saw a woman – Miss Clarke, who had returned from luncheon – and stopped. There was one thing on earth he was afraid of – a woman.

"Bring it out here," he requested.

President Fraser brought it and placed it in the slender hands of the scientist, who examined it closely by a window, turning it over and over. At last he sniffed at it. There was the faint, clinging odor of violet perfume. Then abruptly, irrelevantly, he turned to Fraser.

"How many women employed in the bank?" he asked.

"Three," was the reply; "Miss Clarke, who is my secretary, and two general stenographers in the outer office."

"How many men?"

"Fourteen, including myself."

If the president and Cashier West had been surprised at the actions of The Thinking Machine up to this point, now they were amazed. He thrust the handkerchief at Hatch, took his own handkerchief, briskly scrubbed his hands with it, and also passed that to Hatch.

"Keep those," he commanded.

He sniffed at his hands, then walked into the outer office, straight toward the desk of one of the young women stenographers. He leaned over her, and asked one question:

"What system of shorthand do you write?"

"Pitman," was the astonished reply.

The scientist sniffed. Yes, it was unmistakably a sniff. He left her suddenly and went to the other stenographer. Precisely the same thing happened; standing close to her he asked one question, and at her answer sniffed. Miss Clarke passed through the outer office to mail a letter. She, too, had to answer the question as the scientist squinted into her eyes, and sniffed.

"Ah," he said, at her answer.

Then from one to another of the employees of the bank he went, asking each a few questions. By this time a murmur of amusement was running through the office. Finally The Thinking Machine approached the cage in which sat Dunston, the receiving teller. The young man was bent over his work, absorbed.

"How long have you been employed here?" asked the scientist, suddenly.

Dunston started and glanced around quickly.

"Five years," he responded.

"It must be hot work," said The Thinking Machine. "You're perspiring."

"Am I?" inquired the young man, smilingly.

He drew a crumpled handkerchief from his hip pocket, shook it out, and wiped his forehead.

"Ah!" exclaimed The Thinking Machine, suddenly.

He had caught the faint, subtle perfume of violets – an odor identical with that on the handkerchief found in front of the safe.

III

The Thinking Machine led the way back to the private office of the cashier, with President Fraser, Cashier West and Hatch following.

"Is it possible for anyone to overhear us here?" he asked.

"No," replied the president. "The directors meet here."

"Could anyone outside hear that, for instance?" and with a sudden sweep of his hand he upset a heavy chair.

"I don't know," was the astonished reply. "Why?"

The Thinking Machine went quickly to the door, opened it softly and peered out. Then he closed the door again.

"I suppose I may speak with absolute frankness?" he inquired.

"Certainly," responded the old banker, almost startled. "Certainly."

"You have presented an abstract problem," The Thinking Machine went on, "and I presume you want a solution of it, no matter where it hits?"

"Certainly," the president again assured him, but his tone expressed a grave, haunting fear.

"In that case," and The Thinking Machine turned to the reporter, "Mr Hatch, I want you to ascertain several things for me. First, I want to know if Miss Clarke uses or has ever used violet perfume—if so, when she ceased using it."

"Yes," said the reporter. The bank officials exchanged wondering looks.

"Also, Mr Hatch," and the scientist squinted with his strange eyes straight into the face of the cashier, "go to the home of Mr West, here, see for yourself his laundry mark, and ascertain beyond any question if he has ever, or any member of his family has ever, used violet perfume."

The cashier flushed suddenly.

"I can answer that," he said, hotly. "No."

"I knew you would say that," said The Thinking Machine, curtly. "Please don't interrupt. Do as I say, Mr Hatch."

Accustomed as he was to the peculiar methods of this man, Hatch saw faintly the purpose of the inquiries.

"And the receiving teller?" he asked.

"I know about him," was the reply.

Hatch left the room, closing the door behind him. He heard the bolt shot in the lock as he started away.

"I think it only fair to say here, Professor Van Dusen," explained the president, "that we understand thoroughly that it would have been impossible for Mr West to have had anything to do with or know—"

"Nothing is impossible," interrupted The Thinking Machine.

"But I won't—" began West, angrily.

"Just a moment, please," said The Thinking Machine. "No one has accused you of anything. What I am doing may explain to your satisfaction just how your handkerchief came here and bring about the very thing I suppose you want – exoneration."

The cashier sank back into a chair; President Fraser looked from one to the other. Where there had been worry on his face there was now only wonderment.

"Your handkerchief was found in this office, apparently having been dropped by the persons who blew the safe," and the long, slender fingers of The Thinking Machine were placed tip to tip as he talked. "It was not there the night before. The janitor who swept says so; Dunston, who happened to look, says so; Miss Clarke and Dunston both say they saw you with a handkerchief as you left the bank. Therefore, that handkerchief reached that spot after you left and before the robbery was discovered."

The cashier nodded.

"You say you don't use perfume; that no one in your family uses it. If Mr Hatch verifies this, it will help to exonerate you. But some person who handled that handkerchief after it left your possession and before it appeared here did use perfume. Now who was that person? Who would have had an opportunity?

"We may safely dismiss the possibility that you lost the handkerchief, that it fell into the hands of burglars, that those burglars used perfume, that they brought it to your bank – your own bank, mind you! – and left it. The series of coincidences necessary to bring that about would not have occurred once in a million times."

The Thinking Machine sat silent for several minutes, squinting steadily at the ceiling.

"If it had been lost anywhere, in the laundry, say, the same rule of coincidence I have just applied would almost eliminate it. Therefore, because of an opportunity to get that handkerchief, we will assume – there is – there must be – some one employed in this bank who had some connection with or actually participated in the burglary."

The Thinking Machine spoke with perfect quiet, but the effect was electrical. The aged president staggered to his feet and stood staring at him dully; again the flush of crimson came into the face of the cashier.

"Some one," The Thinking Machine went on, evenly, "who either found the handkerchief and unwittingly lost it at the time of the burglary, or else stole it and deliberately left it. As I said, Mr West seems eliminated. Had he been one of the robbers, he would not wittingly have left his handkerchief; we will still assume that he does not use perfume, therefore personally did not drop the handkerchief where it was found."

"Impossible! I can't believe it, and of my employees—" began Mr Fraser.

"Please don't keep saying things are impossible," snapped The Thinking Machine. "It irritates me exceedingly. It all comes to the one vital question: Who in the bank uses perfume?"

"I don't know," said the two officials.

"I do," said The Thinking Machine. "There are two – only two, Dunston, your receiving teller, and Miss Clarke."

"But they—"

"Dunston uses a violet perfume not like that on the handkerchief, but identical with it," The Thinking Machine went on. "Miss Clarke uses a strong rose perfume."

"But those two persons, above all others in the bank, I trust implicitly," said Mr Fraser, earnestly. "And, besides, they wouldn't know how to blow a safe. The police tell me this was the work of experts."

"Have you, Mr Fraser, attempted to raise, or have you raised lately, any large sum of money?" asked the scientist, suddenly.

"Well, yes," said the banker, "I have. For a week past I have tried to raise ninety thousand dollars on my personal account."

"And you, Mr West?"

The face of the cashier flushed slightly – it might have been at the tone of the question – and there was the least pause.

"No," he answered finally.

"Very well," and the scientist arose, rubbing his hands; "now we'll search your employees."

"What?" exclaimed both men. Then Mr Fraser added: "That would be the height of absurdity; it would never do. Besides, any person who robbed the bank would not carry proofs of the robbery, or even any of the money about with them – to the bank, above all places."

"The bank would be the safest place for it," retorted The Thinking Machine. "It is perfectly possible that a thief in your employ would carry some of the money; indeed, it is doubtful if he would dare do anything else with it. He could see you would have no possible reason for suspecting anyone here – unless it is Mr West."

There was a pause. "I'll do the searching, except the three ladies, of course," he added, blushingly. "With them each combination of two can search the other one."

Mr Fraser and Mr West conversed in low tones for several minutes.

"If the employees will consent I am willing," Mr Fraser explained, at last; "although I see no use of it."

"They will agree," said The Thinking Machine. "Please call them all into this office."

Among some confusion and wonderment the three women and fourteen men of the bank were gathered in the cashier's office, the outer doors being locked. The Thinking Machine addressed them with characteristic terseness.

"In the investigation of the burglary of last night," he explained, "it has been deemed necessary to search all employees of this bank." A murmur of surprise ran around the room. "Those who are innocent will agree readily, of course; will all agree?"

There were whispered consultations on all sides. Dunston flushed angrily; Miss Clarke, standing near Mr Fraser, paled slightly. Dunston looked at her and then spoke.

"And the ladies?" he asked.

"They, too," explained the scientist. "They may search one another – in the other room, of course."

"I for one will not submit to such a proceeding," Dunston declared, bluntly, "not because I fear it, but because it is an insult."

Simultaneously it impressed itself on the bank officials and The Thinking Machine that the one person in the bank who used a perfume identical with that on the handkerchief was the first to object to a search. The cashier and president exchanged startled glances.

"Nor will I," came in the voice of a woman.

The Thinking Machine turned and glanced at her. It was Miss Willis, one of the outside stenographers; Miss Clarke and the other woman were pale, but neither had spoken.

"And the others?" asked The Thinking Machine.

Generally there was acquiescence, and as the men came forward the scientist searched them, perfunctorily, it seemed. Nothing! At last there remained three men, Dunston, West and Fraser. Dunston came forward, compelled to do so by the attitude of his fellows. The three women stood together. The Thinking Machine spoke to them as he searched Dunston.

"If the ladies will retire to the next room they may proceed with their search," he suggested. "If any money is found, bring it to me – nothing else."

"I will not, I will not, I will not," screamed Miss Willis, suddenly. "It's an outrage."

Miss Clarke, deathly white and half fainting, threw up her hands and sank without a sound into the arms of President Fraser. There she burst into tears.

"It is an outrage," she sobbed. She clung to President Fraser, her arms flung upward and her face buried on his bosom. He was soothing her with fatherly words, and stroked her hair awkwardly. The Thinking Machine finished the search of Dunston. Nothing! Then Miss Clarke roused herself and dried her eyes.

"Of course I will have to agree," she said, with a flash of anger in her eyes.

Miss Willis was weeping, but, like Dunston, she was compelled to yield, and the three women went into an adjoining room. There was a tense silence until they reappeared. Each shook her head. The Thinking Machine nearly looked disappointed.

"Dear me!" he exclaimed. "Now, Mr Fraser." He started toward the president, then paused to pick up a scarf pin.

"This is yours," he said. "I saw it fall," and he made as if to search the aged man.

"Well, do you really think it necessary in my case?" asked the president, in consternation, as he drew back, nervously. "I—I am the president, you know."

"The others were searched in your presence, I will search you in their presence," said The Thinking Machine, tartly.

"But – but—" the president stammered.

"Are you afraid?" the scientist demanded.

"Why, of course not," was the hurried answer; "but it seems so – so unusual."

"I think it best," said The Thinking Machine, and before the banker could draw away his slender fingers were in the inside breast pocket, whence they instantly drew out a bundle of money – one hundred $100 bills – ten thousand dollars – with the initials of the receiving teller, "P.D." – "o. k. – R. W."

"Great God!" exclaimed Mr Fraser, ashen white.

"Dear me, dear me!" said The Thinking Machine again. He sniffed curiously at the bundle of bank notes, as a hound might sniff at a trail.

IV

President Fraser was removed to his home in a dangerous condition. His advanced age did not withstand the shock. Now alternately he raved and muttered incoherently, and the old eyes were wide, staring fearfully always. There was a consultation between The Thinking Machine and West after the removal of President Fraser, and the result was another hurried meeting of the board of directors. At that meeting West was placed, temporarily, in command. The police, of course, had been informed of the matter, but no arrest was probable.

Immediately after The Thinking Machine left the bank Hatch appeared and inquired for him. From the bank he went to the home of the scientist. There Professor Van Dusen was bending over a retort, busy with some problem.

"Well?" he demanded, as he glanced up.

"West told the truth," began Hatch. "Neither he nor any member of his family uses perfume; he has few outside acquaintances, is regular in his habits, but is a man of considerable wealth, it appears."

"What is his salary at the bank?" asked The Thinking Machine.

"Fifteen thousand a year," said the reporter. "But he must have a large fortune. He lives like a millionaire."

"He couldn't do that on fifteen thousand dollars a year," mused the scientist. "Did he inherit any money?"

"No," was the reply. "He started as a clerk in the bank and has made himself what he is."

"That means speculation," said The Thinking Machine. "You can't save a fortune from a salary, even fifteen thousand dollars a year. Now, Mr Hatch, find out for me all about his business connections. His source of income particularly I would like to know. Also whether or not he has recently sought to borrow or has received a large sum of money; if he got it and what he did with it. He says he has not sought such a sum. Perhaps he told the truth."

"Yes, and about Miss Clarke—"

"Yes; what about her?" asked The Thinking Machine.

"She occupies a little room in a boarding-house for women in an excellent district," the reporter explained. "She has no friends who call there, at any rate. Occasionally, however, she goes out at night and remains late."

"The perfume?" asked the scientist.

"She uses a perfume, the housekeeper tells me, but she doesn't recall just what kind it is – so many of the young women in the house use it. So I went to her room and looked. There was no perfume there. Her room was considerably disarranged, which seemed to astonish the housekeeper, who declared that she had carefully arranged it about nine o'clock. It was two when I was there."

"How was it disarranged?" asked the scientist.

"The couch cover was jerked awry and the pillows tumbled down, for one thing," said the reporter. "I didn't notice any further."

The Thinking Machine relapsed into silence.

"What happened at the bank?" inquired Hatch.

Briefly the scientist related the facts leading up to the search, the search itself and its startling result. The reporter whistled.

"Do you think Fraser had anything to do with it?"

MYSTERY OF THE RALSTON BANK

"Run out and find out those other things about West," said The Thinking Machine, evasively. "Come back here tonight. It doesn't matter what time."

"But who do you think committed the crime?" insisted the newspaper man.

"I may be able to tell you when you return."

For the time being The Thinking Machine seemed to forget the bank robbery, being busy in his tiny laboratory. He was aroused from his labors by the ringing of the telephone bell.

"Hello," he called. "Yes, Van Dusen. No, I can't come down to the bank now. What is it? Oh, it has disappeared? When? Too bad! How's Mr Fraser? Still unconscious? Too bad! I'll see you tomorrow."

The scientist was still engrossed in some delicate chemical work just after eight o'clock that evening when Martha, his housekeeper and maid of all work, entered.

"Professor," she said, "there's a lady to see you."

"Name?" he asked, without turning.

"She didn't give it, sir."

"There in a moment."

He finished the test he had under way, then left the little laboratory and went into the hall leading to the sitting-room, where unprivileged callers awaited his pleasure. He sniffed a little as he stepped into the hall. At the door of the sitting-room he paused and peered inside. A woman arose and came toward him. It was Miss Clarke.

"Goodevening," he said. "I knew you'd come."

Miss Clarke looked a little surprised, but made no comment.

"I came to give you some information," she said, and her voice was subdued. "I am heartbroken at the awful things which have come out concerning—concerning Mr Fraser. I have been closely associated with him for several months, and I won't believe that he could have had anything to do with this affair, although I know positively that he was as in need of a large sum of money – ninety thousand dollars – because his personal fortune was in danger. Some error in titles to an estate, he told me."

"Yes, yes," said The Thinking Machine.

"Whether he was able to raise this money I don't know," she went on. "I only hope he did without having to—to do that—to have any—"

"To rob his bank," said the scientist, tartly. "Miss Clarke, is young Dunston in love with you?"

The girl's face changed color at the sudden question.

"I don't see—" she began.

"You may not see," said The Thinking Machine, "but I can have him arrested for robbery and convict him."

The girl gazed at him with wide, terror-stricken eyes, and gasped.

"No, no, no," she said, hurriedly. "He could have had nothing to do with that at all."

"Is he in love with you?" again came the question.

There was a pause.

"I've had reason to believe so," she said, finally, "though—"

"And you?"

The girl's face was flaming now, and, squinting into her eyes, the scientist read the answer.

"I understand," he commented, tersely. "Are you going to be married?"

"I could—could never marry him," she gasped suddenly. "No, no," emphatically. "We are not, ever."

She slowly recovered from her confusion, while the scientist continued to squint at her curiously.

"I believe you said you had some information for me?" he asked.

"Y-yes," she faltered. Then more calmly: "Yes. I came to tell you that the package of ten thousand dollars which you took from Mr Fraser's pocket has again disappeared."

MYSTERY OF THE RALSTON BANK

"Yes," said the other, without astonishment.

"It was presumed at the bank that he had taken it home with him, having regained possession of it in some way, but a careful search has failed to reveal it."

"Yes, and what else?"

The girl took a long breath and gazed steadily into the eyes of the scientist, with determination in her own.

"I have come, too, to tell you," she said, "the name of the man who robbed the bank."

V

If Miss Clarke had expected that The Thinking Machine would show either astonishment or enthusiasm, she must have been disappointed, for he neither altered his position nor looked at her. Instead, he was gazing thoughtfully away with lackluster eyes.

"Well?" he asked. "I suppose it's a story. Begin at the beginning."

With a certain well-bred air of timidity, the girl began the story; and occasionally as she talked there was a little tremor of the lips.

"I have been a stenographer and typewriter for seven years," she said, "and in that time I have held only four positions. The first was in a law office in New York, where I was left an orphan to earn my own living; the second was with a manufacturing concern, also in New York. I left there three years ago to accept the position of private secretary to William T. Rankin, president of the—National Bank, at Hartford, Connecticut. I came from there to Boston and later went to work at the Ralston Bank, as private secretary to Mr Fraser. I left the bank in Hartford because of the failure of that concern, following a bank robbery."

The Thinking Machine glanced at her suddenly.

"You may remember from the newspapers—" she began again.

"I never read the newspapers," he said.

"Well, anyway," and there was a shade of impatience at the interruption, "there was a bank burglary there similar to this. Only seventy thousand dollars was stolen, but it was a small institution and the theft precipitated a run which caused a collapse after I had been in that position for only six months."

"How long have you been with the Ralston National?"

"Nine months," was the reply.

"Had you saved any money while working in your other positions?"

"Well, the salary was small—I couldn't have saved much."

"How did you live those two years from the time you left the Hartford Bank until you accepted this position?"

The girl stammered a little.

"I received assistance from friends," she said, finally.

"Go on."

"That bank in Hartford," she continued, with a little gleam of resentment in her eyes, "had a safe similar to the one at the Ralston National, though not so large. It was blown in identically the same way as this one was blown."

"Oh, I see," said the scientist. "Some one was arrested for this, and you want to give me the name of that man?"

"Yes," said the girl. "A professional burglar, William Dineen, was arrested for that robbery and confessed. Later he escaped. After his arrest he boasted of his ability to blow any style of safe. He used an invention of his own for the borings to place the charges. I noticed that safe and I noticed this one. There is a striking similarity in the two."

The Thinking Machine stared at her.

"Why do you tell me?" he asked.

MYSTERY OF THE RALSTON BANK

"Because I understood you were making the investigation for the bank," she responded, unhesitatingly, "and I dreaded the notoriety of telling the police."

"If this William Dineen is at large you believe he did this?"

"I am almost positive."

"Thank you," said The Thinking Machine.

Miss Clarke went away, and late that night Hatch appeared. He looked weary and sank into a chair gratefully, but there was satisfaction in his eye. For an hour or more he talked. At last The Thinking Machine was satisfied, nearly.

"One thing more," he said, in conclusion. "Notify the police to look out for William Dineen, professional bank burglar, and his pals, whose names you can get from the newspapers in connection with a bank robbery in Hartford. They are wanted in connection with this case."

The reporter nodded.

"When Mr Fraser recovers I intend to hold a little party here," the scientist continued. "It will be a surprise party."

It was two days later, and the police were apparently seeking some tangible point from which they could proceed, when The Thinking Machine received word that there had been a change for the better in Mr Fraser's condition. Immediately he sent for Detective Mallory, with whom he held a long conversation. The detective went away tugging at his heavy mustache and smiling. With three other men he disappeared from police haunts that afternoon on a special mission.

That night the little "party" was held in the apartments of The Thinking Machine. President Fraser was first to arrive. He was pale and weak, but there was a fever of impatience in his manner. Then came West, Dunston, Miss Clarke, Miss Willis and Charles Burton, a clerk whose engagement to the pretty Miss Willis had been recently announced.

The party gathered, each staring at the other curiously, with questions in their eyes, until The Thinking Machine entered, rubbing his fingers together briskly. Behind him came

Hatch, bearing a shabby gripsack. The reporter's face showed excitement despite his rigid efforts to repress it. There were some preliminaries, and then the scientist began.

"To come to the matter quickly," he said, in preface, "we will take it for granted that no employee of the Ralston Bank is a professional burglar. But the person who was responsible for that burglary, who shared the money stolen, who planned it and actually assisted in its execution is in this room – now."

Instantly there was consternation, but it found no expression in words, only in the faces of those present.

"Further, I may inform you," went on the scientist, "that no one will be permitted to leave this room until I finish."

"Permitted?" demanded Dunston. "We are not prisoners."

"You will be if I give the word," was the response, and Dunston sat back, dazed. He glanced uneasily at the faces of the others; they glanced uneasily at him.

"The actual facts in the robbery you know," went on The Thinking Machine. "You know that the safe was blown, that a large sum of money was stolen, that Mr West's handkerchief was found near the safe. Now, I'll tell you what I have learned. We will begin with President Fraser.

"Against Mr Fraser is more direct evidence than against anyone else, because in his pocket was found one of the stolen bundles of money, containing ten thousand dollars. Mr Fraser needed ninety thousand dollars previous to the robbery."

"But—" began the old man, with deathlike face.

"Never mind," said the scientist. "Next, Miss Willis." Curious eyes were turned on her, and she, too, grew suddenly white. "Against her is less direct evidence than against anyone else. Miss Willis positively declined to permit a search of her person until she was as compelled to do so by the fact that the other two permitted it. The fact that nothing was found has no bearing on the subject. She did refuse.

"Then Charles Burton," the inexorable voice went on, calmly, as if in mere discussion of a problem of mathematics.

MYSTERY OF THE RALSTON BANK

"Burton is engaged to Miss Willis. He is ambitious. He recently lost twenty thousand dollars in stock speculation – all he had. He needed more money in order to give this girl, who refused to be searched, a comfortable home.

"Next Miss Clarke, secretary to Mr Fraser. Originally she came under consideration through the fact that she used perfume, and that Mr West's handkerchief carried a faint odor of perfume. Now it is a fact that for years Miss Clarke used violet perfume, then on the day following the robbery suddenly began to use strong rose perfume, which smothers a violet odor. Miss Clarke, you will remember, fainted at the time of the search. I may add that a short while ago she was employed in a bank which was robbed in the identical manner of this one."

Miss Clarke sat apparently calm, and even faintly smiling, but her face was white. The Thinking Machine squinted at her a moment, then turned suddenly to Cashier West.

"Here is the man," he said, "whose handkerchief was found, but he does not use perfume, has never used it. He is the man who would have had best opportunity to leave unfastened the window in his private office by which the thieves entered the bank; he is the man who would have had the best opportunity to apply a certain chemical solution to the granite sockets of the steel bars, weakening the granite so they could be pulled out; he is the man who misrepresented facts to me. He told me he did not have and had not tried to raise any especially large sum of money. Yet on the day following the robbery he deposited one hundred and twenty-five thousand dollars in cash in a bank in Chicago. The stolen sum was one hundred and twenty-nine thousand dollars. That man, there."

All eyes were now turned on the cashier. He seemed choking, started to speak, then dropped back into his chair.

"And last, Dunston," resumed The Thinking Machine, and he pointed dramatically at the receiving teller. "He had equal opportunity with Mr West to know of the amount of money in the bank; he refused first to be searched, and you witnessed his act a moment ago. To this man now there clings the identical odor of violet perfume which was on the handkerchief – not a perfume like it, but the identical odor."

There was silence, dumfounded silence, for a long time. No one dared to look at his neighbor now; the reporter felt the tension. At last The Thinking Machine spoke again.

"As I have said, the person who planned and participated in the burglary is now in this room. If that person will stand forth and confess it will mean a vast difference in the length of the term in prison."

Again silence. At last there came a knock at the door, and Martha thrust her head in.

"Two gentlemen and four cops are here," she announced.

"There are the accomplices of the guilty person, the men who actually blew that safe," declared the scientist, dramatically. "Again, will the guilty person confess?"

No one stirred.

VI

There was tense silence for a moment. Dunston was the first to speak.

"This is all a bluff," he said. "I think, Mr Fraser, there are some explanations and apologies due to all of us, particularly to Miss Clarke and Miss Willis," he added, as an afterthought. "It is humiliating, and no good has been done. I had intended asking Miss Clarke to be my wife, and now I assert my right to speak for her. I demand an apology."

Carried away by his own anger and by the pleading face of Miss Clarke and the pain there, the young man turned fiercely on The Thinking Machine. Bewilderment was on the faces of the two banking officials.

"You feel that an explanation is due?" asked The Thinking Machine, meekly.

MYSTERY OF THE RALSTON BANK

"Yes," thundered the young man.

"You shall have it," was the quiet answer, and the stooped figure of the scientist moved across the room to the door. He said something to some one outside and returned.

"Again I'll give you a chance for a confession," he said. "It will shorten your prison term." He was speaking to no one in particular; yet to them all. "The two men who blew the safe are now about to enter this room. After they appear it will be too late."

Startled glances were exchanged, but no one stirred. Then came a knock at the door. Silently The Thinking Machine looked about with a question in his eyes. Still silence, and he threw open the door. Three policemen in uniform and Detective Mallory entered, bringing two prisoners.

"These are the men who blew the safe," The Thinking Machine explained, indicating the prisoners. "Does anyone here recognize them?"

Apparently no one did, for none spoke.

"Do you recognize any person in this room?" he asked of the prisoners.

One of them laughed shortly and said something aside to the other, who smiled. The Thinking Machine was nettled and when he spoke again there was a touch of sarcasm in his voice.

"It may enlighten at least one of you in this room," he said, "to tell you that these two men are Frank Seranno and Gustave Meyer, Mr Meyer being a pupil and former associate of the notorious bank burglar, William Dineen. You may lock them up now," he said to Detective Mallory. "They will confess later."

"Confess!" exclaimed one of them. Both laughed.

The prisoners were led out and Detective Mallory returned to lave in the font of analytical wisdom, although he would not have expressed it in those words. Then The Thinking Machine began at the beginning and told his story.

"I undertook to throw some light on this affair a few hours after its occurrence, at the request of President Fraser, who had once been able to do me a very great favour," he explained. "I went to the bank – you all saw me there – looked over the premises, saw how the thieves had entered the building, looked at the safe and at the spot where the handkerchief was found. To my mind it was demonstrated clearly that the handkerchief appeared there at the time of the burglary. I inquired if there was any draught through the office, seeking in that way to find if the handkerchief might have been lost at some other place in the bank, overlooked by the sweeper and blown to the spot where it was found. There was no draught.

"Next I asked for the handkerchief. Mr Fraser asked me into his office to look at it. I saw a woman – Miss Clarke it was – in there and declined to go. Instead, I examined the handkerchief outside. I don't know that my purpose there can be made clear to you. It was a possibility that there would be perfume on the handkerchief, and the woman in the office might use perfume. I didn't want to confuse the odors. Miss Clarke was not in the bank when I arrived; she had gone to luncheon.

"Instantly I got the handkerchief I noticed the odor of perfume – violet perfume. Perfume is used by a great many women, by very few men. I asked how many women were employed in the bank. There were three. I handed the scented handkerchief to Mr Hatch, removed all odor of the clinging perfume from my hands with my own handkerchief and also handed that to Mr Hatch, so as to completely rid myself of the odor.

"Then I started through the bank and spoke to every person in it, standing close to them so that I might catch the odor if they used it. Miss Clarke was the first person who I found used it – but the perfume she used was a strong rose odor. Then I went on until I came to Mr Dunston. The identical odor of the handkerchief he revealed to me by drawing out his own handkerchief while I talked to him."

MYSTERY OF THE RALSTON BANK 233

Dunston looked a little startled, but said nothing; instead he glanced at Miss Clarke, who sat listening, interestedly. He could not read the expression on her face.

"This much done," continued The Thinking Machine, "we retired to Cashier West's office. There I knew the burglars had entered; there I saw a powerful chemical solution had been applied to the granite around the sockets of the protecting steel bars to soften the stone. Its direct effect is to make it of chalklike consistency. I was also curious to know if any noise made in that room would attract attention in the outer office, so I upset a heavy chair, then looked outside. No one moved or looked back; therefore no one heard.

"Here I explained to President Fraser and to Mr West why I connected some one in the bank with the burglary. It was because of the scent on the handkerchief. It would be tedious to repeat the detailed explanation I had to give them. I sent Mr Hatch to find out, first, if Miss Clarke here had ever used violet perfume instead of rose; also to find out if any members of Mr West's family used any perfume, particularly violet. I knew that Mr Dunston used it.

"Then I asked Mr Fraser if he had sought to raise any large sum of money. He told me the truth. But Mr West did not tell me the truth in answer to a question along the same lines. Now I know why. It was because as cashier of the bank he was not supposed to operate in stocks, yet he has made a fortune at it. He didn't want Fraser to know this, and willfully misrepresented the facts.

"Then came the search. I expected to find just what was found, money, but considerably more of it. Miss Willis objected, Mr Dunston objected and Miss Clarke fainted in the arms of Mr Fraser. I read the motives of each aright. Dunston objected because he is an egotistical young man and, being young, is foolish. He considered it an insult. Miss Willis objected also through a feeling of pride."

The Thinking Machine paused for a moment, locked his fingers behind his head and leaned far back in his chair.

"Shall I tell what happened next?" he asked, "or will you tell it?"

Everyone in the room knew it was a question to the guilty person. Which? Whom? There came no answer, and after a moment The Thinking Machine resumed, quietly, very quietly.

"Miss Clarke fainted in Mr Fraser's arms. While leaning against him, and while he stroked her hair and tried to soothe her, she took from the bosom of her loose shirtwaist a bundle of money, ten thousand dollars, and slipped it into the inside pocket of Mr Fraser's coat."

There was deathlike silence.

"It's a lie!" screamed the girl, and she rose to her feet with anger-distorted face. "It's a lie!"

Dunston arose suddenly and went to her. With his arm about her he turned defiantly to The Thinking Machine, who had not moved or altered his position in the slightest. Dunston said nothing, because there seemed to be nothing to say.

"Into the inside pocket of Mr Fraser's coat," The Thinking Machine repeated. "When she removed her arms his scarf pin clung to the lace on one of her sleeves. That I saw. That pin could not have caught on her sleeve where it did if her hand had not been to the coat pocket. Having passed this sum of money – her pitiful share of the theft – she agreed to the search."

"It's a lie!" shrieked the girl again. And her every tone and every gesture said it was the truth. Dunston gazed into her eyes with horror in his own and his arm fell limply. Still he said nothing.

"Of course nothing was found," the quiet voice went on. "When I discovered the bank notes in Mr Fraser's pocket I smelled of them – seeking the odor, this time not of violet perfume, but of rose perfume. I found it."

MYSTERY OF THE RALSTON BANK 235

Suddenly the girl whose face had shown only anger and defiance leaned over with her head in her hands and wept bitterly. It was a confession. Dunston stood beside her, helplessly; finally his hand was slowly extended and he stroked her hair.

"Go on, please," he said to Professor Van Dusen, meekly. His suffering was no less than hers.

"These facts were important, but not conclusive," said The Thinking Machine, "so next, with Mr Hatch's aid here, I ascertained other things about Miss Clarke. I found out that when she went out to luncheon that day she purchased some powerful rose perfume; that, contrary to custom, she went home; that she used it liberally in her room; and that she destroyed a large bottle of violet perfume which you, Mr Dunston, had given her. I ascertained also that her room was disarranged, particularly the couch. I assume from this that when she went to the office in the morning she did not have the money about her; that she left it hidden in the couch; that through fear of its discovery she rushed back home to get it; that she put it inside her shirtwaist, and there she had it when the search was made. Am I right, Miss Clarke?"

The girl nodded her head and looked up with piteous, tear-stained face.

"That night Miss Clarke called on me. She came ostensibly to tell me that the package of money, ten thousand dollars, had disappeared again. I knew that previously by telephone, and I knew, too, that she had that money then about her. She has it now. Will you give it up?"

Without a word the girl drew out the bundle of money, ten thousand dollars. Detective Mallory took it, held it, amazed for an instant, then passed it to The Thinking Machine, who sniffed at it.

"An odor of strong rose perfume," he said. Then: "Miss Clarke also told me that she had worked in a bank which had been robbed under circumstances identical with this by one William Dineen, and expressed the belief that he had something to do with this. Mr Hatch ascertained that two of Dineen's pals were living in Cambridge. He found their rooms and searched them, later giving the address to the police.

"Now, why did Miss Clarke tell me that? I considered it in all points. She told me either to aid honestly in the effort to catch the thief, or to divert suspicion in another direction. Knowing as much as I did then, I reasoned it was to divert suspicion from you, Mr Dunston, and from herself possibly. Dineen is in prison, and was there three months before this robbery; I believed she knew that. His pals are the two men in the other room; they are the men who aided Dineen in the robbery of the Hartford bank, with Miss Clarke's assistance; they are the men who robbed the Ralston National with her assistance. She herself indicated her profit from the Hartford robbery to me by a remark she made indicating that she had not found it necessary to work for two years from the time she left the Hartford bank until she became Mr Fraser's secretary."

There was a pause. Miss Clarke sat sobbing, while Dunston stood near her studying the toe of his shoe. After awhile the girl became more calm.

"Miss Clarke, would you like to explain anything?" asked The Thinking Machine. His voice was gentle, even deferential.

"Nothing," she said, "except admit it all—all. I have nothing to conceal. I went to the bank, as I went to the bank in Hartford, for the purpose of robbery, with the assistance of those men in the next room. We have worked together for years. I planned this robbery; I had the opportunity, and availed myself of it, to put a solution on the sockets of the steel bars of the window in Mr West's room, which would gradually destroy the granite and make it possible to pull out the bars. This took weeks, but I could reach that room safely from Mr Fraser's.

MYSTERY OF THE RALSTON BANK

"I had the opportunity to leave the window unfastened and did so. I dressed in men's clothing and accompanied those two men to the bank. We crept in the window, after pulling the bars out. The men attacked the night watchman and bound him. The handkerchief of Mr West's I happened to pick up in the office one afternoon a month ago and took it home. There it got the odor of perfume from being in a bureau with my things. On the night we went to the bank I needed something to put about my neck and used it. In the bank I dropped it. We had arranged all details at night, when I met them."

She stopped and looked at Dunston, a long, lingering look, that sent the blood to his face. It was not an appeal; it was nothing save the woman love in her, mingled with desperation.

"I intended to leave the bank in a little while," she went on. "Not immediately, because I was afraid that would attract attention, but after a few weeks. And then, too, I wanted to get forever out of sight of this man," and she indicated Dunston.

"Why?" he asked.

"Because I loved you as no woman ever loved a man before," she said, "and I was not worthy. There was another reason, too – I am married already. This man, Gustave Meyer, is my husband."

She paused and fumbled nervously at the veil fastening at her throat. Silence lay over the room; The Thinking Machine reached behind him and picked up the shabby-looking gripsack which had passed unnoticed.

"Are there any more questions?" the girl asked, at last.

"I think not," said The Thinking Machine.

"And, Mr Dunston, you will give me credit for some good, won't you – some good in that I loved you?" she pleaded.

"My God!" he exclaimed in a sudden burst of feeling.

"Look out!" shouted The Thinking Machine.

He had seen the girl's hand fly to her hat, saw it drawn suddenly away, saw something slender flash at her breast. But it was too late. She had driven a heavy hat pin straight through her breast, piercing the heart. She died in the arms of the man she loved, with his tears on her face.

Detective Mallory appeared before the two prisoners in an adjoining room.

"Miss Clarke has confessed," he said.

"Well, the little devil!" exclaimed Meyer. "I knew some day she would throw us. I'll kill her!"

"It isn't necessary," remarked Mallory.

In the room where the girl lay The Thinking Machine pushed with his foot the shabby-looking grip toward President Fraser and West.

"There's the money," he said.

"Where – how did you get it?"

"Ask Mr Hatch."

"Professor Van Dusen told me to search the rooms of those men in there, find the shabbiest looking bag or receptacle that was securely locked, and bring it to him. I – I did so. I found it under the bed, but I didn't know what was in it until he opened it."

11

MYSTERY OF THE SCARLET THREAD

I

The Thinking Machine-Professor Augustus S. F. X. Van Dusen, Ph.D, LL.D., F.R.S., M.D., etc., scientist and logician-listened intently and without comment to a weird, seemingly inexplicable story. Hutchinson Hatch, reporter, was telling it. The bowed figure of the savant lay at ease in a large chair. The enormous head with its bushy yellow hair was thrown back, the thin, white fingers were pressed tip to tip and the blue eyes, narrowed to mere slits, squinted aggressively upward. The scientist was in a receptive mood.

"From the beginning, every fact you know," he had requested.

"It's all out in the Back Bay," the reporter explained. "There is a big apartment house there, a fashionable establishment, in a side street, just off Commonwealth Avenue. It is five stories in all, and is cut up into small suites, of two and three rooms with a bath. These suites are handsomely, even luxuriously furnished, and are occupied by people who can afford to pay big rents. Generally these are young unmarried men, although in several cases they are husband and wife. It is a house of every modern improvement, elevator service, hall boys, liveried door men, spacious corridors and all that. It has both the gas and electric systems of lighting. Tenants are at liberty to use either or both.

"A young broker, Weldon Henley, occupies one of the handsomest of these suites, being on the second floor, in front. He has met with considerable success in the Street. He is a bachelor and lives there alone. There is no personal servant. He dabbles in photography as a hobby, and is said to be remarkably expert.

"Recently there was a report that he was to be married this Winter to a beautiful Virginia girl who has been visiting Boston from time to time, a Miss Lipscomb–Charlotte Lipscomb, of Richmond. Henley has never denied or affirmed this rumor, although he has been asked about it often. Miss Lipscomb is impossible of access even when she visits Boston. Now she is in Virginia, I understand, but will return to Boston later in the season."

The reporter paused, lighted a cigarette and leaned forward in his chair, gazing steadily into the inscrutable eyes of the scientist.

"When Henley took the suite he requested that all the electric lighting apparatus be removed from his apartments," he went on. "He had taken a long lease of the place, and this was done. Therefore he uses only gas for lighting purposes, and he usually keeps one of his gas jets burning low all night."

"Bad, bad for his health," commented the scientist.

"Now comes the mystery of the affair," the reporter went on. "It was five weeks or so ago Henley retired as usual – about midnight. He locked his door on the inside – he is positive of that – and awoke about four o'clock in the morning nearly asphyxiated by gas. He was barely able to get up and open the window to let in the fresh air. The gas jet he had left burning was out, and the suite was full of gas."

"Accident, possibly," said The Thinking Machine. "A draught through the apartments; a slight diminution of gas pressure; a hundred possibilities."

"So it was presumed," said the reporter. "Of course it would have been impossible for—"

"Nothing is impossible," said the other, tartly. "Don't say that. It annoys me exceedingly."

"Well, then, it seems highly improbable that the door had been opened or that anyone came into the room and did this deliberately," the newspaper man went on, with a slight smile. "So Henley said nothing about this; attributed it to accident. The next night he lighted his gas as usual, but he left it burning a little brighter. The same thing happened again."

"Ah," and The Thinking Machine changed his position a little. "The second time."

"And again he awoke just in time to save himself," said Hatch. "Still he attributed the affair to accident, and determined to avoid a recurrence of the affair by doing away with the gas at night. Then he got a small night lamp and used this for a week or more."

"Why does he have a light at all?" asked the scientist, testily.

"I can hardly answer that," replied Hatch. "I may say, however, that he is of a very nervous temperament, and gets up frequently during the night. He reads occasionally when he can't sleep. In addition to that he has slept with a light going all his life; it's a habit."

"Go on."

"One night he looked for the night lamp, but it had disappeared – at least he couldn't find it – so he lighted the gas again. The fact of the gas having twice before gone out had been dismissed as a serious possibility. Next morning at five o'clock a bell boy, passing through the hall, smelled gas and made a quick investigation. He decided it came from Henley's place, and rapped on the door. There was no answer. It ultimately developed that it was necessary to smash in the door. There on the bed they found Henley unconscious with the gas pouring into the room from the jet which he had left lighted. He was revived in the air, but for several hours was deathly sick."

"Why was the door smashed in?" asked The Thinking Machine. "Why not unlocked?"

"It was done because Henley had firmly barred it," Hatch explained. "He had become suspicious, I suppose, and after the second time he always barred his door and fastened every window before he went to sleep. There may have been a fear that some one used a key to enter."

"Well?" asked the scientist. "After that?"

"Three weeks or so elapsed, bringing the affair down to this morning," Hatch went on. "Then the same thing happened a little differently. For instance, after the third time the gas went out Henley decided to find out for himself what caused it, and so expressed himself to a few friends who knew of the mystery. Then, night after night, he lighted the gas as usual and kept watch. It was never disturbed during all that time, burning steadily all night. What sleep he got was in daytime.

"Last night Henley lay awake for a time; then, exhausted and tired, fell asleep. This morning early he awoke; the room was filled with gas again. In some way my city editor heard of it and asked me to look into the mystery."

That was all. The two men were silent for a long time, and finally The Thinking Machine turned to the reporter.

"Does anyone else in the house keep gas going all night?" he asked.

"I don't know," was the reply. "Most of them, I know, use electricity."

"Nobody else has been overcome as he has been?"

"No. Plumbers have minutely examined the lighting system all over the house and found nothing wrong."

"Does the gas in the house all come through the same meter?"

"Yes, so the manager told me. I supposed it possible that some one shut it off there on these nights long enough to extinguish the lights all over the house, then turned it on again. That is, presuming that it was done purposely. Do you think it was an attempt to kill Henley?"

"It might be," was the reply. "Find out for me just who in the house uses gas; also if anyone else leaves a light burning all night; also what opportunity anyone would have to get at the meter, and then something about Henley's love affair with Miss Lipscomb. Is there anyone else? If so, who? Where does he live? When you find out these things come back here."

That afternoon at one o'clock Hatch returned to the apartments of The Thinking Machine, with excitement plainly apparent on his face.

"Well?" asked the scientist.

"A French girl, Louise Regnier, employed as a maid by Mrs Standing in the house, was found dead in her room on the third floor today at noon," Hatch explained quickly. "It looks like suicide."

"How?" asked The Thinking Machine.

"The people who employed her—husband and wife – have been away for a couple of days," Hatch rushed on. "She was in the suite alone. This noon she had not appeared, there was an odor of gas and the door was broken in. Then she was found dead."

"With the gas turned on?"

"With the gas turned on. She was asphyxiated."

"Dear me, dear me," exclaimed the scientist. He arose and took up his hat. "Let's go and see what this is all about."

II

When Professor Van Dusen and Hatch arrived at the apartment house they had been preceded by the Medical Examiner and the police. Detective Mallory, whom both knew, was moving about in the apartment where the girl had been found dead. The body had been removed and a telegram sent to her employers in New York.

"Too late," said Mallory, as they entered.

"What was it, Mr Mallory?" asked the scientist.

"Suicide," was the reply. "No question of it. It happened in this room," and he led the way into the third room of the suite. "The maid, Miss Regnier, occupied this, and was here alone last night. Mr and Mrs Standing, her employers, have gone to New York for a few days. She was left alone, and killed herself."

Without further questioning The Thinking Machine went over to the bed, from which the girl's body had been taken, and, stooping beside it, picked up a book. It was a novel by "The Duchess." He examined this critically, then, standing on a chair, he examined the gas jet. This done, he stepped down and went to the window of the little room. Finally The Thinking Machine turned to the detective.

"Just how much was the gas turned on?" he asked.

"Turned on full," was the reply.

"Were both the doors of the room locked?"

"Both, yes."

"Any cotton, or cloth, or anything of the sort stuffed in the cracks of the window?"

"No. It's a tight-fitting window, anyway. Are you trying to make a mystery out of this?"

"Cracks in the doors stuffed?" The Thinking Machine went on.

"No." There was a smile about the detective's lips.

The Thinking Machine, on his knees, examined the bottom of one of the doors, that which led into the hall. The lock of this door had been broken when employees burst into the room. Having satisfied himself here and at the bottom of the other door, which connected with the bedroom adjoining, The Thinking Machine again climbed on a chair and examined the doors at the top.

"Both transoms closed, I suppose?" he asked.

"Yes," was the reply. "You can't make anything but suicide out of it," explained the detective. "The Medical Examiner has given that as his opinion – and everything I find indicates it."

"All right," broke in The Thinking Machine abruptly. "Don't let us keep you."

After awhile Detective Mallory went away. Hatch and the scientist went down to the office floor, where they saw the manager. He seemed to be greatly distressed, but was willing to do anything he could in the matter.

"Is your night engineer perfectly trustworthy?" asked The Thinking Machine.

"Perfectly," was the reply. "One of the best and most reliable men I ever met. Alert and wide-awake."

"Can I see him a moment? The night man, I mean?"

"Certainly," was the reply. "He's downstairs. He sleeps there. He's probably up by this time. He sleeps usually till one o'clock in the daytime, being up all night."

"Do you supply gas for your tenants?"

"Both gas and electricity are included in the rent of the suites. Tenants may use one or both."

"And the gas all comes through one meter?"

"Yes, one meter. It's just off the engine room."

"I suppose there's no way of telling just who in the house uses gas?"

"No. Some do and some don't. I don't know."

This was what Hatch had told the scientist. Now together they went to the basement, and there met the night engineer, Charles Burlingame, a tall, powerful, clean-cut man, of alert manner and positive speech. He gazed with a little amusement at the slender, almost childish figure of The Thinking Machine and the grotesquely large head.

"You are in the engine room or near it all night every night?" began The Thinking Machine.

"I haven't missed a night in four years," was the reply.

"Anybody ever come here to see you at night?"

"Never. It's against the rules."

"The manager or a hall boy?"

"Never."

"In the last two months?" The Thinking Machine persisted.

"Not in the last two years," was the positive reply. "I go on duty every night at seven o'clock, and I am on duty until seven in the morning. I don't believe I've seen anybody in the basement here with me between those hours for a year at least."

The Thinking Machine was squinting steadily into the eyes of the engineer, and for a time both were silent. Hatch moved about the scrupulously clean engine room and nodded to the day engineer, who sat leaning back against the wall. Directly in front of him was the steam gauge.

"Have you a fireman?" was The Thinking Machine's next question.

"No. I fire myself," said the night man. "Here's the coal," and he indicated a bin within half a dozen feet of the mouth of the boiler.

"I don't suppose you ever had occasion to handle the gas meter?" insisted The Thinking Machine.

"Never touched it in my life," said the other. "I don't know anything about meters, anyway."

"And you never drop off to sleep at night for a few minutes when you get lonely? Doze, I mean?"

The engineer grinned good-naturedly.

"Never had any desire to, and besides I wouldn't have the chance," he explained. "There's a time check here," – and he indicated it. "I have to punch that every half hour all night to prove that I have been awake."

"Dear me, dear me," exclaimed The Thinking Machine, irritably. He went over and examined the time check – a revolving paper disk with hours marked on it, made to move by the action of a clock, the face of which showed in the middle.

"Besides there's the steam gauge to watch," went on the engineer. "No engineer would dare go to sleep. There might be an explosion."

"Do you know Mr Weldon Henley?" suddenly asked The Thinking Machine.

"Who?" asked Burlingame.

"Weldon Henley?"

"No-o," was the slow response. "Never heard of him. Who is he?"

"One of the tenants, on the second floor, I think."

"Lord, I don't know any of the tenants. What about him?"

"When does the inspector come here to read the meter?"

"I never saw him. I presume in daytime, eh Bill?" and he turned to the day engineer.

"Always in the daytime – usually about noon," said Bill from his corner.

"Any other entrance to the basement except this way – and you could see anyone coming here this way I suppose?"

"Sure I could see 'em. There's no other entrance to the cellar except the coal hole in the sidewalk in front."

"Two big electric lights in front of the building, aren't there?"

"Yes. They go all night."

A slightly puzzled expression crept into the eyes of The Thinking Machine. Hatch knew from the persistency of the questions that he was not satisfied; yet he was not able to fathom or to understand all the queries. In some way they had to do with the possibility of some one having access to the meter.

"Where do you usually sit at night here?" was the next question.

"Over there where Bill's sitting. I always sit there."

The Thinking Machine crossed the room to Bill, a typical, grimy-handed man of his class.

"May I sit there a moment?" he asked.

Bill arose lazily, and The Thinking Machine sank down into the chair. From this point he could see plainly through the opening into the basement proper – there was no door – the gas meter of enormous proportions through which all the gas in the house passed. An electric light in the door made it bright as daylight. The Thinking Machine noted these things, arose, nodded his thanks to the two men and, still with the puzzled expression on his face, led the way upstairs. There the manager was still in his office.

"I presume you examine and know that the time check in the engineer's room is properly punched every half-hour during the night?" he asked.

"Yes. I examine the dial every day – have them here, in fact, each with the date on it."

"May I see them?"

Now the manager was puzzled. He produced the cards, one for each day, and for half an hour The Thinking Machine studied them minutely. At the end of that time, when he arose and Hatch looked at him inquiringly, he saw still the perplexed expression.

After urgent solicitation, the manager admitted them to the apartments of Weldon Henley. Mr Henley himself had gone to his office in State Street. Here The Thinking Machine did several things which aroused the curiosity of the manager, one of which was to minutely study the gas jets. Then The Thinking

MYSTERY OF THE SCARLET THREAD

Machine opened one of the front windows and glanced out into the street. Below fifteen feet was the sidewalk; above was the solid front of the building, broken only by a flagpole which, properly roped, extended from the hall window of the next floor above out over the sidewalk a distance of twelve feet or so.

"Ever use that flagpole?" he asked the manager.

"Rarely," said the manager. "On holidays sometimes – Fourth of July and such times. We have a big flag for it."

From the apartments The Thinking Machine led the way to the hall, up the stairs and to the flagpole. Leaning out of this window, he looked down toward the window of the apartments he had just left. Then he inspected the rope of the flagpole, drawing it through his slender hands slowly and carefully. At last he picked off a slender thread of scarlet and examined it.

"Ah," he exclaimed. Then to Hatch: "Let's go, Mr Hatch. Thank you," this last to the manager, who had been a puzzled witness.

Once on the street, side by side with The Thinking Machine, Hatch was bursting with questions, but he didn't ask them. He knew it would be useless. At last The Thinking Machine broke the silence.

"That girl, Miss Regnier, was murdered," he said suddenly, positively. "There have been four attempts to murder Henley."

"How?" asked Hatch, startled.

"By a scheme so simple that neither you nor I nor the police have ever heard of it being employed," was the astonishing reply. "It is perfectly horrible in its simplicity."

"What was it?" Hatch insisted, eagerly.

"It would be futile to discuss that now," was the rejoinder. "There has been murder. We know how. Now the question is – who? What person would have a motive to kill Henley?"

III

There was a pause as they walked on.

"Where are we going?" asked Hatch finally.

"Come up to my place and let's consider this matter a bit further," replied The Thinking Machine.

Not another word was spoken by either until half an hour later, in the small laboratory. For a long time the scientist was thoughtful – deeply thoughtful. Once he took down a volume from a shelf and Hatch glanced at the title. It was "Gases: Their Properties." After awhile he returned this to the shelf and took down another, on which the reporter caught the title, "Anatomy."

"Now, Mr Hatch," said The Thinking Machine in his perpetually crabbed voice, "we have a most remarkable riddle. It gains this remarkable aspect from its very simplicity. It is not, however, necessary to go into that now. I will make it clear to you when we know the motives.

"As a general rule, the greatest crimes never come to light because the greatest criminals, their perpetrators, are too clever to be caught. Here we have what I might call a great crime committed with a subtle simplicity that is wholly disarming, and a greater crime even than this was planned. This was to murder Weldon Henley. The first thing for you to do is to see Mr Henley and warn him of his danger. Asphyxiation will not be attempted again, but there is the possibility of poison, a pistol shot, a knife, anything almost. As a matter of fact, he is in great peril.

"Superficially, the death of Miss Regnier, the maid, looks to be suicide. Instead it is the fruition of a plan which has been tried time and again against Henley. There is a possibility that Miss Regnier was not an intentional victim of the plot, but the fact remains that she was murdered. Why? Find the motive for the plot to murder Mr Henley and you will know why."

The Thinking Machine reached over to the shelf, took a book, looked at it a moment, then went on:

"The first question to determine positively is: Who hated Weldon Henley sufficiently to desire his death? You say he is a successful man in the Street. Therefore there is a possibility that some enemy there is at the bottom of the affair, yet it seems hardly probable. If by his operations Mr Henley ever happened to wreck another man's fortune find this man and find out all about him. He may be the man. There will be innumerable questions arising from this line of inquiry to a man of your resources. Leave none of them unanswered.

"On the other hand there is Henley's love affair. Had he a rival who might desire his death? Had he any rival? If so, find out all about him. He may be the man who planned all this. Here, too, there will be questions arising which demand answers. Answer them – all of them – fully and clearly before you see me again.

"Was Henley ever a party to a liason of any kind? Find that out, too. A vengeful woman or a discarded sweetheart of a vengeful woman, you know, will go to any extreme. The rumor of his engagement to Miss-Miss—"

"Miss Lipscomb," Hatch supplied.

"The rumor of his engagement to Miss Lipscomb might have caused a woman whom he had once been interested in or who was once interested in him to attempt his life. The subtler murders – that is, the ones which are most attractive as problems – are nearly always the work of a cunning woman. I know nothing about women myself," he hastened to explain; "But Lombroso has taken that attitude. Therefore, see if there is a woman."

Most of these points Hatch had previously seen – seen with the unerring eye of a clever newspaper reporter – yet there were several which had not occurred to him. He nodded his understanding.

"Now the center of the affair, of course," The Thinking Machine continued, "is the apartment house where Henley lives. The person who attempted his life either lives there or has ready access to the place, and frequently spends the night there. This is a vital question for you to answer. I am leaving all this to you because you know better how to do these things than I do. That's all, I think. When these things are all learned come back to me."

The Thinking Machine arose as if the interview were at an end, and Hatch also arose, reluctantly. An idea was beginning to dawn in his mind.

"Does there occur to you that there is any connection whatever between Henley and Miss Regnier?" he asked.

"It is possible," was the reply. "I had thought of that. If there is a connection it is not apparent yet."

"Then how — how was it she — she was killed, or killed herself, whichever may be true, and —"

"The attempt to kill Henley killed her. That's all I can say now."

"That all?" asked Hatch, after a pause.

"No. Warn Mr Henley immediately that he is in grave danger. Remember the person who has planned this will probably go to any extreme. I don't know Mr Henley, of course, but from the fact that he always had a light at night I gather that he is a timid sort of man – not necessarily a coward, but a man lacking in stamina – therefore, one who might better disappear for a week or so until the mystery is cleared up. Above all, impress upon him the importance of the warning."

The Thinking Machine opened his pocketbook and took from it the scarlet thread which he had picked from the rope of the flagpole.

"Here, I believe, is the real clew to the problem," he explained to Hatch. "What does it seem to be?"

Hatch examined it closely.

"I should say a strand from a Turkish bath robe," was his final judgement.

"Possibly. Ask some cloth expert what he makes of it, then if it sounds promising look into it. Find out if by any possibility it can be any part of any garment worn by any person in the apartment house."

"But it's so slight—" Hatch began.

"I know," the other interrupted, tartly. "It's slight, but I believe it is a part of the wearing apparel of the person, man or woman, who has four times attempted to kill Mr Henley and who did kill the girl. Therefore, it is important."

Hatch looked at him quickly.

"Well, how – in what manner – did it come where you found it?"

"Simple enough," said the scientist. "It is a wonder that there were not more pieces of it – that's all."

Perplexed by his instructions. But confident of results, Hatch left The Thinking Machine. What possible connection could this tiny bit of scarlet thread, found on a flagpole, have with one shutting off the gas in Henley's rooms? How did anyone go into Henley's rooms to shut off the gas? How was it Miss Regnier was dead? What was the manner of her death?

A cloth expert in a great department store turned his knowledge on the tiny bit of scarlet for the illumination of Hatch, but he could go no further than to say that it seemed to be part of a Turkish bath robe.

"Man or woman's?" asked Hatch.

"The material from which bath robes are made is the same for both men and women," was the reply. "I can say nothing else. Of course there's not enough of it to even guess at the pattern of the robe."

Then Hatch went to the financial district and was ushered into the office of Weldon Henley, a slender, handsome man of thirty-two or three years, pallid of face and nervous in manner.

He still showed the effect of the gas poisoning, and there was even a trace of a furtive fear—fear of something, he himself didn't know what—in his actions.

Henley talked freely to the newspaper man of certain things, but of other things he was resentfully reticent. He admitted his engagement to Miss Lipscomb, and finally even admitted that Miss Lipscomb's hand had been sought by another man, Regnault Cabell, formerly of Virginia.

"Could you give me his address?" asked Hatch.

"He lives in the same apartment house with me – two floors above," was the reply.

Hatch was startled; startled more than he would have cared to admit.

"Are you on friendly terms with him?" he asked.

"Certainly," said Henley. "I won't say anything further about this matter. It would be unwise for obvious reasons."

"I suppose you consider that this turning on of the gas was an attempt on your life?"

"I can't suppose anything else."

Hatch studied the pallid face closely as he asked the next question.

"Do you know Miss Regnier was found dead today?"

"Dead?" exclaimed the other, and he arose. "Who—what—who is she?"

It seemed a distinct effort for him to regain control of himself.

The reporter detailed then the circumstances of the finding of the girl's body, and the broker listened without comment. From that time forward all the reporter's questions were either parried or else met with a flat refusal to answer. Finally Hatch repeated to him the warning which he had from The Thinking Machine, and feeling that he had accomplished little, went away.

At eight o'clock that night—a night of complete darkness— Henley was found unconscious, lying in a little used walk in the

Common. There was a bullet hole through his left shoulder, and he was bleeding profusely. He was removed to the hospital, where he regained consciousness for just a moment.

"Who shot you?" he was asked.

"None of your business," he replied, and lapsed into unconsciousness.

IV

Entirely unaware of this latest attempt on the life of the broker, Hutchinson Hatch steadily pursued his investigations. They finally led him to an intimate friend of Regnault Cabell. The young Southerner had apartments on the fourth floor of the big house off Commonwealth Avenue, directly over those Henley occupied, but two flights higher up. This friend was a figure in the social set of the Back Bay. He talked to Hatch freely of Cabell.

"He's a good fellow," he explained, "one of the best I ever met, and comes of one of the best families Virginia ever had – a true F. F. V. He's pretty quick tempered and all that, but an excellent chap, and everywhere he has gone here he has made friends."

"He used to be in love with Miss Lipscomb of Virginia, didn't he?" asked Hatch, casually.

"Used to be?" the other repeated with a laugh. "He is in love with her. But recently he understood that she was engaged to Weldon Henley, a broker – you may have heard of him? – and that, I suppose, has dampened his ardor considerably. As a matter of fact, Cabell took the thing to heart. He used to know Miss Lipscomb in Virginia – she comes from another famous family there – and he seemed to think he had a prior claim on her."

Hatch heard all these things as any man might listen to gossip, but each additional fact was sinking into his mind, and each additional fact led his suspicions on deeper into the channel they had chosen.

"Cabell is pretty well to do," his informant went on, "not rich as we count riches in the North, but pretty well to do, and I believe he came to Boston because Miss Lipscomb spent so much of her time here. She is a beautiful young woman of twenty-two and extremely popular in the social world everywhere, particularly in Boston. Then there was the additional fact that Henley was here."

"No chance at all for Cabell?" Hatch suggested.

"Not the slightest," was the reply. "Yet despite the heartbreak he had, he was the first to congratulate Henley on winning her love. And he meant it, too."

"What's his attitude toward Henley now?" asked Hatch. His voice was calm, but there was an underlying tense note imperceptible to the other.

"They meet and speak and move in the same set. There's no love lost on either side, I don't suppose, but there is no trace of any ill feeling."

"Cabell doesn't happen to be a vindictive sort of man?"

"Vindictive?" and the other laughed. "No. He's like a big boy, forgiving, and all that; hot-tempered, though. I could imagine him in a fit of anger making a personal matter of it with Henley, but I don't think he ever did."

The mind of the newspaper man was rapidly focusing on one point; the rush of thoughts, questions and doubts silenced him for a moment. Then:

"How long has Cabell been in Boston?"

"Seven or eight months – that is, he has had apartments here for that long – but he has made several visits South. I suppose it's South. He has a trick of dropping out of sight occasionally. I understand that he intends to go South for good very soon. If I'm not mistaken, he is trying now to rent his suite."

Hatch looked suddenly at his informant; an idea of seeing Cabell and having a legitimate excuse for talking to him had occurred to him.

"I'm looking for a suite," he volunteered at last. "I wonder if you would give me a card of introduction to him? We might get together on it."

Thus it happened that half an hour later, about ten minutes past nine o'clock, Hatch was on his way to the big apartment house. In the office he saw the manager.

"Heard the news?" asked the manager.

"No," Hatch replied. "What is it?"

"Somebody's shot Mr Henley as he was passing through the Common early tonight."

Hatch whistled in amazement.

"Is he dead?"

"No, but he is unconscious. The hospital doctors say it is a nasty wound, but not necessarily dangerous."

"Who shot him? Do they know?"

"He knows, but he won't say."

Amazed and alarmed by this latest development, an accurate fulfillment of The Thinking Machine's prophecy, Hatch stood thoughtful for a moment, then recovering his composure a little asked for Cabell.

"I don't think there's much chance of seeing him," said the manager. "He's going away on the midnight train—going South, to Virginia."

"Going away tonight?" Hatch gasped.

"Yes; it seems to have been rather a sudden determination. He was talking to me here half an hour or so ago, and said something about going away. While he was here the telephone boy told me that Henley had been shot; they had 'phoned from the hospital to inform us. Then Cabell seemed greatly agitated. He said he was going away tonight, if he could catch the midnight train, and now he's packing."

"I suppose the shooting of Henley upset him considerably?" the reporter suggested.

"Yes, I guess it did," was the reply. "They moved in the same set and belonged to the same clubs."

The manager sent Hatch's card of introduction to Cabell's apartments. Hatch went up and was ushered into a suite identical with that of Henley's in every respect save in minor details of furnishings. Cabell stood in the middle of the floor, with his personal belongings scattered about the room; his valet, evidently a Frenchman, was busily engaged in packing.

Cabell's greeting was perfunctorily cordial; he seemed agitated. His face was flushed and from time to time he ran his fingers through his long, brown hair. He stared at Hatch in a preoccupied fashion, then they fell into conversation about the rent of the apartments.

"I'll take almost anything reasonable," Cabell said hurriedly. "You see, I am going away tonight, rather more suddenly than I had intended, and I am anxious to get the lease off my hands. I pay two hundred dollars a month for these just as they are."

"May I look them over?" asked Hatch.

He passed from the front room into the next. Here, on a bed, was piled a huge lot of clothing, and the valet, with deft fingers, was brushing and folding, preparatory to packing. Cabell was directly behind him.

"Quite comfortable, you see," he explained. "There's room enough if you are alone. Are you?"

"Oh, yes," Hatch replied.

"This other room here," Cabell explained, "is not in very tidy shape now. I have been out of the city for several weeks, and—What's the matter?" he demanded suddenly.

Hatch had turned quickly at the words and stared at him, then recovered himself with a start.

"I beg your pardon," he stammered. "I rather thought I saw you in town here a week or so ago – of course I didn't know you – and I was wondering if I could have been mistaken."

"Must have been," said the other easily. "During the time I was away a Miss—, a friend of my sister's, occupied the suite. I'm afraid some of her things are here. She hasn't sent for them as yet. She occupied this room, I think; when I came back a few days ago she took another place and all her things haven't been removed."

"I see," remarked Hatch, casually. "I don't suppose there's any chance of her returning here unexpectedly if I should happen to take her apartments?"

"Not the slightest. She knows I am back, and thinks I am to remain. She was to send for these things."

Hatch gazed about the room ostentatiously. Across a trunk lay a Turkish bath robe with a scarlet stripe in it. He was anxious to get hold of it, to examine it closely. But he didn't dare to, then. Together they returned to the front room.

"I rather like the place," he said, after a pause, "but the price is—"

"Just a moment," Cabell interrupted. "Jean, before you finish packing that suit case be sure to put my bath robe in it. It's in the far room."

Then one question was settled for Hatch. After a moment the valet returned with the bath robe, which had been in the far room. It was Cabell's bath robe. As Jean passed the reporter an end of the robe caught on a corner of the trunk, and, stopping, the reporter unfastened it. A tiny strand of thread clung to the metal; Hatch detached it and stood idly twirling it in his fingers.

"As I was saying," he resumed, "I rather like the place, but the price is too much. Suppose you leave it in the hands of the manager of the house—"

"I had intended doing that," the Southerner interrupted.

"Well, I'll see him about it later," Hatch added.

With a cordial, albeit pre-occupied, handshake, Cabell ushered him out. Hatch went down in the elevator with a feeling of elation; a feeling that he had accomplished something. The manager was waiting to get into the lift.

"Do you happen to remember the name of the young lady who occupied Mr Cabell's suite while he was away?" he asked.

"Miss Austin," said the manager, "but she's not young. She was about forty-five years old, I should judge."

"Did Mr Cabell have his servant Jean with him?"

"Oh, no," said the manager. "The valet gave up the suite to Miss Austin entirely, and until Mr Cabell returned occupied a room in the quarters we have for our own employees."

"Was Miss Austin ailing in any way?" asked Hatch. "I saw a large number of medicine bottles upstairs."

"I don't know what was the matter with her," replied the manager, with a little puzzled frown. "She certainly was not a woman of sound mental balance – that is, she was eccentric, and all that. I think rather it was an act of charity for Mr Cabell to let her have the suite in his absence. Certainly we didn't want her."

Hatch passed out and burst in eagerly upon The Thinking Machine in his laboratory.

"Here," he said, and triumphantly he extended the tiny scarlet strand which he had received from The Thinking Machine, and the other of the identical color which came from Cabell's bath robe. "Is that the same?"

The Thinking Machine placed them under the microscope and examined them immediately. Later he submitted them to a chemical test.

"It is the same," he said, finally.

"Then the mystery is solved," said Hatch, conclusively.

V

The Thinking Machine stared steadily into the eager, exultant eyes of the newspaper man until Hatch at last began to fear that he had been precipitate. After awhile, under close scrutiny, the reporter began to feel convinced that he had made a mistake –

he didn't quite see where, but it must be there, and the exultant manner passed. The voice of The Thinking Machine was like a cold shower.

"Remember, Mr Hatch," he said, critically, "that unless every possible question has been considered one cannot boast of a solution. Is there any possible question lingering yet in your mind?"

The reporter silently considered that for a moment, then:

"Well, I have the main facts, anyway. There may be one or two minor questions left, but the principal ones are answered."

"Then tell me, to the minutest detail, what you have learned, what has happened."

Professor Van Dusen sank back in his old, familiar pose in the large arm chair and Hatch related what he had learned and what he surmised. He related, too, the peculiar circumstances surrounding the wounding of Henley, and right on down to the beginning and end of the interview with Cabell in the latter's apartments. The Thinking Machine was silent for a time, then there came a host of questions.

"Do you know where the woman – Miss Austin – is now?" was the first.

"No," Hatch had to admit.

"Or her precise mental condition?"

"No."

"Or her exact relationship to Cabell?"

"No."

"Do you know, then, what the valet, Jean, knows of the affair?"

"No, not that," said the reporter, and his face flushed under the close questioning. "He was out of the suite every night."

"Therefore might have been the very one who turned on the gas," the other put in testily.

"So far as I can learn, nobody could have gone into that room and turned on the gas," said the reporter, somewhat aggressively. "Henley barred the doors and windows and kept watch, night after night."

"Yet the moment he was exhausted and fell asleep the gas was turned on to kill him," said The Thinking Machine; "thus we see that he was watched more closely than he watched."

"I see what you mean now," said Hatch, after a long pause.

"I should like to know what Henley and Cabell and the valet knew of the girl who was found dead," The Thinking Machine suggested. "Further, I should like to know if there was a good – sized mirror – not one set in a bureau or dresser – either in Henley's room or the apartments where the girl was found. Find out this for me and – never mind. I'll go with you."

The scientist left the room. When he returned he wore his coat and hat. Hatch arose mechanically to follow. For a block or more they walked along, neither speaking. The Thinking Machine was the first to break the silence:

"You believe Cabell is the man who attempted to kill Henley?"

"Frankly, yes," replied the newspaper man.

"Why?"

"Because he had the motive – disappointed love."

"How?"

"I don't know," Hatch confessed. "The doors of the Henley suite were closed. I don't see how anybody passed them."

"And the girl? Who killed her? How? Why?"

Disconsolately Hatch shook his head as he walked on. The Thinking Machine interpreted his silence aright.

"Don't jump at conclusions," he advised sharply. "You were confident Cabell was to blame for this – and he might have been, I don't know yet – but you can suggest nothing to show how he did it. I have told you before that imagination is half of logic."

At last the lights of the big apartment house where Henley lived came in sight. Hatch shrugged his shoulders. He had grave doubts—based on what he knew—whether The Thinking Machine would be able to see Cabell. It was nearly eleven o'clock and Cabell was to leave for the South at midnight.

"Is Mr Cabell here?" asked the scientist of the elevator boy.

"Yes, just about to go, though. He won't see anyone."

"Hand him this note," instructed The Thinking Machine, and he scribbled something on a piece of paper. "He'll see us."

The boy took the paper and the elevator shot up to the fourth floor. After awhile he returned.

"He'll see you," he said.

"Is he unpacking?"

"After he read your note twice he told his valet to unpack," the boy replied.

"Ah, I thought so," said The Thinking Machine.

With Hatch, mystified and puzzled, following, The Thinking Machine entered the elevator to step out a second or so later on the fourth floor. As they left the car they saw the door of Cabell's apartment standing open; Cabell was in the door. Hatch traced a glimmer of anxiety in the eyes of the young man.

"Professor Van Dusen?" Cabell inquired.

"Yes," said the scientist. "It was of the utmost importance that I should see you, otherwise I should not have come at this time of night."

With a wave of his hand Cabell passed that detail.

"I was anxious to get away at midnight," he explained, "but, of course, now I shan't go, in view of your note. I have ordered my valet to unpack my things, at least until tomorrow."

The reporter and the scientist passed into the luxuriously furnished apartments. Jean, the valet, was bending over a suit case as they entered, removing some things he had been carefully placing there. He didn't look back or pay the least attention to the visitors.

"This is your valet?" asked The Thinking Machine.

"Yes," said the young man.

"French, isn't he?"

"Yes."

"Speak English at all?"

"Very badly," said Cabell. "I use French when I talk to him."

"Does he know that you are accused of murder?" asked The Thinking Machine, in a quiet, conversational tone.

The effect of the remark on Cabell was startling. He staggered back a step or so as if he had been struck in the face, and a crimson flush overspread his brow. Jean, the valet, straightened up suddenly and looked around. There was a queer expression, too, in his eyes; an expression which Hatch could not fathom.

"Murder?" gasped Cabell, at last.

"Yes, he speaks English all right," remarked The Thinking Machine. "Now, Mr Cabell, will you please tell me just who Miss Austin is, and where she is, and her mental condition? Believe me, it may save you a great deal of trouble. What I said in the note is not exaggerated."

The young man turned suddenly and began to pace back and forth across the room. After a few minutes he paused before The Thinking Machine, who stood impatiently waiting for an answer.

"I'll tell you, yes," said Cabell, firmly. "Miss Austin is a middle-aged woman whom my sister befriended several times – was, in fact, my sister's governess when she was a child. Of late years she has not been wholly right mentally, and has suffered a great deal of privation. I had about concluded arrangements to put her in a private sanitarium. I permitted her to remain in these rooms in my absence, South. I did not take Jean – he lived in the quarters of the other employees of the place, and gave the apartment entirely to Miss Austin. It was simply an act of charity."

"What was the cause of your sudden determination to go South to-night?" asked the scientist.

"I won't answer that question," was the sullen reply.

There was a long, tense silence. Jean, the valet, came and went several times.

"How long has Miss Austin known Mr Henley?"

"Presumably since she has been in these apartments," was the reply.

"Are you sure you are not Miss Austin?" demanded the scientist.

The question was almost staggering, not only to Cabell, but to Hatch. Suddenly, with flaming face, the young Southerner leaped forward as if to strike down The Thinking Machine.

"That won't do any good," said the scientist, coldly. "Are you sure you are not Miss Austin?" he repeated.

"Certainly I am not Miss Austin," responded Cabell, fiercely.

"Have you a mirror in these apartments about twelve inches by twelve inches?" asked The Thinking Machine, irrelevantly.

"I—I don't know," stammered the young man. "I – have we, Jean?"

"Oui," replied the valet.

"Yes," snapped The Thinking Machine. "Talk English, please. May I see it?"

The valet, without a word but with a sullen glance at the questioner, turned and left the room. He returned after a moment with the mirror. The Thinking Machine carefully examined the frame, top and bottom and on both sides. At last he looked up; again the valet was bending over a suit case.

"Do you use gas in these apartments?" the scientist asked suddenly.

"No," was the bewildered response. "What is all this, anyway?"

Without answering, The Thinking Machine drew a chair up under the chandelier where the gas and electric fixtures were and began to finger the gas tips. After awhile he climbed down and passed into the next room, with Hatch and Cabell, both hopelessly mystified, following. There the scientist went through the same process of fingering the gas jets. Finally, one of the gas tips came out in his hand.

"Ah," he exclaimed, suddenly, and Hatch knew the note of triumph in it. The jet from which the tip came was just on a level with his shoulder, set between a dressing table and a window. He leaned over and squinted at the gas pipe closely. Then he returned to the room where the valet was.

"Now, Jean," he began, in an even, calm voice, "please tell me if you did or did not kill Miss Regnier purposely?"

"I don't know what you mean," said the servant sullenly, angrily, as he turned on the scientist.

"You speak very good English now," was The Thinking Machine's terse comment. "Mr Hatch, lock the door and use this 'phone to call the police."

Hatch turned to do as he was bid and saw a flash of steel in young Cabell's hand, which was drawn suddenly from a hip pocket. It was a revolver. The weapon glittered in the light, and Hatch flung himself forward. There was a sharp report, and a bullet was buried in the floor.

VI

Then came a fierce, hard fight for possession of the revolver. It ended with the weapon in Hatch's hand, and both he and Cabell blowing from the effort they had expended. Jean, the valet, had turned at the sound of the shot and started toward the door leading into the hall. The Thinking Machine had stepped in front of him, and now stood there with his back to the door. Physically he would have been a child in the hands of the valet, yet there was a look in his eyes which stopped him.

"Now, Mr Hatch," said the scientist quietly, a touch of irony in his voice, "hand me the revolver, then 'phone for Detective Mallory to come here immediately. Tell him we have a murderer – and if he can't come at once get some other detective whom you know."

"Murderer!" gasped Cabell.

Uncontrollable rage was blazing in the eyes of the valet, and he made as if to throw The Thinking Machine aside, despite the revolver, when Hatch was at the telephone. As Jean started forward, however, Cabell stopped him with a quick, stern gesture. Suddenly the young Southerner turned on The Thinking Machine; but it was with a question.

"What does it all mean?" he asked, bewildered.

"It means that that man there," and The Thinking Machine indicated the valet by a nod of his head, "is a murderer – that he killed Louise Regnier; that he shot Welden Henley on Boston Common, and that, with the aid of Miss Regnier, he had four times previously attempted to kill Mr Henley. Is he coming, Mr Hatch?"

"Yes," was the reply. "He says he'll be here directly."

"Do you deny it?" demanded The Thinking Machine of the valet.

"I've done nothing," said the valet sullenly. "I'm going out of here."

Like an infuriated animal he rushed forward. Hatch and Cabell seized him and bore him to the floor. There, after a frantic struggle, he was bound and the other three men sat down to wait for Detective Mallory. Cabell sank back in his chair with a perplexed frown on his face. From time to time he glanced at Jean. The flush of anger which had been on the valet's face was gone now; instead there was the pallor of fear.

"Won't you tell us?" pleaded Cabell impatiently.

"When Detective Mallory comes and takes his prisoner," said The Thinking Machine.

Ten minutes later they heard a quick step in the hall outside and Hatch opened the door. Detective Mallory entered and looked from one to another inquiringly.

"That's your prisoner, Mr Mallory," said the scientist, coldly. "I charge him with the murder of Miss Regnier, whom you were so confident committed suicide; I charge him with five attempts on the life of Weldon Henley, four times by gas poisoning, in which Miss Regnier was his accomplice, and once by shooting. He is the man who shot Mr Henley."

The Thinking Machine arose and walked over to the prostate man, handing the revolver to Hatch. He glared down at Jean fiercely.

"Will you tell how you did it or shall I?" he demanded.

His answer was a sullen, defiant glare. He turned and picked up the square mirror which the valet had produced previously.

"That's where the screw was, isn't it?" he asked, as he indicated a small hole in the frame of the mirror. Jean stared at it and his head sank forward hopelessly. "And this is the bath robe you wore, isn't it?" he demanded again, and from the suit case he pulled out the garment with the scarlet stripe.

"I guess you got me all right," was the sullen reply.

"It might be better for you if you told the story then?" suggested The Thinking Machine.

"You know so much about it, tell it yourself."

"Very well," was the calm rejoinder. "I will. If I make any mistake you will correct me."

For a long time no one spoke. The Thinking Machine had dropped back into a chair and was staring through his thick glasses at the ceiling; his finger tips were pressed tightly together. At last he began:

"There are certain trivial gaps which only the imagination can supply until the matter is gone into more fully. I should have supplied these myself, but the arrest of this man, Jean, was precipitated by the attempted hurried departure of Mr Cabell for the South tonight, and I did not have time to go into the ease to the fullest extent.

"Thus, we begin with the fact that there were several clever attempts made to murder Mr Henley. This was by putting out the gas which he habitually left burning in his room. It happened four times in all; thus proving that it was an attempt to kill him. If it had been only once it might have been accident, even twice it might have been accident, but the same accident does not happen four times at the same time of night.

"Mr Henley finally grew to regard the strange extinguishing of the gas as an effort to kill him, and carefully locked and barred his door and windows each night. He believed that some one came into his apartments and put out the light, leaving the gas flow. This, of course, was not true. Yet the gas was put out. How? My first idea, a natural one, was that it was turned off for an instant at the meter, when the light would go out, then turned on again. This, I convinced myself, was not true. Therefore still the question—how?

"It is a fact – I don't know how widely known it is – but it is a fact that every gas light in this house might be extinguished at the same time from this room without leaving it. How? Simply by removing that gas jet tip and blowing into the gas pipe. It would not leave a jet in the building burning. It is due to the fact that the lung power is greater than the pressure of the gas in the pipes, and forces it out.

"Thus we have the method employed to extinguish the light in Mr Henley's rooms, and all the barred and locked doors and windows would not stop it. At the same time it threatened the life of every other person in the house – that is, every other person who used gas. It was probably for this reason that the attempt was always made late at night, I should say three or four o'clock. That's when it was done, isn't it?" he asked suddenly of the valet.

Staring at The Thinking Machine in open-mouthed astonishment the valet nodded his acquiescence before he was fully aware of it.

"Yes, that's right," The Thinking Machine resumed complacently. "This was easily found out—comparatively. The next question was how was a watch kept on Mr Henley? It would have done no good to extinguish the gas before he was asleep, or to have turned it on when he was not in his rooms. It might have led to a speedy discovery of just how the thing was done.

"There's a spring lock on the door of Mr Henley's apartment. Therefore it would have been impossible for anyone to peep through the keyhole. There are no cracks through which one might see. How was this watch kept? How was the plotter to satisfy himself positively of the time when Mr Henley was asleep? How was it that the gas was put out at no time of the score or more nights Mr Henley himself kept watch? Obviously he was watched through a window.

"No one could climb out on the window ledge and look into Mr Henley's apartments. No one could see into that apartment from the street – that is, could see whether Mr Henley was asleep or even in bed. They could see the light. Watch was kept with the aid offered by the flagpole, supplemented with a mirror – this mirror. A screw was driven into the frame – it has been removed now – it was swung on the flagpole rope and pulled out to the end of the pole, facing the building. To a man standing in the hall window of the third floor it offered precisely the angle necessary to reflect the interior of Mr Henley's suite, possibly even showed him in bed through a narrow opening in the curtain. There is no shade on the windows of that suite; heavy curtains instead. Is that right?"

Again the prisoner was surprised into a mute acquiescence.

"I saw the possibility of these things, and I saw, too, that at three or four o'clock in the morning it would be perfectly possible for a person to move about the upper halls of this house without being seen. If he wore a heavy bath robe, with a hood, say, no one would recognize him even if he were seen, and besides the garb would not cause suspicion. This bath robe has a hood.

"Now, in working the mirror back and forth on the flagpole at night a tiny scarlet thread was pulled out of the robe and clung to the rope. I found this thread; later Mr Hatch found an identical thread in these apartments. Both came from that bath robe. Plain logic shows that the person who blew down the gas pipes worked the mirror trick; the person who worked the mirror trick left the thread; the thread comes back to the bath robe – that bath robe there," he pointed dramatically. "Thus the person who desired Henley's death was in these apartments, or had easy access to them."

He paused for a moment and there was a tense silence. A great light was coming to Hatch, slowly but surely. The brain that had followed all this was unlimited in possibilities.

"Even before we traced the origin of the crime to this room," went on the scientist, quietly now, "attention had been attracted here, particularly to you, Mr Cabell. It was through the love affair, of which Miss Lipscomb was the center. Mr Hatch learned that you and Henley had been rivals for her hand. It was that, even before this scarlet thread was found, which indicated that you might have some knowledge of the affair, directly or indirectly.

"You are not a malicious or revengeful man, Mr Cabell. But you are hot-tempered—extremely so. You demonstrated that just now, when, angry and not understanding, but feeling that your honor was at stake, you shot a hole in the floor."

"What?" asked Detective Mallory.

"A little accident," explained The Thinking Machine quickly. "Not being a malicious or revengeful man, you are not the man to deliberately go ahead and make elaborate plans for the murder of Henley. In a moment of passion you might have killed him – but never deliberately as the result of premeditation. Besides you were out of town. Who was then in these apartments? Who had access to these apartments? Who might have used your bath robe? Your valet, possibly Miss Austin. Which? Now, let's see how we reached this conclusion which led to the valet.

"Miss Regnier was found dead. It was not suicide. How did I know? Because she had been reading with the gas light at its full. If she had been reading by the gas light, how was it then that it went out and suffocated her before she could arise and shut it off? Obviously she must have fallen asleep over her book and left the light burning.

"If she was in this plot to kill Henley, why did she light the jet in her room? There might have been some defect in the electric bulb in her room which she had just discovered. Therefore she lighted the gas, intending to extinguish it – turn it off entirely – later. But she fell asleep. Therefore when the valet here blew into the pipe, intending to kill Mr Henley, he unwittingly killed the woman he loved – Miss Regnier. It was perfectly possible, meanwhile, that she did not know of the attempt to be made that particular night, although she had participated in the others, knowing that Henley had night after night sat up to watch the light in his rooms.

"The facts, as I knew them, showed no connection between Miss Regnier and this man at that time—nor any connection between Miss Regnier and Henley. It might have been that the person who blew the gas out of the pipe from these rooms knew nothing whatever of Miss Regnier, just as he didn't know who else he might have killed in the building.

"But I had her death and the manner of it. I had eliminated you, Mr Cabell. Therefore there remained Miss Austin and the valet. Miss Austin was eccentric—insane, if you will. Would she have any motive for killing Henley? I could imagine none. Love? Probably not. Money? They had nothing in common on that ground. What? Nothing that I could see. Therefore, for the moment, I passed Miss Austin by, after asking you, Mr Cabell, if you were Miss Austin.

"What remained? The valet. Motive? Several possible ones, one or two probable. He is French, or says he is. Miss Regnier is French. Therefore I had arrived at the conclusion that they knew each other as people of the same nationality will in a house of this sort. And remember, I had passed by Mr Cabell and Miss Austin, so the valet was the only one left; he could use the bath robe.

"Well, the motive. Frankly that was the only difficult point in the entire problem – difficult because there were so many possibilities. And each possibility that suggested itself suggested also a woman. Jealousy? There must be a woman. Hate? Probably a woman. Attempted extortion? With the aid of a woman. No other motive which would lead to so elaborate a plot of murder would come forward. Who was the woman? Miss Regnier.

"Did Miss Regnier know Henley? Mr Hatch had reason to believe he knew her because of his actions when informed of her death. Knew her how? People of such relatively different planes of life can know each other – or do know each other – only on one plane. Henley is a typical young man, fast, I dare say, and liberal. Perhaps, then, there had been a liason. When I saw this possibility I had my motives – all of them – jealousy, hate and possibly attempted extortion as well.

"What was more possible than Mr Henley and Miss Regnier had been acquainted? All liasons are secret ones. Suppose she had been cast off because of the engagement to a young woman of Henley's own level? Suppose she had confided in the valet here? Do you see? Motives enough for any crime, however diabolical. The attempts on Henley's life possibly followed an attempted extortion of money. The shot which wounded Henley was fired by this man, Jean. Why? Because the woman who had cause to hate Henley was dead. Then the man? He was alive and vindictive. Henley knew who shot him, and knew why, but he'll never say it publicly. He can't afford to. It would ruin him. I think probably that's all. Do you want to add anything?" he asked the valet.

"No," was the fierce reply. "I'm sorry I didn't kill him, that's all. It was all about as you said, though God knows how you found it out," he added, desperately.

"Are you a Frenchman?"

"I was born in New York, but lived in France for eleven years. I first knew Louise there."

Silence fell upon the little group. Then Hatch asked a question:

"You told me, Professor, that there would be no other attempt to kill Henley by extinguishing the gas. How did you know that?"

"Because one person – the wrong person – had been killed that way," was the reply. "For this reason it was hardly likely that another attempt of that sort would be made. You had no intention of killing Louise Regnier, had you, Jean?"

"No, God help me, no."

"It was all done in these apartments," The Thinking Machine added, turning to Cabell, "at the gas jet from which I took the tip. It had been only loosely replaced and the metal was tarnished where the lips had dampened it."

"It must take great lung power to do a thing like that," remarked Detective Mallory.

"You would be amazed to know how easily it is done," said the scientist. "Try it some time."

The Thinking Machine arose and picked up his hat; Hatch did the same. Then the reporter turned to Cabell.

"Would you mind telling me why you were so anxious to get away tonight?" he asked.

"Well, no," Cabell explained, and there was a rush of red to his face. "It's because I received a telegram from Virginia – Miss Lipscomb, in fact. Some of Henley's past had come to her knowledge and the telegram told me that the engagement was broken. On top of this came the information that Henley had been shot and – I was considerably agitated."

The Thinking Machine and Hatch were walking along the street.

"What did you write in the note you sent to Cabell that made him start to unpack?" asked the reporter, curiously.

"There are some things that it wouldn't be well for everyone to know," was the enigmatic response. "Perhaps it would be just as well for you to overlook this little omission."

"Of course, of course," replied the reporter, wonderingly.

12

PROBLEM OF CONVICT NO. 97

Martha opened the door. Her distinguished master, Professor Augustus S. F. X. Van Dusen – The Thinking Machine – lay senseless on the floor. His upturned face, always drawn and pale, was deathly white now, the thin straight lips were colorless, the eyelids drooping, and the profuse yellow hair was tumbled back from the enormous brow in disorder. His arms were outstretched on either side helplessly, and the slender white hands were still and inert. The fading light from the windows over the laboratory table beat down upon the pitifully small figure, and so for the moment Martha stood with distended eyes gazing in terror and apprehension. She was not of the screaming kind, but a great lump rose in her old throat. Then, with fear tearing at her heart, she swooped the slender, child-like figure up in her strong arms and laid it on a couch.

"Glory be!" she exclaimed, and there was devotion in the tone—devotion to this eminent man of science whom she had served so long. "What could have happened to the poor, poor man?"

For another moment she stood looking upon the pallid face, then the necessity of action impressed itself upon her. The heart was still beating, – she convinced herself of that, – and he was breathing. Perhaps he had only fainted. She grasped at the idea hopefully, and turned, seeking water. There was a faucet over a sink at the end of the long table, and innumerable graduated glasses; but even in her excited condition Martha knew better than to use one of them. All sorts of chemicals had been in them – poisons too. With another quick glance at the little scientist she rushed out of the room, as she had entered, bent on getting water.

When she appeared again at the open door with pitcher and drinking glass she paused a second time in amazement. The distinguished scientist was sitting cross legged on the couch, thoughtfully caressing the back of his head.

"Martha, did anyone call?" he inquired.

"Lor', sir! what did happen to you?" she burst out amazedly.

"Oh, a little accident," he explained irritably. "Did anyone call?"

"No, sir. How do you feel now, sir?"

"Don't disturb yourself about me, my good woman; I'm all right," The Thinking Machine assured her, and put his feet to the floor. "You are sure no one was here?"

"Yes, sir. Lor'! you was that white when I picked you up from the floor there—"

"Was I lying on my back or my face?"

"Flat of your back, sir, all sprawled out. I thought you was dead, sir."

Again The Thinking Machine thoughtfully caressed the back of his head, and Martha rattled on verbosely, indicating just where and how he had been lying when she opened the door.

"Are you sure that you didn't hear any sound?" again queried the scientist.

"Nothing, sir."

"Any sudden jar?"

"Nothing, sir, nothing. I was just laying the tea things, sir, and opened the door to tell you it was ready."

She poured a glass of water from the pitcher, and The Thinking Machine moistened his lips, to which the color was slowly returning.

"Martha," he directed, "go see if the front door is closed, please."

Martha went out. "Yes, sir," she reported on her return.

"Locked?"

"Yes, sir."

The Thinking Machine arose and straightened up, almost himself again. Then he went over to the laboratory table and peered squintingly into a mirror which hung there, after which he wandered all over his apartments, examining windows, trying doors, and stopping occasionally to stare curiously about at objects which had been familiar for years. He turned; Martha was just behind him, looking on wonderingly.

"Lost something, sir?" she asked solicitously.

"You are sure you didn't hear any sound of any sort?" he asked in turn.

"Not a thing, sir."

Then The Thinking Machine went to the telephone. In a minute or so he was in conversation with Hutchinson Hatch, newspaper reporter.

"Heard of any jail delivery at Chisholm prison?" he inquired.

"No," replied the reporter. "Why?"

"There has been an escape," said the scientist positively.

"Who was it?" demanded the reporter eagerly. "How did it happen?"

"The prisoner's name is Philip Gilfoil. I don't know how he got out, but he is out."

"Philip Gilfoil?" Hatch repeated. "He's the forger who—"

"Yes, the forger," said The Thinking Machine abruptly. "He's out. You might go over and investigate, then come by and see me."

Hatch spoke to his city editor and rushed out. Half an hour later he was at Chisholm prison, a vast spreading structure of granite in the suburbs, and in conversation with the warden, an old acquaintance.

"Who was it that escaped?" Hatch began briskly.

"Escaped?" repeated the warden with a momentary start, and then he laughed. "Nobody."

"You have been keeping Philip Gilfoil here, haven't you?"

"I am keeping Philip Gilfoil here," was the grim response. "He is No. 97, and is now in Cell 9."

"How long since you have seen him?" the reporter insisted.

"Ten minutes," was the ready response.

The reporter was staring at him steadily; but the warden's eyes met his frankly. There have been instances where denials of this sort have been made offhand with the idea of preventing the public from knowing the truth as long as possible. Hatch knew of several.

"May I see Gilfoil?" he inquired coldly.

"Sure," replied the warden cheerfully. "Come on and I'll show you."

He escorted the newspaper man along the corridor to Cell 9. "Ninety-seven, are you there?" he called.

"Where'd you expect I'd be?" grumbled some one inside.

"Come to the door for a minute."

There was a movement inside the cell, and the figure of a man approached the door out of the gloom. It had been several months since Hatch had seen Philip Gilfoil; but there was not the slightest question in his mind about the identity of this man. It was Gilfoil – the same sharp, hooked nose, the same thin lipped mouth, everything the same save now that the prison pallor was upon him. There was frank surprise in the reporter's face.

"Do you know me, Gilfoil?" he inquired.

"I'll never forget you," replied the prisoner. There was anything but a kindly expression in the voice. "You're the fellow who helped to send me here – you and the old professor chap."

Hatch led the way back to the warden's office. "Look here, warden!" he remarked pointedly, accusingly. "I want to know the real facts. Has that man been out of his cell since he has been here?"

"No, except for exercise," was the reply. "All the prisoners are allowed a certain time each day for that."

"I mean has he never been out of the prison?"

"Not on your life!" declared the warden. "He's in for eight years, and he doesn't get out till that's up."

"I have reason to believe – the best reason in the world to believe – that he has been out," insisted the reporter.

"You are talking through your hat, Hatch," said the warden, and he laughed with the utmost good nature. "What's the matter, anyway?"

Hatch didn't choose to tell him. He went instead to a telephone and called up The Thinking Machine.

"You are mistaken about Gilfoil having escaped," he told the scientist. "He is still in Chisholm prison."

"Did you see him?" came the irritable demand.

"Saw him and talked to him," replied the reporter. "He was in Cell 9 not five minutes ago."

There was a long silence. Hatch could imagine what it meant – The Thinking Machine was turning this over and over in his mind.

"You are mistaken, Mr Hatch," came the surprising statement at last in the same irritable, querulous voice. "Gilfoil is not in his cell. I know he is not. There is no need to argue about it. Goodby."

It so happened that Professor Augustus S. F. X. Van Dusen was well acquainted with the warden of Chisholm prison. Thus it was that when he called at the prison half an hour or so after Hatch had gone he was received with more courtesy and attention than would have been the case if he had been a casual visitor. The warden shook hands with him and there was a pleasant reminiscent grin on his face.

"I want to find out something about this man Gilfoil," the scientist began abruptly.

"You too?" remarked the warden. "Hutchinson Hatch was here a little while ago inquiring about him."

"Yes, I sent him," said the scientist. "He tells me that Gilfoil is still here?"

"He is still here," said the warden emphatically. "He's been here for nearly a year, and will remain here for another seven years. Hatch seemed to have an impression that he had escaped. Do you happen to know where he got that idea?"

The Thinking Machine squinted into his face for an instant inscrutably, then glanced up at the clock. It was eighteen minutes past eight o'clock.

"Are you sure that Gilfoil is in his cell?" he demanded curtly.

"I know he is – in Cell 9." The warden tilted his cigar to an angle which was only a little less than aggressive, and glared at his visitor curiously. This constant questioning as to Convict 97, and the implied doubt behind it, was anything but soothing. The Thinking Machine dropped back into a chair, and the watery blue eyes were turned upward. The warden knew the attitude.

"How long have you had Gilfoil?" queried The Thinking Machine after a moment.

"A little more than ten months."

"Well behaved prisoner?"

"Well, yes, now he is. When he first came he was rather an unpleasant customer, and was given to profanity, but lately he has realized the uselessness of it all, and now, I may say, he is a model of decency. That's the usual course with prisoners; they are bad at first, and then in nine cases out of ten they settle down and behave themselves."

"Naturally," mused the scientist. "Just when did you first notice this change for the better in his conduct?"

"Oh, a month or six weeks ago," was the reply.

"Was it a gradual change or a sudden change?"

"I couldn't say, really," responded the wondering warden. "I suppose it might be called a sudden change. I noticed one day that he didn't swear at me as I passed his cell, and that was unusual."

The Thinking Machine straightened up in his chair suddenly and squinted belligerently at the official for an instant. Then he sank back again, and his eyes wandered upward. "Do you happen to remember that first date he didn't swear at you?"

The warden laughed. "It didn't make any particular impression on my mind. It was a month or six weeks ago."

"Has he sworn at you since?" the scientist went on.

"No, I don't think anyone has heard him swear since. He's been remarkably well behaved."

"Any callers?"

"Well, not for a long time. A physician came here to see him twice. There was something the matter with his throat, I think."

"How did it happen that the prison physician didn't attend him?" demanded The Thinking Machine curiously.

"He asked that an outside physician be called," was the response. "He had twelve or fifteen dollars here in the office, and I paid the physician out of that."

Some new line of thought had evidently been awakened in the scientist's mind; for there came a subtle change in the drawn face, and for a long time he was silent.

"Do you happen to remember," he asked slowly at last, "if the physician was called in before or after he stopped swearing?"

"After, I think," the warden replied wearily. "What the deuce is all this about, anyway?" he demanded flatly after a moment.

"Throat trouble, you said. How did it affect him?"

"Made him a little hoarse, that's all. The doctor told me it wasn't anything particularly – probably the dampness in the cell or something."

"And did you know the doctor who was called – know him personally?" demanded The Thinking Machine, and there was a strange, new gleam in the narrow eyes.

"Yes, quite well. I've known him for years. I let him in and let him out."

The crabbed little scientist seemed almost disappointed. He dropped back again into the depths of the chair.

"Do you want to see Gilfoil?" asked the warden.

"Not yet," was the reply; "but I should like you to walk down the corridor very, very softly and flash your light in Cell 9 and see if Convict 97 is there?"

The warden came to his feet suddenly. There was something in the tone which startled him; but the momentary shock was followed instantly by a little nervous laugh. No man knew better than he that Convict 97 was still there, yet to please this whimsical visitor he lighted his dark lantern and went out. He was gone only a couple of minutes, and when he returned there was a queer expression on his face – almost an awed expression.

"Well?" queried the scientist. "Was he asleep."

"No," replied the warden, "he wasn't. He was down on his knees beside his cot, praying."

The Thinking Machine arose and paced back and forth across the office two or three times. At last he turned to the warden. "Really, I hate to put you to so much trouble," he said; "but believe me it is in the interests of justice. I should like personally to visit Cell 9 say in an hour from now after Convict 97 is asleep. Meanwhile, don't let me disturb you. Go on about your affairs; I'll wait."

And then and there The Thinking Machine gave the warden a lesson in perfect repose. He glanced at the clock, – the hands indicated eight-forty, – then sat down again, and for one hour he sat there without the slightest movement to indicate even a casual interest in anybody or anything. The warden, busy with some accounts, glanced around curiously at the diminutive figure half a dozen times; once or twice he imagined his visitor had fallen asleep, but the blue eyes behind the thick spectacles, narrow as they were, belied this idea. It was precisely twenty-one minutes of ten o'clock when The Thinking Machine arose.

"Now, please," he requested.

Without a word of protest the warden relighted the dark lantern, opened the doors leading into the corridor of the prison, and they went on to Cell 9. They paused at the door. There was utter silence in the huge prison, broken only by the regular, rhythmic breathing of Convict 97. At a motion from The Thinking Machine the warden softly unlocked the cell door, and they entered.

"Silence, please," whispered the scientist.

He took the lantern from the warden's unresisting hand, and going softly to the cot turned the light full into the face of the sleeping man. For a second or so he gazed steadily at the features upturned thus to him, then the brilliant light seemed to disturb the sleeper, for his eyelids twitched, and finally opened with a start.

"Do you know me, Gilfoil?" demanded The Thinking Machine suddenly, and he leaned forward so that the cutting rays of light should illumine has own features.

"Yes," the prisoner replied shortly.

"What's my name?" insisted the scientist.

"Van Dusen," was the prompt reply. "I know you, all right." Convict 97 raised himself on an elbow and met the eyes of the other two men without a quiver.

"What size shoe do you wear?" demanded the scientist.

"None of your business!" growled the convict.

The Thinking Machine turned the lantern to the floor and found the shoes the prisoner had laid aside on retiring. He picked them up and examined them carefully, after which he replaced them, nodded to the warden, and they went out. The prisoner lay for a long time, resting on his elbow, seeking to pierce the gloom of the cell and corridor beyond with wide awake eyes, then, sighing, lay down again.

"Let me see Gilfoil's pedigree, and I shall not annoy you further," The Thinking Machine requested, once they were in the warden's office again. The record book was forthcoming. The scientist copied, accurately and at length, everything written therein concerning Philip Gilfoil. "And last," he requested, "the name, please, of the physician who called to see Convict 97?"

"Dr Heindell," replied the Warden, – "Dr Delmore L. Heindell."

The Thinking Machine replaced his notebook in his pocket, planted his hat more firmly on the great shock of yellow hair, and slowly began to draw on his gloves.

"What is all this thing about Gilfoil, anyhow?" demanded the warden desperately. "Be good enough to inform me what the deuce you and Hatch have been driving at?"

"You are, I believe, an able, careful, conscientious man," said The Thinking Machine, "and I don't know that under the circumstances you can be blamed for what has happened; but the man you have in Cell 9 is not Philip Gilfoil. I don't know who your Convict 97 is; but Philip Gilfoil hasn't been in Chisholm prison for weeks. Goodnight."

And the crabbed little scientist went on his way.

For the third time Hutchinson Hatch rapped upon the little door. The echo reverberated through the house; but there came no answering sound. The modest cottage in a quiet street of a fashionable suburb seemed wholly deserted, yet as he stepped back to the edge of the veranda he could see a faint light trickling through closely drawn shutters on the second floor.

Surely there must be some one there, the reporter reasoned, or that light would not be burning. And if some one was there, why wouldn't they answer? As he looked the trickling light remained still, and then he went to the door and tried it. It was unlocked. He merely ascertained that the door yielded readily under his hand, then he rapped for the fourth time. No answer yet.

He was just turning away from the door, when suddenly it opened before him, a single arm shot out from the gloom of the hall, and before he could retreat had closed on the collar of his coat. He was hauled into the house despite an instinctive resistance, then the door banged behind him. He could see nothing; the darkness was intense. But still that powerful hand gripped his collar.

"I'll fix your clock, young fellow, right now!" said a man's voice.

Then, even as he struggled, he was conscious of a heavy blow on the point of the chin, strange lights dancing fantastically before his eyes; he felt himself sinking, sinking, and then he knew no more.

When he recovered consciousness he lay stretched full length upon a couch on a strange room. His head seemed bursting, and the rosy light of dawn through the window caused a tense pain in his eyes. For half a minute he lay still, until he had remembered those singular events which had preceded this, and then he started up. He was leaning on one elbow surveying the room, when he became conscious of the rustling of skirts. He turned; a woman was advancing toward him – a woman of apparently thirty years, in whose sweet face lay some heavy, desperate grief.

Involuntarily Hatch struggled to his feet – perhaps it was a spirit of defense, perhaps a natural gallantry. She paused and stood looking at him.

"What happened?" he demanded flatly. "What am I doing here?"

The woman's eyes grew suddenly moist, and her lips trembled. "I'm glad it was no worse," she said hopelessly.

"Who are you?" Hatch asked curiously.

"Please don't ask," she pleaded. "Please don't! If you are able to go, please go now while you may."

The reporter wasn't at all certain that he wanted to go. He was himself again now, confident, alert, with new strength rushing through his veins, and a naturally inquisitive mind fully aroused. If it was only a poke in the jaw he got, it didn't matter much. He had had those before, and besides here was something which demanded an explanation.

"Who was the man who struck me last night?" he asked.

"Please go!" the woman pleaded. "Believe me, you must. I can't explain anything – it's all horrible and unreal and hideous!" Tears were streaming down the wan cheeks now, and the hands closed and unclosed spasmodically.

Hatch sat down. "I am not going yet," he said. "Tell me about it."

"There is nothing I can tell – nothing!" the woman sobbed.

She buried her face in her hands and wept softly. Then Hatch saw a great bruised spot across her cheek and neck – it might have been the mark of a lash. Whatever particular kind of trouble he was in, he told himself, he was not alone, for she too was a victim.

"You must tell me about it," he insisted.

"I can't, I can't!" she wailed.

And then a cringing, awful fear came into her tear stained face, as she lifted her head to listen. There was the sound of footsteps outside the door.

"He'll kill you, he'll kill you!" whispered the woman.

Hatch set his lips grimly, motioned her to silence, and stepped toward the door. A heavy chair stood there. He weighed it judicially in his hands, and glanced toward the woman reassuringly. She had dropped down on the couch and had buried her face in a pillow; her slender form was shaking with sobs. Hatch raised the chair above his head and closed his hands on it fiercely.

There was a slight rattle as some one turned the knob of the door. Then it opened and a man entered. Hatch stared at the profile with amazed eyes.

"By George!" he exclaimed.

Then he brought the chair down with all the strength of two well muscled arms. The man sank to the floor without a sound; the woman straightened up, screamed once, and fell forward in a dead faint.

It was about ten o'clock that morning when The Thinking Machine and Hutchinson Hatch, together with a powerful cabman, dragged a man into the warden's office at Chisholm prison.

"Here's your man, Philip Gilfoil," said The Thinking Machine tersely.

"Gilfoil!" the warden almost shouted. "Did he escape?"

And a moment later two guards came into the warden's office with Convict 97 between them. There were two Philip Gilfoils, if one might trust the evidence of a sense of sight; the first with dissipated, brutally lined face, and the other with the prison pallor upon him and with deep grief written indelibly in his eyes.

"They are brothers, gentlemen – twin brothers," explained The Thinking Machine. He turned to the man in prison garb, the man from Cell 9. "This is the Rev. Dr Phineas Gilfoil, pastor of a fashionable little church in a suburb, and," he turned upon the man whom they had brought there in the cab, "this is Philip Gilfoil, forger – this is Convict 97."

The warden and the prison guards stood stupefied, gazing from one to the other of the two men. The facial lines were identical; physically they had been cast in the same mold.

"The only real difference between them, except a radical mental difference, is the size of their feet," The Thinking Machine went on. "Philip Gilfoil, the forger, the real Convict 97, who has been out of this prison for five weeks and four days, wears a number eight and a half shoe, according to your own records Mr Warden; the Rev. Phineas Gilfoil, who has been in his brothers place, Cell 9, for five weeks and four days, wears a number seven shoe. See here!"

He stooped suddenly, lifted one of Dr Gilfoil's feet and slipped one shoe off without even untying it. It showed no impression of the foot at all in the upper part, it was so large. Dr Gilfoil dropped back weakly into a chair without a word and buried his face in his hands; Philip Gilfoil, the forger, his head still awhirl with the fumes of liquor, took one step toward his brother, then sat down and glared from one to the other defiantly.

"But how-what-when did they change places?" demanded the warden stammeringly. The whole thing was a nightmare to him.

"Precisely five weeks and four days ago," replied The Thinking Machine. "Your records show that. On your own books, in your own handwriting, is a complete solution of the problem, although you didn't know it," he added magnanimously. "Everything is there. Let me see the book a moment."

The squint eyes ran rapidly down a page, and stopped at a written entry opposite the pedigree record.

'Sept. 3. – Miss P. Gilfoil, sister, permitted half-hour's conversation with 97 in afternoon. Brought permission from chairman of Prison Commission.'

"That's the record of the escape," continued The Thinking Machine. "Philip Gilfoil has no sister, therefore the person who called was the Rev. Dr Phineas Gilfoil, an only brother, and he wore woman's clothing. He went to that cell willingly and for the specific purpose of changing places with his brother, –

the motive doesn't appear, – and was to remain in the cell for a time agreed upon. The necessary changes of clothing were made, instructions which were to enable the minister to impersonate his brother were given, – and they were elaborate, – then Philip Gilfoil, Convict 97, walked out as a woman. I dare say he invited a close scrutiny; it was perfectly safe because of his remarkable resemblance to the man he had left behind."

Amazement in the warden's eyes was giving way to anger at the trick of which he had been the victim. He turned to the guards who had stood by silently.

"Take this man back!" he directed, and indicated Philip Gilfoil. "Put him where he belongs!" Then he turned toward the white faced minister. "I shall deliver you over to the police."

Philip Gilfoil was led away; then the warden reached for the telephone receiver.

"Now, just a moment, please," requested The Thinking Machine, and he sat down. "You have your prisoner now, safely enough, and here you are about to turn over to the police a man whose every act of life has been a good one. Remember that for a moment, please."

"But why should he change places with my prisoner?" blazed the warden. "That makes him liable too. The statutes are specific on—"

"The Rev. Dr Gilfoil has done one of the most amazing, not to say heroic, things that I ever heard of," interrupted the scientist. "Now, wait a minute. He, a man of position, of reputation, of unquestioned morals, a good man, deliberately incarcerates himself for the sake of a criminal brother who, in this man's eyes, must be free for a short time at any rate. The reason of this, the necessity, while urgent, still doesn't appear. Dr Gilfoil trusted his brother, criminal though he was, to return to his cell in four weeks and finish his sentence. The exchange of prisoners then was to be made in the same manner. That the criminal brother did not return, as he agreed, but that Dr Gilfoil was loyal to him even then and lived up to the lie, can only reflect credit upon Dr Gilfoil for a self sacrifice which is almost beyond us prosaic people of this day."

"I did it because—" Dr Gilfoil began hoarsely, his voice quivering with emotion. It was the first time he had spoken.

"It doesn't matter why you did it," interrupted The Thinking Machine. "You did it for love of a brother, and he betrayed you – betrayed you to the point of his taking possession of your house while maudlin from drink, to the point of striking your wife like the coward he is, and of making a temporary prisoner of Mr Hatch here, who had gone to your home to investigate. It is due to Mr Hatch's personal courage that your wife is freed from him, – she was practically a prisoner, – and that he is now in his cell again."

Dr Gilfoil's face went pallid for an instant, and he staggered to his feet, with lips tightly pressed together, fighting back an emotion which nearly overwhelmed him. After a moment came a strange softening of his features, and he stood staring out the window into the prison yard with upraised eyes.

"That's all of it," said the scientist, after a moment. "I don't think, Mr Warden, that justice would demand the imprisonment of this man. I believe it would be far better to let the matter remain just between ourselves. It will not happen again, and—"

"But it was a crime," interrupted the warden.

"Technically, yes," admitted The Thinking Machine; "but we can overlook even a crime, if it does no harm, and if it is inspired by the motive which prompted this one. Think of it for a moment in that light."

There was a long silence in the little office. The Thinking Machine sat with upturned eyes and fingers pressed tip to tip; Dr Gilfoil's eyes roved from the drawn, inscrutable face of the scientist to the warden; Hatch's brow was furrowed with wrinkles of perplexity.

"How did you find out about this escape first?" asked the reporter curiously.

"I knew Philip Gilfoil had escaped, because I saw him," replied The Thinking Machine tersely. "He came to my place, evidently to kill me. I was in my laboratory. He came up behind me to strike me down. I glanced into a mirror above my work table, saw him, and tried to avoid the blow. It caught me in the back of the head, and I fell unconscious. Martha made some noise outside which must have frightened Gilfoil, for he fled. The front door locked behind him—it's a spring lock. But I had recognized the escaped prisoner perfectly, – never forget faces, – and I knew he had the motive to kill me because I had been instrumental in sending him here.

"I told you merely that Gilfoil had escaped and sent you here to inquire. Afterward I came myself, because I knew Philip Gilfoil was not in that cell. I found out many additional facts, among them a sudden change for the better in the prisoner's behavior, which confirmed my knowledge that it was Philip Gilfoil who had attacked me. I sought to surprise Dr Gilfoil here into a betrayal of identity by a visit to his cell at night. But his loyalty to his brother and his perfect self possession enabled him to play the role. He recognized me as he recognized you, Mr Hatch, because we can imagine that Philip Gilfoil had been careful in his plans and had instructed him to look out for us.

"Everything else came from the record book. This gave me Philip Gilfoil's pedigree, mentioned Phineas Gilfoil, without stating his vocation, and gave a clue to his place of residence. You followed up that end, Mr Hatch, while I called on Dr Heindell who had treated the prisoner for a bad throat. He informed me that there was nothing at all the matter with the prisoner's throat, so a plain problem in addition brought me a definite knowledge of what had happened. In conclusion, I may say that Dr Gilfoil planned only a four weeks' stay here. I know that because you told me he had gone on a four weeks' vacation."

The minister's eyes again settled on the face of the warden. That official had been turning the matter over in his mind, evidently at length, as he listened. Finally he spoke.

"You had better go back to the cell, Dr Gilfoil," he said respectfully, "and change clothing with your brother. You couldn't wear that prison suit in the street safely."

13

PROBLEM OF THE BROKEN BRACELET

The girl in the green mask leaned against the foot of the bed and idly fingered a revolver which lay in the palm of her daintily gloved hand. The dim glow of the night lamp enveloped her softly, and added a sinister glint to the bright steel of the weapon. Cowering in the bed was another figure – the figure of a woman. Sheets and blankets were drawn up tightly to her chin, and startled eyes peered anxiously, as if fascinated, at the revolver.

"Now please don't scream!" warned the masked girl. Her voice was quite casual, the tone in which one might have discussed an affair of far removed personal interest. "It would be perfectly useless, and besides dangerous."

"Who are you?" gasped the woman in the bed, staring horror stricken at the inscrutable mask of her visitor. "What do you want?"

A faint flicker of amusement lay in the shadowy eyes of the masked girl, and her red lips twitched slightly. "I don't think I can be mistaken," she said inquiringly. "This is Miss Isabel Leigh Harding?"

"Y-yes," was the chattering reply.

"Originally of Virginia?"

"Yes."

"Great-granddaughter of William Tremaine Harding, an officer in the Continental Army about 1775?"

The inflection of the questioning voice had risen almost imperceptibly; but the tone remained coldly, exquisitely courteous. At the last question the masked girl leaned forward a little expectantly.

"Yes," faltered Miss Harding faintly.

"Good, very good," commented the masked girl, and there was a note of repressed triumph in her voice. "I congratulate you, Miss Harding, upon your self possession. Under the same circumstances most women would have begun by screaming. I should have myself."

"But who are you?" demanded Miss Harding again. "How did you get in here? What do you want?"

She sat bolt upright in bed, with less of fear now than curiosity in her manner, and her luxuriant hair tumbled about her semibare shoulders in profuse dishevelment.

At the sudden movement the masked girl took a firmer grip on the revolver, and moved it forward a little threateningly. "Now please don't make any mistake!" she advised Miss Harding pleasantly. "You will notice that I have drawn the bell rope up beyond your reach and knotted it. The servants are on the floor above in the extreme rear, and I doubt if they would hear a scream. Your companion is away for the night, and besides there is this." She tapped her weapon significantly. "Furthermore, you may notice that the lamp is beyond your reach; so that you cannot extinguish it as long as you remain in bed."

Miss Harding saw all these things, and was convinced.

"Now as to your question," continued the masked girl quietly. "My identity is of absolutely no concern or importance to you. You would not even recognize my name if I gave it to you. How did I get here? By opening an unfastened window in the drawing room on the first floor and walking in. I shall leave it unlatched when I go; so perhaps you had better have some one fasten it, otherwise thieves may enter." She smiled a little at the astonishment in Miss Harding's face. "Now as to why I am here and what I want."

She sat down on the foot of the bed, drew her cloak more closely about her, and folded her hands in her lap. Miss Harding placed a pillow and lounged against it comfortably, watching her visitor in astonishment. Except for the mask and the revolver, it might have been a cozy chat in any woman's boudoir.

"I came here to borrow from you – borrow, understand," the masked girl went on, "the least valuable article in your jewel box."

"My jewel box!" gasped Miss Harding suddenly. She had just thought of it, and glanced around at the table where it lay open.

"Don't alarm yourself," the masked girl remarked reassuringly; "I have removed nothing from it."

The light of the lamp fell full upon the open casket whence radiated multicolored flashes of gems. Miss Harding craned her neck a little to see, and seeing sank back against her pillow with a sigh of relief.

"As I said, I came to borrow one thing," the masked girl continued evenly. "If I cannot borrow it, I shall take it."

Miss Harding sat for a moment in mute contemplation of her visitor. She was searching her mind for some tangible explanation of this nightmarish thing. After awhile she shook her head, meaning thereby that even conjecture was futile. "What particular article do you want?" she asked finally.

"Specifically by letter, from the prison in which he was executed by order of the British commander, your great-grandfather, William Tremaine Harding, left a gold bracelet, a plain band, to your grandfather," the masked girl explained; "Your grandfather, at that time a child, received the bracelet, when twenty-one years old, from the persons who held it in trust for him, and on his death, March 25, 1853, left it to your father. Your father died intestate in April, 1898, and the bracelet passed into your mother's keeping, there being no son. Your mother died within the last year. Therefore, the bracelet is now, or should be, in your possession. You see," she concluded, "I have taken pains to acquaint myself with your family history."

"You have," Miss Harding assented. "And may I ask why you want this bracelet?"

"I should answer that it was no concern of yours."

"You said borrow it, I believe?"

"Either I will borrow it or take it."

"Is there any certainty that it will ever be returned? And if so, when?"

"You will have to take my word for that, of course," replied the masked girl. "I shall return it within a few days."

Miss Harding glanced at her jewel box. "Have you looked there?" she inquired.

"Yes," replied the masked girl. "It isn't there."

"Not there?" repeated Miss Harding.

"If it had been there I should have taken it and gone away without disturbing you," the masked girl went on. "Its absence is what caused me to wake you."

"Not there!" said Miss Harding again wonderingly, and she moved as if to get up.

"Don't do that, please!" warned the masked girl quickly. "I shall hand you the box if you like."

She arose and passed the casket to Miss Harding, who spilled out the contents in her lap.

"Why, it is gone!" she exclaimed.

"Yes, from there," said the other a little grimly. "Now please tell me immediately where it is. It will save trouble."

"I don't know," replied Miss Harding hopelessly.

The masked girl stared at her coldly for a moment, then drew back the hammer of the revolver until it clicked.

Miss Harding stared in sudden terror.

"All this is merely time wasted," said the masked girl sternly, coldly. "Either the bracelet or this!" Again she tapped the revolver.

"If it is not here, I don't know where it is," Miss Harding rushed on desperately. "I placed it here at ten o'clock tonight – here in this box – when I undressed. I don't know – I can't imagine—"

The masked girl tapped the revolver again several times with one gloved finger. "The bracelet!" she demanded impatiently.

Fear was in Miss Harding's eyes now, and she made a helpless, pleading gesture with both white hands. "You wouldn't kill me—murder me!" she gasped. "I don't know. I – Here, take the other jewels. I can't tell you."

"The other jewels are of absolutely no use to me," said the girl coldly. "I want only the bracelet."

"On my honor," faltered Miss Harding, "I don't know where it is. I can't imagine what has happened to it. I – I—" she stopped helplessly.

The masked girl raised the weapon threateningly, and Miss Harding stared in cringing horror.

"Please, please, I don't know!" she pleaded hysterically.

For a little while the masked girl was thoughtfully silent. One shoe tapped the floor rhythmically; the eyes were contracted. "I believe you," she said slowly at last. She arose suddenly and drew her coat closely about her. "Goodnight," she added as she started toward the door. There she turned back. "It would not be wise for you to give an alarm for at least half an hour. Then you had better have some one latch the window in the drawing room. I shall leave it unfastened. Goodnight."

And she was gone.

PROBLEM OF THE BROKEN BRACELET 299

Hutchinson Hatch, reporter, had just finished relating the story to The Thinking Machine, incident by incident, as it had been reported to Chief of Detectives Mallory, when the eminent scientist's aged servant, Martha, tapped on the door of the reception room and entered with a card.

"A lady to see you, sir," she announced.

The scientist extended one slender white hand, took the card, and glanced at it.

"Your story is merely what Miss Harding told the police?" he inquired of the reporter. "You didn't get it from Miss Harding herself?"

"No, I didn't see her."

"Show the lady in, Martha," directed The Thinking Machine. She turned and went out, and he passed the card to the reporter.

"By George! it's Miss Harding herself!" Hatch exclaimed. "Now we can get it all straight."

There was a little pause, and Martha ushered a young woman into the room. She was girlish, slender, daintily yet immaculately attired, with deep brown eyes, firmly molded chin and mouth, and wavy hair. Hatch's expression of curiosity gave way to one of frank admiration as he regarded her. There was only the most impersonal sort of interest in the watery blue eyes of The Thinking Machine. She stood for a moment with gaze alternating between the distinguished man of science and the reporter.

"I am Mr Van Dusen," explained The Thinking Machine. "Allow me, Miss Harding – Mr Hatch."

The girl smiled and offered a gloved hand cordially to each of the two men. The Thinking Machine merely touched it respectfully; Hatch shook it warmly. The eyes were veiled demurely for an instant, then the lids were lifted suddenly, and she favored the newspaper man with a gaze that sent the blood to his cheeks.

"Be seated, Miss Harding," the scientist invited.

"I hardly know just what I came to say, and just how to say it," she began uncertainly, and smiled a little. "And anyway I had hoped that you were alone; so—"

"You may speak with perfect freedom before Mr Hatch," interrupted The Thinking Machine. "Perhaps I shall be able to aid you; but first will you repeat the history of the bracelet as nearly as you can in the words of the masked woman who called upon you so – so unconventionally."

The girl's brows were lifted inquiringly, with a sort of start.

"We were discussing the case when your card was brought in," continued The Thinking Machine tersely. "We shall continue from that point, if you will be so good."

The young woman recited the history of the bracelet, slowly and carefully.

"And that statement of the case is correct?" queried the scientist.

"Absolutely, so far as I know," was the reply.

"And as I understand it, you were in the house alone; that is, alone except for the servants?"

"Yes; I live there alone, except for a companion and two servants. The servants were not within the sound of my voice, even if I had screamed, and Miss Talbott, my companion, it happened, was out for the night."

The Thinking Machine had dropped back into his chair, with squint eyes turned upward, and long white fingers pressed tip to tip. He sat thus silently for a long time. The girl at last broke the silence.

"Naturally I was a little surprised," she remarked falteringly, "that I should have appeared just in time to interrupt a discussion of the singular happenings in my home last night; but really—"

"This bracelet," interrupted the little scientist again. "It was of oval form, perhaps, with no stones set in it, or anything of that sort – merely a band that fastened with an invisible hinge. That's right, I believe?"

"Quite right, yes," replied the girl readily.

It occurred to Hatch suddenly that he himself did not know – in fact, had not inquired – the shape of the bracelet. He knew only that it was gold, and of no great value. Knowing nothing about what it looked like, he had not described it to The Thinking Machine; therefore he raised his eyes inquiringly now. The drawn face of the scientist was inscrutable.

"As I started to say," the girl went on, "the bracelet and the events of last night have no direct connection with the purpose of my visit here."

"Indeed?" commented the scientist.

"No; I came to see if you could assist me in another way. For instance," and she fumbled in her pocket book, "I happened to know, Professor Van Dusen, of some of the remarkable things you have accomplished, and I should like to ask if you can throw any light on this for me."

She drew from the pocketbook a crumpled, yellow sheet of paper – a strip perhaps an inch wide, thin as tissue, glazed, and extraordinarily wrinkled. The Thinking Machine squinted at its manifold irregularities for an instant curiously, nodded, sniffed at it, then slowly began to unfold it, smoothing it out carefully as he went. Hatch leaned forward eagerly and stared. He was a little more than astonished at the end to find that the sheet was blank. The Thinking Machine examined both sides of the paper thoughtfully.

"And where did you find the bracelet at last?" he inquired casually.

"I have reason to believe," the girl rushed on suddenly, regardless of the question, "that this strip of paper has been substituted for one of real value, – I may say one of great value, – and I don't know how to proceed, unless—"

"Where did you find the bracelet?" demanded The Thinking Machine again impatiently.

Hatch would have hesitated a long time before he would have said the girl was disconcerted at the question, or that there had been any real change in the expression of her pretty face. And yet—

"After the masked woman had gone," she went on calmly, "I summoned the servants and we made a search. We found the bracelet at last. I thought I had tossed it into my jewel box when I removed it last night; but it seems I was careless enough to let it fall down behind my dressing table, and it was there all the time the – the masked woman was in my room."

"And when did you make this discovery?" asked The Thinking Machine.

"Within a few minutes after she went out."

"In making your search, you were guided, perhaps, by a belief that in the natural course of events the bracelet could not have disappeared from your jewel box unless some one had entered the room before the masked woman entered; and further that if anyone had entered you would have been awakened?"

"Precisely." There was another pause. "And now please," she went on, "what does this blank strip of paper mean?"

"You had expected something with writing on it, of course?"

"That's just what I had expected," and she laughed nervously. "You may rest assured I was considerably surprised at finding that."

"I can imagine you were," remarked the scientist dryly.

The conversation had reached a point where Hatch was hopelessly lost. The young woman and the scientist were talking with mutual understanding of things that seemed to have no connection with anything that had gone before. What was the paper anyway? Where did it come from? What connection did it have with the affairs of the previous night? How did—

"Mr Hatch, a match, please," requested The Thinking Machine.

Wonderingly the reporter produced one and handed it over. The imperturbable man of science lighted it and thrust the mysterious paper into the blaze. The girl arose with a sudden, startled cry, and snatched at the paper desperately, extinguishing the match as she did so. The Thinking Machine turned disapproving eyes on her.

"I thought you were going to burn it!" she gasped.

"There is not the slightest danger of that, Miss Harding," declared The Thinking Machine coldly. He examined the blank sheet again. "This way, please."

He arose and led the way into his tiny laboratory across the narrow hall, with the girl following. Hatch trailed behind, wondering vaguely what it was all about. A small brazier flashed into flame as The Thinking Machine applied a match, and curious eyes peered over his shoulders as he held the blank strip, now smoothed out, so that the rising heat would strike it.

For a long time three pairs of eyes were fastened on the mysterious paper, all with understanding now, but nothing appeared. Hatch glanced round at the young woman. Her face wore an expression of tense excitement. The red lips were slightly parted in anticipation, the eyes sparkling, and the cheeks flushed deeply. In staring at her the reporter forgot for the instant everything else, until suddenly:

"There! There! Do you see?"

The exclamation burst from her triumphantly, as faint, scrawly lines grew on the strip suspended over the brazier. Totally oblivious of their presence apparently, The Thinking Machine was squinting steadily at the paper, which was slowly crinkling up into wavy lines under the influence of the heat. Gradually the edges were charring, and the odor of scorched paper filled the room. Still the scientist held the paper over the fire. Just as it seemed inevitable that it would burst into flame, he withdrew it and turned to the girl.

"There was no substitution," he remarked tersely. "It is sympathetic ink."

"What does it say?" demanded the young woman abruptly. "What does it mean?"

The Thinking Machine spread the scorched strip of paper on the table before them carefully, and for a long time studied it minutely.

"Really, my dear young woman, I don't know," he said crabbedly at last. "It may take days to find out what it means."

"But something's written there! Read it!" the girl insisted.

"Read it for yourself," said the scientist impatiently. "I am frank to say it's beyond me as it is now. No, don't touch it. It will crumble to pieces."

Faintly, yet decipherable under a magnifying glass, the three were able to make out this on the paper:

Stonehedge-idim-sérpa'l ed serueh siort tnaeG ed etéT al rap eétej erbmo'l ed tniop ud zerit sruO'd rehcoR ud eueuq ud dron ua sdeip tnec. W.F.H.

"What does it mean? What does it mean?" demanded the young woman impatiently. "What does it mean?"

The sudden hardening of her tone caused both Hatch and The Thinking Machine to turn and stare at her. Some strange change had come over her face. There was chagrin, perhaps, and there was more than that, – a merciless glitter in the brown eyes, a grim expression about the chin and mouth, a greedy closing and unclosing of the small, well shaped hands.

"I presume it's a cipher of some sort," remarked The Thinking Machine curtly. "It may take time to read it and to learn definitely just where the treasure is hidden, and you may have to wait for—"

"Treasure!" exclaimed the girl. "Did you say treasure? There is treasure, then?"

The Thinking Machine shrugged his shoulders. "What else?" he asked. "Now, please, let me see the bracelet."

"The bracelet!" the girl repeated, and again Hatch noted that quick change of expression on the pretty face. "I – er – must you see it? I – er—" And she stopped.

"It is absolutely necessary, if I make anything of this," and the scientist indicated the charred paper. "You have it in your pocketbook, of course."

The girl stepped forward suddenly and leaned over the laboratory table, intently studying the mysterious strip of paper. At last she raised her head as if she had reached a decision.

"I have only a – a part of the bracelet," she announced, "only half. It was unavoidably broken, and—"

"Only half?" interrupted The Thinking Machine, and he squinted coldly into the young woman's eyes.

"Here it is," she said at last, desperately almost. "I don't know where the other half is; it would be useless to ask me."

She drew an aged, badly scratched half circlet of gold from her pocketbook, handed it to the scientist, then went and looked out the window. He examined it – the delicate decorative tracings, then the invisible hinge where the bracelet had been rudely torn apart. Twice he raised his squint eyes and stared at the girl as she stood silhouetted against the light of the window. When he spoke again there was a deeper note in his voice – a singular softening, an unusual deference.

"I shall read the cipher of course, Miss Harding," he said slowly. "It may take an hour, or it may take a week, I don't know." Again he scrutinized the charred paper. "Do you speak French?" he inquired suddenly.

"Enough to understand and to make myself understood," replied the girl. "Why?"

The Thinking Machine scribbled off a copy of the cipher and handed it to her.

"I'll communicate with you when I reach a conclusion," he remarked. "Please leave your address on your card here," and he handed her the card and pencil.

"You know my home address," she said. "Perhaps it would be better for me to call this afternoon late or tomorrow."

"I'd prefer to have your address," said the scientist. "As I say, I don't know when I shall be able to speak definitely."

The girl paused for a moment and tapped the blunt end of the pencil against her white teeth thoughtfully with her left hand. "As a matter of fact," she said at last, "I am not returning home now. The events of last night have shaken me considerably, and I am now on my way to Blank Rock, a little sea shore town where I shall remain for a few days. My address there will be the High Tower."

"Write it down, please!" directed The Thinking Machine tersely. The girl stared at him strangely, with a challenge in her eyes, then leaned over the table to write. Before the pencil had touched the card, however, she changed her mind and handed both to Hatch, with a smile.

"Please write it for me," she requested. "I write a wretched hand anyway, and besides I have on my gloves." She turned again to the little scientist, who stood squinting over her head. "Thank you so much for your trouble," she said in conclusion. "You can reach me at this address either by wire or letter for the next fortnight."

And a few minutes later she was gone. For awhile The Thinking Machine was silent as he again studied the faint writing on the strip of paper.

"The cipher," he remarked to Hatch at last, "is no cipher at all; it's so simple. But there are some other things I shall have to find out first, and – suppose you drop by early tomorrow to see me."

Half an hour later The Thinking Machine went to the telephone, and after running through the book called a number.

"Is Miss Harding home yet?" he demanded, when an answer came.

"No, sir," was the reply, in a woman's voice.

"Would you mind telling me, please, if she is left handed?"

"Why, no, sir. She's right handed. Who is this?"

"I knew it, of course. Goodbye."

The Thinking Machine was squinting into the inquiring eyes of Hutchinson Hatch.

"The reason why the police are so frequently unsuccessful in explaining the mysteries of crime," he remarked, "is not through lack of natural intelligence, or through lack of a birth given aptitude for the work, but through the lack of an absolutely accurate knowledge which is wide enough to enable them to proceed. Now here is a case in point. It starts with a cipher, goes into an intricate astronomical calculation, and from that into simple geometry. The difficulty with the detectives is not that they could not work out each of these as it was presented, perhaps with the aid of some outsider, but that they would not recognize the existence of the three phases of the problem in the first place.

"You have heard me say frequently, Mr Hatch, that logic is inevitable – as inevitable as that two and two make four not sometimes, but all the time. That is true; but it must have an indisputable starting point, – the one unit which is unassailable. In this case unit produces unit in order, and the proper array of these units gives a coherent answer. Let me demonstrate briefly just what I mean.

"A masked woman, employing the method at least of a thief, demands a certain bracelet of this Miss – Miss Harding. (Is that her name?) She doesn't want jewels; she wants that bracelet. Whatever other conjectures may be advanced, the one dominant fact is that that bracelet, itself of little comparative value, is worth more than all the rest to her, – the masked woman, I mean, – and she has endangered liberty and perhaps life to get it. Why? The history of the bracelet as she herself stated it to Miss Harding gives the answer. A man in prison, under sentence of death, had that bracelet at one time. We can conjecture immediately, therefore, that the masked woman knew that the fact of its having been in this man's possession gave him an opportunity at least of so marking the bracelet, – or of confiding in it, I may say, a valuable secret. One's first thought, therefore, is of treasure—hidden treasure. We shall go further and say treasure hidden by a Continental officer to prevent its falling into other hands as loot. This officer under sentence of death, and therefore cut off from all communication with the outside, took a desperate means of communicating the location of the treasure to his heirs.

That is clear, isn't it?" The reporter nodded.

"I described the bracelet, – you heard me, – and yet I had never seen it, nor had I a description of it. That description was merely a forward step, a preliminary test of the truth of the first assumptions. I reasoned that the bracelet must be of a type which could be employed to carry a message safely past prying eyes; and there is really only one sort which is feasible, and that is the one I described. These bracelets are always hollow, the invisible hinges hold them together on one side, and they lock on the other. It would be perfectly possible, therefore, to write the message the prisoner wanted to send out on a strip of tissue paper, or any thin paper, and cram it into the bracelet at the lock end. In that event it would certainly pass minute inspection; the only difficulty would be for the outside person to find it. That was a chance; but it was all a chance anyway.

"When the young woman came here and produced a strip of thin paper, apparently blank, with the multitude of wrinkles in it, I immediately saw that that paper had been recovered from the bracelet. It was old, yellow, and worn. Therefore, blank or not, that was the message which the prisoner had sent out. You saw me hold it over the brazier, and saw the characters appear. It was sympathetic ink, of course.

"Hard to make in prison, you say? Not at all. Writing either with lemon juice or milk, once dry, is perfectly invisible on paper; but when exposed to heat at any time afterward, it will appear. That is a chemical truth.

"Now the thing that appeared was a cipher – an absurd one, still a cipher. Extraordinary precaution of the prisoner who was about to die! This cipher – let me see exactly," and the scientist spelled it out:

"'Stonehedge-idim-sérpa'l ed serueh siort tnaeG ed etéT al rap eétej erbmo'l ed tniop ud zerit sruO'd rehcoR ud eueuq ud dron ua sdeip tnec'

"If you know anything of languages, Mr Hatch," he continued, "you know that French is the only language where the apostrophe and the accent marks play a very important part. A moment's study of this particular cipher therefore convinced me that it was in French. I tried the simple expedient of reading it backward, with this result:

"'Stonehedge. Cent pieds au nord du queue du Rocher d'Ours tirez du point de l'ombre jetée par La Téte de Geant trois heures de l'aprés-midi.'

"Here, therefore, was a sensible statement in French, which translated freely into English is simply:

'Stonehedge. Hundred feet due north from tail Bear Rock through apex (or point) of shadow cast by Giant's Head, three p.m.'

"I had read the cipher and knew its English before I gave a copy of it to the young woman who was here. I specifically asked her if she knew French, to give her a clue by which she might interpret the cipher herself. And thus I blazed the way within a few minutes to the point where astronomical and geometrical calculations were next. Please bear in mind that this message from the dead was not dated.

"Now, about the young woman herself," continued the scientist after a moment. "The statement of how she came to find the bracelet was obviously untrue; particularly are we convinced of this when she cannot, or will not, explain how it was broken. Therefore, another field is open for scrutiny. The bracelet was broken. If we assume that it is the bracelet, and there is no reason to doubt it, and we know it is in her possession, we know also that more than one person had been searching for it. We know positively that that other person – not the masked girl, but the one who had preceded her to Miss Harding's room on the same night – got the bracelet from Miss Harding, and we are safe in assuming that it passed out of that other person's hand by force. The bracelet had been literally torn apart at the hinge. In other words, there had been a physical contest, and one piece of the circlet – the piece with the message – passed out of the hands of the person who had preceded the masked woman and stolen the bracelet.

"But this is by the way. Stonehedge is the name of the old Tremaine Harding estate, about twenty miles out, and there the Tremaine Harding family valuables were hidden by William Tremaine Harding, who died by bullet, a martyr to the cause of freedom. We shall get the treasure this afternoon, after I have settled one or two dates and made the astronomical and geometrical calculations which are necessary."

There was silence for a minute or more, broken at last by the impatient "Honk, honk!" of an automobile outside.

"We'll go now," announced The Thinking Machine as he arose. "There is a car for us."

He led the way out, Hatch following. A heavy touring car, with three seats, driven by a young woman, was waiting at the door. The woman was a stranger to the reporter; but there was no introduction.

"Did you get the date of Captain Harding's imprisonment?" asked The Thinking Machine.

"Yes," was the reply, – "June 3, 1776."

The Thinking Machine clambered in, Hatch following silently, and the car rushed away. It paused in a suburb long enough to pick up two workmen with picks and shovels, who took their places in the back seat, and then the automobile with its strange company – a pretty woman, a newspaper reporter, a distinguished scientist, and two laborers – proceeded on its way. Hatch, alone in the second seat, heard only one remark by the scientist, and this was:

"Of course she was clever enough to read the cipher, after I gave her the hint that it was in French; so we shall find that the place has been dug over; but there is only one chance in three hundred and sixty-five that the treasure was found. I give her credit for extraordinary cleverness; but not enough to make the necessary astronomical calculations."

A run of an hour and a half brought them to Stonehedge, a huge old estate with ramshackle dwelling and acres of rock ridden ground. Away off in the northwest corner were two large stones – Bear Rock and Giants Head – rising fifteen or twenty feet above the ground. The car was driven over a rough road and stopped near them.

"You see, she did read the cipher," remarked the scientist placidly. "Workmen have already been here."

Straight ahead of them was an excavation ten feet or more square. Hatch peered into it, while The Thinking Machine busied himself by planting a stake at the so-called tail of Bear Rock. Then he glanced at his watch, – it was half past two o'clock, – and sat down with the young woman in the shadow of Giants Head. Hatch lounged on the ground near them, and the workmen made themselves comfortable in their own way.

"We can't do anything till three o'clock," remarked The Thinking Machine.

"And just what shall we do then?" inquired the young woman expectantly. It was the first time she had spoken since they started.

"It is rather difficult to explain," said The Thinking Machine. "The hole there proves that the young woman read the cipher, of course. Now here briefly is why the treasure was not found. Today is September 17.

A measurement was made, according to instructions, from the tail of Bear Rock through the apex of the shadow of Giants Head precisely at three o'clock yesterday, one hundred feet due north, or as near north as possible. The hole shows the end of the hundred-foot line. Now, we know that Captain Harding was imprisoned on June 3, 1776; we know he buried the treasure before that date; we have a right to assume that it was only shortly before. On June 3 of any year the apex of the shadow will be in a totally different place from September 17, because of the movement of the earth about the sun and the relative changes in the sun's position. What we must do now is to find precisely where the shadow falls at three o'clock today, then make our calculations to show where it will fall say one week before June 3. Do you follow me? In other words, a difference of half a foot in the location of the apex of the shadow will make a difference of many feet at the end of one hundred feet when we follow the cipher."

At precisely three o'clock The Thinking Machine noted the position of the shadow, and then began a calculation which covered two sheets of blank paper which Hatch had in his pocket.

"This is correct," said The Thinking Machine at last as he arose and planted another stake in the ground. "There is a chance of course that we miss fire the first time because of possible seismic disturbances at sometime past or of a change in the surface of the ground; but this is mathematically correct."

Then, with the assistance of the newspaper man and the young woman, he drew his hundred-foot line, and planted a third stake.

"Dig here!" he told the workmen.

One hour later the long lost family plate and jewels of the ancient Harding family had been unearthed. The Thinking Machine and the others stooped over the rotting box which had been brought to the surface and noted the contents. Roughly the value was above two hundred thousand dollars.

"And I think that is all, Miss Harding," said the scientist at last. "It is yours. Load it into your car there and drive home."

"Miss Harding!" Hatch repeated quickly, with a glance at the young woman. "Miss Harding?"

The Thinking Machine turned and squinted at the reporter for a moment. "Didn't you know that the young woman who called on me was not Miss Harding?" he demanded. "It was evident in her every act, – in her failing to explain the broken bracelet; and in the fact that she was left handed. You must have noticed that. Well, this is Miss Harding, and she is right handed."

The girl smiled at Hatch's astonishment.

"Then the other young woman merely impersonated Miss Harding?" he asked at last.

"That is all, and cleverly," replied The Thinking Machine. "She merely wanted me to read the cipher for her. I put her on the track of reading it herself purposely, and she and the persons associated with her are responsible for the excavation over there."

"But who is the other young woman?"

"She is the one who visited Miss Harding, wearing a mask."

"But what is her name?"

"I'm sure I haven't the faintest idea, Mr Hatch," responded the little scientist shortly. "We have her to thank, however, for placing a solution of the affair into our hands. Who she is and what she is, is of no real consequence, particularly as Miss Harding has this."

The scientist indicated the box with one small foot, then turned and clambered into the waiting automobile.

14

PROBLEM OF THE CROSS MARK

It was an unsolved mystery, apparently a riddle without an answer, in which Watson Richards, the distinguished character actor, happened to play a principal part. The story was told at the Mummers Club one dull afternoon. Richards' listeners were three other actors, a celebrated poet, and a newspaper reporter named Hutchinson Hatch.

"You know there are few men in the profession today who really amount to anything who haven't had their hard knocks. Well, my hard times came early, and lasted a long time. So it was just about three years ago to a day that a real crisis came in my affairs. It seemed the end. I had gone one day without food, had bunked in the park that night, and here it was two o'clock in the afternoon of another day. It was dismal enough.

"I was standing on a corner, gazing moodily across the street at the display window of a restaurant, rapidly approaching the don't care stage. Some one came up behind and touched me on the shoulder. I turned listlessly enough, and found myself facing a stranger – a clean cut, well groomed man of some forty years.

"'Is this Mr Watson Richards, the character actor?' he asked.

"'Yes,' I replied.

"'I have been looking for you everywhere,' he explained briefly. 'I want to engage you to do a part for one performance. Are you at liberty?'

"You chaps know what that meant to me just at that moment. Certainly the words dispelled some unpleasant possibilities I had been considering.

"'I am at liberty—yes,' I replied. 'Be glad to do it. What sort of part is it?'

"'An old man,' he informed me. 'Just one performance, you know. Perhaps you'd better come up town with me and see Mr Hallman right now.'

"I agreed with a readiness which approached eagerness, and he called a passing cab. Hallman was perhaps the manager, or stage manager, I thought. We had driven on for a block in the general direction of up town, my companion chatting pleasantly. Finally he offered me a cigar. I accepted it. I know now that cigar was drugged, because I had hardly taken more than two or three puffs from it when I lost myself completely.

"The next thing I remember distinctly was of stepping out of the cab – I think the stranger assisted me – and going into a house. I don't know where it was – I didn't know then – didn't know even the street. I was dizzy, giddy. And suddenly I stood before a tall, keen faced, clean shaven man. He was Hallman. The stranger introduced me and then left the room. Hallman regarded me keenly for several minutes, and somehow under that scrutiny my dormant faculties were aroused. I had thrown away the cigar at the door.

"'You play character parts?' Hallman began.

"'Yes, all the usual things,' I told him. 'I'm rather obscure, but—'

"'I know,' he interrupted; 'but I have seen your work, and like it. I have been told too that you are remarkably clever at make-up.'

"I think I blushed, – I hope I did, anyway, – I know I nodded. He paused to stare at me for a long time.

"'For instance,' he went on finally, 'you would have no difficulty at all in making up as a man of seventy-five years?'

"'Not the slightest,' I answered. 'I have played such parts.'

"'Yes, yes, I know,' and he seemed a little impatient. 'Well, your make-up is the matter which is most important here. I want you for only one performance; but the make-up must be perfect, you understand.' Again he stopped and stared at me. 'The pay will be one hundred dollars for the one performance.'

"He drew out a drawer of a desk and produced a photograph. He looked at it, then at me, several times, and finally placed it in my hands.

"'Can you make up to look precisely like that?' he asked quietly.

"I studied the photograph closely. It was that of a man about seventy-five years old, of rather a long cast of features, not unlike the general shape of my own face. He had white hair, and was clean shaven. It was simple enough, with the proper wig, a make-up box, and a mirror.

"'I can,' I told Hallman.

"'Would you mind putting on the make-up here now for my inspection?' he inquired.

"'Certainly not,' I replied. It did not strike me at the moment as unusual. 'But I'll need the wig and paints.'

"'Here they are,' said Hallman abruptly, and produced them. 'There's a mirror in front of you. Go ahead.'

"I examined the wig and compared it with the photograph. It was as near perfect as I had ever seen. The make-up box was new and the most complete I ever saw. It didn't occur to me until a long time afterward that it had never been used before. So I went to work. Hallman paced up and down nervously behind me. At the end of twenty minutes I turned upon him a face which was so much like the photograph that I might have posed for it. He stared at me in amazement.

"'By George!' he exclaimed. 'That's it! It's marvelous!' Then he turned and opened the door. 'Come in, Frank,' he called, and the man who had conducted me there entered. Hallman indicated me with a wave of his hand. 'How is it?' he asked.

"Frank, whoever he was, also seemed astonished. Then that passed and a queer expression appeared on his face. You may imagine that I awaited their verdict anxiously.

"'Perfect – absolutely perfect,' said Frank at last.

"'Perhaps the only thing,' Hallman mused critically, 'is that it isn't quite pale enough.'

"'Easily remedied,' I replied, and turned again to the make-up box. A moment later I turned back to the two men. Simple enough, you know – it was one of those pallid, pasty faced make-ups – the old man on the verge of the grave, and all that sort of thing—good deal of pearl powder.

"'That's it!' the two men exclaimed.

"The man Frank looked at Hallman inquiringly.

"'Go ahead,' said Hallman, and Frank left the room.

"Hallman went over, closed and locked the door, after which he came back and sat down in front of me, staring at me for a long time in silence. At length he opened an upper drawer of the desk and glanced in. A revolver lay there, right under his hand. I know now he intended that I should see it.

"'Now, Mr Richards,' he said at last very slowly, 'what we want you to do is very simple, and as I said there's a hundred dollars in it. I know your circumstances perfectly – you need the hundred dollars.' He offered me a cigar, and foolishly enough I accepted it. 'The part you are to play is that of an old man, who is ill in bed, speechless, utterly helpless. You are dying, and you are to play the part. Use your eyes all you want; but don't speak!'

"Gradually the dizziness I had felt before was coming upon me again. As I said, I know now it was the cigar; but I kept on smoking.

"'There will be no rehearsal,' Hallman went on, and now I knew he was fingering the revolver I had seen in the desk; but it made no particular impression on me. 'If I ask you questions, you may nod an affirmative, but don't speak! Do only what I say, and nothing else!'

"Full realization was upon me now; but everything was growing hazy again. I remember I fought the feeling for a moment; then it seemed to overwhelm me, and I was utterly helpless under the dominating power of that man.

"'When am I to play the part?' I remember asking.

"'Now!' said Hallman suddenly, and he rose. 'I'm afraid you don't fully understand me yet, Mr Richards. If you play the part properly, you get the hundred dollars; if you don't, this!'

"He meant the revolver. I stared at it dumbly, overcome by a helpless terror, and tried to stand up. Then there came a blank, for how long I don't know. The next thing I remember I was lying in bed, propped up against several pillows. I opened my eyes feebly enough, and there wasn't any acting about it either, because whoever drugged those cigars knew his business.

"There in front of me was Hallman, with a grief stricken expression on his face which made all my art seem amateurish. There was another man there too (not Frank), and a woman who seemed to be about forty years old. I couldn't see their faces – I wouldn't even be able to suggest a description of them, because the room was almost dark. Just the faintest flicker of light came through the drawn curtains; but I could see Hallman's devilish face all right. These three conversed together in low tones – sick room voices – but I couldn't hear, and doubt if I could have followed their conversation if I had heard.

"Finally the door opened and a girl entered. I have seen many women, but – well, she was peculiarly fascinating. She gave one little cry, rushed toward the bed impulsively, dropped on her knees beside it, and buried her face in the sheets. She was shaking with sobs.

"Then I knew – intuitively, perhaps, but I knew – that in some way I was being used to injure that girl. A sudden feeling of fearful anger seized upon me, but I couldn't move to save my soul. Hallman must have caught the blaze in my eyes, for he came forward on the other side of the bed, and, under cover of a handkerchief which he had been using rather ostentatiously, pressed the revolver against my side.

"But I wouldn't be made a tool of. In my dazed condition I know I was seized with a desperate desire to fight it out – to make him kill me if he had to, but I would not deceive the girl. I knew if I could jerk my head down on the pillow it would disarrange the wig, and perhaps she would see. I couldn't. I might pass my hands across my make-up and smear it. But I couldn't lift my hands. I was struggling to speak, and couldn't.

"Then somehow I lost myself again. Hazily I remember that somebody placed a paper in front of me on a book – a legal-looking document – and guided my hand across it; but that isn't clear. I was helpless, inert, so much clay in the hands of this man Hallman. Then everything faded – slowly, slowly. My impression was that I was actually dying; my eyelids closed of themselves; and the last thing I saw was the shining gold of that girl's hair as she sobbed there beside me.

"That's all of it. When I became fully conscious again a policeman was shaking me. I was sitting on a bench in the park. He swore at me volubly, and I got up and moved slowly along the path with my hands in my pockets. Something was clenched in one hand. I drew it out and looked at it. It was a hundred-dollar bill. I remember I got something to eat; and I woke up in a hospital.

"Well, that's the story. Make what you like of it. It can never be solved, of course. It was three years ago. You fellows know what I have done in that time. Well, I'd give it all, every bit of it, to meet that girl again (I should know her), tell her what I know, and make her believe that it was no fault of mine."

Hutchinson Hatch related the circumstances casually one afternoon a day or so later to Professor Augustus S. F. X. Van Dusen – The Thinking Machine.

That eminent man of science listened petulantly, as he listened to all things. "It happened in this city?" he inquired at the end.

"Yes."

"But Richards has no idea what part of the city?"

"Not the slightest. I imagine that the drugged cigar and a naturally weakened condition made him lose his bearings while in the cab."

"I dare say," commented the scientist. "And of course he has never seen Hallman again?"

"No – he would have mentioned it if he had."

"Does Richards remember the exact date of the affair?"

"I dare say he does, though he didn't mention it," replied the reporter.

"Suppose you see Richards and get the date — exactly, if possible," remarked The Thinking Machine. "You might telephone it to me. Perhaps —" and he shrugged his slender shoulders.

"You think there is a possibility of solving the riddle?" demanded the reporter eagerly.

"Certainly," snapped The Thinking Machine. "It requires no solution. It is ridiculously simple, – obvious, I might say, – and yet I dare say the girl Richards referred to has been the victim of some huge plot. It's worth looking into for her sake."

"Remember, it happened three years ago," Hatch suggested tentatively.

"It wouldn't matter particularly if it happened three hundred years ago," declared the scientist. "Logic, Mr Hatch, remains the same through all the ages – from Adam and Eve to us. Two and two made four in the Garden of Eden just as they do now in a counting house. Therefore, the solution, I say, is absurdly simple. The only problem is to discover the identity of the principals in the affair – and a child could do that."

Later that afternoon Hatch telephoned to The Thinking Machine from the Mummers Club.

"That date you asked for was May 19, three years ago," said the reporter.

"Very well," commented The Thinking Machine. "Drop by to-morrow afternoon. Perhaps we can solve the riddle for Richards."

Hatch called late the following afternoon, as directed, but The Thinking Machine was not in.

"He went out about nine o'clock, and hasn't returned yet," the scientist's aged servant, Martha, informed him.

That night about ten o'clock Hatch used the telephone in a second attempt to reach The Thinking Machine.

"He hasn't come in yet," Martha told him over the wire. "He said he would be back for luncheon; but he isn't here yet."

Hatch replaced the receiver thoughtfully on the hook. Early the following morning he again used the telephone, and there was a note of anxiety in Martha's voice when she answered.

"He hasn't come yet, sir," she explained. "Please, what ought I to do? I'm afraid something has happened to him."

"Don't do anything yet," replied Hatch. "I dare say he'll return to-day."

Again at noon, at six o'clock, and at eleven that night Hatch called Martha on the telephone. Still the scientist had not appeared. Hatch too was worried now; yet how should he proceed? He didn't know, and he hesitated to think of the possibilities. On the morrow, however, something must be done – he would take the matter to Detective Mallory at police headquarters if necessary.

But this was made unnecessary unexpectedly by the arrival next morning of a letter from The Thinking Machine. As he read, an expression of utter bewilderment spread over Hatch's face. Tersely the letter was like this:

Employ an expert burglar, a careful, clever man. At two o'clock of the night following the receipt of this letter go with him to the alley which runs behind No. 810 Blank Street. Enter this house with him from the rear, go up two flights of stairs, and let him pick the lock of the third door on the left from the head of the stairs. Silence above everything. Don't shoot if possible to avoid it.

Van Dusen.

P.S. Put some ham sandwiches in your pocket.

Hatch stared at the note in blank bewilderment for a long time; but he obeyed orders. Thus it came to pass that at ten minutes of two o'clock that night he boosted the notorious Blindy Bates – a man of rare accomplishments in his profession, who at the moment happened to be out of prison – to the top of the rear fence of No. 810 Blank Street. Bates hauled up the reporter, and they leaped down lightly inside the yard.

The back door was simplicity itself to the gifted Bates, and yielded in less than sixty seconds from the moment he laid his hand upon it. Then came a sneaking, noiseless advance along the lower hall, to the accompaniment of innumerable thrills up and down Hatch's spinal column; up the first flight safely, with Blindy Bates leading the way; then along the hall and up the second flight. There was absolutely not a sound in the house — they moved like ghosts.

At the top of the second flight Bates shot a gleam of light from his dark lantern along the hall. The third door it was. And a moment later he was concentrating every faculty on the three locks of this door. Still there had been not the slightest sound. The one spot in the darkness was the bull's eye of the lantern as it illuminated the lock. The first lock was unfastened, then the second, and finally the third. Bates didn't open the door – he merely stepped back – and the door opened as of its own volition. Involuntarily Hatch's hand closed fiercely on his revolver, and Bates's ready weapon glittered a little in the darkness.

"Thanks," came after a moment, in the quiet, querulous voice of The Thinking Machine. "Mr Hatch, did you bring those sandwiches?"

Half an hour later The Thinking Machine and Hatch appeared at police headquarters. Being naturally of a retiring, unostentatious disposition, Bates did not accompany them; instead, he went his way fingering a bill of moderately large denomination.

Detective Mallory was at home in bed; but Detective Cunningham, another shining light, received his distinguished visitor and Hatch.

"There's a man named Howard Guerin now asleep in his state room aboard the steamer Austriana, which sails at five o'clock this morning – just an hour and a half from now – for Hamburg," began The Thinking Machine without any preface. "Please have him arrested immediately."

"What charge?" asked the detective.

"Really, it's of no consequence," replied The Thinking Machine. "Attempted murder, conspiracy, embezzlement, fraud – whatever you like. I can prove any or all of them."

"I'll go after him myself," said the detective.

"And there is also a young woman aboard," continued The Thinking Machine, – "a Miss Hilda Fanshawe. Please have her detained, not arrested, and keep a close guard on her – not to prevent escape, but to protect her."

"Tell us some of the particulars of it," asked the detective.

"I haven't slept in more than forty-eight hours," replied The Thinking Machine. "I'll explain it all this afternoon, after I've rested a while."

The Thinking Machine, for the benefit of Detective Mallory and his satellites, recited briefly the salient points of the story told by the actor, Watson Richards. His listeners were Howard Guerin, tall, keen faced, and clean shaven; Miss Hilda Fanshawe, whose pretty face reflected her every thought; Hutchinson Hatch, and three or four headquarters men. Every eye was upon the drawn face of the diminutive scientist, as he sat far back in his chair, with squint eyes turned upward, and fingertips pressed together.

"From the facts as he stated them, we know beyond all question, in the very beginning, that Mr Richards was used as a tool to further some conspiracy or fraud," explained The Thinking Machine. "That was obvious. So the first thing to do was to learn the identity of those persons who played the principal parts in it. From Mr Richards' story we apparently had nothing, yet it gave us practically the names and addresses of the persons at the bottom of the thing.

"How? To find how, we'll have to consider the purpose of the conspiracy. An actor—an artist in facial impersonation, we might say—is picked up in the street and compelled to go through the mummery of a death bed scene while stupefied with drugs. Obviously this was arranged for the benefit of some person who must be convinced that he or she had witnessed a dissolution and the signature of a will, perhaps,—and a will signed under the eyes of that person for whose benefit the farce was acted.

"So we assume a will was signed. We know, within reason, that the mummery was arranged for the benefit of a young woman—Miss Fanshawe here. From the intricacy and daring of the plot, it was pretty safe to assume that a large sum of money was involved. As a matter of fact, there was – more than a million. Now, here is where we take an abstract problem and establish the identity of the actors in it. That will was signed by compulsory forgery, if I may use the phrase, by an utter stranger—

a man who could not have known the handwriting of the man whose name he signed, and who was in a condition that makes it preposterous to imagine that he even attempted to sign that name. Yet the will was signed, and the conspirators had to have a signature that would bear inspection. Now, what have we left?

"When a person is incapable of signing his or her name, physically or by reason of no education, the law accepts a cross mark as a signature, when properly witnessed. We know Mr Richards couldn't have known or imitated the signature of the old man he impersonated; but he did sign – therefore a cross mark, which could have been established beyond question in a court of law. Now, you see how I established the identity of the persons in this fraud. I got the date of the incident from Mr Richards, then a trip to the surrogate's office told me all I wanted to know. What will had been filed for probate about that date which bore the cross mark as a signature? The records answered the question instantly – John Wallace Lawrence.

"I glanced over the will. It specifically allowed Miss Hilda Fanshawe a trivial thousand dollars a year, and yet she was Lawrence's adopted daughter. See how the joints began to fit together? Further, the will left the bulk of the property to Howard Guerin, a Mrs Francis, – since deceased, by the way, – and one Frank Hughes. The men were his nephews, the woman his niece. The joints continued to fit nicely, therefore the problem was solved. It was an easy matter to find these people, once I knew their names. I found Guerin – Mr Richards knew him as Hallman – and asked him about the matter. From the fact that he locked me up in a room of his house and kept me prisoner for two days I was convinced that he was the principal conspirator, and so it proves."

Again there was silence. Detective Mallory took three long breaths, and asked a question. "But where was John Wallace Lawrence when this thing happened?"

"Miss Fanshawe had been in Europe, and was rushing home, knowing that her adopted father was dying," The Thinking Machine explained. "As a matter of fact, when she returned Mr Lawrence was dead – he died the day before the farce which had been arranged for her benefit, and at the moment his body lay in an up stairs room. He was buried two days later – a day after the farce had been played – and she attended his funeral. You see there was no reason why she should have suspected anything. I don't happen to know the provisions of Lawrence's real will, but I dare say it left practically everything to her. The thousand-dollar allowance by the conspirators was a sop to stop possible legal action."

The door of the room opened, and a uniformed man thrust his head in. "Mr Richards wants to see Professor Van Dusen," he announced.

Immediately behind him came the actor. He stopped in the door and stared at Guerin for a moment.

"Why, hello, Hallman!" he remarked pleasantly. Then his eyes fell upon the girl, and a flash of recognition lighted them.

"Miss Fanshawe, permit me, Mr Richards," said The Thinking Machine. "You have met before. This is the gentleman you saw die."

"And where is Frank Hughes?" asked Detective Mallory.

"In South Africa," replied the scientist. "I learned a great deal while I was a prisoner."

A deeply troubled expression suddenly appeared on Hutchinson Hatch's face that night when he was writing the story for his newspaper, and he went to the telephone and called The Thinking Machine.

"If you were guarded so closely as a prisoner in that room, how on earth did you mail that letter to me?" he inquired.

"Guerin came in to say some unpleasant things," came the reply, "and placed several letters he intended to post on the table for a moment. The letter for you was already written and stamped, and I was seeking a way to mail it, so I put it with his letters and he mailed it for me."

Hatch burst out laughing.

15

THE JACKDAW

Monsieur Jean Saint Rocheville lived by his wits, and, being rather witty, he lived rather well. In the beginning he hadn't been Monsieur Jean St. Rocheville at all. Born Jones, christened James Aloysius, nicknamed Jimmie, he had been, first, a pickpocket. Sheer ability lifted him above that; and it came to pass that he graduated from all the cruder professions—second-story work, burglary, and what not—until now, when we meet him, he was a social brigand famous under many names.

For instance, in two cities of the West he was being industriously sought as Wilhelm Van Der Wyde, and was described as of the æsthetic, musical type—young, thick-spectacled, clean-shaven, long-haired, and pale blond, speaking English badly and profusely.

In New York, the police knew him as Hubert Montgomery Wade, card sharp and utterer of worthless checks; and described him as taciturn, past middle age, with fluffy, iron-gray hair, full iron-gray beard, and a singularly pallid face. As we see him, he seemed about thirty, slim, elegant, aristocratic of feature, with close-cut brown hair, carefully waxed mustache, and a suggestion of an imperial. Also, he spoke English with a slight accent.

Monsieur St. Rocheville was smiling as he strode through the spacious estate of Idlewild, whipping his light cane in the early-morning air of a balmy June day. On the whole, he had little to complain of in the way the world was wagging. True, he had failed, at his first attempt, to possess himself of the superb diamond necklace of his hostess, Mrs Wardlaw Browne; but it had not been a discreditable failure; there had been no unpleasant features connected therewith, no exposure; not even a shadow of suspicion. Perhaps, after all, he had been hasty. His invitation had several weeks to run; and meanwhile here were all the luxuries of a splendid country place at his command—motors, horses, tennis, golf, to say nothing of a house full of charming women and several execrable players of auction, who insisted on gambling for high stakes. And auction, Monsieur St. Rocheville might have said, was his middle name.

Idly meditating upon all these pleasant things, St. Rocheville dropped down upon a seat in the shade of a hedge overlooking the rose garden, lighted a cigarette, and fell to watching the curious evolutions of three great velvet-black birds swimming in the air above him. Now they rose in a vast spiral, up, up until they were mere specks against the blue void, only to drop sheerly almost to the earth before their wings stayed them; now with motionless pinions, floating away in immense circles; again darting hither and yon swiftly as an arrow flies, weaving strange patterns in the air. Something here for the Wright brothers to learn, Monsieur St. Rocheville thought lazily.

Came finally an odd whistle from the direction of the house behind him. The three birds swooped down with a rush and vanished beyond the hedge. Curiously St. Rocheville peered through the thick-growing screen. On a second-story balcony stood a girl with one of the birds perched upon each shoulder, and the third at rest on her hand.

"Well, by George!" exclaimed St. Rocheville.

As he looked, the girl flipped something into the air. The birds dived for it simultaneously, immediately returning to their perches. Fascinated, he looked on as the trick was repeated. So this was she, to whom he had heard some one refer as the Jackdaw Girl – the young lady he had caught staring at him so oddly the night before, just after her arrival. He had been introduced to her between rubbers – a charming, piquant wisp of a creature, with big, innocent eyes and cameo features, much given to gay little bursts of laughter. Her name? Oh, yes. Fayerwether – Drusila Fayerwether.

St. Rocheville ventured into the open. Miss Fayerwether smiled, and flung a titbit of some sort directly at his feet. The birds came for it like huge black projectiles. Involuntarily he took a step backward. She laughed.

"They won't hurt you, really," she assured him mockingly. "They are quite tame. Let me show you." She held aloft a slice of toast; the powerful black wings quivered expectantly. "No," she commanded. The toast fell at St. Rocheville's feet. Neither of the birds stirred. "Hold it in your left hand," she directed. Mechanically the astonished young man obeyed. "Extend your right and keep it steady." He did so. "Now, Blitz!"

It was a command. The bird from her left shoulder, the largest of the three, came hurtling toward St. Rocheville with a shrill scream. For an instant the giant wings beat about his ears, then the talons closed on his right hand in no gentle grip, and man and bird stared at each other. To the young man there was something evil and cruel in the beady, fixed eyes; in the poise of the head on the glistening, snakelike neck; in the merciless claws. And, gad, what a beak! It was a thing to tear with, to mutilate, destroy.

St. Rocheville shuddered. The whole performance was creepy and uncanny. It chilled his blood. It seemed out of all proportion, this exquisite, dainty, pink-and-white girl, and the sinister, somber, winged things—

He drew a breath of relief when Blitz, having solemnly gobbled up his toast, flew away to his mistress.

"They are my pets," she said affectionately. "Aren't they beautiful? Blitz and Jack and Jill I call them."

"Strange pets they are, mademoiselle," remarked St. Rocheville gravely. "How did you come to choose them?"

"Why, I've known them always," she replied. "Blitz here is old enough, and I dare say wise enough, to be my grandfather. He is nearly sixty, and was in my family thirty-five years before I was born. He used to stalk solemnly around my cradle like a soldier on guard, and swear dreadfully. He talks a little when he will – half a dozen words or so. Jack and Jill are younger. From their conduct, I should say they haven't yet reached the age of discretion."

"Would you mind telling me," he questioned curiously, "how a person would proceed to tame a—a flock of flying machines like that?"

"Sugar," replied Miss Fayerwether tersely. "They will do anything for sugar."

"Sugar!" Blitz screamed harshly, ruffling his silky plumage. "Sugar!"

Monsieur St. Rocheville went away to keep a tennis engagement. Miss Fayerwether disappeared into her room, leaving the three birds perched on the rail of the balcony. On the court, Rex Miller was waiting for St. Rocheville with a question:

"Meet the new girl last night? Miss Fayerwether?"

"Yes."

"They say she's a bird charmer," Rex went on. "She charmed me, all right. Gad, I always knew I was a bird!"

In his own apartments again, St. Rocheville, hot from his exertions on the tennis court, was preparing for a cold plunge, when Blitz fluttered in at the window and perched himself familiarly on the back of a chair.

"Hello!" said St. Rocheville.

"Hello!" Blitz replied promptly.

Astonished, the young man burst out laughing – a laugh which died under the steady glare of the beady eyes. Again, for some unaccountable reason, he was possessed of that singular feeling of horror he had felt at first. He shook it off impatiently and entered the bathroom, leaving Blitz in possession.

He returned just in time to see the big bird darting through the window with something bright dangling from the powerful beak. He knew instantly what it was – his watch! He had left it on a table, and the bird had taken advantage of his absence to steal it. He started toward the window on a run; but, struck by a sudden thought, he stopped, and stood staring into the open, the while he permitted an idea to seep in. Finally he dropped into a chair, his agile mind teeming with possibilities.

Suppose—just suppose—Blitz had been taught to steal? Absurd, of course! Blitz was probably an upright, moral enough bird according to his own lights; but couldn't he be taught to steal? Either Blitz or another bird like him? He had heard somewhere that magpies would filch any glittering thing and secrete it. Why not jackdaws? Weren't they the same thing, after all? He didn't know.

A tame bird, properly trained, cunning, wary, with an innate faculty of making acquaintances, and powerful on the wing!

St. Rocheville forgot all about his watch in contemplation of a new idea. By George, it was worth an experiment, anyway!

There was a light tapping at his door.

"Monsieur St. Rocheville!" some one called.

"Yes?" he answered.

"It is I, Miss Fayerwether. I think I have your watch here. One of my birds came in my window with it from this direction. Your window was open, so I imagine he—he stole it."

St. Rocheville pulled his bath robe about him and peered out. Miss Fayerwether, with disturbed face, held the watch toward him – the great, solemn-looking bird was perched upon one shoulder.

"Hello!" Blitz greeted him socially.

"It is my watch, yes," said St. Rocheville. "Blitz paid me a visit and took it away with him."

"Naughty, naughty!" and Miss Fayerwether shook one rosy finger under the bird's nose. "He embarrasses me awfully sometimes," she confided. "I can't keep him confined all the time; and he has a trick of picking up any bright thing and bringing it to me."

"Please don't let it disturb you," St. Rocheville begged. "As for you, Monsieur Blitz, I'll keep my eye on you."

Miss Fayerwether vanished down the hall, scolding.

So Blitz had a trick of picking up bright things, eh? Monsieur St. Rocheville was pleased to know it. It was only a question, then, of training the bird to bring the thing he picked up to the right place. Assuredly here was an experiment worth while. In failure or success he was safe. No sane person could blame him for the immoral acts of a bird.

St. Rocheville seemed to have conquered his aversion to Blitz and Jack and Jill, for during the next week he spent hours with them; and hours, too, with their charming mistress. Sometimes he would play games with the birds—curious games – always in the absence of Miss Fayerwether. He would toss bright bits of glass, or even a finger ring, into the grass, or into the open window of his room, and the birds would go hurtling off to search. At length they came to know that there would be a lump of sugar for each on their return, with two pieces for the bird who brought the ring. St. Rocheville found it an absorbing game. He played it for hour after hour, for day after day.

All these things immediately preceded the first public knowledge of that series of robberies within a district of which

Idlewild was the center. Miss Fayerwether, it seemed, was the first victim. She had either lost, or mislaid, she said, a diamond and ruby bracelet, and asked Mrs Wardlaw Browne to have her servants look for it. She pooh-poohed the idea of theft. She had been careless, that was all. Yes, the bracelet was quite valuable; but it would doubtless come to light. She wouldn't have mentioned it at all except for the fact that it was an heirloom.

This politely phrased request opened the floodgates of revelation. Rex Miller had lost a rare scarab stickpin; the elderly Mrs Scott was minus three valuable rings and an aquamarine hair ornament; Claudia Chanoler had been robbed of a rope of pearls worth thousands—robbed was the word she used; an emerald cameo, the property of Agatha Blalock, was missing. Following closely upon these mysterious happenings came word to Mrs Wardlaw Browne of similar happening at the nearby estates of friends. A dozen valuable trinkets had vanished from the Willows where the Melville Pages had a house party; and at Sagamore, Mrs Willets was bewailing the loss of an emerald bracelet which represented a small fortune.

The explosion came the night Mrs Wardlaw Browne's diamond necklace was stolen. There had been an unpleasant scene of some sort in the card room. Rex Miller seemed to think that there was more than luck in the cards Monsieur St. Rocheville held; and he intimated as much. All things considered, Monsieur St. Rocheville behaved superbly. Being the only winner at the table, he tore the score into bits, and it fluttered to the floor. The other gentlemen understood that he disdained to accept money so long as a doubt remained. So the game ended abruptly, and they joined the ladies in the drawing-room. Ten minutes later Mrs Wardlaw Browne's necklace vanished utterly.

So ultimately it came to pass that The Thinking Machine—more properly, Professor Augustus S. F. X. Van Dusen, Ph.D., F.R.S., M.D., LL.D., et cetera, et cetera, logician, analyst, and master mind in the sciences – turned his crabbed genius upon the problem. He consented to do so at the request of Hutchinson Hatch, newspaper reporter; and, singularly enough, it was Monsieur Jean St. Rocheville in person who brought the matter to the reporter's attention. Together they went to The Thinking Machine.

"You know," St. Rocheville took the trouble to explain, "every time I read of a robbery of this sort, either in a newspaper or in fiction, some foreign nobleman is always the villain in the piece." He shrugged his shoulders. "It is an honor I do not desire."

"You are a nobleman, then?" queried The Thinking Machine. The narrowed, pale-blue, squinting eyes were fixed tensely upon the young man's face.

"No." St. Rocheville smiled.

"Extraordinary," murmured the little scientist. "And who are you?"

"My father and my father's father are bankers in France." St. Rocheville lied gracefully. "The situation at Idlewild is—"

"Where?" The Thinking Machine interrupted curtly.

"Idlewild."

"I mean, where is your father a banker?"

"Paris."

"In what capacity? What's his position?"

"Managing director."

"What bank?"

"Crédit Lyonnaise."

The Thinking Machine nodded his satisfaction and dropped his enormous head, with its thick, straw-coloured thatch, back against the chair comfortably, his slim fingers coming to rest precisely tip to tip. Monsieur St. Rocheville stared at him curiously. Obviously here was a person who was not to be trifled with. However, he felt he had passed his preliminary examination, unexpected as it was, with great credit. Not once had he forgotten his dialect; not for a fraction of a second had he hesitated in answering the abrupt questions. Ability to lie readily is a great convenience.

"Now," The Thinking Machine commanded, his squinting eyes turned upward, "what happened at Idlewild?"

Inadvertently or otherwise, St. Rocheville failed to refer, even remotely, to the three great velvet-black birds — Blitz and Jack and Jill – in his narrative of events at Idlewild. It was rather a chronological statement of the thefts as they had been reported, with no suggestion as to the manner in which they might have been committed.

"Now," and St. Rocheville spoke slowly, as one who wanted to be certain of his words, "I come down to those things which happened immediately before the disappearance of Mrs Wardlaw Browne's necklace. Frankly my own statement will place me in rather a compromising position – that is, my real motive may not be understood – but it is better that I should tell you in the beginning things that you will surely find out."

"Decidedly better," The Thinking Machine agreed dryly. He didn't alter his position.

"Well, you must know that at Idlewild the men play auction a great deal, and—"

"Auction?" The Thinking Machine repeated. "What is auction, Mr Hatch?"

"Auction bridge," the reporter told him. "A game of cards – a variation of whist."

Monsieur St., Rocheville stared from the wizened little scientist to the reporter incredulously. He would not have believed a person could have lived in a civilized country and not know what auction was. Perhaps he wouldn't have believed, either, that The Thinking Machine never read a newspaper. So circumscribed is our own viewpoint.

"At Idlewild the men play auction a great deal," The Thinking Machine prompted. "Go on."

"Auction, yes," St. Rocheville resumed. "It happens sometimes that the stakes are rather high. On the night Mrs Wardlaw Browne's necklace was stolen, four of us were playing in the card room – a Mr Gordon and myself as partners against a Mr Miller and Franklin Chanoler, the financier." He hesitated slightly. "Mr Miller had been losing, and in a burst of temper he intimated that—that I – that I – er—"

"Had been cheating," The Thinking Machine supplied crabbedly. "Go on."

"As a result of that little unpleasantness," St. Rocheville continued, "the game ended, and we joined the ladies. Now, please understand that it is not my wish to retaliate upon Mr Miller. I have explained my motive – I don't want to be made a scapegoat. I do want the actual facts to come out." Some subtle change passed across his face. "Mr Miller," he said measuredly, "stole Mrs Wardlaw Browne's necklace!"

"Miller," Hatch repeated. "Do you mean Rex Miller?"

"That's his name, yes – Rex Miller."

"Rex Miller? The son of John W. Miller, the millionaire?" Hatch came to his feet excitedly.

"Rex Miller is his name, yes," St. Rocheville shrugged his shoulders.

"Oh, that's impossible!" Hatch declared.

"Nothing is impossible, Mr Hatch," interrupted The Thinking Machine tartly. "Sit down. You annoy me." He shifted his pale-blue eyes, and squinted at Monsieur St. Rocheville through his thick spectacles. "How do you know Mr Miller stole the necklace?"

"I saw him slip it into the pocket of his dress coat," St. Rocheville declared flatly. "Naturally, I had an idea that, when he drew Mrs Wardlaw Browne aside immediately after we came out of the card room, it was his intention to—to denounce me as a card sharp. You may imagine that I was watching them both closely, because my honor was at stake. I wanted to see how she took it. It seems that he said nothing whatever to her about the card game; but he did steal the necklace. I saw him hiding it."

Fell a long silence. With inscrutable face The Thinking Machine sat staring at the ceiling. Twice St. Rocheville shifted his position uneasily. He was wondering if his story had been convincing. Adroit mixture of truth and falsehood that it was, he failed to see a single defect in it. Hatch, too, was staring curiously at the scientist.

"I understand perfectly your hesitation in going into details," said The Thinking Machine at last. "Under all the circumstances your motive might be misconstrued; but I think you have made me understand." He rose suddenly. "That's all," he said. "I'll look into the matter to-morrow."

Monsieur St. Rocheville was about to take his departure, when The Thinking Machine stopped him for a last question.

"You used a phrase just now," he said. "I am anxious to get it exactly — something about your father and your father's father—"

"Oh! I said" – Monsieur St. Rocheville obliged – "that my father and my father's father were bankers in Paris."

"That's it," said the little scientist. "Thanks. Goodday."

Monsieur St. Rocheville went out. The Thinking Machine scribbled something on a sheet of paper and handed it to the reporter.

"Attend to that when you get to your office," he directed. Hatch read it, and his eyes opened wide. "Also, do you happen to know a native Frenchman who speaks perfect English?"

"I do; yes."

"Look him up, and ask him to repeat the phrase, 'My father and my father's father.'"

"Why?" inquired the reporter blankly.

"When he says it you'll know why. Immediately this other matter is attended to come back here."

Monsieur St. Rocheville's troubled meditations were disturbed by the appearance of Miss Fayerwether around a bend in the walk. Fluttering about her were her pets, Blitz and Jack and Jill. One after another they would swoop down, gobble up a beakful of sugar from her open hand, then sail off in a circle. There was something in the sight of Miss Fayerwether to dispel troubled meditations. She was gowned in a filmy white, clinging stuff, with a wide, flapping sun hat, her cheeks glowing with the sun's reflection, her big, innocent eyes repeating the marvelous blue of the sky.

Monsieur St. Rocheville, at sight of her, arose, bowed formally, and made way for her beside him. She sat down, to be instantly submerged in a fluttering cloud of black wings.

"Go away," she ordered. "I have no more sugar. See?" and she extended her empty hands.

The giant birds wandered off seeking what they might find; and for a time the girl and the young man sat silent. Twice Miss Fayerwether's eyes sought St. Rocheville's; twice she caught him staring straight into her face.

"Detectives were here today," she remarked at last.

"Yes, I know," said St. Rocheville.

"They had a long talk with Mrs Wardlaw Browne, and insisted on searching the house – that is, the rooms of the guests – but she would not permit it."

"She made a mistake."

"You mean that some one of the guests—"

"I mean there is a thief here somewhere," said St. Rocheville; "and he should be unmasked." (And this from Jimmie Jones, erstwhile pickpocket, burglar, and what not – Jimmie Jones, alias Wilhelm Van Der Wyde, alias Hubert Montgomery Wade, alias Jean St. Rocheville.) "I am willing for them to search my room; you are willing for them to search your room – the others should be."

The young man's lips were tightly set; there was an uncompromising glint in his eyes. His simulation had been so perfect that even he was feeling the righteous indignation of the hopelessly moral. Whatever else he felt didn't appear at the moment. Miss Fayerwether was gazing dreamily into the void.

"Have you ever been to Chicago?" she queried irrelevantly at last.

"No," said Monsieur St. Rocheville. As a matter of fact, Chicago was one of the cities in which there was being made even then an industrious search for Wilhelm Van Der Wyde.

"Or Denver?" the girl continued dreamily.

That was another city in which Wilhelm Van Der Wyde was badly wanted. Monsieur St. Rocheville turned upon Miss Fayerwether suspiciously.

"No," he declared. "Why?"

"No reason – I was merely curious," she replied carelessly. And then again irrelevantly: "Nothing has been stolen from you?"

For answer, St. Rocheville held out his left hand. A heavy diamond solitaire which he usually wore on his little finger was missing. The print of the ring on the flesh was still visible.

"Oh!" exclaimed Miss Fayerwether; and again: "Oh!" She looked startled. St. Rocheville didn't recall that he had ever seen just such an expression before. "When was your ring stolen? How?"

"I removed it when I got into my bath," St. Rocheville explained. "My window was closed, but my door was unlocked. When I came out of the bath the ring had disappeared – that's all."

"Well" – and there was a flash of indignation in the girl's eyes – "you can't blame that on Blitz, anyway."

"I'm not trying to," said St. Rocheville. "I said my window was closed. My door was closed but unlocked. I don't think Blitz can open a door, can he?"

Miss Fayerwether didn't answer. Once she was almost on the point of saying something further; and, for an instant, there was mute appeal in the innocent eyes as her slim white hand lay on the young man's arm. Then she changed her mind and went on to her room, the birds fluttering along after.

Strange thoughts came to Monsieur St. Rocheville. The light touch on his arm had thrilled him curiously. He found himself staring off moodily in the direction of her window. Also he caught himself remembering the marvelous blue of her eyes! He didn't recall at the moment that he had ever noticed the colour of any one's eyes before.

'Twas an hour after dinner when The Thinking Machine, accompanied by Detective Mallory, the bright light of the Bureau of Criminal Investigation, and one of his satellites, Blanton by name, with Hutchinson Hatch trailing, appeared at Idlewild. It may have been mere accident that St. Rocheville met them as they stepped out of the automobile.

"I neglected to tell you," he remarked to the scientist, "that young Miller has been losing heavily at auction of late; and I hear that he has had some sort of a row with his father about his allowance."

"I understand," The Thinking Machine nodded.

"Also," St. Rocheville ran on, "there has been at least one other theft here since I saw you. A diamond ring of mine was stolen from my room while I was in the bath. I wouldn't venture to say who took it."

"I know," The Thinking Machine assured him curtly. "I will have it in my hand in ten minutes."

Indignant at the intrusion of the police in what she was pleased to term her personal affairs – the detectives who had been there before were from a private agency – Mrs Wardlaw Browne bustled into the room where The Thinking Machine and his party waited. Monsieur St. Rocheville effaced himself.

"Pray what does this mean?" Mrs Wardlaw Browne demanded.

"It means, madam, that we have a search warrant, and intend to go through your house, if necessary." The Thinking Machine informed her crustily. Through the half-open door he caught a glimpse of a slender figure – a mere wisp of a girl with big, wonder-stuck eyes. "Mallory, close that door. You, madam," – this to Mrs Wardlaw Browne – "can assist us by answering a few questions."

Mrs Wardlaw Browne was of the tall, gaunt, haughty type; thin to scrawniness, enormously rich, and possessed of all the arrogance that riches bring. She studied the faces of the four men contemptuously; then, with a little resigned expression, sat down.

"Just how did you lose your necklace?" The Thinking Machine began abruptly. "Did you drop it? Was it taken from your neck? Are you sure you had it on?"

"I know I had it on," was the reply. "I did not drop it. It was taken from my neck."

"Did you, by any chance, wear a low-neck gown on the evening it was taken?" The little scientist's squinting eyes were fixed upon her tensely.

"I never wear décolleté," came the frigid response.

With his great head pillowed upon the back of his chair, his thin fingers tip to tip, and his eyes turned upward, The Thinking Machine sat in silence for a minute or more, the while tiny, cobwebby lines appeared in his domelike brow.

"Can you," he inquired finally, "summon a servant without leaving this room?"

"There is a bell, yes." Mrs Wardlaw Browne was forgetting to be haughty in a certain fascination which grew upon her as she gazed at this little man.

"Will you ring it, please?"

Mrs Wardlaw Browne arose, touched a button, and sat down again. A moment later a footman entered.

"Tell Mr Rex Miller," The Thinking Machine directed, "that Mrs Wardlaw Browne would like to see him immediately in this room."

The footman bowed and withdrew. Followed an interminable wait—interminable, at least, to Detective Mallory, who impatiently clicked his handcuffs together. Mrs Wardlaw Browne yawned to hide the curiosity that was consuming her.

The door opened, and Rex Miller entered. He stood for a moment staring at the silent party, and finally:

"Did you send for me, Mrs Browne?"

"I did," said The Thinking Machine. "Sit down, please." Rex sank into a chair mechanically. "Mr Blanton" – the scientist neither raised his voice nor lowered his eyes – "you will undertake to see that Mr Miller doesn't leave this room. Mr Mallory, you will search Mr Miller's apartments. Somewhere there you will find Mrs Wardlaw Browne's diamond necklace; also a man's diamond ring."

Rex came to his feet with writhing hands, a thundercloud in his face. Mrs Wardlaw Browne burst into inarticulate expostulations. Blanton drew a revolver and laid it across his knee. Mallory bustled out. Hatch merely waited. Silence came; a silence so tense, so strained that Mrs Wardlaw Browne was tempted to scream. At last there were footsteps, the door from the hall was thrown open, and Mallory, triumphant, appeared.

"I have them," he announced grimly. The necklace, a radiant, glittering thing, was dangling from one finger. The ring lay in his open palm. "And now, Mr Rex Miller" – he fished out his handcuffs and started toward the young man – "if you'll hold out your—"

"Oh, sit down, Mallory!" commanded The Thinking Machine impatiently.

Loitering in a hallway, where he could keep an eye on the stairs leading from the lower part of the house, Monsieur St. Rocheville saw Miss Fayerwether creep stealthily up, silent-footed, chalk-white of face, and come racing toward him across the heavy velvet carpet. For the reason that she would surely see him, he walked toward her, amazed and a little perturbed at something in her manner.

"What's the matter?" inquired St. Rocheville calmly.

"Oh, it's you!" Miss Fayerwether's hand flew to her heart. She was frightened, gasping. "Nothing!"

"But something must be the matter," he insisted. "You are white as a sheet."

With an apparent effort the girl regained control of herself, and stood staring at him mutely. 'Twas in that moment that Monsieur St. Rocheville saw for the first time some strange, new expression in the big, innocent eyes – they seemed to grow hard, worldly, all-wise even as he looked.

"There are detectives in the house," she said.

"I know it. What about it?"

"They have a warrant, and intend to search every room."

"Well?" St. Rocheville refused to get excited about it.

"Including, I imagine, yours and mine."

"I'm willing. I dare say you are."

For an instant the girl's self-possession seemed to desert her completely. Her eyes closed as if in pain, and she swayed a little. St. Rocheville thrust out an arm protectingly. When she lifted her face again St. Rocheville read terror therein.

"If-if they search my room," she faltered, "I-I am lost!"

"How? Why? What do you mean?"

"I don't know that I could make any one else understand," she went on swiftly. "The birds, you know – Blitz and Jack and Jill. You saw, and I explained to you, a trick they have of-of thieving; stealing bright things."

She stopped. In his impatience St. Rocheville seized her by the arm and shook her soundly.

"Well?" he demanded.

"Nearly every jewel that has been stolen is hidden now in my room," she confessed. "I knew nothing of it until yesterday, when I came across them. Then, after all the excitement about the thefts, I was afraid to return the things, and I could think of no way to proceed. So, you see, if they search my room it will—"

St. Rocheville was possessed of an agile mind; resourceful as it was agile. Suddenly he remembered two questions the girl had asked the day before – questions about Chicago and Denver. His teeth snapped. He thrust out a hand, and, opening the nearest door – he didn't happen to know whose room it was – he dragged her in, and turned on the electric light. Then their eyes met squarely.

"You are the thief, then?" he demanded. "Don't lie to me! You are the thief?"

"The things are in my room." She was sobbing a little. "The birds—"

"You are the thief!" There was a curious note of exultation in his voice. "And you do know something about Chicago and Denver?"

"I know that you are Wilhelm Van Der Wyde," she flashed defiantly. "I recognized you at once. I saw you in old Charles' 'fence' there once when you were not aware of it. I could never be mistaken in your eyes."

Monsieur St. Rocheville laughed blithely; came a faint answering smile, and he gathered her into his arms.

"I've always needed a partner," he said.

"Mr Miller," The Thinking Machine was saying placidly, "isn't the thief at all." He raised his hand to still a clamor of ejaculation. "Monsieur Rocheville, so called, stole the necklace, at least, and concealed it, with a ring from his own finger, in Mr Miller's apartment." Again he raised his hand. "Mr Miller caught Monsieur St. Rocheville cheating at cards, and practically denounced him. Monsieur St. Rocheville took his revenge by undertaking to fasten the jewel thefts upon Mr Miller. He imagined, shallowly enough, that if the necklace should be found in Mr Miller's room the police would look no farther. It is barely possible that the police wouldn't have looked farther."

Mrs Wardlaw Browne's aristocratic mouth had dropped open in sheer astonishment. Detective Mallory looked bewildered, dazed. Rex Miller's face was an animated interrogation mark.

"Then who is the thief?" Mallory found voice to express the burning question.

"I'm sure I don't know," The Thinking Machine confessed frankly. "I think, perhaps, it was Monsieur St. Rocheville, so called; but there's nothing to connect him — Please sit down, Mallory. You annoy me. It would do no good to search his apartment. If he stole anything, it isn't here now; besides—"

The door opened suddenly, and the footman appeared.

"Miss Fayerwether is badly hurt, ma'am," he explained hurriedly. "She seems to have fallen from her window. We found her outside, unconscious."

Mrs Wardlaw Browne went out hurriedly. Obeying an almost imperceptible nod of The Thinking Machine's head, Detective Mallory followed her. The scientist turned to Detective Blanton.

"Get St. Rocheville," he directed tersely.

Ten minutes later Mallory returned. In one hand he held a small chamois bag. The contents thereof he spilled upon a table. The Thinking Machine glanced around, saw a glittering heap of jewels, then resumed his steady scrutiny of the ceiling.

"The girl had them?"

"Yes," replied the detective. "She tried to escape from her room by sliding down a rope made of sheets. It broke, and she fell."

"Badly hurt?"

"Only a sprained ankle, and shock."

Blanton flung himself in.

"St. Rocheville's gone," he announced hurriedly. "I imagine he cut for it. Went away in one of the automobiles."

When Miss Fayerwether recovered consciousness, and the sharp agony in her ankle had become a mere dull pain, she found herself in some large room, rank with the odor of strange chemical messes. As a matter of fact, it was The Thinking Machine's laboratory; and the three men present were the little scientist in person, Mallory, and Hatch. Blanton had gone on to police headquarters to send out a general alarm for Monsieur St. Rocheville.

"There was no mystery about it," she heard The Thinking Machine saying. "That is, no mystery that the simplest rules of logic wouldn't instantly dissipate. A man, presumably French, but speaking English almost perfectly, comes into this room and betrays himself as an imposter five minutes afterward by using, without a trace of accent, the one phrase in all our language which no Frenchman, unless he is reared from infancy in an English-speaking country, can pronounce as it should be pronounced. This man used the phrase: 'My father and my father's father;' and he pronounced it as either of us would have pronounced it. The French can master our 'th' only with difficulty, and then only at the beginning of a word; otherwise their 'th' becomes almost like our 'z.'

"From the beginning, therefore, I imagined our so-called Monsieur St. Rocheville an imposter. Being an imposter, he was a liar. I proved he was a liar when I made him state who his father was. At my suggestion, Mr Hatch cabled to Paris, demonstrated that there is not, and never has been a Monsieur

St. Rocheville connected with the Crédit Lyonnaise; and, this much established, St. Rocheville's story collapsed utterly. He had been accused of cheating at cards; and in retaliation he tried to shift the thefts upon Mr Miller. He had seen Mr Miller, so he said, steal the necklace. His obvious purpose in this was to bring about a search of Mr Miller's apartment, where he had carefully planted the necklace, also his own ring. The remainder of the story you all know."

Miss Fayerwether had listened breathlessly, with closed eyes. The Thinking Machine arose and came over to her. For an instant his slender, cool hand rested on her brow; and in that instant she fought the fight. She was caught. St. Rocheville, alias Van Der Wyde, was free. He had tried to help her. She was to have gathered the jewels together, escaped through her window to avoid attracting attention, and joined him in the waiting automobile. He was free. She would allow him to remain free. Love, be it said, makes martyrs of us all.

"I stole the jewels," she said quietly. "Monsieur St. Rocheville knew nothing of the thefts. My birds—"

That was all. The door opened and closed. Monsieur St. Rocheville stood before them with a vicious-looking, snub-nosed, automatic pistol in his hand.

"Put up your hands!" he commanded curtly. "You, Mallory, you! Put them up, I say! Put them up!" Mallory put them up. "And you, too! Put them up!" The Thinking Machine and Hutchinson Hatch obeyed unanimously. "Now, Miss Fayerwether, can you walk?"

"I think so." She struggled to her feet.

"Very well." There was a deadly calm in his manner. "Take Mallory's gun, his keys, his handcuffs, and his police whistle. Careful now! Stand on the far side of him. I may have to kill him." The girl obeyed deftly. "Are the handcuffs unlocked? Good! Snap one end around his right wrist. Now, Mallory, lower your right hand!"

"I'll be—" the enraged detective began.

"Lower your right hand." The pistol clicked. "Now, Miss Fayerwether, snap the other end of the handcuff around the leg of his chair, above the rungs." It was done, neatly and quickly. "And I think that will hold you for a few minutes, Mallory. Now, Miss Fayerwether, there's an automobile outside. The motor is running. Get in the car. Take your time. Safely in, honk the horn three times."

The girl hobbled out. Monsieur St. Rocheville took advantage of the pause to sneer a little at the three men— Mallory safely shackled to a heavy chair, which would effectually stop immediate pursuit; Hatch with his hands anxiously stretched into the air, The Thinking Machine placidly meeting his gaze, eye to eye.

"I'll get you yet!" Mallory bellowed in impotent rage.

"Oh, perhaps." Outside, the automobile horn sounded thrice. "Until then, au revoir!" and Monsieur St. Rocheville vanished as silently as he had come.

"There's loyalty for you," observed The Thinking Machine, as if astonished.

"Love, not loyalty," Hatch declared. "He's crazy about her. Nothing on earth would have brought him back but love."

"Love!" mused the little scientist. "A most interesting phenomena. I shall have to look into it some time."

As I have said, Monsieur St. Rocheville was a young man of resource and daring. Later that night he burglariously entered the room Miss Fayerwether had occupied at Idlewild, and took Blitz and Jack and Jill away with him, cage and all.

16

PROBLEM OF THE CRYSTAL GAZER

With hideous, goggling eyes the great god Budd sat cross-legged on a pedestal and stared stolidly into the semi-darkness. He saw, by the wavering light of a peacock lamp which swooped down from the ceiling with wings outstretched, what might have been a nook in a palace of East India. Draperies hung here, there, everywhere; richly embroidered divans sprawled about; fierce tiger rugs glared up from the floor; grotesque idols grinned mirthlessly in unexpected corners; strange arms were grouped on the walls. Outside the trolley cars clanged blatantly.

The single human figure was a distinct contradiction of all else. It was that of a man in evening dress, smoking. He was fifty, perhaps sixty, years old with the ruddy colour of one who has lived a great deal out of doors. There was only a touch of gray in his abundant hair and moustache. His eyes were steady and clear, and indolent.

For a long time he sat, then the draperies to his right parted and a girl entered. She was a part of the picture of which the man was a contradiction. Her lustrous black hair flowed about her shoulders; lambent mysteries lay in her eyes. Her dress was the dress of the East. For a moment she stood looking at the man and then entered with light tread.

"Varick Sahib," she said, timidly, as if it were a greeting. "Do I intrude?" Her voice was softly guttural with the accent of her native tongue.

"Oh no, Jadeh. Come in," said the man.

She smiled frankly and sat down on a hassock near him.

"My brother?" she asked.

"He is in the cabinet."

Varick had merely glanced at her and then continued his thoughtful gaze into vacancy. From time to time she looked up at him shyly, with a touch of eagerness, but there was no answering interest in his manner. His thoughts were far away.

"May I ask what brings you this time, Sahib?" she inquired at last.

"A little deal in the market," responded Varick, carelessly. "It seems to have puzzled Adhem as much as it did me. He has been in the cabinet for half an hour."

He stared on musingly as he smoked, then dropped his eyes to the slender, graceful figure of Jadeh. With knees clasped in her hands she leaned back on the hassock deeply thoughtful. Her head was tilted upward and the flickering light fell full on her face. It crossed Varick's mind that she was pretty, and he was about to say so as he would have said it to any other woman, when the curtains behind them were thrown apart and they both glanced around.

Another man – an East Indian – entered. This man was Adhem Singh, the crystal gazer, in the ostentatious robes of a seer. He, too, was a part of the picture. There was an expression of apprehension, mingled with some other impalpable quality on his strong face.

"Well, Adhem?" inquired Varick.

"I have seen strange things, Sahib," replied the seer, solemnly. "The crystal tells me of danger."

"Danger?" repeated Varick with a slight lifting of his brows. "Oh well, in that case I shall keep out of it."

"Not danger to your business, Sahib," the crystal gazer went on with troubled face, "but danger in another way."

The girl, Jadeh, looked at him with quick, startled eyes and asked some question in her native tongue. He answered in the same language, and she rose suddenly with terror stricken face to fling herself at Varick's feet, weeping. Varick seemed to understand too, and looked at the seer in apprehension.

"Death?" he exclaimed. "What do you mean?"

Adhem was silent for a moment and bowed his head respectfully before the steady, inquiring gaze of the white man.

"Pardon, Sahib," he said at last. "I did not remember that you understood my language."

"What is it?" insisted Varick, abruptly. "Tell me."

"I cannot, Sahib."

"You must," declared the other. He had arisen commandingly. "You must."

The crystal gazer crossed to him and stood for an instant with his hand on the white man's shoulder, and his eyes studying the fear he found in the white man's face.

"The crystal, Sahib," he began. "It tells me that-that-"

"No, no, brother," pleaded the girl.

"Go on," Varick commanded.

"It grieves me to say that which will pain one whom I love as I do you, Sahib," said the seer, slowly. "Perhaps you had rather see for yourself?"

"Well, let me see then," said Varick. "Is it in the crystal?"

"Yes, by the grace of the gods."

"But I can't see anything there," Varick remembered. "I've tried scores of times."

"I believe this will he different, Sahib," said Adhem, quietly. "Can you stand a shock?"

Varick shook himself a little impatiently.

"Of course," he replied. "Yes, yes."

"A very serious shock?"

PROBLEM OF THE CRYSTAL GAZER

Again there was an impatient twist of Varick's shoulders.

"Yes, I can stand anything," he exclaimed shortly. "What is it? Let me see."

He strode toward that point in the draperies where Adhem had entered while the girl on her knees, sought with entreating hands to stop him.

"No, no, no," she pleaded. "No."

"Don't do that," Varick expostulated in annoyance, but gently he stooped and lifted her to her feet. "I am not a child – or a fool."

He threw aside the curtains. As they fell softly behind him he heard a pitiful little cry of grief from Jadeh and set his teeth together hard.

He stood in the crystal cabinet. It was somewhat larger than an ordinary closet and had been made impenetrable to the light by hangings of black velvet. For awhile he stood still so that his eyes might become accustomed to the utter blackness, and gradually the sinister fascinating crystal ball appeared, faintly visible by its own mystic luminosity. It rested on a pedestal of black velvet.

Varick was accustomed to his surroundings – he had been in the cabinet many times. Now he dropped down on a stool in front of the table whereon the crystal lay and leaning forward on his arms stared into its limpid depths. Unblinkingly for one, two, three minutes he sat there with his thoughts in a chaos.

After awhile there came a change in the ball. It seemed to glow with a growing light other than its own. Suddenly it darkened completely, and out of this utter darkness grew shadowy, vague forms to which he could give no name. Finally a veil seemed lifted for the globe grew brighter and he leaned forward, eagerly, fearfully. Another veil melted away and a still brighter light illumined the ball.

Now Varick was able to make out objects. Here was a table littered with books and papers, there a chair, yonder a shadowy mantel. Gradually the light grew until his tensely fixed eyes pained him, but he stared steadily on. Another quick brightness came and the objects all became clear. He studied them incredulously for a few seconds, and then he recognized what he saw. It was a room – his study – miles away in his apartments.

A sudden numb chilliness seized him but he closed his teeth hard and gazed on. The outlines of the crystal were disappearing, now they were gone and he saw more. A door opened and a man entered the room into which he was looking. Varick gave a little gasp as he recognized the man. It was – himself. He watched the man – himself – as he moved about the study aimlessly for a time as if deeply troubled, then as he dropped into a chair at the desk. Varick read clearly on the vision – face those emotions which he was suffering in person. As he looked the man made some hopeless gesture with his hands – his hands – and leaned forward on the desk with his head on his arms. Varick shuddered.

For a long time, it seemed, the man sat motionless, then Varick became conscious of another figure – a man – in the room. This figure had come into the vision from his own view point. His face was averted – Varick did not recognize the figure, but he saw something else and started in terror. A knife was in the hand of the unknown, and he was creeping stealthily toward the unconscious figure in the chair – himself – with the weapon raised.

An inarticulate cry burst from Varick's colourless lips – a cry of warning – as he saw the unknown creep on, on, on toward – himself. He saw the figure that was himself move a little and the unknown leaped. The upraised knife swept down and was buried to the handle. Again a cry, an unintelligible shriek, burst from Varick's lips; his heart fluttered and perspiration poured from his face. With incoherent mutterings he sank forward helplessly.

How long he remained there he didn't know, but at last he compelled himself to look again. The crystal glittered coldly on its pedestal of velvet but that hideous thing which had been there was gone. The thought came to him to bring it back, to see more, but repulsive fear, terror seized upon him. He rose and staggered out of the cabinet. His face was pallid and his hands clasped and unclasped nervously.

Jadeh was lying on a divan sobbing. She leaped to her feet when he entered, and looking into his face she knew. Again she buried her face in her hands and wept afresh. Adhem stood with moody eyes fixed on the great god Budd.

"I saw – I understand," said Varick between his teeth, "but – I don't believe it."

"The crystal never lies, Sahib," said the seer, sorrowfully.

"But it can't be – that," Varick declared protestingly.

"Be careful, Sahib, oh, be careful," urged the girl.

"Of course I shall be careful," said Varick, shortly. Suddenly he turned to the crystal gazer and there was a menace in his tone. "Did such a thing ever appear to you before?"

"Only once, Sahib."

"And did it come true?"

Adhem inclined his head, slowly.

"I may see you tomorrow," exclaimed Varick suddenly. "This room is stifling. I must go out."

With twitching hands he drew on a light coat over his evening dress, picked up his hat and rushed out into the world of realities. The crystal gazer stood for a moment while Jadeh clung to his arm, tremblingly.

"It is as the gods will," he said sadly, at last.

Professor Augustus S. F. X. Van Dusen – The Thinking Machine – received Howard Varick in the small reception room and invited him to a seat. Varick's face was ashen; there were dark lines under his eyes and in them there was the glitter of an ungovernable terror. Every move showed the nervousness which gripped him. The Thinking Machine squinted at him curiously, then dropped back into his big chair.

For several minutes Varick said nothing; he seemed to be struggling to control himself. Suddenly he burst out:

"I'm going to die some day next week. Is there any way to prevent it?"

The Thinking Machine turned his great yellow head and looked at him in a manner which nearly indicated surprise.

"Of course if you've made up your mind to do it," he said irritably, "I don't see what can be done." There was a trace of irony in his voice, a coldness which brought Varick around a little. "Just how is it going to happen?"

"I shall be murdered – stabbed in the back – by a man whom I don't know," Varick rushed on desperately.

"Dear me, dear me, how unfortunate," commented the scientist. "Tell me something about it. But here—" He arose and went into his laboratory. After a moment he returned and handed a glass of some effervescent liquid to Varick, who gulped it down. "Take a minute to pull yourself together," instructed the scientist.

He resumed his seat and sat silent with his long, slender fingers pressed tip to tip. Gradually Varick recovered. It was a fierce fight for the mastery of emotion.

"Now," directed The Thinking Machine at last, "tell me about it."

Varick told just what happened lucidly enough, and The Thinking Machine listened with polite interest. Once or twice he turned and looked at his visitor.

"Do you believe in any psychic force?" Varick asked once.

"I don't disbelieve in anything until I have proven that it cannot be," was the answer. "The God who hung a sun up there has done other things which we will never understand." There was a little pause, then: "How did you meet this man, Adhem Singh?"

"I have been interested for years in the psychic, the occult, the things we don't understand," Varick replied. "I have a comfortable fortune, no occupation, no dependents and made this a sort of hobby. I have studied it superficially all over the world. I met Adhem Singh in India ten years ago, afterwards in England where he went through Oxford with some financial assistance from me, and later here. Two years ago he convinced me that there was something in crystal gazing – call it telepathy, self hypnotism, sub-conscious mental action – what you will. Since then the science, I can call it nothing else, has guided me in every important act of my life."

"Through Adhem Singh?"

"Yes."

"And under a pledge of secrecy, I imagine – that is secrecy as to the nature of his revelations?"

"Yes."

"Any taint of insanity in your family?"

Varick wondered whether the question was in the nature of insolent reproof, or was a request for information. He construed it as the latter.

"No," he answered. "Never a touch of it."

"How often have you consulted Mr Singh?"

"Many times. There have been occasions when he would tell me nothing because, he explained, the crystal told him nothing. There have been other times when he advised me correctly. He has never given me bad advice even in intricate stock operations, therefore I have been compelled to believe him in all things."

"You were never able to see anything yourself in the crystal until this vision of death, last Tuesday night you say?"

"That was the first."

"How do you know the murder is to take place at any given time – that is next week, as you say?"

"That is the information Adhem Singh gave me," was the reply. "He can read the visions—they mean more to him than—"

"In other words, he makes it a profession?" interrupted the scientist.

"Yes."

"Go on."

"The horror of the thing impressed me so – both of us – that he has at my request twice invoked the vision since that night. He, like you, wanted to know when it would happen. There is a calendar by weeks in my study; that is, only one week is shown on it at a time. The last time the vision appeared he noted this calendar. The week was that beginning next Sunday, the 21st of this month. The only conclusion we could reach was it would happen during that week."

The Thinking Machine arose and paced back and forth across the room deeply thoughtful. At last he stopped before his visitor.

"It's perfectly amazing," he commented emphatically. "It approaches nearer to the unbelievable than anything I have ever heard of."

Varick's response was a look that was almost grateful.

"You believe it impossible then?" he asked, eagerly.

"Nothing is impossible," declared the other aggressively. "Now, Mr Varick, you are firmly convinced that what you saw was prophetic? That you will die in that manner, in that place?"

"I can't believe anything else – I can't," was the response.

"And you have no idea of the identity of the murderer – to – be, if I may use that phrase?"

"Not the slightest. The figure was wholly unfamiliar to me."

"And you know – you know – that the room you saw in the crystal was yours?"

"I know that absolutely. Rugs, furniture, mantel, books, everything was mine."

The Thinking Machine was again silent for a time.

"In that event," he said at last, "the affair is perfectly simple. Will you place yourself in my hands and obey my directions implicitly?"

"Yes." There was an eager, hopeful note in Varick's voice now.

"I am going to try to disarrange the affairs of Fate a little bit," explained the scientist gravely. "I don't know what will happen but it will be interesting to try to throw the inevitable, the pre-ordained I might say, out of gear, won't it?"

With a quizzical, grim expression about his thin lips The Thinking Machine went to the telephone in an adjoining room and called some one. Varick heard neither the name nor what was said, merely the mumble of the irritable voice. He glanced up as the scientist returned.

"Have you any servants – a valet for instance?" asked the scientist.

"Yes, I have an aged servant, a valet, but he is now in France, I gave him a little vacation. I really don't need one now as I live in an apartment house – almost a hotel."

"I don't suppose you happen to have three or four thousand dollars in your pocket?"

"No, not so much as that," was the puzzled reply. "If it's your fee—"

"I never accept fees," interrupted the scientist. "I interest myself in affairs like these because I like them. They are good mental exercise. Please draw a cheque for, say four thousand dollars, to Hutchinson Hatch."

"Who is he?" asked Varick. There was no reply. The cheque was drawn and handed over without further comment.

It was fifteen or twenty minutes later that a cab pulled up in front of the house. Hutchinson Hatch, reporter, and another man whom he introduced as Philip Byrne were ushered in. As Hatch shook hands with Varick The Thinking Machine compared them mentally. They were relatively of the same size and he bobbed his head as if satisfied.

"Now, Mr Hatch," he instructed, "take this cheque and get it cashed immediately, then return here. Not a word to anybody."

Hatch went out and Byrne discussed politics with Varick until he returned with the money. The Thinking Machine thrust the bills into Byrne's hand and he counted it, afterward stowing it away in a pocket.

"Now, Mr Varick, the keys to your apartment, please," asked the scientist.

They were handed over and he placed them in his pocket. Then he turned to Varick.

"From this time on," he said, "your name is John Smith. You are going on a trip, beginning immediately, with Mr Byrne here. You are not to send a letter, a postal, a telegram or a package to anyone; you are to buy nothing, you are to write no checks, you are not to speak to or recognize anyone, you are not to telephone or attempt in any manner to communicate with anyone, not even me. You are to obey Mr Byrne in everything he says."

Varick's eyes had grown wider and wider as he listened.

"But my affairs – my business?" he protested.

"It is a matter of your life or death," said The Thinking Machine shortly.

For a moment Varick wavered a little. He felt that he was being treated like a child.

"As you say," he said finally.

"Now, Mr Byrne," continued the scientist, "you heard those instructions. It is your duty to enforce them. You must lose this man and yourself. Take him away somewhere to another place. There is enough money there for ordinary purposes. When you learn that there has been an arrest in connection with a certain threat against Mr Varick, come back to Boston – to me – and bring him. That's all."

Mr Byrne arose with a business like air.

"Come on, Mr Smith," he commanded.

Varick followed him out of the room.

Here was a table littered with books and papers, there a chair, yonder a shadowy mantel * * * * A door opened and a man entered the room * * * * moved about the study aimlessly for a time as if deeply troubled, then dropped into a chair at the desk * * * * made some hopeless gesture with his hands and leaned forward on the desk with his head on his arms * * * * another figure in the room * * * * knife in his hand * * * * creeping stealthily toward the unconscious figure in the chair with the knife raised * * * * the unknown crept on, on, on * * * *

There was a blinding flash, a gush of flame and smoke, a sharp click and through the fog came the unexcited voice of Hutchinson Hatch, reporter.

"Stay right where you are, please."

"That ought to be a good picture," said The Thinking Machine.

The smoke cleared and he saw Adhem Singh standing watching with deep concern a revolver in the hand of Hatch, who had suddenly arisen from the desk in Varick's room. The Thinking Machine rubbed his hands briskly.

"Ah, I thought it was you," he said to the crystal gazer. "Put down the knife, please. That's right. It seems a little bold to have interfered with what was to be like this, but you wanted too much detail, Mr Singh. You might have murdered your friend if you hadn't gone into so much trivial theatrics."

"I suppose I am a prisoner?" asked the crystal gazer.

"You are," The Thinking Machine assured him cheerfully. "You are charged with the attempted murder of Mr Varick. Your wife will be a prisoner in another half hour with all those who were with you in the conspiracy."

He turned to Hatch, who was smiling broadly. The reporter was thinking of that wonderful flash-light photograph in the camera that The Thinking Machine held, – the only photograph in the world, so far as he knew, of a man in the act of attempting an assassination.

"Now, Mr Hatch," the scientist went on, "I will 'phone to Detective Mallory to come here and get this gentleman, and also to send men and arrest every person to be found in Mr Singh's home. If this man tries to run—shoot."

The scientist went out and Hatch devoted his attention to his sullen prisoner. He asked half a dozen questions and receiving no answers he gave it up as hopeless. After awhile Detective Mallory appeared in his usual state of restrained astonishment and the crystal grazer was led away.

Then Hatch and The Thinking Machine went to the Adhem Singh house. The police had preceded them and gone away with four prisoners, among them the girl Jadeh. They obtained an entrance through the courtesy of a policeman left in charge and sought out the crystal cabinet. Together they bowed over the glittering globe as Hatch held a match.

"But I still don't see how it was done," said the reporter after they had looked at the crystal.

The Thinking Machine lifted the ball and replaced it on its pedestal half a dozen times apparently trying to locate a slight click. Then he fumbled all around the table, above and below. At his suggestion Hatch lifted the ball very slowly, while the scientist slid his slender fingers beneath it.

"Ah," he exclaimed at last. "I thought so. It's clever, Mr Hatch, clever. Just stand here a few minutes in the dark and I'll see if I can operate it for you."

He disappeared and Hatch stood staring at the crystal until he was developing a severe case of the creeps himself. Just then a light flashed in the crystal, which had been only dimly visible, and he found himself looking into – the room in Howard Varick's apartments, miles away. As he looked, startled, he saw The Thinking Machine appear in the crystal and wave his arms. The creepiness passed instantly in the face of this obvious attempt to attract his attention.

It was later that afternoon that The Thinking Machine turned the light of his analytical genius on the problem for the benefit of Hatch and Detective Mallory.

"Charlatanism is a luxury which costs the peoples of the world incredible sums," he began. "It had its beginning, of course, in the dark ages when man's mind grasped at some tangible evidence of an Infinite Power, and through its very eagerness was easily satisfied. Then quacks began to prey upon man, and do to this day under many guises and under many names. This condition will continue until enlightenment has become so general that man will realize the absurdity of such a thing as Nature, or the other world's forces, going out of its way to tell him whether a certain stock will go up or down. A sense of humour ought to convince him that disembodied spirits do not come back and rap on tables in answer to asinine questions. These things are merely prostitutions of the Divine Revelations."

Hatch smiled a little at the lecture platform tone, and Detective Mallory chewed his cigar uncomfortably. He was there to find out something about crime; this thing was over his head.

"This is merely preliminary," The Thinking Machine went on after a moment. "Now as to this crystal gazing affair — a little reason, a little logic. When Mr Varick came to me I saw he was an intelligent man who had devoted years to a study of the so-called occult. Being intelligent he was not easily hoodwinked, yet he had been hoodwinked for years, therefore I could see that the man who did it must be far beyond the blundering fool usually found in these affairs.

"Now Mr Varick, personally, had never seen anything in any crystal – remember that – until this 'vision' of death. When I knew this I knew that 'vision' was stamped as quackery; the mere fact of him seeing it proved that, but the quackery was so circumstantial that he was convinced. Thus we have quackery.

Why? For a fee? I can imagine successful guesses on the stock market bringing fees to Adhem Singh, but the 'vision' of a man's death is not the way to his pocket-book. If not for a fee—then what?

"A deeper motive was instantly apparent. Mr Varick was wealthy, he had known Singh and had been friendly with him for years, had supplied him with funds to go through Oxford, and he had no family or dependents. Therefore it seemed probable that a will, or perhaps in another way, Singh would benefit by Mr Varick's death. There was a motive for the 'vision,' which might have been at first an effort to scare him to death, because he had a bad heart. I saw all these things when Mr Varick talked to me first, several days after he saw the 'vision' but did not suggest them to him. Had I done so he would not have believed so sordid a thing, for he believed in Singh, and would probably have gone his way to be murdered or to die of fright as Singh intended.

"Knowing these things there was only the labour of trapping a clever man. Now the Hindu mind works in strange channels. It loves the mystic, the theatric, and I imagined that having gone so far Singh would attempt to bring the 'vision' to a reality. He presumed, of course, that Mr Varick would keep the matter to himself.

"The question of saving Varick's life was trifling. If he was to die at a given time in a given room the thing to do was to place him beyond possible reach of that room at that time. I 'phoned to you, Mr Hatch, and asked you to bring me a private detective who would obey orders, and you brought Mr Byrne. You heard my instructions to him. It was necessary to hide Mr Varick's identity and my elaborate directions were to prevent anyone getting the slightest clue as to him having gone, or as to where he was. I don't know where he is now.

"Immediately Mr Varick was off my hands, I had Martha, my housekeeper, write a note to Singh explaining that Mr

PROBLEM OF THE CRYSTAL GAZER

Varick was ill, and confined to his room, and for the present was unable to see anyone. In this note a date was specified when he would call on Singh. Martha wrote, of course, as a trained nurse who was in attendance merely in day time. All these points were made perfectly clear to Singh.

"That done, it was only a matter of patience. Mr Hatch and I went to Mr Varick's apartments each night – I had Martha there in day time to answer questions – and waited, in hiding. Mr Hatch is about Varick's size and a wig helped us along. What happened then you know. I may add that when Mr Varick told me the story I commented on it as being almost unbelievable. He understood, as I meant he should, that I referred to the 'vision.' I really meant that the elaborate scheme which Singh had evolved was unbelievable. He might have killed him just as well with a drop of poison or something equally pleasant."

The Thinking Machine stopped as if that were all.

"But the crystal?" asked Hatch. "How did that work? How was it I saw you?"

"That was a little ingenious and rather expensive," said The Thinking Machine, "so expensive that Singh must have expected to get a large sum from success. I can best describe the manufacture of the 'vision' as a variation of the principle of the camera obscura. It was done with lenses of various sorts and a multitude of mirrors, and required the assistance of two other men – those who were taken from Singh's house with Jadeh.

"First, the room in Mr Varick's apartments was duplicated in the basement of Singh's house, even to rugs, books and wall decorations. There two men rehearsed the murder scene that Mr Varick saw. They were disguised of course. You have looked through the wrong end of a telescope of course? Well, the original reduction of the murder scene to a size where all of it would appear in a small mirror was accomplished that way. From this small mirror there ran pipes with a series of mirrors and lenses, through the house, carrying the reflection of what was happening below, so vaguely though that features were barely distinguishable. This pipe ran up inside one of the legs of the table on which the crystal rested, and then, by reflection to the pedestal.

"You, Mr Hatch, saw me lift that crystal several times and each time you might have noticed the click. I was trying to find then, how the reflection reached it. When you lifted it slowly and I put my fingers under it I knew. There was a small trap in the pedestal, covered with velvet. This closed automatically and presented a solid surface when the crystal was lifted, and opened when the crystal was replaced. Thus the reflection reached the crystal which reversed it the last time and made it appear right side up to the watcher. The apparent growth of the light in the crystal was caused below. Some one simply removed several sheets of gauze, one at a time, from in front of the first lens."

"Well!" exclaimed Detective Mallory. "That's the most elaborate affair I ever heard of."

"Quite right," commented the scientist, "but we don't know how many victims Singh had. Of course any 'vision' was possible with a change of scene in the basement. I imagine it was a profitable investment because there are many fools in this world."

"What did the girl have to do with it?" asked Hatch.

"That I don't know," replied the scientist. "She was pretty. Perhaps she was used as a sort of bait to attract a certain class of men. She was really Singh's wife I imagine, not his sister. She was a prominent figure in the mummery with Varick of course. With her aid Singh was able to lend great effectiveness to the general scheme."

A couple of days later Howard Varick returned to the city in tow of Philip Byrne. The Thinking Machine asked Mr Varick only one question of consequence.

"How much money did you intend to leave Singh?"

"About two hundred and fifty thousand dollars," was the reply. "It was to be used under his direction in furthering an investigation into the psychic. He and I had planned just how it was to be spent."

Personally Mr Varick is no longer interested in the occult.

17

PROBLEM OF THE DESERTED HOUSE

The telephone bell rang sharply, twice. Professor Augustus S.F.X. Van Dusen – The Thinking Machine – opened his eyes from a sound sleep, rose from the bed, turned on an electric light, and squinted at the clock on the table. It was just half-past one; he had been asleep for only a little more than an hour. He slid his small feet into a pair of soft slippers and went to the telephone.

"Hello!" he called irritably.

"Is that Professor Van Dusen?" came the answer in a man's voice – a voice tense with nervous excitement, and so quick in enunciation that the words tumbled over one another.

"Yes," replied the scientist. "What is it?"

"It's a matter of life and death!" came the hurried response in the same hasty tone. "Can you come at once and—" The instrument buzzed and sputtered incoherently, and the remainder of the question was lost.

For an instant The Thinking Machine listened intently, seeking to interpret the interruption; then the sputtering ceased and the wire was silent. "Who is this talking?" he demanded.

The answer was almost a shout; it was as if the speaker was strangling, and the words came explosively, with a distinct effort. "My name is—"

And that was all. The voice was swallowed up suddenly in the deafening crack of an explosion of some sort – a pistol shot! Involuntarily The Thinking Machine dodged. The receiver sang shrilly in his ear, and the transmitter vibrated audibly; then the instrument was mute again – the connection was broken.

"Hello, hello!" the scientist called again and again; but there was no answer. He moved the hook up and down several times to attract Central's attention. But that brought no response. Whatever had happened had at least temporarily rendered his own line lifeless. "Dear me! Dear me!" he grumbled petulantly. "Most extraordinary!"

For a time he stood thoughtfully staring at the instrument; then went over and sat down on the edge of the bed. Sleep was banished now. Here was a problem, and a strange one! Every faculty of his wonderful brain was concentrated upon it. The minutes sped on as he sat there turning it all over in his mind, analyzing it, regarding it from every possible viewpoint, while tiny wrinkles were growing in the enormous brow. Finally he concluded to try the telephone again. Perhaps it had only been momentarily deadened by the shock. He returned to the instrument and picked up the receiver. The rhythmic buzz of the wire told him instantly that the line was working. Central answered promptly.

"Can you tell me the number which was just connected with this?" he inquired. "We were interrupted."

"I'll see if I can get it," was the reply.

"It's of the utmost importance," he went on to explain tersely; "a matter of life and death, even."

"I'll do what I can," Central assured him; "but there is no record of the calls, you know, and there may have been fifty in the last ten or fifteen minutes, and of course the operators don't remember them." She obligingly gave him a quarter of an hour as she sought some clue to the number.

The Thinking Machine waited patiently for the report, staring dumbly at the transmitter meanwhile, and at last it came. No one remembered the number; there was no record of it. Central was sorry. With a curt word of thanks the scientist called for one of the big newspaper offices and asked for Hutchinson Hatch, reporter.

"Mr Hatch isn't in," came the response.

"Do you know where he is?" queried the scientist, and there was a shadow of anxiety in the perpetually irritated voice.

"No; home, I suppose."

The man of science drew long, quick breath – it might have been one of uneasiness – and called the newspaper man's home number. Of course the mysterious message over the telephone had not been from Hatch. It was not the reporter's voice, he was positive of that, and yet there was the bare chance that—

"Hello!" Hatch growled amiably but sleepily over the wire.

The Thinking Machine's drawn face showed a vague relief as he recognized the tone. "That you, Mr Hatch?" he asked.

"Yes."

"In any trouble?"

"Trouble?" repeated the reporter in evident surprise. "No. Who is this?"

"Van Dusen," was the response. "Goodnight."

Mechanically, unconsciously almost, The Thinking Machine began dressing. The ever active, resourceful brain, plunged so suddenly into this maze of mystery, was fully awake now and was groping through the fog of possibilities and conjecture, feeling for some starting point in this singular problem which had been thrust upon it so strangely. And evidently at last there came some inspiration; for the eminent scientist started hurriedly out the front door into the night, pausing on the steps to remember that in his haste he had forgotten to exchange his slippers for shoes, and that he was bare headed.

PROBLEM OF THE DESERTED HOUSE

Fifteen minutes later the night operator in chief at the branch telephone exchange was favored with a personal call from Professor Augustus S. F. X. Van Dusen. There was a conference of five minutes or so, after which the scientist was led back through the operating room and ushered into a long high ceilinged apartment where thousands of telephone wires were centered – a web woven of thin strands, each of which led ultimately to the long table where a dozen or more girls were on watch. He went into that room at five minutes of two o'clock; he came out at seventeen minutes after four and appeared before the night operator in the outer office.

"I found it," he announced shortly. "Please, now, let me speak to police headquarters – either Detective Mallory or Detective Cunningham."

Detective Cunningham answered.

"This is Van Dusen," the scientist told him. "I should like to know if any murder or attempted murder has been reported to the police to-night?"

"No," replied the detective. "Why?"

"I was afraid not," mused The Thinking Machine enigmatically. "Has there been any call for police assistance anywhere?"

"No."

"Between one and two o'clock?" insisted the scientist.

"There hasn't been a call tonight," was the reply. "What's it all about?"

"I don't know – yet," said the scientist. "Goodnight."

The Thinking Machine went out after a few minutes, pausing on the curb in the brilliant glare of a street lamp to jot down a number on his cuff. When he looked up a cab was just passing. He hailed it, gave an address to the driver, and a moment later the vehicle went clattering down the street. When it stopped at last before a dark, four-story house, the cabman sat still for a moment expecting his passenger to alight.

But nothing happened; so he jumped down and peered into the gloom of the vehicle. Dimly he was able to make out the small figure of the scientist huddled up in a corner of the cab with his huge yellow head thrown back, and slender white fingers pressed tip to tip.

"Here we are, sir," announced the driver.

"Yes, yes, to be sure!" exclaimed the scientist hurriedly. "I quite forgot. You needn't wait."

The vehicle was driven off as The Thinking Machine ascended the brown stone steps of the house and pulled the bell. There was no answer, no sound inside, and he pulled it the second time, then the third. Finally, leaning forward with his ear pressed against the door, he pulled the bell the fourth time. This evidently convinced him that the cord inside was disconnected, and he tried the door. It was locked.

Without an instant's hesitation he ran down the steps to the basement entrance in an areaway. There was no bell there, and he tried the knob tentatively. It turned, and he stepped into a damp, smelly hallway, unrelieved by one glint of light. He closed the door noiselessly behind him, and stood for a little while listening. Then he did peculiar thing. He produced a small electric pocket lamp, and holding it as far to the left as he could reach, with the lens pointing ahead of him, pressed the button. A single white ray cleft the darkness, revealing a bare, littered floor, moldy walls, a couple of doors, and stairs leading up.

He spent five cautious minutes perhaps in the basement. There was no sign of recent human habitation, nothing but accumulated litter, and dust and dirt. Then he went up the stairs to the floor above. Here he spent another five minutes, with only an occasional flash of light, always at arm's length to extreme right or left, to tell him there was yet no sign of occupancy. Then another flight of stairs to the second floor. Still there was no sound, no trace of anyone, no indication of a living thing.

His first glimpse of the third floor confirmed at first glance all those impressions of desertion he had gathered below. The front room was identical with the one below, the front hall room was identical; but there was a difference in the large rear room. The dust and litter of the floor seemed worn into a sort of path from the top of the stairs, and following this path toward the back he came upon – a telephone!

"Forty-one-seventeen," he read, as the instrument stood revealed, bathed in the light from the electric bulb. Then he glanced down at his cuff and repeated, "Forty-one-seventeen."

With every sense alert for one disturbing sound, he spent two full minutes examining the instrument. He seemed to be seeking some mark upon it, – the scar of a bullet, perhaps, – and as the scrutiny continued fruitless, the tiny wrinkles, which had momentarily disappeared from his face, appeared there again, and deepened perceptibly. The receiver was on the hook, the transmitter seemed to be in perfect condition, and the walls round the box were smooth. Finally he allowed the light to fade, then picked up the receiver and held it to his ear. His sensitive fingers instantly became aware of tiny particles of dust on the smooth black surface; and the line was dead. Central did not answer. Yet this was the telephone from which he had been called!

Again he examined the instrument under the light, with something akin to perplexity on his drawn face; then allowed his eyes to follow the silken wire as it led up, across the room, and out the window. Did it go up or down? Probably up, possibly down. He had just taken two steps toward that window, with the purpose of answering this question definitely, when he heard a sound somewhere off in the house and stopped.

The light faded, and utter gloom swooped down upon him as he listened. What he heard apparently was the tread of feet at a distance, somewhere below. They seemed to be approaching. Now they were in the lower hall, and grew clatteringly distinct in the emptiness of the house; then the tread sounded on the stairs, the certain, quick step of one who knew his way perfectly. Now the sound was at the door – now finally in the room. Yet there was not one ray of light.

For a little time The Thinking Machine stood motionless, invisible in the enshrouding darkness, until the footsteps seemed almost upon him. Then suddenly his right arm was extended full length from his body, the electric bulb blazed in his hand, and slashed around the room. By every evidence of the sense of sound the flash should have revealed something – perhaps the figure of a man. But there was nothing! The room was vacant, save for himself. And even while the light flared he heard the steps again. The light went out, he took four quick, noiseless steps to his left, and stood there for a moment puzzled.

Then he understood. The mysterious tread was stilled now, as if the person had stopped, and it remained still for several minutes. The Thinking Machine crept silently, cautiously, toward the door and stepped out into the hall. Leaning over the stair rail, he listened. And after awhile the tread sounded again. He drew back into the shadow of a linen closet as the sound grew nearer – stood stock – still staring into blank nothingness as it was almost upon him; then the footsteps receded gradually along the hall, down the stairs, growing fainter, until the receding echo was lost in the silence of the night.

Whereupon The Thinking Machine went boldly up the stairs to the fourth floor, the top. He mounted confidently, as if expecting something to reward his scrutiny; but his eyes rested only upon the bleak desolation of unoccupied apartments. He went straight to the rear room, above the one he had just left, and directly across to one of the windows. Faint, rosy streaks of dawn slashed the east – just enough natural light to show dimly a silken wire hanging down from the middle of the window outside. He opened the window, drew in the wire, and examined it carefully under the electric light, and nodded as if he understood.

Finally he turned abruptly and retraced his steps to the first floor. There he paused to examine the knob of the front door; then went on down into the basement. Instead of examining the door there, however, he turned back under the stairs. There he found another door – a door to the subcellar, standing open a scant few inches. A damp, moldy smell came up. After a moment he pushed the door open slowly and ventured one foot forward in the darkness. It found a step, and he began to descend. The fourth step down creaked suddenly, and he paused to listen intently. Utter silence!

Then on down, ten, eleven, twelve, fourteen, steps, and his foot struck soft, yielding earth. Safely on the ground again, in the protecting gloom, he stood still for a long time, peering blindly around him. At last a blaze of light leaped from the electric bulb, which was extended far from the body to the right, and The Thinking Machine drew a quick breath. It might have been surprise; for within the glow of the light lay the figure of a young man, a boy almost, flat of his back on the muddy earth, with eyes blinking in the glare. His feet were bound tight together with a rope, and his hands were evidently fastened behind him.

Are you the gentleman who telephoned for me?" inquired The Thinking Machine calmly.

There was no answer, and yet the prostrate man was fully conscious, as proved by the moving eyes and a twitching of his limbs.

"Well?" demanded the scientist impatiently. "Can't you talk?"

His answer was a flash of flame, the crash of a revolver at short range, and the light dropped, automatically extinguished as the pressure on the button was removed. Upon this came the sound of a body falling. There was a long drawn gasp, and again silence.

"For God's sake, Cranston!" came the explosive voice of a man after a moment. "You've killed him!"

"Well, I'm not in this game to spend the rest of my life in jail," was the answer, almost a snarl. "I didn't want to kill anybody; but if I had to, all right. If it hadn't been for this kid here, we'd have been all right anyway. I've got a good mind to give him one too, while I'm at it!"

"Well, why don't you?" came a third voice. It was taunting, cold, unafraid.

"Oh, shut up!"

Feet moved uncertainly, feelingly, over the soft earth and stumbled upon the inert, limp figure of The Thinking Machine, lying face down on the ground, almost at the feet of the bound man. One of the men who had spoken stooped, and his fingers touched the still, slim body. He withdrew his hands quickly.

"Is he dead?" some one asked.

"My God, man! Why did you do it?" exclaimed the man who had spoken first, and there was a passionate undertone in his voice. "I never dreamed that this thing would lead to – to murder!"

"It hardly seems to be a time to debate why I did it," was the brutal response; "so much as it is to decide what we'll do now that it is done. We might drop this body in the coal bin in the basement until we finish up here; but what shall we do with the boy? We are both guilty – he saw it. He wanted to tell the other. What will he do now?"

"He'll tell it just so surely as he lives," the bound man answered for himself.

"In that case there's only one thing to do," declared Cranston flatly. "We'd better make a double job of this, leave them both here, and get away."

"Don't kill me – don't kill me!" whined the young man suddenly. "I won't ever tell – I promise! Don't kill me!"

"Oh, shut up!" snarled Cranston. "We'll attend to you later. Got a match?"

"Don't strike a light," commanded the other man sharply, fearfully. "No, don't! Why, man, suppose – suppose your shot had struck him in – in the face. God!"

"Well, help me lift it," asked Cranston shortly.

And between them they carried the childlike body of the eminent man of science through the darkness to the stairs, up the stairs and through the basement to the back. The dawn was growing now, and the pallid, drawn face of The Thinking Machine was dimly visible by a light from the window. The eyes were wide open, glassy; the mouth agape slightly. Overcome by a newborn terror, – hideous fear, – the two men flung the body brutally into an open coal bin, slammed down the cover, and went stumbling, clattering, out of the room.

It was something less than half an hour later that the lid of the coal bin was raised from inside, and The Thinking Machine clambered out. He paused for a moment, to rub his knees and elbows ruefully and stretch his cramped limbs.

"Dear me! Dear me!" he grumbled to himself. "I really must be more careful."

And then straight back to the entrance of the subcellar he went. It was lighter outside now, and he walked with the assurance of one who saw where he went, yet noiselessly. But the door of the stairs leading down still revealed only a yawning, black hole. He went on without the slightest hesitation, remembering to step over the fourth step, which had squeaked once before. In the gloom below, standing on the earth again, he listened for many minutes.

Assured at last that he was alone, he groped about the floor for his electric light, and finally found it. Without fear or apparent caution he examined the huge, dark, damp room. On each side were thrown up banks of dirt that seemed to have been dug recently, and here before him was where the bound man had lain. And over there he started forward eagerly when he saw it – was a telephone! The transmitter box had been wrecked by what seemed to be a bullet. As he saw it he nodded his head comprehendingly.

From there he went on around some masonry. Here was a passage of some sort. He flashed the light into it. It had been dug out of the solid earth, and its existence evidently accounted for the heaps of dirt in the subcellar. Still he didn't hesitate. Straight along the passage he went, wary of step, and stooping occasionally to avoid striking his head against the earth above him. Ten, fifteen, twenty, feet he went, and still the gloomy, foul smelling hole lay ahead of him, leading to—what? At about thirty-five feet from the subcellar there was a sharp turn, – he thought at first it was the end of the tunnel, – then the passage straightened out again, and there was another fifteen or twenty feet, growing smaller and smaller as he went forward.

Suddenly the tunnel stopped. The Thinking Machine found himself flattening his nose against a door of some sort. He allowed his light to fade, then dimly, through a cranny, he saw a faint glow outside. This seemed to be his destination, wherever it was, – and he paused thoughtfully. Obviously the light outside was electric, and if electric light might not some one be in there? A subterranean chamber of some sort, perhaps? His fingers ran around the edge of the door, loosened a fastening, and he peered out. Then, assured again, he opened the door wide, and stepped out into a brilliant glare.

He was in the subway. He stood blinking incredulously. Here to his right the shining rails went winding off round a curve in the far distance; and to the left was a quicker turn in the line of the excavation. In neither direction was there anything that looked like a station.

"Really, this is most extraordinary!" he exclaimed.

Then and there the eminent man of science paused to consider this weird thing from all possible viewpoints. It was unbelievable, positively nightmarish; yet true enough, for here he stood in the subway. There was no question about that; for in the distance was the roar of a train, and he discreetly withdrew into the little door, closing it carefully behind him until it had passed.

Finally he popped out again, closed the door behind him, paused only to admire the skill with which a portion of the tiling in the tunnel had been utilized as a door, then went on across the tracks. It was still early morning; the trains were as yet few and far between; so he had a little leisure for the minute examination he made of the tiled walls opposite the closed door. It was perhaps ten minutes before he found a tile that was loose. He hauled at it until it came out in his hand, revealing a dark aperture beyond.

Within fifteen minutes, therefore, from the time he undertook the search for the second door he was standing in another narrow, earthy tunnel which beckoned him on. With the ever ready light to guide him, and still proceeding with caution, he advanced for possibly thirty feet; then came a turn. Round the turn he found himself in a sort of room – another cellar, perhaps. He permitted his light to go out, and stood listening, straining his squint eyes. After a time he was satisfied and flashed his light again.

Directly before him were half a dozen rough steps, leading up to what seemed to be a trap door. He had barely time to notice this and to see that the trap door was hanging open, when there came a cyclonic rush toward him out of the darkness, from the direction of his right, something whizzed past his head, causing him to drop the precious light, and instinctively he ran up the steps. The gloom above was no more dangerous, he thought, than the gloom below, and he went on, finally passing through the trap and standing on a hard floor above.

There was the sound of a fierce, desperate struggle down there somewhere, cursing, blasphemy, then the noise of feet on the steps coming toward him, and the trap door closed with the heavy, resonant clang of iron. He was alone, his light lost. A sudden strange, awful silence closed down around him, a silence alive with suggestion of unseen, unknown dangers. He stood for a moment, then sank down upon the floor wearily.

Cashier Randall stood beside the ponderous door of the vault, watch in hand. It was two minutes of ten o'clock. At precisely ten the time lock on the massive steel structure, built into the solid masonry of the bank, would bring the mechanism into position for the combination to work. Already the various clerks and tellers were at their posts; books and money were in the vault. At length there came a whir and a sharp click in the heavy door, and the cashier whirled the combination. A few minutes later he pulled open the outer door with a perceptible effort, then turned his attention to the combination lock on the second door. This yielded more readily; but there was still another door, the third to be unlocked. Altogether the task of opening the huge vault required something like six minutes.

Finally Cashier Randall threw open the light third door, then touched an electric button to his right. Instantly the gloom of the structure was dispelled by a flood of light, and he started back in amazement. Almost at his feet, on the floor of the vault, was the huddled figure of a man. Dead? Or unconscious? Certainly there was no movement to indicate life, and the cashier stepped backward into the office with blanched face.

Others came crowding round and saw, and startled glances were exchanged.

"You, Carroll and Young, lift him out, please," requested the cashier quietly. "Don't make any noise about it. Take him to my office."

The order was obeyed in silence. Then Cashier Randall in person went into the vault and ran hurriedly through the piles of money which lay there. He came out at last and spoke to one of the paying tellers.

PROBLEM OF THE DESERTED HOUSE

"The money is all right," he said, with a relieved expression in his face. "Have it all counted carefully, please, and report to me."

He retired into his private office and closed the door behind him. Carroll and Young stood staring down curiously at the man who now lay stretched full length on the couch. They looked at the cashier inquiringly.

"I think it's a matter for the police," continued the cashier after a moment and he picked up the receiver of the telephone.

"But how – how did he get in the vault?" stammered Carroll.

"I don't know. Hello! Police headquarters, please."

"Anything missing, sir?" inquired Young.

"Not so far as we know," was the reply. "Don't make any excitement about it, please. He is breathing yet, isn't he?"

"Yes," answered Carroll. "He doesn't seem to be hurt – just unconscious."

"Lack of air," said the cashier. "He must have been in there all night. It's enough to kill him. Hello! I want to speak to the chief of detectives. Mr Mallory, yes. This is the Grandison National Bank, Mr Mallory. Can you come down at once, please, and investigate a matter of great importance?"

Fifteen minutes later Detective Mallory walked into the cashier's private office. Instantly his eyes fell upon the recumbent figure on the couch, and there came with the glimpse a strange, startled expression.

"Well, for" — he blurted. "Where did you get hold of him?"

"I found him in the vault just now when I opened it," was the reply. "Do you know him?"

"Know him?" bellowed Detective Mallory. "Know him? Why it's Professor Van Dusen, a distinguished scientist. He's the fellow they call The Thinking Machine sometimes." He paused incredulously. "Have you sent for a doctor? Well, send for one quick!"

With the tender care of a mother for her child the detective hovered about the couch whereon The Thinking Machine lay, having first opened the window, and pausing now and then to swear roundly at the physician's delay in arriving. And at last the doctor came. Quick restoratives brought the scientist to consciousness within a few minutes.

"Ah, Mr Mallory!" he remarked weakly. "Please have the doors locked, and put somebody you can trust on guard. Don't let anyone out. I'll explain in a minute or so."

The detective rushed out of the room, returning a moment later. He found The Thinking Machine talking to the cashier.

"Have you a man named Cranston employed here in the bank?"

"Yes," replied the cashier.

"Arrest him, Mr Mallory," directed The Thinking Machine. "Doctor, just the least bit of nitroglycerin, please, in my left arm, here. And, also, Mr Mallory, arrest any particular chum of this man Cranston; also a young man, almost a boy, possibly employed here – probably a relative or closely connected with Cranston's chum. That will do, doctor. Thanks! Anything stolen?"

The detective glanced inquiringly at the cashier.

"No," replied that official.

The Thinking Machine dropped back on the couch, closed his eyes, and lay silent for a moment.

"Pretty bad pulse, doctor," he remarked at last. "Charge your hypodermic again. What bank is this, Mr Mallory?"

"Grandison National," the detective informed him. "What happened to you? How did it come you were in the vault?"

"It was awful, Mr Mallory – awful, believe me!" was the reply. "I'll tell you about it after awhile. Meanwhile be sure to get Cranston and—"

And he fainted.

Twenty-four hours' rest in his own home, under the watchful eye of a physician, restored The Thinking Machine to a physical condition almost normal. But the whys and wherefors of his mysterious presence in the vault of the bank were still matters of eager speculation, but speculation only, to both the police and the bank officials. His last words, before being removed to his own apartments, had been a warning against the further use of the vault; but no explanation accompanied it.

Meanwhile Detective Mallory and his men rounded up three prisoners – Harry Cranston, a middle aged and long trusted employee of the bank; David Ellis Burge, a young mechanical engineer with whom Cranston had been upon terms of great intimacy for many months; and Richard Folsom, a stalwart young nephew of Burge's, himself a student of mechanical engineering. They were held upon charges born in the fertile mind of Detective Mallory, carefully isolated from one another and from the outside.

The Thinking Machine told his story in detail, incident by incident, from the moment of the telephone call until the trap door closed behind him and he found himself in the vault of a bank. His listeners, Detective Mallory, President Hall and Cashier Randall of the Grandison National, and Hutchinson Hatch, reporter, absorbed it in utter amazement.

"Certainly it was the most elusive problem that has ever come under my observation," declared the diminutive man of science. "It was so elusive, so compelling, that I indiscreetly placed my life in danger twice, and I didn't know definitely what it all meant until I knew I was in the vault. No man may know that slow suffocation, that hideous gasping for breath as minute after minute went by, unless he has felt it. And, gentlemen, if I had been killed one of the most valuable minds in the sciences would have been lost. It would have been nothing less than a catastrophe." He paused and settled back into that position which was so familiar to at least two of his hearers.

"When I got the telephone call," he resumed after a moment, "it told me several things beyond the obvious. The logic of it all – and logic, gentlemen, is incontrovertible – was that some man was in danger, in danger even as he talked to me, that he had tried to reach me, seeking help, that the first interruption on the wire came because perhaps he was being choked, and that the second came – the shot which wrecked the instrument – as a desperate expedient to prevent further conversation. The scene was quite clear in my mind.

"The wire was dead then. Central didn't know the number. There was no way to get that number save by the tedious process of testing the wires in the exchange, and that might have taken days. It took only two hours or so, fortunately; but I got the number at last from which I was called; that is, I got a wire which was inexplicably dead, and assumed the rest. The number of that wire was forty-one-seventeen. The records showed the street and number of the house where it came from. Therefore I went there. Before I went I took the precaution of calling up police headquarters to see if any report of a murder or attempted murder or anything unusual had come in. Nothing had come in. This fact in itself was elucidating, because vaguely it indicated that I had been called, rather than the police, because – well, perhaps because it was not desirable for the police to know.

"Well, as I explained, I searched the house; and by the way, Mr Mallory, I don't know if you know the advantages of always holding your dark lantern as far away from your body as possible when going into dangerous places; because if there is danger, a shot, say, the natural impulse of the person who shoots is to aim at the light. Incidentally this precaution saved my life in the cellar, when I feigned death. But I'm going a little ahead of myself.

"I found telephone number forty-one-seventeen, and there was a heavy coat of dust on the receiver. Obviously it had not been recently used. The line was dead, it is true, but the instrument was in perfect condition. There was no sign of a bullet mark anywhere round or near it. If the bullet that was fired had killed the man who had been using the line, it would not have deadened the wire; therefore instantly I saw that the line had been tapped somewhere; that this instrument had been cut off from it, and the instrument which was demolished was the one on the branch wire.

"I knew this, and was going to the window to see if the wire led up or down, when I heard some one approaching. I first supposed that the person, whoever it was, was in the room with me, the steps were so distinct; but when I flashed the light, intending at least to see him, I knew he was above me. One loses the sense of direction of sound, particularly in the dark; and it is an incontestable fact that footsteps, or any sound above, can be heard more clearly than the same sound below. Therefore I knew that some one was in the room above me. For what purpose? Possibly to disconnect the branch wire on the telephone line.

"I waited until the person, whoever it was, came down and went his way; then I found the wire, and saw where the connection had been made on it. Then I went straight down to the subcellar. There I saw this Folsom lying on the ground, bound. He was not gagged; yet he didn't answer my questions; obviously because he knew if he did he would place himself in danger. The shot was fired at me, or rather at my light, and I went through the farce which ultimately placed me in a coal bin. Then I began to get a definite idea of things from the conversation, when Cranston's name was mentioned several times.

"Folsom persisted in an outspoken declaration to reveal everything he knew, including the story of my murder. He insisted until he placed himself in grave danger, and then, under cover of utter darkness, I extended one hand and pinched him twice on the ankle. He knew then that I was not dead, that I had heard, and did the very thing I wanted him to do – begged for his life. It was a bit of justifiable duplicity. I knew if he was the man his every act so far had indicated that he would humbug Cranston and the other man into letting him go, or at least not committing another murder. Subsequent developments showed that this conjecture was correct.

"From the coal bin I went back to the subcellar, knowing positively now that there would be no one there. Those men were frightened when they left me, and men run from fright. What they would do with young Folsom I didn't know. There, with my electric light, I found the branch telephone. The transmitter box had been ruined by a shot, as I imagined. So, thus far at least, the logic of the affair was taking me some place.

"And then I followed that tunnel through the subway into another tunnel. I should not have ventured into that second tunnel had I not been fairly confident that no one else was there. In that I was mistaken. I don't know now, but I imagine that young Folsom was temporarily being held prisoner there, and that possibly Cranston was on guard. Anyway, there was a fight, and the trap door was open – the trap door into the vault. And I don't know yet whether Folsom and Cranston, if they were there, even knew I was at hand. Certainly the trap door, once closed behind me, was not opened again. And you know the rest of it." Again there was a pause, and the scientist twiddled his fingers idly.

"Now it all comes down to this," he concluded at last. "Cranston dragged Burge in to the affair, – Burge is a mechanical engineer, and a good one was needed to do this work, – they rented the house, and went to work. It took weeks, perhaps months, to do it all. Folsom in some way learned of it, and he is an honest man. He took a desperate means of getting the information into my hands, instead of the hands of the police. Why the telephone was in the house I don't know –

perhaps it was already there, perhaps they had it put in. Anyway, of your prisoners, Mr Mallory, this young Folsom is guilty only of an attempt to shield his uncle, Burge, while Cranston is the ringleader, and Burge the man who achieved the immense task of getting under the vault of the bank.

"This vault has a floor of cement, cut into small squares. The trap door is in that floor, and so perfectly concealed in the lines of the squares that it is invisible unless submitted to a close scrutiny, just as the doors in the tiled walls of the subway were invisible to a casual observer. They overcame tremendous difficulties, these two men, in cutting through the immense foundation of the vault, even the steel itself, but remember that they worked at night for weeks and weeks, and were making no mistakes. They did not actually rob the bank because, I imagine, they were awaiting the deposit there of some immense sum. Is that correct, Mr Hall?"

President Hall started suddenly. "Yes, in a week or so we were expecting a shipment of gold from Europe – nearly three million dollars," he explained. "Think of it!"

Detective Mallory whistled. "Phew! What a haul it would have been!"

"Now, Mr Mallory, either of these three men, if properly approached, will confess the whole thing substantially as I have told it," remarked The Thinking Machine. "But I would advise that Folsom be allowed to go. He is really a very decent sort of young man."

When they had all gone except Hatch, the eminent man of science went over and laid one hand upon the reporter's shoulder and squinted straight into his eyes for a moment. "You know, Mr Hatch," he said, and there was a strange note in the irritable voice, "my first fear, when the telephone call came, was that it was you. You must be careful – very careful, always."

Love Golden Age crime fiction? Have you checked out the full yellowback range?

From Locked door mysteries to blind detectives through first women detectives, the yellowback reissues is one of the largest selections of classic crime fictions, in the original format with a modern clean easy read page layout. A sampling below.

For more details and a full list of titles:
visit https://www.hachetteindia.com/home/yellowbacks

H. Rider Haggard MR. MEESON'S WILL 	**Melville Davisson Post** MASTER OF MYSTERIES THE COMPLETE UNCLE ABNER COLLECTION 	**Jack London** THE ASSASSINATION BUREAU LTD. 
Baroness Orczy THE SKIN O' MY TOOTH 	**Earl Derr Biggers** SEVEN KEYS TO BALDPATE 	**Horace Walpole** THE CASTLE OF OTRANTO 
Sexton Blake THE SEXTON BLAKE COLLECTION VOLUME 1 	**Francis Beeding** THE HOUSE OF DR. EDWARDES 	**A. E. W. Mason** AT THE VILLA ROSE 
Fergus Hume THE MILLIONAIRE MYSTERY 	**Donald Henderson** A VOICE LIKE VELVET 	**Richard Hallas** YOU PLAY THE BLACK AND THE RED COMES UP

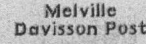

Assembling the greatest detectives all together

Covering the full range and history of detective fiction. From Zadig, *The Moonstone*, and Dupin through Sherlock Holmes, Loveday Brooke, Montague Egg, Lord Peter Wimsey, *The Thinking Machine*, Father Brown down to Solar Pons.

For more details and a full list of titles:
visit https://www.hachetteindia.com/home/yellowbacks

WELCOME BACK TO THE GOLDEN AGE